Joy in the Morning

Joy in the Morning

BY BETTY SMITH

HARPER & ROW, PUBLISHERS

New York, Evanston, and London

LIBRARY OF CONGRESS CATALOG CARD NUMBER: 62–14560

Weeping may endure for a night,
but joy cometh in the morning.
                    —Psalm 30:5

Joy in the Morning

Chapter One

It was an out-of-date town hall in an up-to-date progressive college town in a midwestern state. The corridor was long and dark with narrow benches at intervals against the wall, and a brass cuspidor by each bench.

Although the year was 1927 and few men chewed tobacco any more, no one had the authority to get rid of the cuspidors. So they stood there. Each morning the janitor polished them and put a fresh half inch of water in each as janitors had done before him for the past fifty years.

One of the benches was occupied by a boy named Carl and a girl named Annie. There was a small, red, very new suitcase on the bench next to the girl. She gave it a possessive pat from time to time. The boy chain-smoked, which made him seem nervous even though he wasn't.

Although he was known as Carl Brown, the boy had started life as Carlton Braun—the Carlton after the father's boss. Mr. Braun had worked for Mr. Carlton since the age of twelve. The work was hard, the hours long, the pay low, and the raises scarce.

Whenever he asked the boss for a raise, Mr. Carlton would put his arm around Mr. Braun's shoulder and tell him in a mel-

1

low voice, not to worry, son. He'd be taken care of, son. When he, Mr. Carlton, passed away, there'd be some bonds in that there safe, son, made out to William Braun.

So when the baby was born, they named him Carlton so the boss would be sure to remember the bonds. When the boy was six years old, Mr. Carlton died. When they opened that there safe, there were no bonds for William Braun, son. The disappointed father reduced the boy's name to Carl.

During the war, when people were running around hollering, "Down with the Kaiser!" and changing sauerkraut to liberty cabbage, Mr. Braun, by due process of law, had his name changed to Brown. Although he had been born in Germany, he wanted no one to mistake which side he was on.

Thus evolved the name Carl Brown.

There was no complication about the girl's name, Annie McGairy. She had been christened Annie, after her German-born maternal grandmother, and the McGairy, of course, was donated by her father, who had been born in Dublin, Ireland.

Carl was a handsome boy—tall, blond, and with a manly look of maturity which made him seem older than his twenty years. His clothes were cheap, but he wore them so well that they looked expensive. He was neat in a casual way. Altogether, he was an attractive young man whom one couldn't help but notice.

Annie was eighteen but looked like a child of fourteen who had borrowed her sister's clothes for the day. She was small, slender but well made, and had long, pretty light-brown hair which she wore in a knot at the back of her head. She had nice clear skin, a mobile mouth, and sad gray eyes. She wasn't a girl you'd notice especially except when she spoke. Then you'd *have* to notice her.

They sat close together on the bench, holding hands and waiting to be married. From time to time there was a little hiss as Carl threw a half-smoked cigarette into the cuspidor. At each hiss Annie squeezed his hand and said, "Nervous?" Each time he squeezed back and said, "No. You?" Each time she said, "A little." Then they squeezed hands together.

A woman clerk came toward them and Carl started to rise. "Keep your seat," said the woman pleasantly.

"Will we have to wait much longer?" asked Carl, looking at his watch. "We don't want to miss the game."

"Judge Calamus doesn't usually come in on a Saturday," said the clerk. "But he's making an exception in your case. We got in touch with him at his home and he'll be over in a few minutes."

"Good!"

"Now: You have the license?" Carl started to get it from his inside coat pocket. "Oh, I don't need to see it. Just checking," she said. "Where you folks from?"

"Brooklyn," he said.

"Both of you?"

Carl nodded. "But I've been here a year."

"He goes to college here," said Annie proudly.

"Med school?" asked the clerk.

"Law school," he said.

"That's nice," she said vaguely. She turned to Annie. "And how long have you been here?"

"Two hours," said Annie.

"She came in on the night train from New York," explained Carl.

"Then our Middle West must seem strange to you," she said to Annie.

"Oh, no. I had an idea what it would be like. I read books that were laid in the Middle West—like *Winesburg, Ohio* and *Main Street* and *Sister Carrie*. And to me the Middle West didn't seem much different than where I lived. Why, *Sister Carrie* could have been laid in Brooklyn as well as in Chicago."

Carl pressed Annie's hand in warning and she stopped talking. Annie noticed the clerk was staring at her in a strange way.

"Oh! Yes, well . . ." The clerk sounded confused. She started back to her office, saying over her shoulder, "The judge will expect a little something for his trouble, you know."

"I understand," said Carl.

"Carl, did I say something wrong?" Annie asked anxiously.

"No, sweetheart."

"Then why did you want me to stop talking?"

"I didn't want her hanging around."

He didn't want to tell Annie that the clerk had been astonished by Annie's accent. Carl had a slight Brooklyn accent, but Annie's was broad, complicated by an intruding Irish brogue.

"Well, she talks funny too," said Annie suddenly.

It was uncanny how at times Annie seemed to know Carl's thoughts. It made him uneasy. "Oh, you'll get used to the way they talk," he said, "the way they'll get used to the way you, I mean *we*, talk."

"I know that sometimes I don't say things right, but I'll learn, Carl. You'll see. I'm a person who learns very quick."

"Quick-*ly!*" His correction was automatic.

She had been about to say: Don't ever be ashamed of me. She changed it to: "Don't you worry about me."

"Worry? Never! Why, you're smart, Annie. You just don't know how very smart you are."

"No, Carl. I only went to school up to the eighth grade."

"You're as smart as most college graduates."

"You're just saying that."

"No, sweetheart. I mean it."

"I'll learn, Carl. You'll see."

"Don't learn too much now. I don't want my wife to be a big shot."

"Nothing like that. I'm not ambitious or anything. But I certainly want to know enough so you won't be ashamed of me when you get to be a great lawyer or maybe a governor."

"Why not President?" he said jokingly. "I guess you don't have much faith in me."

"You know what I mean, Carl."

"I know, sweetheart. But I love you just the way you are." He kissed her cheek.

"This waiting makes me nervous. What time is it by your watch?" she said.

"Ten after eleven. Damn it, the game starts at one-thirty and I've got to get rid of your suitcase and we have to have lunch and . . ."

"And I'd hate to miss the game," she said. "I never saw a football game, but I'm all ready for it." She touched the yellow chrysanthemum with its ribbon bow of the college colors, which Carl had pinned to her coat when she stepped off the train, and held up the little blue pennant he had put into her hand, waved it, and whispered, "Rah! Rah! Rah!"

The clerk came and said the judge had arrived and would they follow her? And take the suitcase along. Not that anyone would actually steal it, she explained, but you never could tell with so many strangers in town for the game.

The name was on the door: *Willis J. Calamus.* Under it *Justice of Peace* and down in the corner *Notary Public.* Carl made a snide remark about a notary calling himself judge, and Annie said, sh-h, he might hear you.

The judge seemed to take up all the space in the small office —his stomach was so fat. Annie expected he would be wearing a robe as judges did in the movies. Instead he wore roomy pants with lots of seat to them, a clean but carelessly ironed shirt and an unbuttoned alpaca coat, which rode up in the back and sagged down in the front as though the pockets were full of iron filings.

The judge sent the clerk out to dig up a certain Miss Vi for the other witness. He took the license from Carl and went behind the counter to read it. First he patted himself while he looked in the air. That was how he searched for his glasses. Eventually he found them in his shirt pocket. He made a ceremony of adjusting the glasses on his nose. Nervously, Carl took his cigarettes from his pocket. The judge stared at the pack, then stared at Carl. Carl returned the pack to his pocket.

The judge breathed heavily as he read the license word for word, looking up at Carl or Annie at intervals as if deciding which one was the culprit. Carl fretted with impatience and Annie became lost in her thoughts.

This can't be real, she thought. Where is my veil? My white dress? Where is my quiet church with the sun coming in the windows and the organ playing and Mama there, crying, but proud all the same?

Carl couldn't stand the wait much longer. He lifted his wrist to check the time. The judge stopped reading to stare at Carl. Insultingly, Carl shook the watch and held it to his ear. The judge gave him a long look before he resumed reading the license.

God must know, thought Annie, I did my best to get married in the right way—in a church with Mama there and my little brothers and the neighbors there and Arlene for my bridesmaid. I told Mama . . .

"Mama, I'll be eighteen next Wednesday."

"How time flies!"

"Carl and I want to get married."

"Don't talk silly. You're only a kid."

"I stopped being a kid when I was fourteen; when I got my first job."

"Never mind. You're still a kid."

"I want to get married in church. With you there, Mama."

"Now you get that idea right out of your head. You're not getting married in a church or anywhere."

"Mama, please don't make me get married on the sly in City Hall."

"Such foolish talk and you haven't seen that boy in over a year."

"He was here all summer."

"And you went out with him?"

"Yes."

"Without telling your mother?"

"I was afraid you'd tell Dan."

"Listen, Annie. You think you want to marry Carl. But you're too young to know your own mind. Carl's not for you. Someday the right man will come along and you'll be glad you waited."

"I can't wait, Mama. I *got* to get married."

"You got to? Did you say you *got* to?"

"It's not what you think, Mama."

"Tell me what I think. Tell me."

"You're hurting my arm, Mama."

"I said, tell me!"

"It's better that you don't know."

"When was your last period?"

"Don't say ugly things, Mama."

"Don't you tell me what to say, you . . . you tramp!"

"Mama, if you say that again . . ."

"Tramp!"

"You went too far, Mama."

"How dare you raise your hand to me! When I think . . . when I think how I suffered bringing you into the world; the sacrifices I made for you . . ."

"Don't cry, Mama. Please don't cry."

"All the thanks I get. If your father could hear the way you talk to me . . ."

"My father is dead."

"Dan is your father. He's more your father than your own was. Why do you think I married Dan? A man twenty years older than me? I didn't love him. Respect, yes. But not love."

"Why did you marry without love, Mama?"

"To give my children a father; a man who would see to it that they had a good home, plenty to eat, decent clothes . . ."

7   *

"But, Mama, about Dan . . ."

"What about Dan?"

"Nothing."

"What, Annie? I know you don't like him. Why?"

"The way he looks at me—kisses me good night when I'm in bed."

"He kisses all you children good night."

"But I'm not a child."

"To him, you're a baby."

"I'm a woman."

"Not in his eyes. He loves you the way he loves your little brothers. He never had any children of his own. He's such a good man. . . . Ah, Annie, don't cry. Don't cry . . ."

Carl was pressing her hand and whispering, "Stop daydreaming, sweetheart."

She came to with a start. She heard the judge ask Carl if he was Carl Brown and she heard Carl say yes.

"And your age?"

"Twenty."

"And you, young lady, are Annie McGairy?"

"Yes, sir."

"And *your* age?"

"Eighteen."

"How long have you been eighteen?"

"Since last Wednesday."

"You have your birth certificate?"

"No, sir. But . . ."

The judge folded the license and pushed it toward Carl. "Come back when she grows up, son."

"The license states the young lady's correct age, sir." Carl pushed the license back.

"So? Perhaps you were able to fool the clerk who issued it," said the judge. "But not me. No, sir! Not me. The young lady doesn't look a day over fourteen and this is not Tennessee, you know. We have statutes in this state forbidding the marriage of minor children." He pushed the license back to Carl.

Annie, who had been delving in her overloaded handbag, now came up with a slip of paper which she gave to Carl. It was her baptismal certificate. Carl surmised that her mother wouldn't give her the birth certificate and that Annie had got this from her minister. He put the certificate on top of the license and for the last time the license was pushed across the counter.

The clerk came in just then, followed by Miss Vi. Miss Vi was a little, middle-aged, eager-looking woman. She stood on tiptoes to look over the clerk's shoulder at the bridal couple. She caught Annie's eye, smiled and winked. Annie returned the smile but didn't wink back because she wasn't sure whether it had been a wink or a tic—the little woman was so jerky—and Annie didn't want to hurt her feelings if it was a tic.

"Ready if you are, judge," said the clerk gaily, trying to get a festive mood into the proceedings.

The judge came from behind the counter and told everyone where to stand. Then he paused and evaluated his grouping. He made a few changes; stepped back to check. He frowned. Something wasn't right. Ah! The pennant Annie was holding.

"I'll take that, young lady." He put the pennant on the counter.

He looked around and slapped his pockets, wondering where his book was. The clerk got it from behind the counter. The judge turned the pages one by one—forever, it seemed to Carl— looking for the marriage ceremony.

"I believe we're ready," he said. He looked around. Since no one contradicted him, he proceeded. "Take her right hand, Mr. Brown." Their hands fumbled at each other, and it ended up with Carl holding her left hand. "The right hand, boy. The right hand."

Miss Vi winked at Annie. Annie winked back, deciding that

9 *

Miss Vi didn't have a tic after all. The marriage ceremony got under way. Annie listened with rapt attention as if memorizing every word. The judge came to. "And do you, Annie McGairy, take . . ."

The last time I'll be called Annie McGairy, she thought dreamily. The judge waited. Carl pressed Annie's hand. "I do! I do! Yes!" she said loudly.

Carl grinned down at her, Miss Vi winked, the clerk rolled her eyes in exasperation, and the judge scowled at the whole bunch of them.

The ring slid on easily because it was too big for her. (But you'll grow into it, Carl had told her when she tried it on that morning.) Annie was surprised that it felt so cold because gold always looked so warm.

Suddenly it was over. She was married to Carl until death did them part. She clasped her hands together and whirled around once like a child at play. The clerk shook Carl's hand, congratulated him, and then wished Annie all the luck in the world. Miss Vi did the same. Impulsively, Annie threw her arms around the little woman and hugged her. The judge waved the marriage certificate to dry the ink of the signatures before he extended it to them with a little flourish. Carl stepped forward to take it.

"It belongs to the little lady," said the judge. Everyone smiled. Annie took the certificate and pressed it to her breast, smiling up at the judge with misty eyes. "I believe," said the judge, "that I have the privilege of kissing the bride." He came at Annie.

Annie threw herself at Carl and buried her face in his coat. "Don't let him touch me," she whispered hysterically. "He's like my stepfather. Looks like . . ." She trembled, and whimpered, "Mama! Mama!"

"Calling for Mama already?" said the clerk, exchanging looks with Miss Vi.

"After all," said Carl, "she's never been away from home before."

"Well, I don't blame the little thing for missing her mother, then," said Miss Vi.

"Oh, don't mind me," said Annie. "I just got a little homesick all of a sudden."

Carl picked up her suitcase and said, "I thank you all. We both thank you."

The judge looked upset, the witnesses smiled cynically at each other. Annie pressed Carl's hand to remind him of the little something for the judge. "Oh, I almost forgot!" said Carl. The judge looked relieved.

Annie held the suitcase while Carl took two one-dollar bills from his wallet. He gave them to the judge one at a time. The judge kept his hand outstretched and waited. Carl snapped his wallet shut. The judge looked sourly at the two worn-out bills in his hand. Carl gave a big sigh of relief. The ordeal was over.

"Let's go, Mrs. Brown," he said.

"Good-by all," said Annie. "And thanks a whole lot!"

The clerk closed the door after them. "Another premature baby on the way, I suppose," she said.

"Come now," said Miss Vi. "Aren't most first babies premature?"

"Damned kids," said the judge, stuffing the two bills into his pants pocket, "damned kids can't wait. Have to beat the gong."

Thus were the newlyweds blessed.

They paused on the top step of the Town Hall because Carl needed a cigarette badly. The sun was bright but the air was cool. Annie thought the air smelled like apples, and Carl said that was logical because there were thousands of apple orchards in the state and now everybody was making cider in order to have applejack in the winter.

Annie wanted to know where all the people came from. Everywhere, he told her. It was the biggest football game of the year. They looked down on the crowds—groups passing each other as they went in opposite directions. There were students with out-

11   *

of-town dates. You knew the girls were from out of town because they were carefully dressed in new outfits. There were coeds wearing the routine college outfit—dark pleated skirt, loose, dark pull-over sweater, thick white socks, and saddle shoes. The shoes were fashionably dirty. There were groups of college men, different from the average student, wearing ankle-length raccoon coats and pork-pie hats, and with a flask of bathtub gin in a hip pants pocket.

"The townies call them the rah-rah boys," explained Carl.

"Why?" she asked.

"Because they're frat men." There was contempt in his voice.

"It all don't seem real."

"That's because you've never been in a college town before."

"I mean that I went in this building as Miss McGairy and came out Mrs. Brown. All because a man I never saw before read something out of a book, we're married until one of us dies, and we can have children, and you can't sleep with another woman . . ."

"And you can only sleep with me. It cuts both ways, wonder girl."

"But it was so quick! It takes longer to buy a hat than to get married. I don't *feel* married."

"Listen, my child bride: That piece of paper pressed to your bosom is a legal document—signed, sealed, and delivered. It means we're married in the eyes of God, man, the nation, and the world."

"Honest?"

"I'll prove it." He put his arms around her.

"Not here, Carl. All those people . . ."

"Why not? Pretend we're back in Brooklyn. We did most of our kissing on the street there. Come on, now." She lifted her face for his kiss.

A passing group of frat men stopped to watch the embrace. One of them took a cheer leader's stance and led the rest in the bloodcurdling on-to-victory yell.

"And," said Carl, "seems like we're married in the eyes of the university too."

"You said it," agreed Annie.

They started across the campus. Carl was going to leave her suitcase in his former dorm room. He had rented a room in a private house, but it wasn't available until evening because it was rented for the day to some visiting alumni.

They came to a curve in the campus walk. "Take my hand," he said, "and close your eyes. Back up. Just a little. That's good. Now squatty voo." She sat down on a bench. "Now open your eyes."

She looked around. "What, Carl?"

"There!" He pointed to a magnificent edifice which loomed up out of the bare-limbed trees. It had wide white marble steps and huge white columns.

"What's that building, Carl?"

"It happens to be the University Library."

"No! I can't believe it! It's beautiful! Just beautiful! Like something in history. Oh, how I'd love to see the inside!"

"You will, sweetheart."

"Oh, Carl," she said imploringly, "I guess they wouldn't let me take books out of there, would they? Seeing I don't belong to the college?"

"I don't see why not. I'll give you my card."

"Will you?" She hugged his arm. "Oh, Carl, this is the most wonderful wedding present in the world!"

That reminded him of the small wedding present he had for her. He put his hand in his pocket to get it, but changed his mind. No use diluting her ecstasy over the library, he decided. He'd give it to her before they went to bed.

He looked at his watch. "We have a little time. Let's sit here awhile and organize our future. Okay?"

"Okay!" They sat close together on the bench.

"First, let's talk about money and get that the hell out of the way."

"I've got nearly six dollars left," she said eagerly, "from my last pay, after the train and all. And seventy-five dollars in my bankbook—nearly seventy-eight with interest." She dug the bankbook out of her handbag.

"Put it away, Annie dear. It's your own money and we are not going to use it to pay bills."

He reported on his financial position. Tuition paid until June. His meals no problem. He earned three meals a day working as bus boy at the Townly Cafeteria. He earned five dollars for delivery of the college newspaper from six to eight in the morning. And his mother had been sending him five a week.

Ten dollars clear, thought Annie. He must have been able to save a lot. As if he knew her thoughts, he said, "I suppose I should have saved some of that. But I needed . . ."

He had needed shoes and socks and underwear and shirts and a new tie once in a while. Tennis balls and his racket restrung—ice skates sharpened . . .

"And haircuts," contributed Annie.

"Trims," he admitted. "Twice a month. A pack of cigarettes a day. And, oh, toothbrushes and toothpaste, the Sunday paper, notebooks, stamps, stationery, and a movie once in a while with the fellers with a hot dog and near-beer afterwards. Oh, and laundry and . . ."

"Money sure flies, don't it, Carl?"

"You can say that again." He took her hand in both of his. "I might as well tell this, Annie, before you find it out from someone else." He took a deep breath. "I took a girl to a class dance."

"How many times?"

"Just once. That meant a taxi both ways and a corsage and a midnight supper."

She had to swallow very hard before she could say: "That's none of my business, Carl. We were not married then. Just engaged. Naturally, that doesn't count."

"But, sweetheart, I had to take a girl out once in a while or the fellers would think I was queer. Besides, we were not alone. There was a party of us."

"I suppose," she said formally, "I, too, should make a similar confession. Unfortunately, however, I have nothing to tell. I considered it wouldn't be fair to . . . oh, never mind."

"Now, Annie dear. Now."

She moved away from him on the bench. "Were you able to save any money?"

"How could I? I had to buy textbooks, and they cost like hell even if they are secondhand."

"And corsages cost like hell, too, don't they?"

"Know something?" He grinned. "I think you are jealous."

"Yes, I am."

"Jealousy is a sign of inferiority."

"All right, then: I'm inferior."

"Let's cut out this nonsense, Annie. Okay?"

"Okay. Just so it doesn't happen again."

"I swear!"

"Okay, then."

"Do you think we can get along on ten dollars a week?"

"We'll only have five. Your mother's not going to send you money when she knows you're married."

"Oh, I don't know. She may be a little upset when she hears the news, but she'll get over it. All she wants in the world is for me to be happy."

"With her."

"You've got her all wrong, sweetheart. You'll like Mom after you get to know her. After all, you only saw her once."

She had been fifteen then, the time he took her to see his mother. The Browns lived in a neighborhood like Annie's and had the same type of flat. But the Brown home was different; neat—no clutter. Annie's home was pretty untidy. But then both

Annie and her mother worked away from home and the two little brothers all but took the place apart. Now, Carl's mother had nothing to do except keep house. And the family was grown up. Tessie, Carl's forty-year-old spinster sister, kept her room neat and Carl had kept his neat.

In Annie's house the parlor was used only for company. In the Brown house the parlor was turned over to Carl as a bed-sitting room. When Annie had commented on it, Mrs. Brown had said the best was none too good for her only son.

Carl took Annie into his room. He was anxious to show her his awards and trophies—a medal for winning a hundred-yard dash; a silver cup for fancy-figure ice skating, and the framed picture of the Y.M.C.A. basketball team with Carl sitting in the middle and holding the ball because he had been captain that year.

But Annie was most interested in the little bookcase he had made "in shop" in the seventh grade, and the books it held. She was impressed when he said he owned all the books. Annie had never owned a book. He told her to choose any one she wanted as a present.

She knelt before the bookcase as though it were an altar. She crossed her hands on her breast in an ecstasy of delicious indecision. Should she take the volume of *Sherlock Holmes* because it had a lot of reading to it? Or the slim volume of *Sonnets from the Portuguese* because it was so beautiful—soft green leather binding and tasseled, gold cord bookmark?

Carl looked down at the heavy coil of hair at the back of her head, held in place by two bone hairpins. On an impulse, he pulled out the pins. She jumped up with a yelp when she felt her hair cascade down her back. She demanded her hairpins, and he challenged her to try to get them.

She chased him around the room. He high-jumped a Morris chair and vaulted over his narrow bed. She started across the bed after him but lost her footing in the soft bedclothes and fell sprawling on the bed.

He leaned over Annie and said, "Now I got you where I want you." At that precise moment his mother came in.

"My God!" she said.

Annie sat up, her hair disordered, face flushed, and tried to pull her short, tight skirt down over her knees.

"Take it easy, Mom," said Carl. "It's not what you think."

"I'm ashamed of you, Carl. So ashamed," his mother said. "And what kind of girl is that to lie in your bed, with her skirts up around her neck and all?"

"Listen, Mom, I took her hairpins and her hair fell down and . . ."

"I don't want to hear any more. I think she'd better go home."

"Don't worry," said Annie. "I'm going and glad to go." She snatched her pins out of his hand. "And as for you, Carl, I never want to see you again. And that goes double for your mother." She walked out with her head high.

He found her down in the vestibule, tears in her eyes and the pins in her mouth, trying to coil up her hair. Her hands were trembling. Clumsily, he helped her get the pins in.

"I told Mom how it had happened and made her believe it. And she's awfully sorry, Annie, and wants you to come back and stay for supper."

"I'd choke on her food."

"But you can understand, Annie, how Mom got the wrong idea—you on the bed, me almost on top of you?"

"She could have listened when you tried to tell her how it happened, couldn't she? But no! She *wanted* to think it was something dirty because she hated me from the first moment she saw me and she got a lot of satisfaction out of treating me like a prostitute."

"She said she was sorry."

"An easy thing to say after she had the fun of telling me off. Does she think 'sorry' is a word like a rubber eraser she can use to rub out the dirty way she thought of me and the things she said?"

17   *

Annie had cried then; cried so long that Carl had to skip his night school class to take her to see Charlie Chaplin.

Annie sighed now, remembering. "That's true. I only saw her once. If I had gone back for supper, it might have been different."

"Be fair, Annie. What about your mother? Did she put out the red carpet for me? Not so you'd notice it. She treated me like Carl the Ripper, out to ruin her innocent baby. But I never hated her for that. I figured that she was worried because you were only a little kid and she was afraid I'd get you into trouble."

"I guess there'll always be mother-in-law trouble," she said.

"Ah, no. I think they'll come around in time. And if they don't, what of it? We've got to live our life the way they had to live theirs." He wanted a cigarette, but the package was empty. He balled it up and threw it away. "Damn it, I'm out of cigarettes."

"Wait!" She got a new pack out of her handbag. "Here. I bought them just before I got on the train so that in case you ran out I could surprise you."

"You're a sweetheart." He stretched out his legs, spread his arms along the back of the bench and drew deeply on his cigarette. Somewhere a bell tolled the half hour.

"Happy?" he asked.

"Contented."

"When are you going to start being happy?"

"Oh, I was happy this morning when I got off the train and saw you. But now I'm contented."

"What's the difference between happiness and contentment, wise guy?"

"Well, happy is like when somebody gives you a big lump of something wonderful and it's too big to hold. So you pull off a piece from time to time to hold in your hand. That's being contented. Anyway, that's the way I look at it."

"Know what you are?"

"What?"

* 18

"A personality kid. Know what that means?"

"Does that mean being full of being a person?" she asked.

"I hadn't thought of that, but that's exactly what it means." He ground out his cigarette and put an arm around her. "Know something? We've been married nearly an hour now, and I haven't slept with you yet. Now, there's a nice thick bush over there and nobody's looking. How about it?"

"Carl, you're just terrible!" She pretended to be shocked, but her giggle gave her away.

He lifted a strand of her hair and kissed her ear. "Did that give you a thrill?" he asked.

"Do it again," she said. He laughed and did it again.

"For such a sad, sad girl," he said, "you are very funny." He lifted his wrist to check the time. She put her hand over the watch.

"It's twelve-thirty, Carl, and you know it. You don't have to look at the watch every minute."

Annie didn't like the watch. She knew his mother had given it to him for Christmas and sometimes when he looked at it she remembered again the time she was on the bed and his mother had thought . . .

"What's on your mind?" he asked.

"Food."

"Tell you what: Let's skip the game, sweetheart. We can't make it anyway. I'll have no trouble selling the tickets. And we'll use the money to have the best wedding lunch in town. What do you say?"

"I say, grand!"

She freshened up in the library washroom while Carl went to the dorm to store her suitcase. He came back with the weekly letter from his mother. It had the usual five-dollar money order enclosed.

"Let your mother know you're married, Carl, before she sends you more money."

"I think I ought to prepare her first; write that you're here and we're thinking of getting married, and follow that up with a letter saying we are married."

"I think it's better to let her know right away."

"It might be a bit of a shock. Let me do it my way, Annie."

"Well, I'm going to wire my mother right away."

She sent a wire saying she was married and happy. Carl wrote on a card that Annie was with him and they were thinking of marrying. He put the card in a stamped envelope and mailed it.

He had no trouble selling his football tickets. He stood in front of the Sport Shop and held them out. In a few seconds he had sold them for six dollars. Since he had got his ticket for nothing, and bought a dorm mate's ticket for a dollar, Carl was pleased with his five-dollar profit—that is, until he saw the man to whom he had sold the tickets resell them to someone else for eight dollars.

They went to the nicest restaurant in town and had the most expensive lunch on the menu; seventy-five cents. Carl ordered a bottle of near-beer and two glasses. It wasn't champagne, he said, but a luxury just the same at thirty-five cents a bottle. Annie didn't like it, so Carl drank the whole bottle.

The place was almost empty, and the waiter, suspecting they were newly married, hovered over them and served them with a flourish. Carl and Annie had little to say to each other during the meal because both were very hungry. After Carl's second cup of coffee and Annie's second piece of pie à la mode, they relaxed. Carl lit a cigarette, leaned back in his chair, and sighed contentedly.

"This is the life," he said. "Good food, well served in a fine restaurant instead of an eat-and-run cafeteria. A whole lazy afternoon ahead; no split seconds to make a class and my Annie here with me."

"I'm sure glad I'm not rich," she said, "because I'd be used to

* 20

things like that and I'd never have that, you know: 'First fine glorious rapture'?"

"You sure like to live, don't you, Annie?"

"You talk funny. *Everybody* likes to live."

"Do me a favor?"

"Sure."

"Don't ever change. Stay the way you are."

"Oh, I *couldn't* give you a guarantee on that. No."

"Why not, Annie?"

"Well, the world is full of people."

"No kidding!"

"And people are persons."

"You mean individuals."

"All right. Individual persons. Persons change. A person gets old and old makes him different. So he changes whether he wants to or not."

"I ask you a simple question, my girl, and you go all away around the mulberry bush."

"All I'm saying is, persons have to change. I am a person. I will change."

"And all I'm saying is: Deep down don't change."

"You mean funnel-melody?"

He laughed until he coughed. When he got his breath, he said, "That word happens to be pronounced fun-da-ment-ally."

She looked at the waiter, hoping he had not heard her blunder and Carl's correction. But the waiter was grinning and Annie hung her head.

"It's a word in a book I read. I never heard anybody say it and it's the first time I ever tried. So I thought I was saying it right. But I'm," she had to wait for the right word to come to her, "but I'm grateful for the correction."

"Ah, I'm sorry, sweetheart. So sorry. But you asked me always to correct you when . . ."

"But not in front of people. It makes me feel . . . oh, I don't know . . ." Her voice trailed off. "But you know what I mean."

They went back to their campus bench and spent the afternoon recalling incidents which Annie referred to a little gaudily as "from out of our past."

"Just think," she said, "if I hadn't started that serial in that magazine and didn't have to go to the library to see if the new number was there with the ending . . ."

"And," he said, "if on that special night my sister hadn't pestered me to go and see if *Black Oxen* was in yet . . ."

"We might never have met," they said simultaneously. That possibility gave them the shudders. "And if . . ." they said together.

"Let me talk, Carl. If you hadn't walked me home that night, we would not be married today."

"I had to walk you home. I was afraid you'd be raped on one of those dark streets—a cute little fourteen-year-old kid like you."

"Kid nothing! I was holding down a full-time job at the time. I could've taken care of myself."

"I bet!"

"And, you know, when you left me at my door you acted as though you didn't want to see me again and I felt just *terrible?*"

"I didn't want anything to do with you. I was a man of sixteen at the time and you were too young for me."

"What made you change your mind?"

"Well, when I said good-by and meant it, you gave me a great big smile and said, *'So long for a while.'* What could I do?"

"Say! Remember, Carl, that Sunday we rode back and forth all day on the Staten Island ferry on the one fare? And we had a box of soda crackers to throw to the gulls and they flew back and forth all day, following us?"

"Hey, Annie, remember that Sunday at Coney Island?"

"Do I! Face to face, looking at each other and laying in the sand."

"We had to lie in the sand. If we sat up for a second, some

couple would plop down in the space we left and we'd have to sit back to back with strangers. That Sunday was murder."

"But the ocean was there."

"It must have been. I heard it but I didn't see it. All that crowd."

"Carl, here's something I bet you don't remember: That Sunday when we were in Manhattan—just walking around. And we were waiting for traffic on Broadway and Forty-second Street and you said if I really loved you, I'd give you a great big kiss right there on Broadway in front of all the people?"

"And you did! Was I embarrassed!"

"Liar! Now what else? Let me think a minute, Carl."

He took a moment to think, too. He thought of the dark vestibules of Brooklyn. An evening with her had always excited him physically. The pressing of hands; sitting thigh to thigh in the movies or the trolley car; a furtive kiss on a dark street; a tentative hand on her breast in a dark movie house. The desperation at evening's end—the pulling her into a dark vestibule to hold her in a passionate embrace—always on edge lest someone would go into or come out of the house. He shook his head from side to side, thinking of it.

"What are you thinking about, Carl?"

"How we were never alone together because there was no place we *could* be alone together. All our love-making in public: On the street; in subways, trolley cars, movies, vestibules. . . . Always like animals looking for a dark corner . . ."

"But we weren't the only ones, Carl. It was that way with everybody. Even older people who looked at us in a funny way when we kissed on the street: They used to do the same as we did. Only they didn't remember or didn't want to remember."

"No, they don't do the things we did out here."

"Oh, Carl, all people are human. Even kids. And I bet you the ones out here do as much petting as we did."

"But with a difference, sweetheart. Sure, the same old petting,

23   *

courting, love-making—whatever you want to call it—goes on here. But there's the stadium where they can go nights and be alone in the dark. And on a warm spring night there's the river and you can rent a canoe for two."

"Yes, I can see how things would be different in a place like this. Funny! A person lives one way and he thinks all people live that way because there is no other way. Then he goes away somewhere and sees there are other ways to live."

Another cigarette, another time of silence, then from the stadium a muffled roar. "We must be winning," he said.

"Oh, you mean the game."

"Annie?" He took her hand in both of his. "Maybe you don't know what you're in for. Things could get mighty tough."

"No tougher than I'm used to, Carl."

"There might be times when we won't know where the next meal is coming from."

"Not if I get a job."

"You can't count on that. Count on working. Something might come up."

"You mean like a baby? Oh, we'd manage some way. I'd nurse it of course and we wouldn't need extra money for its food."

"It's not as simple as that. We mustn't have a baby right away, sweetheart."

"But I don't know how not to have one."

"I asked around. I found out. So I'll take care of that. I just wanted you to know why we couldn't have a baby."

"There's nothing to worry about, then. I'll get a job first thing."

"And join the growing list of women putting a husband through college."

"What's wrong with that?"

"I don't like it."

"Carl, I'm used to working. I've been working four years. And for what? Nothing. Now I'll get something out of it."

"You mean I will. I'll get a law degree. But what will you get out of it?"

"A good start for my children. Their father will be a lawyer."

"But what will *you* get?"

"I've already got it. Just to be here in this wonderful place with you. Just to get away from"—she caught herself before saying, My stepfather—"where I was. Ah, I've gotten so much already."

"I hope you'll never be sorry."

"I'll never be sorry, Carl. No matter what."

The game was over. People swarmed all over the campus. He got her suitcase and his own stuff from the dorm. She had to carry her own suitcase because he had two of his own and was burdened down with a pair of ice skates hanging over his shoulder and a tennis racket under his arm.

That's a part of him I don't know, she thought. The way he skates good enough to win a silver cup and runs fast enough to get a medal and that Japanese boy from Hawaii he plays tennis with Saturday afternoons. I could never fit in with that part of his life. Imagine me playing tennis! Why, I can't even play ping-pong!

Annie was impressed with the house, especially the wide porch which looked like a living room to her with its wicker chairs and table. And there was a wooden swing hanging from chains.

They set their stuff down on the porch and he took her in his arms. "In five minutes," he whispered, "we'll be in bed together. Give me a good, hard, long kiss to tide me over."

She did.

But it was not to be. The landlady was very nice about it, but what could she do? she asked. The room was rented for the *day* and it was *still* day. Yes, she could see that Mrs. Brown was very tired. Would Mrs. Brown care to rest on the landlady's bed? Annie shook her head, no, and Carl said they'd wait. Well, they were welcome to wait in the living room. And now if they would excuse her? She had a cake to ice.

Ill at ease, they sat apart on the sofa. He lit a cigarette, but

25   *

Annie pointed out that there were no ashtrays around and maybe the landlady didn't like people to smoke in the room. They went out on the porch and sat in the swing. Adjusting herself to sit close to Carl, she started the swing to swaying. This irritated him.

"Don't swing, damn it!" he said. He was instantly sorry. "Don't mind me, sweetheart."

"I know how you feel, Carl, because I feel the same way."

"You don't know and you don't feel the same. You *can't* know how a man feels. A woman can bide her time and wait. But a man . . . Me! All keyed up waiting . . . waiting all day . . . waiting years. It's enough to drive a man crazy!"

"I know. Carl, I'll go get a Coke and leave you alone for a few minutes." She started to leave the swing.

"Like hell you will!"

"Don't holler at me, now," she said. "It's not my fault."

He grabbed her roughly and almost pulled her on top of him. He kissed her eyes, her ears, her mouth and the hollow at the base of her neck. He shoved his hand down her blouse and took hold of one of her breasts.

"No, Carl! Don't!"

"Let me," he begged.

"No! People are passing and any minute the landlady might come out."

"Back home, you didn't care how many people passed; who came in or out of a vestibule. What's so different about this place?"

"It's more open—got more air," she said inanely.

The silly remark infuriated him. Fury, added to sexual frustration, made him wild. He grabbed the top of her blouse and tore it down to her waist. The little buttons spattered on the floor. When he began pulling off her jacket, she opened her mouth to scream, but he got his hand over her mouth just in time. She put her two hands flat on his chest and shoved him out of the swing. He stood before her and the swing, on the rebound, clipped his

* 26

knees. He felt like murdering somebody. She started to cry then —great gulping sobs. It was the last straw.

"God damn it!" he said, his teeth tight together. "I'm going to settle this once and for all!" He stamped into the house.

Annie sat in the crazily rocking swing, tears running down her face as her trembling fingers tried to button her suit jacket over her exposed breasts. Her hat had fallen off in the scuffle. Standing up to get it made the swing rebound and it banged her square in the backside, forcing her down on her knees. The indignity of it was too much for tears. She laughed hysterically— laughed and laughed!

Carl came out of the house whistling happily because the landlady had told him she had explained their situation to the men in the room and they'd been very nice about it and were getting ready to leave and Carl and Annie could have the room in about fifteen minutes.

His happy whistling went off into a long whistle of surprise when he saw Annie, kneeling on the floor, her hat on backwards, her jacket buttoned awry, dirty tear streaks on her cheeks, and her arm over her mouth to stifle her wild laughter.

"Cry-sake, Annie! What happened?"

"The swing hit me!"

He got her to her feet, buttoned her jacket properly, set her hat on straight, dusted off her skirt and mopped at her face with his handkerchief, all the while castigating himself.

He didn't know what had got into him, he told her—acting that way. He was a pig, a dog, a louse, and even a son-of-a-bitch. And hanging was too good for him and she had every right to leave him but he hoped she wouldn't.

"No use running yourself down, Carl," she said in a tired voice. "It doesn't help."

"But it makes me feel better." She gave him a long look, then turned her head away, saying nothing.

She said nothing all the way to the lunchroom where he took

27   *

her for a sandwich and coffee while waiting for the room to be made ready. She said nothing all through their little supper. He knew she was very angry and was thinking things out and when she had them all thought out she'd give it to him. He didn't enjoy his supper, anticipating it.

She drank the last of her coffee and folded her paper napkin as carefully as she'd fold a damask one.

"Carl?"

"Yes, my sweetheart." He took her hand. She pulled it away.

"Ah, don't, Annie. Don't! Don't be mad at me. I'm so sorry and I love you so much."

"Carl, I'm a person. I'm a person that don't like to be grabbed in a swing." He waited for her to continue. "That's all," she said.

He was relieved that it wasn't worse. "I'll remember," he said.

"Also remember never to come grabbing at me any time, any place."

"I'll remember," he repeated.

She had no more to say to him and was silent on the way home. By the time they got back to the house, it was almost dark. The swing loomed up darkly on the porch. Annie gave it a dirty look. Carl, hoping to make her smile, offered to give it a good swift kick if she said so. She gave him no response.

It was a typical student's room; larger than most, however, with three windows, a double bed, a study table and chair, a rocking chair, and a bookcase half filled with Carl's books which he had carried over the day before. There was a dresser with a mirror. Carl called her attention to a little iced wedding cake and two plates and a knife, sitting on the dresser. Annie broke her silence. She clasped her hands and looked up at him with shining eyes.

"Oh, Carl! You *didn't!*"

"No. I wish I had. The landlady made it for us. She said a wedding wasn't a wedding without a cake. You know, Annie, I went into that kitchen meaning to give her hell because the room

* 28

wasn't ready? But what does she do but show me the cake she had made for us. It sure took the wind out of my sails. Let's have a piece." He gave her the knife. "You cut it."

"Put your hand on mine while I cut it. That's how people do. I saw it in a movie about a wedding at West Point."

He put his hand on hers, and she cut two pieces and put each on a plate. Well, it wasn't a tiered cake and there wasn't a sword to cut it with and Carl wore no uniform and she wasn't wearing a bouffante white dress and an heirloom veil, but it was a wonderful cake just the same.

Annie ate two pieces and then licked her fingers, one by one. She looked around for a towel or something to wipe them on. Carl let her wipe them on his shirt. It was dirty anyhow, he said.

"What's her name?" she asked.

"The landlady? Mrs. Hansmon."

"I'll be right back."

The landlady was in the kitchen—putting it to bed, she said. Annie was reminded of her dead father, who had been a printer. He used to talk about putting the paper to bed.

"I came down to thank you for the cake, Mrs. Hansmon."

"Oh, that! It was nothing."

"It's beautiful! I'll remember it all my life."

"Pshaw! Only a little cake. The room all right?"

"Just grand!"

"Well, if you ever need anything . . ."

"And if I can ever do anything for you in return for the cake . . ."

"Why, thank you, Mrs. Brown."

"People what I like, well, I like them to call me Annie."

"Annie, then. You're a nice girl, Annie, and you've got a nice husband."

"I know." The landlady put her hand on the light string and waited for Annie to leave. "Mrs. Hansmon?"

"Yes, Annie?"

"Could I ask you a personal question?"

"Well," hedged the landlady, certain that Annie was going to ask about contraceptives, "that depends."

"I just want to ask do you understand the way I talk?"

"Why, naturally."

"That's all. I'm glad. Thanks and good night." Annie ran back up the stairs.

She's a real nice girl, thought the landlady as she gave the light string a jerk. But kind of strange.

Carl, stripped to the waist, was pacing the floor. He had pulled down the shades, turned back the bedspread, and his pajamas, a new pair, were on the bed. Annie rushed in and started to describe her visit with Mrs. Hansmon. He wouldn't let her talk. He took her in his arms and kissed her urgently.

"Let me at least take my hat off," she said.

"Oh, Annie, please don't stall. I've been waiting all day!"

She started to unbutton her coat. She swayed a little. "I guess I'm kind of dizzy," she said.

"You poor little thing! You're about out on your feet. Sit in the rocker and I'll take your shoes off." She sat down. He pulled off her high-heeled pumps. Annie, feeling through her skirt, got her garters unfastened. He pulled off her silk stockings. "Such little feet to do so much walking," he murmured as he rubbed them. "Could you stand up for a minute, Annie, and let me take your jacket off?"

She stood up. "I want to do it myself." She turned her back to him and started to undo the buttons.

He felt sorry for her and decided to give her a little break. "Look, Annie. I'll go take a shower and undress in the bathroom and give you a chance to get ready for bed all by yourself. Okay?"

"All right. And thanks, Carl."

When he got back wearing his new pajamas, she was standing

in the middle of the room, toothbrush in one hand, tin of tooth powder in the other. She was wearing her new white nightgown and robe. He put his arms around her. She stood rigid.

"What's wrong, sweetheart? Don't you love me any more?"

"I've got to wash my teeth."

"Later."

"Now!" she said stubbornly.

He grabbed the knot of coiled hair at the nape of her neck, pulled her head back roughly and put a bruising kiss on her slightly opened mouth. With all her strength, she pushed him away from her.

"Oh, stop this nonsense, Annie."

"I told you not to grab at me. And I'm not going to sleep with you."

"But we're married now, sweetheart."

"I'm still not going to sleep with you."

"Why? Tell me."

"Because you'll hurt me. I know it."

"Go wash your teeth, sweetheart," he said quietly. She left.

He wondered what in hell had gone wrong? Everything, he answered himself. She had gone through too much.

And why, oh, why had he started that talk about how tough things might get and they mustn't have a baby right away? That could have waited. And worst of all, the way he'd lost his head in that damned swing! The swing did it, he decided. Scared her to death.

But was it especially the swing? Could it be that in all their years of embracing, kissing, touching, discussing sex often and thoroughly, she had been conditioned into feeling that the preliminaries were the whole thing? And that consummation wasn't necessary?

All this clinical analysis knocked most of the desire out of him. When Annie came back, he made no move to go to her. "Go to bed, Annie," he said. "I won't bother you." But she re-

31   *

mained standing near the door, still foolishly clutching her toothbrush and powder. He needed a cigarette badly and went to the closet to get one from his coat. At his first move, she started and dropped the tin of powder. "Take it easy, sweetheart. I'm just getting a cigarette." He felt a pang when he heard her sigh of relief.

He got a cigarette and remembered the wedding gift he had for her. He brought it out and placed the little box on the dresser. "I bought a wedding present for you and like a dope I forgot to give it to you." He made a point of going over to the window, away from the dresser, to light his cigarette. "Don't you want to see what it is?" he asked.

Slowly she went to the dresser and picked up the package. "But I didn't get anything for you," she said.

"Good! That makes me one up on you."

She opened the box. In it was a thin little gold chain with a golden heart with an infinitesimal diamond chip.

"It's beautiful!" She went to him and kissed his cheek. "Put it on for me," she said. She turned her back and he put it on for her. "It's cold," she said. "Beautifully cold."

He took her hand. "Annie, will you sit on my lap awhile?" He felt her stiffen. "I don't want anything else—just to pretend you're my baby." She gave him a wary look. "I've never had a baby, you know."

"I should hope not!" She smiled a little. "Carl, I shouldn't have been so mean—asking you what you did with all your money. You were saving it for my locket."

"You weren't mean. You acted exactly like a wife, which is as it should be." She sat on his lap then. "Put your little head on my shoulder and relax," he said.

She snuggled her head against his neck and he rocked with one arm holding her, and with his other hand he patted her backside. After a while of this, she said it felt good.

"Want me to get you a cigarette?" she asked.

"I don't need one." He thought of what he should say. Finally, he said, "Annie, I may be crude at times, even rough. But funnel-melody . . ." He waited for her to smile.

"That word," she said, imitating him, "happens to be pro-nounced fun-da-ment-ally."

He ventured to give her a big hug. She did not protest. "Fundamentally, I am not a monster. So don't be afraid of me. I am Carl, who loves you. I'm the guy you married this morning. Remember? I love you and I wouldn't hurt you for anything in the world."

"I know. But you frightened me when you grabbed me. And then, I got a little panicky. I never slept with a man before, and I didn't know what I was supposed to do. Because I never slept with a man," she repeated.

"Neither have I. With a woman, I mean. I mean, you know what I mean. So I don't know any more about it than you do. We'll just have to help each other."

"Carl!" She sat upright. "You mean you never . . ."

"If I had, I would have known better than to just grab you all of a sudden."

"But I thought all men slept around."

"Not all. Not me, anyhow. But don't tell anyone. They'll think something's wrong with me."

"Who do I know to tell? Besides, I think it's pretty wonderful that I'm going to be your first girl—that way." She cuddled closer to him. "Tell me about it," she said.

So he rocked her and patted her and told as much as he knew about the sex act, and she fell asleep in his arms while he was talking.

He looked down at her in her cheap little bridal nightclothes with the factory creases still in the material and thought of what hopes and dreams she had chosen them with. She still clutched her new toothbrush in her hand. When he tried to remove it, her hand tightened on it in her sleep. Her hair was in disorder.

there were black circles under her eyes. The skin of her eyelids was so thin that the lids looked transparent.

Overwhelming tenderness took the place of passion. She is so strong within herself, he thought, but so uncertain outside. But, just the same, she plows into life with both feet. Deep down, she believes in herself, but outwardly she's full of fear and doubts. She's so helpless . . . helpless . . .

He, too, was drifting off to sleep. However, just before sleep came, he had a cold, clear thought. Later he couldn't remember whether he had actually had the thought or had dreamed it.

Helpless? he thought incredulously. Why, that girl could fight a buzz saw!

An hour later, or was it two, he was awakened by someone pulling his arms. Annie was trying to get him up out of the rocker. "Wake up, Carl," she said, "and come to bed like a good boy."

He saw her through a haze. She had bathed, brushed her hair, braided it and tied a white ribbon on each braid. She had discarded her robe and stood before him in her transparent nightgown and she smelled of baby talcum powder.

She got him on his feet. He swayed sleepily. She put her arms around him and pretended, with many a grunt, that she was trying to lift him off the floor.

"Must I carry you?" she asked.

"I'm awake now. I'll walk."

She stood on tiptoe in her bare feet and put little kisses all over his face. "Hurry up!" she whispered.

He took off his pajama jacket and went into the closet to hang it up. From the closet, he said, "If I turn the light out, will you take off your nightgown, sweetheart?"

"It's already off," she said.

Chapter Two

Carl didn't have to deliver papers on Sunday, but he did **have** to work in the cafeteria. When he came home at ten, Annie was still sleeping. He bent down and kissed her. She awakened suddenly, crying out, "Mama!"

"Cry-sake, Annie!" Carl was startled.

"Oh, it's only you!" she said in wide-awake relief.

"Were you expecting the Sheik of Araby?"

"I forgot I was here. I thought I was in my bed at home."

He had brought her breakfast; a small Mason jar of coffee and a sweet roll. He had her eat it in bed. She said it made her feel like a rich woman—breakfast in bed. Home, she said, her mother wouldn't let her eat in bed, saying that drew bugs. Carl said his mother used to insist he have breakfast in bed so he could rest a few minutes more. "And how I hated it!" he said.

"She spoiled you. Don't expect *me* to."

He hung up his coat and whistled "When My Baby Smiles at Me" as he pulled down the knot of his tie and pulled his shirt up out of his pants. She finished her breakfast and started to get out of bed.

"Oh, no, you don't, Mrs. Brown!"

He had to get out of bed at eleven to work the lunch shift. He wanted her to promise to stay there until he returned. She refused. But she did promise to get back into bed when he returned.

She bathed and dressed, did up her hair, made the bed, straightened up the room and then there was nothing more to do. She went through the books in the bookcase, but all it held was the dictionary and secondhand volumes of Blackstone's *Commentaries*. She read a page and found it dull. She felt a great respect for Carl. He not only could read the stuff, but he understood it, too.

Time hung heavy on her hands, and she was so glad when Carl came home that she threw herself at him.

"We lost!" he said dramatically.

"Lost what?"

"The game. Yesterday."

"Oh, *that!*"

"Oh, that, she says, and I had a quarter bet on us winning."

"Serves you right. Gambling!"

He had brought a sandwich and a bottle of milk for her, and the Sunday papers. She thought he looked tired, and she helped him off with his coat. Hanging it in the closet, she was aware of the odor of grease trapped in the tweed fabric. She took a bite of the sandwich, pronounced it good, put it down and went to the bed to fold back the bedspread. She took off her shoes.

"Sit down, Annie dear, and eat your lunch first while I take a look at the sports page." He sat in the rocker, his hands relaxed on the unopened newspaper.

She finished her sandwich and milk. He still hadn't looked at the paper. "Aren't you going to read about the game, Carl?"

"In a minute."

"You look so tired."

"It's been a hectic weekend," he said.

She sat at his feet. "Let me take your shoes off, darling." His heart turned over. She so rarely used a word of endearment.

She removed his shoes and socks. His feet felt hot to her, and she blew on them to cool them off. He looked down at her.

"I love you, Annie," he said quietly.

In answer, she put her arms around his legs and pressed her cheek against them. It was a moment of peace—of contentment—of knowing each other well.

They didn't get to read the paper. It was the last day of their honeymoon, and they had so much to talk about. They wouldn't see much of each other during the week; what with his paper route and cafeteria job and classes and law library between classes, he'd be gone from six in the morning until eight at night. And then he'd have to study at home until ten.

"So you won't see much of me," he said.

"Just so I know you're in the world."

"Will you be lonesome?"

"Just for you."

"Do you miss your mother, Annie?"

"I'm too worried about what she'll say about our marriage."

"What about your stepfather? Miss him?"

"No!" Her "no" was so explosive that he knew better than to question her further.

"Your brothers?"

"I miss them. I used to take them to the movies every Sunday and buy them a cone. Do they miss me? I wonder. Will they cry when Mama tells them I've gone away for good?"

"Never mind, sweetheart. You'll see them again. Maybe they'll come stay with us at the governor's mansion."

"You really mean you'll be governor?"

"Why not? Dreaming is free in this country. You'll wear silks and satins, and I'll buy you diamonds."

"I have all the diamonds I'll ever want." She touched the necklace he'd given her.

"Pearls?"

"All I want is a pair of jade earrings."

"What do you know about jade?"

37   *

"I read a story about a lady spy, and she always wore jade earrings. And look! I already have holes in my ears."

"I always say, better a hole in the ear than a hole in the head. That's what I always say."

He took her to the cafeteria for supper. The place was almost a block long, and the front was all plate glass. It was dark except for the long counter in the rear. Rising steam indicated that the food was already in the containers. The counter girls in their white uniforms and perky white headbands were already at their stations, talking up and down the counters to each other.

"Why no customers?" asked Annie.

"It's not open yet."

"How do the bus boys get in?"

"The help goes through the kitchen. We better go in. We have to eat before the customers come."

They went through a garbage-smelling alley to get to the kitchen. Carl called out a hello everybody as he hung up his coat. The kitchen smelled of hot grease. So that's why his coat smells that way, thought Annie.

The head chef, who practically ran the cafeteria, was sitting alone at a little table, having a bowl of clear soup. He was theatrically immaculate in white pants, apron, jacket, and a towering white chef's hat. Carl introduced Annie.

"Mr. Felix comes from Holland," explained Carl.

Mr. Felix gallantly rose and pulled off his chef's hat. He had thick white hair, fine and wavy, like the hair of Christmas tree angels, and a white goatee to match. He bowed low over Annie's hand.

"I got a sweetheart is just like you," he said. "She has tea room in Chicago. We work and save our money so we should get married and then we go back to the old country with our money together and live rich there."

"That's wonderful," said Annie, "but don't let us keep you standing, Mr. Felix, while your soup gets cold."

"Your girl has the heart for people," he told Carl. "Now, Annie Brown, you sit and have soup from me." She looked inquiringly at Carl. Carl pulled out a chair for her. "I go now," said Mr. Felix, "and get for you and fresh for me." He took his bowl over to the big black cooking range.

"But, Carl, he didn't ask you," she whispered.

"Protocol."

"What's that?"

"*That* is: The help does not eat with the boss chef."

Mr. Felix came back with two bowls of soup and Carl left.

"Soup! Is all I eat all day," explained Mr. Felix. "Comes this way: All day I taste the sauce, bite the meat, smell the cauliflower, and pinch the pastry. So I can't eat those stuffs. Only soup."

"That must be why you have such nice clear skin and pink cheeks, Mr. Felix."

"Not so nice like yours," he said gallantly. "I wait for you, Annie Brown."

"Excuse me." She picked up her spoon. He waited until she took a spoonful before he picked up his spoon.

"You like it?"

"It's *good!*"

"From turtles, it comes. With sherry wine in."

"It's *very* good!"

"You don't care it's from turtles? Some ladies think that is strange to eat."

"Oh, I'm used to strange food. You see, where I went to school there were Jewish girls, Italian girls, and we brought our lunch —sandwiches. Mama made me jelly sandwiches. The Jewish girls had things like fish with stuffing and the Italian girls brought chopped peppers and onion and tomatoes all mixed together and garlic instead of salt, and hard bread so the stuff wouldn't leak through. And we used to swap sandwiches. That's how I got to like strange food."

39 *

"Annie Brown, you are a woman of the world." Something struck him and he laughed ho! ho! ho! shaking all over like a department store Santa Claus.

"I love this turtle soup, Mr. Felix."

"From live turtles comes my soup. In the back room is box with wet grass in. I catch live flies, my turtles should eat. From them comes the soup. Only for me. Not the customers."

"Live flies?" Annie put her spoon down.

"I like to do that," he said simply. "You would like to see my turtles eat flies I catch?"

"I guess I'm not woman of the world enough for that," she said.

Again he let out the ho! ho! ho! "Eat your soup, Annie Brown. There is babies in it."

"Baby turtles?" she said, aghast.

"No." He looked around like a conspirator and lowered his voice. "No. But what makes you want to do the thing what makes you get babies."

"Good God!" she blurted out.

Mr. Felix leaned back in his chair with a satisfied, relaxed look on his face. Frantically, Annie looked around for Carl. Carl, who had changed into a white jacket, had been watching them. He had heard the counter girls complain about the dirty things the chef whispered to them.

He was at Annie's side instantly. He pressed her hand indicating that she was not to make a scene.

"I'll take my child bride off your hands now, Mr. Felix," he said.

Mr. Felix paid no attention to him or to Annie. He didn't even look up when they left.

Carl took her out into the alley. He asked what had happened. She told him. A muscle worked in his cheek as he listened. When she had finished, he started for the kitchen. She grabbed his arm.

"What are you going to do, Carl?"

"I'm going to take care of the impotent old bastard."

"No! You might lose your job."

"To hell with my job!"

"And it might get around what he said to me. And I'd feel ashamed." He hesitated. "Besides, if you hit him, he might report it to the college and they'd see only his side of it and you might get kicked out of school."

She had something there. He recalled the interview with the Dean of the Law School. He had told the Dean he was going to marry. The Dean had been against it. Again he heard the Dean say: "The slightest lowering of grades, the merest infraction . . . the consequences will be severe."

"Besides," Annie said, "maybe it was my fault. Mama always said I was too free with strangers."

"Ah, no, Annie. Your mother's wrong. You're a friendly, warmhearted girl who likes people. No decent person would take advantage of that."

The cafeteria was about to open, and he had to have his supper now or forfeit it.

They went down the counter with their trays, and Carl introduced her to the counter girls, who smiled and wished them luck and the salad girl said may all their troubles be little ones, and everybody laughed.

Carl introduced her to his very special friend, who was in charge of the coffee urn at the end of the counter. Mrs. Ridinski was a stout, sweet-faced, middle-aged Polish woman. It was evident that she was very fond of Carl.

"So, Carl, you went and got married on me," she said, pretending sadness. Carl hung his head in mock shame. "And you said you'd always be true to me." She wiped away an imaginary tear.

"Her mother held a shotgun on me. What could I do?"

"All fooling aside, Carl," said Mrs. Ridinski, "she's a cute little thing."

"At least *she* thinks so," said Carl.

Annie said, "Don't you believe a word he says, Mrs. Ridinski."

"Too late you tell me," sighed the woman. "But learn from me, Annie. Don't let him break your heart, the way he broke my poor heart."

The cashier was banging open rolls of coins and putting nickels, dimes, and quarters into separate compartments of the cash register. Carl put a quarter on the ledge for Annie's supper. The cashier refused to accept it.

"It's on me," he said gallantly. "Congratulations."

As Carl arranged their food on a little corner table for two, he said, "At least there are *some* nice people in the world."

They had little to say to each other during the meal; both, as usual, being very hungry. Carl, a fast eater, finished first. Annie dawdled over her coffee, watching the other four bus boys at a nearby table. Carl pressed her thigh under the table.

"What?" she asked, startled.

"Drink your good coffee, Annie Brown," he said. "There is babies in it."

Annie laughed until the tears came. The counter girls smiled at each other, the bus boys turned around and smiled, and Mrs. Ridinski waved her hand at Carl and Annie. Carl, pleased, smiled at everyone.

Suddenly all the lights went on. The counter girls stood at attention, each holding a plate like a soldier holding a rifle at inspection. The doors flew open, people gushed in, and in seconds there was a line snaking down the counter. Then came the first ping of the cash register. The cafeteria was open for business.

The other bus boys, who had been hunched over their plates like quarterbacks getting the captain's signals, now straightened. As if obeying a signal, each boy piled his dirty dishes in a pyramid, marched out to the kitchen with it, and returned trundling a rubber-tired cart.

Carl stood up to finish his coffee, made his pyramid and left, saying, "Don't go away, now, Annie."

"I'll wait till you're through, Carl."

For two hours she watched him trundle his cart from table to table, clearing remnants of what had been food off the plates, stacking them, collecting the "silverware," dumping the dregs of coffee cups, slashing left-over water onto the marble tabletop and wiping it dry with a cloth that grew dirtier by the minute.

He worked with no expression on his face. He neither looked at, smiled at, nor spoke to anyone. He was not Carl Brown, newly married husband; not a student specializing in corporate law. And certainly not a potential governor.

He was one of five bus boys working for the privilege of eating.

Chapter Three

She climbed back into bed to read the note Carl had left for her.

Mrs. C. Brown, dear madam:

I congratulate you on turning out to be a wonderful wife. I am aware of my sagacity in choosing you out of one million and three women anxious to marry me.

It was with some anguish I left you this morning. Time will lag ere I see you again. Be so gracious as to meet me in the alley at eight. I crave the boon of strolling home with you. Do not deny me this ecstasy. I am, dearest of dear ones,

Yours until Niagara falls.

Carl Brown, Esquire

She smiled and read the note again. It was fun to receive letters and notes. That reminded her. She'd write to her mother, giving her new address. She meant to write a short note, but poor Annie was like a person possessed when she had a pen in her hand and a blank sheet of paper before her. She wrote and wrote. Was it one hour? Two? She began having a headache, lacking breakfast. Hurriedly, she ended the letter.

Well I wrote enough for now. Here's a dollar for Freddy and Tommy to share. You tell them I miss them and love them. And don't forget I love you, Mama, and you got to love me, too, because I was your first born baby. You got to love me even though I ran away from you . . .

The donated campus campanile struck the quarter hour. She wondered, a quarter to what? I must get a clock. Without a clock to make the day into certain times, a day is just a big bowl of mush, she thought.

She read the "female wanted" ads in yesterday's Sunday paper. Most called for *woman to do light housekeeping and take care of two children while mother works.* Light housekeeping, mused Annie cynically. I just bet it's light. There were a few ads for *office girl must know shorthand.* One ad she tore from the paper. *Wanted girl part-time office work.*

She had a cup of coffee and a doughnut at a little lunchroom around the corner. She phoned from there. A woman answered.

"Can you take dictation?"

"No. But . . ."

"Can you type?"

"No. But I could learn."

"Sorry."

"Wait! I learn awful quick."

The woman hung up.

Annie went downtown and wrote out an ad for the morning paper. *Student's wife wants office work whole or part time.* She gave Mrs. Hansmon's phone number. Then she went to the bank to have her savings transferred. She had to leave her bankbook there, and the man said it might take a week. She stopped in the dime store to get an ashtray for Carl and had lunch there. The menu was the same as the one in the Brooklyn dime store where she had lunched with her friend Arlene. The turkey dinner—thin slices of cold turkey meat and mashed potatoes, covered

45 *

with hot gray gravy, the tiny paper cup of cranberry sauce, and the good coffee—was the same, too.

Yes, it was like being back home in Brooklyn again, except the people pronounced words different. Orange drink, for example. Here they said *ore-ranch*; in Brooklyn it was *ah-rinch*. What made the accent different? The water they drank? Because they weren't near the ocean? The sharper, more pungent air? *What?*

She left a nickel tip. Her mother had been against Annie's tipping. She said Annie liked to show off. Carl was against it, too. He said it degraded the person to whom it was offered and that made Annie feel superior. But Annie knew why she tipped. It made her feel magnificent! And that feeling was worth a nickel any day. She justified the extravagance by saying that's what she'd pay for a pack of gum—if she chewed gum. She smiled. An elderly woman, passing behind the counter with a tray of upside-down freshly washed cups, smiled back at Annie. They sure are nice and friendly out here in the Middle West, thought Annie.

She found a hardware store. "I want a cheap alarm clock," she said. "Not *cheap*, cheap. I mean"—she waited to get the word —"inexpensive."

"Our cheapest clock is ninety-eight cents."

"Could I see it?"

The clerk took a clock from a carton, set the time, wound it, and placed it on the counter. The clock ticked hysterically as if delighted at being free of the carton.

"Now we have a better clock," said the clerk. "Costs a little more, but listen!" He set up the better clock. "Notice the difference? You can hardly hear it tick."

"You'd hear it all right," said Annie, "if you stood it on a piece of tin like you did the cheap one. I'll take the ninety-eight-cent one."

"That's up to you. But you're throwing your money away."

"Why do you have such clocks, then, in your store if you think they're no good?"

He shrugged. "Well, I guess to demonstrate that for a few cents more a customer can get a clock that doesn't tick so loud."

"I happen to be a customer," she said, "that *likes* a clock that ticks loud." The clerk started to wrap it. "I want the box, too. It belongs to the clock."

She walked down the street holding the clock to her breast. She suited her steps to the ticking, which made her walk in short, choppy steps. A passing pedestrian gave her a curious look.

I better cut it out, she admonished herself, or people will think I'm the Japanese Sand Man in person.

She stopped to admire the display in a florist's window: huge chrysanthemums in black bowls and roses in clear glass vases. Up front, in the middle of the window, was a brass container holding a few sprigs of shiny, orange-red berries centered in open yellow husks. She just *had* to know the name of those berries. She went into the store.

"What can I do for you?" asked a tall, thin, slightly effeminate young man.

"Those berries you got in the window: what's their name?"

"Bittersweet."

"What a beautiful name! It suits them so. They grow in yards around here?"

"No. They come from up in the north country."

"Where up north?"

"Oh, past the big lakes; past . . . You acquainted with the northern part of the state?"

"I just got here two days ago."

"I see." He cocked his ear as if listening.

"That's not me breathing," she explained. "That's a clock I bought. A nice clock."

"I see," he said again. "Are you French?"

"No. I'm Brooklyn." Before he could say it, she said it. "You see?" That made him smile, which had been her intention. "What is it like up there where the bittersweet grows?"

"Used to be great lumber country up there. Thousands of

47　*

acres of proud trees. Then came the lumberjacks." He sighed. "If I could write, I'd write a book about it. Call it *The Rape of the Forests.*"

"You mean they chopped all the trees down?"

"They did."

"Are they still chopping them down?"

"The murderous ax no longer rings out in the silent forest," he said dramatically.

"Gee!" she said. "That sounds like a poem."

Encouraged, he went on: "They denuded God's own paradise and left in their wake a purgatory of ugly stumps."

"And the stumps still stand there?"

"After a fashion. They were dug up, upended, and arranged close together to form fences. And tenderly, the bittersweet grows over them like God's own blessing on the miles and miles of gnarled meandering fences."

"Who found the bittersweet and trained it to grow over the upside-down stumps?"

"Well, folklore has it that there was a giant of a man . . ."

"I know! I know!" she interrupted excitedly. "Paul Bunyan did it. Paul Bunyan and his blue ox, Babe." The florist looked at her with cold distaste. "I'm sorry," she said. "You wanted to say it, didn't you?" He said nothing. "Of course, I don't really know. I read about Paul Bunyan once, and I put two and two together."

"I see," he said. Icicles hung on the two words.

She sighed, feeling that the rapport between them was over. "Not to take up any more of your time," she said, "how much is a bunch of that bittersweet?"

"Ten cents."

She could hardly believe they were so cheap. "I'll take a bunch."

While he placed the sprigs on a square of slick green paper, the bottom of which he twisted into a cornucopia, she looked at his name printed backwards on the window.

"That will be a wonderful book, Mr. Byrd. I mean the one you're going to write about the forest."

"It was just a passing thought."

"Oh, no! You must write it, Mr. Byrd. You are a wonderful writer. I *know*. Just by the way you talk!"

"It is kind of you to say so," he said formally. Then he broke down. "Do you *really* think so?" he asked wistfully.

"I'm dead sure of it," she said solemnly.

"Thank you." He looked away from her. "Incidentally," he said casually, "I'm driving up to the north country next Sunday. Perhaps you'd like to come along? See Paul Bunyan's country?"

"Oh, I couldn't! You see," she said proudly, "I'm married!"

"And," he said sadly, "I am not."

"Well, good-by." She put a dime on the counter and went away. It was a long time before he picked up the dime.

One more purchase, a pack of cigarettes in case Carl ran out, and she was home. She pulled off her pumps. High heels were not for walking most of the day. She checked the heels. Suppose one broke off! She'd be done for. She had no other shoes. Saddle shoes for me, she decided, as soon as my bank account comes here.

She washed the Mason jar that had held coffee the day before and polished it to a gleam with tissue from the roll in the bathroom. The bittersweet looked pretty in it. The ashtray went on the study table, where it caught a beam of sun coming in the window. She changed her mind about surprising Carl with the cigarettes. They belonged with the ashtray.

But it took the clock to pull everything together. Its ticking made the room come to life. Annie loved the loud ticking. City bred, she was used to sound—harmony of sound. The sound of the El. Ashcans slammed down at dawn. The chant of the street hucksters and the high thin sound of children at play on the street. The ticking of the clock made her feel just right.

There was a glass tray on the dresser holding two water tumblers. It didn't look right. She removed the tumblers and arranged her toilet articles on the tray. A box of talcum powder, a box of face powder. A jar of cold cream and a lipstick. All dime store products. And her comb! Real tortoise shell! Carl had bought it for her as a birthday present two years ago. It had cost all of a dollar! She held it up to the light. It was like translucent honey with a darker streak running through it. As always, the comb thrilled her. Her hairbrush, a pink celluloid affair with missing tufts, just didn't belong on the tray with the comb. "Back you go, old baldy," she said aloud to the brush and dropped it into the drawer.

She wondered how the room would look to a stranger. She decided to test it. She went out, closing the door, and walked down the hall, then came back. Hand on doorknob, she took a deep breath, closed her eyes, and walked in. She opened her eyes. The sunbeam on the glass ashtray threw off colored, shimmering glints. The bittersweet, duplicated in the mirror, seemed to fill the room with color. Her makeup things looked dainty—and the clock! With its short legs spraddled out, its shiny tin sides and honest open face, it seemed like an old friend. Annie sat on the bed, her hands clasped between her knees, and whispered, "It's beautiful! It's just too beautiful!"

Just then, the campus campanile struck two. Annie's clock showed exactly two! She stood up in awe. To think, she thought; just to *think!* A little ninety-eight-cent clock tells the exact same time as that million-dollar clock on the campus! It's like a miracle.

Elation was followed by despair as she noticed a run in one of her stockings. She berated herself for walking around in her stocking feet. Silk stockings were a luxury. She had had two pairs that morning. Now she had a pair and a half. She got out her pad and wrote:

*   50

Things to buy
(1) 2 pair woolen socks. White. Like coeds
(2) Saddle shoes!
(3) New hairbrush (?)

Now it was time to go to the library. She prepared for it the way a girl prepares for a party. She bathed and dusted herself with talcum powder; put on fresh makeup. She changed into her other slip, brassière, and pair of step-ins. She brushed her hair, annoyed with the defective brush and aware that no matter how she arranged her long hair, she'd look out of place among the bob-haired coeds. She made another entry on her list:

(4) Get hair bobbed (Ask Carl first)

She thought it over and crossed out ask-Carl-first.

She felt proud walking across the campus. I bet, she thought, no other girl in my old neighborhood ever *saw* a campus—much less walked across one. Then she saw a gray-uniformed man with a big stick coming toward her. She became uneasy. Was she allowed on the campus without Carl? Would she be chased off because she was not a college student?

As a child, she'd been chased off the grass in the park; chased off the school grounds after school hours; chased off a street not in her own district by the kids who lived on that street.

She got Carl's library card out of her handbag to show it to the man. But all he was interested in was impaling leaves and papers on the nail at the end of his stick and putting them in a bag he carried.

Annie climbed the wide steps and entered the library with the exultant reverence an art lover has entering the Louvre for the first time. She believed what Carl had told her—that there were more than a million books in that library.

The great vaulted rooms had the same grand smell the one-room library back there in Brooklyn had had: a mixture of ink, paste, leather, apples and wax; all dominated by a faint moss scent.

She went from room to room, floor to floor, stack to stack, reveling in books, books, books. She loved books. She loved them with her senses and her intellect. The way they smelled and looked; the way they felt in her hands; the way the pages seemed to murmur as she turned them. Everything there is in the world, she thought, is in books. Things that people said and did and the way they thought and acted even from away back. Away back! Long before Jesus was born, even. Everything that ever happened or could happen or didn't happen is in these books. Everything since the world began.

It was like old times to Annie to come upon *David Copperfield* in the "D" rack. She smiled at the book and said, "Hello, David," then looked around embarrassed, hoping no one had heard her.

She had first read the book when she was twelve. Before that, she had read fairy tales and novels about well-to-do Victorian families and minor classics available in the little neighborhood library. She had found *David Copperfield* there, and it had made a great impact on her. It was the first realistic book about a city that she'd read up to that time.

She decided to take it out, now, read it again to see if she still liked it after a lapse of six years. From the "L" rack she took out *Babbitt*. She had read *Main Street*, had been impressed by a new kind of writing, and looked forward to reading this book.

Her third book was a slim volume of one-act plays. Annie had seen many short plays in vaudeville. She knew of them as "skits." She had never seen a play in print. Of course there were Shakespeare's plays, but she considered them poetry.

The check-out librarian did not challenge her, as Annie had feared.

Annie walked back across the campus, holding the books in her arm and swaying a bit, as she had seen the coeds do. Happily, she believed she might be mistaken for a coed. She had to change her mind when some classes let out. Most of the coeds wore what was almost a uniform: dark pleated skirts, loose pull-over sweaters, a string of "pearls," saddle shoes and socks. Annie felt out of place in her city clothes. I'll never be one of them, she thought sadly. I'll never belong.

Nevertheless, on arriving home she made more entries on her list of things to buy.

      (4) Dark pleated skirt
      (5) Pull-over sweater
      (6) String of pearls

Then she sat down and read for two hours.

Carl was waiting for her outside the cafeteria. He put his arms around her and kissed her, and for the first time she was embarrassed at being kissed in public. As they walked home hand in hand, he asked how she had put in the day.

"I bought some things I needed and got three books from the library and I wrote to my mother."

"Is that all?"

"That's all. And what kind of a day did you have, Carl?"

"Oh," he said nonchalantly, "I chased my secretary around the desk all afternoon but couldn't catch her. She was wearing her track shoes. Seriously, though, I put in a hell of a day sitting in class, trying to concentrate on corporate law when I wanted to be home with my wife."

He didn't notice the changes in the room until Annie called his attention to them. He said he *thought* the room looked different but he didn't know why. Yes, it looked very nice.

"I'm glad you have something to read," he said. "I've got to put in a couple of hours of hard labor and I won't be much company for you. Folly's going to throw a quiz at us tomorrow."

"Who's Folly?"

"Prof Folsom."

"Does he get mad when you call him Folly?"

"He doesn't know we do."

"Why do you call him that?"

"Because we all like him."

He prepared for the ritual of study in this new place. He checked the table and found it a little unsteady. He wedged an empty matchbook under one of the legs. He put his day's notes on the table, got a textbook from the bookcase, and sharpened a pencil.

"When you get home tomorrow," she said, "I'll have your pencils sharpened for you and the table set for studying."

"Oh, if you go into town tomorrow, will you get me a desk blotter?"

"Yes, *sir!* Any special color?"

"Green will be fine."

"Anything else?"

"Can't think of anything else. Oh! and thanks for the cigarettes." He sat down and opened his book.

"I wish I could sit next to you and hold your pens."

"What pens?"

"You know. Like Dora in *David Copperfield?*"

"That's right. I'd forgotten. So long since I read it."

She hated to relinquish him to his studies. "What's the test in, Carl?"

"Oh, the quiz! Torts."

"What's torts? A little cake? But it can't be."

"Look it up, sweetheart, like a big girl."

Tort: it said in the dictionary. *A wrongful act, injury or damage for which a civil action can be brought.* Under that was the same word with an "e" attached and that meant a small cake. So, thought Annie smugly, I'm not as dumb as I think I am. She turned to face Carl, but he was holding his pencil and seemed to be waiting.

"You study," she said. "Don't mind me."

"I'll wait until you get settled, first." She took the book of one-act plays from the dresser, slipped off her pumps, and sat down in the rocker.

She read *The Valiant*, turning the pages very carefully so they wouldn't rustle. She was immediately absorbed in the play. She came to the part where she *knew* the boy was the girl's brother. She had a definite thrill. As if he had timed it, Carl banged his hand down on the table. She jumped up, dropping the book.

"What is it, Carl?" she asked, her heart beating fast.

"That damned clock! Ticks so damned loud I might as well be studying in a boiler factory."

She ran to the closet, got her jacket, wrapped the clock in it and put it in the bottom drawer. "Shh, now!" she whispered to the clock as she closed the drawer.

"I should have bought the one that didn't tick so loud," she said. "But I liked this one better."

"Come here, sweetheart." She went to him. He put his arm around her waist and she leaned against him. "I'm sorry I got upset about the clock. But listen, Annie, it's going to be very hard on you sitting still in this little room nights. But I've *got* to study nights. There's not enough free time in the day. And I've *got* to concentrate. I don't have a retentive memory like you have. I have to memorize everything—word for word."

"Not to start a fight," she said, "but how could you ever study in the dorm all full of boys?"

"I didn't. I studied at the library. I had a carrel there." He hoped she wouldn't ask what a carrel was.

"What's a carrel?" she asked. "I mean aside from being a Christmas song?"

"A carrel," he said patiently, "is a quiet cubbyhole."

"Thanks." She kissed the top of his head. "I won't bother you any more. I'll sit on the bed and read."

A few nights later, inspired by the one-act plays she had read, she decided to write a play. First, she planned, I must get a good name so I know what I'm writing about. She concentrated on a title but none came up. The thing to do, she decided, is to write the play first and then, whatever it's about, I will give it that name. Now what'll I write about? How about Carl and me? Not the way we are, but if we were different people living in a different way. First I'll give us different names. After some thought, she decided on Linda and Lance. Now where will I lay it? This room? I'll figure that out later. I'll write down the conversations first and put the other stuff in after. She began writing a play.

LANCE

Sit close to me, dearest of dears, while I study torts.
(She sits.)

LINDA

Oh, Lance, I wish I could hold pens for you. Like Dora.

LANCE

Dora?
(He thinks.)
Ah, yes. Good old David Copperfield.
(He smiles a faraway smile.)
We must read the book again, one day. Together this time, my pretty Linda. Once more we'll walk down Memory Lane with dear old Peggoty and wonderful Macawber and blackhearted Uriah Heep.

LINDA

Don't forget, Lance. You have a torts test tomorrow.

LANCE

(He corrects her like she asked him to do.)
Quiz.

LINDA

(Is grateful like always.)
Thank you, Lance.
(Now while her voice is playful, her intentions are serious.)
Now settle down and study torts like a good boy.
(He studies torts. But the nearness of her; the scent of her perfume, distracts him.)
(She feels this.)

* 56

I'm afraid I distract you, Lance. I'll go away.

(She gets up.)

LANCE

(He gets in a panic. He jumps up.)

No! Don't go away! Never go away for I could not live without you, my dear one.

LINDA

(She makes her voice quiet.)

And I? I would die without you.

LANCE

Come into my arms, my love.

LINDA

(She does so. They get in a passionate embrace. She gets weak but holds on to common sense.)

But your torts! remember your torts!

LANCE

(His voice is strong.)

To hell with my torts! To hell with ambition! To hell with running for governor. You are my ambition. You are my claim to fame and fortune!

(The embrace gets very passionate now.)

And there Annie was stuck. She didn't know how to go on from there. In real life, she figured, they'd get undressed and go to bed together. But you couldn't do that in a play.

Just then the campus campanile struck nine. Annie resumed writing:

(From somewhere a clock chimes the hour. The sound is that of silver bells. The room gets darker and the curtain falls down.)

ACT TWO

It is many years later. The place is the governor's mansion. Linda and Lance are rich now. She wears jade earrings. They are walking down Memory Lane.

LINDA

Remember the time, long years ago, when you said my clock sounded like a boiler factory?

57   *

LANCE

And how you cried when I cursed it.

LINDA

(Quiet voice.)
I never cry.

LANCE

Ah, you cry, Linda. In your heart you cry.

LINDA

(She whispers in awe.)
How wise you are.

LANCE

Wise? Ah, no. Stupid, rather. Yes, stupid!

LINDA

How can you say that? You! The governor of a great state?

LANCE

Perhaps I was the youngest man ever to pass the bar examinations. Perhaps I am the youngest governor this or any state ever had. Perhaps I am as stated in the newspapers—intelligent, ethical, and against capital punishment.

(He waits before he says:)
But in my heart I'm stupid.

Annie held her breath. A title was coming! It was still cloudy, but the clouds were breaking up. She waited . . . waited . . . All of a sudden the title was there! The right title; the one and only title! Forgetting that Carl was studying, she threw her arms in the air and called out:

"I got it, Carl! The name for my play! It came to me just like that!" She snapped her fingers. "*The Stupid Heart!* How do you like it?"

Then all hell broke loose.

Carl slammed his book shut and shoved it away from him. It fell on the floor and took the ashtray along with it. The ashtray broke in half.

"Cry-sake, Annie, can't you be still at least five minutes?"

"Cry-sake! I got to breathe, don't I?"

"I'm sorry," he mumbled.

"That I got to breathe?"

"You know I have to study, Annie. I'll get kicked out if I don't keep my grades up. Why are you making it so hard for me?"

"What was I doing? Something so terrible that first you had to curse and then bust the ashtray?"

"I didn't break it. It fell off the table."

"Never mind! You did a bad thing to me. I was having fun writing down conversations and then you hollered at me, like I was doing something just terrible."

"Put yourself in my place, Annie."

"Put yourself in *mine*. I'm here in a strange place without friends or relatives and I feel I don't belong here and never will be allowed to belong here. And you don't care!" She started for the door.

"Where you going, Annie?"

"Never you mind!" She was gone.

He was about to follow her but changed his mind. Since she hadn't bothered with a coat, she probably went to chat with the landlady.

The room was very quiet with Annie gone—so quiet he could hear the muffled tick of the clock in the drawer where she put it every night. He had the whole room to himself now. He could study without distraction. He went back to the table and picked up his book and the pieces of ashtray. He picked up the pack of cigarettes she had bought to surprise him. He felt a pang, thinking of her thoughtfulness. He opened his book, then closed it. He found that he didn't want to study now. He wanted Annie.

He went over to the bed and picked up and read her manuscript. He couldn't help smiling at the stilted dialogue. And yet . . . yet, there was something about her writing. She had written of the other evening—not as it had been, but the way it might have been. Something like a fairy tale.

59 *

He sat on the bed, looking down, his hands clasped between his knees, and tried to think things out. He loved Annie. But how could they possibly get along cooped up in one room? They ought to have a larger place—at least two rooms. That would mean higher rent, though, and where would the money come from?

He couldn't take on any more work without dropping out of school. And as for Annie's getting a job . . . couldn't count on that. The steady jobs were had by the town girls. Self-help coeds had all the part-time jobs.

Was it right to have married her? He came back to that. Everyone had been against it; no one had been for it. His mother had been against it. You're too young, she said. She's a nice girl for all I know, but she's not for you.

Annie's mother had been against it. Sure she wanted her daughter to marry someday—when she had more sense. And let's have no more silly talk about marrying that Brown fellow, she said. Why, he can't even support himself, much less a wife.

The Dean of the Law School had been against it—was still against it.

"Sit down, Brown."

"Thank you, sir." Carl sat down and waited while the Dean looked over the papers in a folder which had Carl's name on it.

"Your record is good," said the Dean. "Good grades; no adverse conduct record." He closed the folder. "Now what did you wish to see me about, Brown?"

Carl didn't know exactly how to tell him. "There's a possibility . . . I mean, I am planning . . ."

"Financial problems?" asked the Dean.

"In a way."

"Considering your good record, I believe a small loan could be arranged."

"Thank you, sir. But I didn't come to see you about that. I am planning to marry."

"And drop out of school?"

"No, sir. I plan on getting my degree."

The Dean frowned. "We do not approve of student marriages."

"But, sir, several married students are taking law, or medicine."

"True. Some years back, when the World War ended, we had an influx of married students—ex-servicemen whose education had been interrupted. A precedent was set. . . ." The Dean paused. "Brown, is there a necessity for your marriage?"

"No, sir. If there were, I would not have asked for this appointment. I would have dropped out and married."

The Dean seemed pleased with the answer. However, he said, "How old are you?"

"Twenty, sir." Impulsively he added, "I've known the young lady four years, sir." The Dean's eyebrows went up a little.

"Let me see." The Dean opened the folder. "At sixteen you had finished high school. At eighteen you had completed, or I might say accumulated, two years of college credits—the minimum number of credits to qualify for admission to third-year law. I take it your parents were not in a financial condition to put you through law school. You are obliged to work between classes; study when you can find the time. In addition, you wish to take on the responsibility of a wife. Evidently the study of law is a by-product to you."

"As long as my grades . . ." began Carl. The Dean put up his hand in a stop signal.

"Law," he said, "is more than good grades; it is more than a profession. Like medicine, it is a dedication. It should come first in a young man's life. Everything else should be set aside."

"If you will pardon me, sir," said Carl, "I am not studying for the priesthood. And I think of the law as a dedicated *profession* rather than a *dedication*. To try to become a good, successful, and ethical lawyer should be a great thing in a man's life. But I don't see why, sir, it should be the whole of his life."

"Well put!" said the Dean. "Tell me, Brown, why you chose corporate law as your major."

61   *

"Because of the rapidly growing auto industry in the state. Existing statutes and precedents are fast becoming obsolete and . . ."

"And in short, you wish to make precedent rather than follow it."

"Yes, sir."

"How do you plan to start?"

"Well, first I'd have to get my diploma and pass the bar exams."

"Setting up a practice is not easy. You cannot get together a hundred dollars, rent a vacated store, buy a secondhand desk, have a telephone installed, and put a sign in the window, stating: *Corporate Law Practiced Here.*"

"No, sir." Carl smiled. "I plan to try to get accepted as a junior partner in a well-established law firm."

"That is extremely difficult. And even if by some rare chance you could get into such a firm, the salary for the first few years is small—I might say almost nonexistent. And," clinched the Dean, "young men with responsibilities, such as a wife and perhaps children, have little chance of being accepted."

"I know the worst. I'll do my best," said Carl.

"Have you reconsidered putting off your marriage until after graduation?"

"No, sir."

The Dean threw his hands in the air, shook his head impatiently, and stood up. Carl stood up.

"Well," said the Dean, "I cannot expel you for marrying. But you understand that as a married man you will not be considered for a scholarship to get you through next year—your last year—nor for a tuition loan?"

"Yes, sir."

"Your work will be carefully watched. Also your conduct. The slightest falling off in grades; the merest infraction . . . the consequences will be quite severe."

"I understand, sir."

The Dean walked to the door with Carl. "When do you plan to marry, Brown?"

"Next week. The young lady will be of age then."

The Dean shook his head and sighed deeply. Carl made his usual thank-you speech. The Dean told him he'd be expected to report once a month; to consult the secretary as to day and time.

Then the Dean did something quite unexpected. He extended his hand and gave Carl a warm handshake. "Good luck, Carl," he said. "I know how it is." He lowered his voice. "I, too, married while I was in law school."

He closed the door after Carl.

Now, pacing the floor and waiting for Annie to come back, Carl thought over his interview with the Dean. He sure put it on the line, he thought. And he was right. It would be impossible to live on five dollars a week in one room. Even if they could, it wouldn't work out. Their marriage would be destroyed or he would fail in his courses. Probably both, and he'd end up with nothing—no wife, no career.

The sensible thing to do was for Annie to go home and wait out the time until he graduated. They could spend the summer together . . .

No! He had to have Annie with him. All the time. He loved her and wanted to sleep with her. It was as simple as that. Their marriage was perfect as far as sex was concerned. She was a warm, talkative, even naïve child during the day and a warm, passionate woman in bed at night. No, he'd made no mistake about marrying Annie and he would not give her up—even for a year. He'd give up the law first.

Maybe he could keep both! He could drop out of school for a year, get a job over in Herdstone. (He understood they paid five dollars a day in the auto factories.) They'd live simply, save

63   *

their money, and he could return to school the next year. He'd get a refund on this year's tuition. That would get them started. He made up his mind then and there to drop out of school. He had to tell Annie right away.

He went downstairs to get her. But the landlady said Annie hadn't been with her. In fact, she hadn't even seen Annie since the night they had arrived.

Carl got upset. Where was she? She had left without her jacket. Could it be she was walking the cold streets in her thin blouse and skirt? Why, she might catch her death of cold. . . . He ran upstairs to get his coat in order to go out and find her.

She was standing at the dresser, putting her manuscript in the drawer.

"Annie! Where have you been?" He shook her a little roughly in his relief at her return.

"Out," she said. "I went out so you could study."

He gathered her in his arms, carried her to the rocker and made her sit on his lap. She felt awfully cold. No wonder. No coat, no sweater.

"Don't ever run out again in this kind of weather without a coat. You could have frozen to death."

"Oh, I'm not a dope. I came home when it got too cold for me."

"What I mean to say is, don't you ever walk out on me again no matter what I say or do. You just try to put up with me. Hear?" She said nothing. He held her tighter, thinking it made her warmer. He rocked and patted her for a little while.

"Do you love me, Annie?"

"I love you, Carl."

"Would you love me if I was a factory worker?"

"Of course. But you're not a factory worker. You are going to be a lawyer. You *got* to be a lawyer. I told the children their father's a lawyer."

"What children?"

"The children I'm going to have."

"*We're* going to have."

"*I'm* the one going to have them. You can watch."

"All joking aside, sweetheart, I've got to drop out of school."

"Don't be silly, Carl. Just because we had a little fight . . ."

"No, Annie. I've made up my mind. The Dean was right."

"Oh, he was only testing you; trying to find out if you had enough guts to be a lawyer."

"How do you know?"

"I don't know how I know. I just *know*."

"We can't make it, Annie. We just can't."

"We'll make it, Carl."

"Please tell me how."

"We'll take it one day at a time. Get through each day as it comes up and tackle the next when it gets here."

"That wouldn't work out."

"It's working out right now. We have the best part of a week licked so far, don't we?"

"Yes, but . . ."

"Oh, Carl, think of the wonderful days we've had—how nice Mrs. Ridinski was and the cashier. Why, that canceled out Mr. Felix. And Carl . . . Carl darling, think how wonderful it is to be in bed together. Why, that makes up for all the worries."

"Yes, sweetheart, I know. But I've *got* to drop out of school; get a steady job. It will only be for a year. I'll get back in school."

"You'll never get back. People never get back to what they left." He had nothing to say to that. "Carl?" She waited. He didn't respond. "Carl, look at me!" He looked down at her face. "Listen! And listen good! You leave school and I leave you!"

"No, you wouldn't, sweetheart. You promised."

"Never mind what I promised. If you drop out, it will be because of me. I'll know it. And I'll leave you. I swear it!"

She got off his lap, got her toilet articles and went to the bathroom, to let him think things over alone.

When she came back in her noiseless way, he was sitting with his arms on the table, his head down on his arms. He jerked his head up when he smelled her talcum powder, hoping she had not seen him that way.

"Things aren't as bad as they look, Carl. My savings will be here Monday—at the latest."

"You'll need that for winter clothes, Annie."

"Not all of the seventy-five dollars. There'll be enough left to get us through until I get a job." She went to him and pressed his head against her breast. "You don't really want to drop out of school, do you?" Suddenly, the place on the nightgown where his head was resting felt wet. It couldn't be, she thought. Men just don't cry.

"Oh, what's the matter, darling?" she asked.

"Nothing, except I'm happy." He got up and took her in his arms. "I'm happy because I've got you and because I might not have to drop out of school right away. And now I have a feeling that the Dean, as you said, was testing me—was not as hard on me as I thought. And . . ."

"Everything's all right," she said. "And let's go to bed. I'm so tired. I must have walked miles today—to town and back, and at least ten times around the block tonight."

"And wrote a play," he said, hoping to make her smile.

"That didn't make me tired, and I don't think the walking did, really. It was thinking things out that wore me out." She got her mangled hairbrush from the drawer.

"Here! Let me help you, sweetheart."

He took the brush and gave her hair an awkward brush or two, braided her hair into two lumps and wound the ribbons around them as though tying up a package. He put her to bed, carefully tucking the blanket about her. As he was getting his pajamas and shaving things together, he said, "You know, I could give up smoking, save half a dollar or so a week."

"No. You depend so much on a cigarette. You'd be a nervous wreck without them. But you don't have to throw them away

* 66

after one puff, Carl. If you smoked them all the way down you wouldn't have to buy a pack nearly every day."

"I'll do that," he said. "Now I'll be right back. Don't go away."

He washed up and shaved. When he got back, she was sound asleep.

Chapter Four

It was still dark when Annie awakened the next morning. She was anxious to know the time. Rather than awaken Carl, she got out of bed, tiptoed to the dresser, knelt down and opened the bottom drawer inch by inch.

A voice came out of the darkness. "Some people buy clocks just to hide them."

She jumped a little. "Is that you, Carl?"

"Who else? Whom are you expecting?"

"You scared me. I thought you were sound asleep. Anyhow, do you have the time?"

"Yes, I have the time." He threw back the covers and got out of bed.

"Well, why don't you tell me?"

"You didn't ask me. You asked me if I *had* the time, that's all."

"One thing I hate," she said, "is a wise guy first thing in the morning."

The campanile struck six. Annie took her clock to the window where there was some light. "The college clock is fast," she said. "My clock says five to."

"There's an off-chance your clock is slow."

68

"You'd be slow, too, if you had to spend the night in the bottom drawer."

"You're a nut," he said.

"Just call me Hazel."

He groaned. "That gag's hard to take on an empty stomach."

So they teased each other and laughed and had fun and it seemed as if the night before had never been.

She made a deal with him: She'd walk as far as the print shop where he got his papers, if he'd sit with her while she had breakfast. They went to the lunchroom around the corner. She had a thick wedge of cheesecake to go with her coffee.

"How you can get that down first thing in the morning is beyond me."

"It's filling." She pried off a big piece with her spoon.

"I can't look!" he said.

They said good-by at the print shop. "I'll see you tonight then? Outside the cafeteria?" he said.

"Okay." She gave him a good-by kiss. "Good luck in your torts quiz."

"Want to know what quiz means?"

"No."

"So I'll tell you anyhow. It's college slang for test and derives from the word inquisition."

"Oh, who cares so early in the morning?" She started walking backwards away from him.

"Good-by for a while, sweetheart."

"Ah, reward!" she called back with a wave. "That's French. It means 'so long.'" He pretended to lunge at her. "What time you got?" she asked. He looked at his watch to check. When he looked up, she was gone; she had turned a corner and disappeared.

He had a feeling of loss. It had always been so, the way she had of suddenly vanishing. She'd walk to the steps of the night college in Brooklyn, and when he turned his back for a second

69   *

to open the door, she'd be gone. But I know now, he thought, she'll always come back. I'll see her again tonight. She'll be waiting for me . . .

He whistled happily as he delivered his papers, tossing each at a house with right good will. He was so happy he didn't quite know how to handle it. The nightmare of dropping out of school was gone; Annie'd had no nagging hangover from the night's quarrel. And the Dean was all right.

He strode into the cafeteria with a big grin for everybody and kidded the counter girls as he piled up a big breakfast on his tray. Mrs. Ridinski looked over her shoulder as she drew a cup of coffee for him.

"You're full of beans today," she said. "Married life must agree with you."

"And how! You ought to try it sometime, sweetheart."

"I'll have to ask my husband first." She laughed as though she had said something very funny. Carl laughed too, and the counter girls smiled.

The streets were empty. It was as if everyone was sleeping and Annie was alone in the world. She liked that feeling. It wasn't quite seven o'clock in the morning, and Annie decided she wouldn't go back to the room just yet. She walked over to the campus. That was quiet and empty, too.

She sat on what she considered her wedding bench. She could see the library from there and she loved to look at the beautiful building. The sun, still low in the sky, was bright but didn't give much warmth. After all, it was near the end of October. The air smelled of pine needles even though there were no pine trees on the campus.

She wondered if the smell came from the north country where new pine trees must be growing to replace the ones that had been felled. Is there a wind from there, she wondered, blowing that smell all the way here? She thought of the bittersweet and wondered whether the florist had started writing *The Rape of the Forest.*

She was aware of the sky. In some places, where there were no buildings, it seemed to touch the ground. Home, she thought, I had to lie on my back on the roof and look up to see as much of the sky as I can see here, sitting down and looking straight ahead.

Just to think, she mused, some people are born to this. Before they're a day old, even, it's fixed that they live in a place like this; fixed that they go tc college.

Carl's the lucky one. He wasn't born to this. But he got here just the same. It wasn't fixed that he'd go to college to learn to be a lawyer. But he's doing it! And I'm lucky, too. I am here. Sitting here . . . going to the library. It's almost like going to college.

The campanile chimed the hour. Suddenly the campus came to life. Students converged from all directions. They came from fraternity houses, sororities, and dormitories; from private homes, from rented rooms.

The boys carried a book or two gripped in a swinging hand, and the girls carried their books in their arms. They walked along, in pairs and in groups. They talked and laughed and raised a hand in greeting and called out "Hi!" to each other or "What do you say?"

Annie envied their casual ways, which came from bred-in assurance. She envied the way they dressed; plainly, but expensively. The costly sweaters, the good shoes. She felt out of place in her too obviously styled suit and foolish hat with the nose veil and her tight kid gloves. She thought of her lack of education; of her wrong use of words; of her mispronunciation of words she knew; of her grammar. She knew she didn't belong She felt that she never would belong.

She got up and went away.

"So you remembered to get me a blotter," said Carl.
"I got a new ashtray too."

71   *

"Here's a free kiss for being a good girl." He looked around. "But where are my cigarettes?"

"What did you do with the pack I bought you yesterday?"

"What did you do with the hundred dollars I gave you yesterday?"

"Bought you a pack of cigarettes. Here." He lit up one immediately. "How'd you make out in the quiz?"

"A minus."

"What was the minus for?"

"I forgot to dot an *i*."

"Oh, you!" She shoved him against the table. He caught the ashtray just in time.

"Watch it, kid." He started to grind out his cigarette in the retrieved ashtray.

She grabbed his hand. "Uh, uh," she said. "You promised to smoke them down to the bottom."

"Okay! Okay! Stop nagging me." He straightened the bent cigarette. "Get any calls from your ad?"

"Just one. The man said he needed a part-time office girl. You know, run errands? Like buying stamps and such? Putting water in the cooler? Filing? A dollar a day."

"Did you take it?"

"Well, he said he had to interview another girl first and he'd call me tomorrow."

"Don't count on it, sweetheart." Carl made preparations to study.

"Carl, is it all right with you if I go out for a few minutes?"

"What's his name?"

"Stop it! I mean to get something for sandwiches so I don't have to go out for lunch tomorrow and miss the phone call?"

"All right. But wear your coat this time." She got her handbag from the drawer and started to put the clock away. "Leave it out, Annie," he said. "I might as well get used to the damn thing." He leaned over to check the matchbook under the wobbly table.

When he looked up, she was gone.

She found a little, dimly lighted grocery store a block away. She said, "Good evening and how's business these days?"

Without looking up, the man said coldly. "Why are you interested?"

She reacted instantly to the rebuff. "I'm not interested. Just nosy. I'd like . . ." She changed the verb. He wasn't worthy of it. "I want a loaf of bread and four slices of that cheese." No wonder the place is dark and empty, she thought, the way he's so impolite to customers!

She stopped at a drugstore for a Coke to give Carl a little more time to study by himself. She took her shoes off before she entered their room. But he heard her come in. He reached out and took her hand.

"Annie, you didn't go out on my account?"

"No. I really needed this stuff." She placed the bread and cheese on the window sill.

"Because I just can't study if you're away."

"I'm here now. And tonight I'll be quiet."

She was as good as her word. She sat on the bed and started to read *Babbitt* and was immediately absorbed in the book. She read, he studied. The room was quiet except for the ticking of the clock. A high falsetto voice broke the silence.

"Oh, Lance, I wish I could hold pens for you like Dora." Then a guttural voice: "Ah, no, I'm not wise I'm stupid. I got a stupid heart, a stupid liver, stupid kidneys."

It was Carl, reading her manuscript and improvising on her dialogue. She got off the bed. "I don't think that's very funny, Carl," she said coldly.

"Hey, look!" he said in his own voice. He made a horrible grimace. "Is my faraway smile on straight?" he asked.

"Give me my play back. Please, Carl."

He held it high in the air. "Come and get it!"

"You damn fool!" She lunged at him and they wrestled across

the table for the manuscript. In the scuffle, the new ashtray fell to the floor and it, too, broke in half.

"You did it this time," he said. She grabbed the manuscript and started to tear it in half. He held her hand and made her stop. "Ah, sweetheart, don't destroy it. I didn't mean to make fun of it. It's cute. Honest."

"It isn't meant to be cute. Now stop acting so silly, Carl, and get back to your torts."

"What torts? Tell me what torts? You are my tort; my one and only tort. The first time I laid eyes on you, I said to myself: She's the tortiest tort in the world. And she's for me."

Annie couldn't help but laugh at that. "You dope," she said affectionately.

"*Mister* Dope to you." He grabbed her arm. "Say mister or I'll pull your arm off."

"All right, Mr. Dope. Now let me go."

He released her. She put the manuscript away in the drawer. Carl sat in the rocker and patted his knee. "Come here," he said.

"No."

"Please, Annie?"

"I said no!"

To the tune of "Melancholy Baby" he improvised: "Come to me, my melancholy tortsie."

Annie couldn't resist that. She sang back: "You shut up or we'll be through."

They went into hysterical laughter and started improvising words to other popular songs of the day.

Somehow, they had to give way after the tension of the last few days. They had worried about family reaction to their marriage; about money; about having a baby. Carl had worried about his quiz; about Annie and about the possibility of dropping out of school. And Annie had worried because he worried; because of their ugly first quarrel. She had worried about not fitting in—about whether she was good enough for Carl.

So they had to break down somehow. And they did. They laughed and sang and romped around and acted like a couple of carefree kids. And before they went to bed, they ate up all the cheese and most of the bread.

Chapter Five

It was early morning the next day. Annie's hat, gloves, and handbag were on the bed. She was prepared to leave for work as soon as the man called. By noon he had not called. Annie made a hurried trip to the grocery store to get some food after giving the landlady instructions in case the telephone rang.

The grocer said, "You're the one wanted to know last night how business was."

"I don't care how business is," said Annie.

"I'll tell you. It's bad."

"That's tough," she said, with what she hoped was a sneer. "I want a glass of currant jelly."

"It only comes in jars."

"All *right!* Just so you sell it to me." She paid him, saying, "I don't know why I come here."

What makes him so grouchy? she wondered. Well, maybe his wife won't sleep with him—not that I blame her—and he takes it out on the customers.

She was halfway through her first jelly sandwich when the phone rang in the hall downstairs. Annie poised at the top of the stairs. Protocol demanded that the landlady answer the phone and summon Annie if the call was for her. Mrs. Hansmon seemed to take forever before she came out of the kitchen and then she had to stand in the hallway wiping her hands on her apron. Before the landlady finished saying hello, Annie was halfway down the stairs. But it was only the neighbor lady calling about a bake sale.

Annie *had* to have that job. She had worked herself up into thinking that Carl's law degree depended on her having that job. She tried to hoax the phone into ringing. If I can walk ten times around the room with my eyes shut and not bump into anything, it will ring, she told herself. She walked around with her eyes shut and the phone did not ring. She tried other charms and spells. The phone did not ring.

She thought of her office friend Arlene, who had waited for a very special ring. And it had not come. Now she knew how her friend must have suffered, and Annie felt closer to her.

Arlene was a sweet, plain-faced, shy girl who had never had a boy friend. The other girls felt sorry for her. One of the girls had a plain, shy brother. She arranged a party in order that Arlene might meet the shy brother. Nothing much happened. Arlene and the boy sat across the room from each other. He looked at Arlene when she wasn't looking, and she looked at him when he wasn't looking. At leaving time the boy, probably prodded by his sister, said, "I'll give you a ring sometime, Arlene."

Arlene was a changed girl when she showed up at the office next day. Her hair was done up in a new becoming way. Her eyes glowed, there was a drift of pink in her cheeks and she was almost pretty. She hummed happily as she filed letters.

But as the week passed without the "ring" materializing, Arlene lost her glow, along with her hopes and dreams, and went back to being her old plain, quiet self.

Trouble was, thought Annie, she counted too much on getting that call like I'm counting on it. But I have to count on it. Carl's staying in school depends on it.

The afternoon waned and Annie knew there'd be no phone call that day. But hope died hard in her. He'll call tomorrow, she assured herself. He's trying out the other girl first, and she won't be right for the job and he'll call me.

The next day she went to the store to get an apple to go with her jelly sandwich lunch. "Yesterday," said the grocer, "you said you wondered why you came here."

"I'm dying to find out," she said sarcastically.

"I'll tell you: because it's handy for you."

"What's your name?" she asked.

"Why?"

"I like to know the names of people I don't like." She took her apple and left. That'll hold him, she thought.

Annie disliked him. In a vague but complicated way she felt it was the grocer's fault that the man hadn't called about the job. Annie was used to people responding to her friendly overtures. The grocer had not responded. This made Annie feel inferior; made her doubt her abilities; made her lose confidence in herself. She believed her state of mind went on thought waves to the man who had a job to give. The man didn't want an office girl who was not sure of herself. That's why he hadn't phoned.

However, the phone did ring just before noon. Annie waited on the top step. "Who?" asked the landlady. A pause. "I'll see." She called up the stairs, "Annie-e-e?"

"Right here!" The landlady was startled. Annie was right behind her.

"For you, Annie," said the landlady needlessly. She went back to the kitchen.

"Hello?" said Annie brisk and businesslike.

"Annie?"

"Oh! It's only you, Carl."

"Cry-sake, Annie, you've got to cut out that 'only you' business. It makes me feel odd."

"I thought it was the man about the job."

"Reason I called you: you know I usually play tennis with my Japanese friend on Saturdays?"

"What's his name?"

Carl told her. It sounded like Horatio Jonesie. "Anyway, he asked me if I wanted to play this coming Saturday afternoon."

"You going to?"

"Well, Saturday we'll be married a week and I thought we might like to celebrate—you and I. I don't *have* to play tennis."

"You play, Carl. I'll come and watch you."

"It will be the last time this year. The courts close next week."

"Well, don't miss it. Where you calling from?"

"The cafeteria. Love me?"

"Yes."

"Say it."

"I love you."

"Good-by, Linda, my dearest of dears." He laughed and hung up before she could get in the last word.

Well, Annie never did get her phone call.

A letter came from her mother in the afternoon mail. Annie had never had a letter from her mother. She knew how her mother spoke, but had no idea how she wrote. Her mother lacked education but was by no means illiterate. Like Annie, she was very articulate. Unlike Annie, she never groped for the right word. When she was stuck, she invented a word.

Dear Daughter.
   I write to you,
   You are bad to run away from home after all the years I schnunched and sockofissed to bring you up right.
   But you came up wrong.
   I plant a pink rose seed and what grows is a dandy line.
   Yes, that.
   Now you are married you say.
   I say what is done is done.
   Now I tell you this because I am your mother.

When a baby comes don't bladder it all over.

Keep it dark because it is nobodys business the baby comes before he should come.

Then move to new place where nobody knows you so they shouldnt count on their fingers about you.

I see hard times for you in the tea leaves.

I am your mother.

So I do not pray that you have all the hard times I had.

I pray for you only to get half the hard times your mother had because that is the only way you will ever know how bad it was what you did to your mother.

"Don't put a curse on me, Mama," Annie whimpered aloud. She read the letter again; objectively this time.

Mama sure knows how to write, thought Annie. Each sentence is a thought; each thought a paragraph. She got in what is, what was, and what she thinks might be.

The letter made Annie feel a sad tenderness toward her mother. She told Carl about it when he got home. She asked him to read the letter.

"She is more hurt than angry," he said.

"But, Carl, did she have to wish me hard luck?"

"Nobody has to wish that, Annie. That comes for free."

"I guess we'll hear from your mother soon, Carl."

"God knows what she'll write."

"She'll run me down good."

"Oh, you know how mothers are, Annie."

"My mother didn't run you down."

"Your mother didn't even mention my name! As far as she's concerned, I'm dead."

"I hope your mother don't mention my name."

"Annie, let's face it. There's going to be a big fight when Mom's letter comes. So don't let's fight ahead of time. Okay?"

"Okay."

The Japanese brought the letter over Saturday afternoon when he came to pick up Carl for tennis. Annie itched to know what

Carl's mother had written. But she had to wait until evening.

Carl's friend called her Mrs. Brown. Annie did not respond, "Call me Annie," as she did when she wanted to be friends. Carl was disappointed. He had so much wanted his friend and his wife to like each other. Annie felt ill at ease with the friend. His English was perfect, and immediately Annie became self-conscious of her own ungrammatical speech. She was unable to take part in the conversation, even though the polite Japanese tried to draw her into the conversation.

She sat on a bench and watched them play tennis. She didn't know how the game was scored and she soon lost interest. Also, her neck hurt pivoting from side to side in order to follow the ball back and forth.

She was more interested in the girl playing on the adjoining court. The girl was pretty and wore a short white, pleated skirt and loose white sweater. She smiled a lot at her partner and had a way of tossing her head and making her short hair bounce as she smiled. Annie wanted to be like that. She tried tossing her head, but her tightly coiled hair wouldn't budge.

The girl missed a ball and it rolled toward Carl. Carl let his own ball go by in order to pick up hers. He extended it with a smile. The girl let him hold it a second while she tossed her head, made her hair bounce, and looked up at Carl. Taking the ball, she made her hair bounce again as she nodded her thanks. Annie decided definitely that she'd have her hair bobbed as soon as her money came.

After the game, Carl suggested that his friend come home with them and have a Coke or something. Annie stood mute. She did not second the invitation. Carl was embarrassed, but the Japanese boy did the tactful thing. He assured them it was a great honor to be invited to their home, but a previous engagement . . .

Walking home, Carl said, "You didn't have a good time, did you, sweetheart?" She admitted she hadn't. "Do you want to tell me all about it?" he asked.

She wanted to tell him how inferior and out of place she had

81   *

felt; the degrading agony of knowing she was stupid and didn't fit in. But she just couldn't run herself down.

She said, "It's just that I'm not experienced in talking to Japanese people. And I don't know much about ath-a-letics." He did not correct her pronunciation. No use adding to her depression. "And I'm sorry, Carl, I didn't invite him to our place. But my mind was on your mother's letter waiting there for us."

"Oh, that's what's bothering you." He felt relieved.

"And furthermore," she said out of the blue, "I *am* going to get my hair bobbed."

"Now what brought that on?"

"Never mind. Besides, we're home now."

She wanted him to read the letter right away. But he hedged. Let him take off his tennis shoes first, and he had to have a shower.

"Do all that after you read the letter first."

"Annie, sit on my lap a little while, won't you? And let's make a little love before we have a big fight over the letter."

"Oh, I'm not going to start a fight, no matter what she writes. And even if we do have a fight, let's get it over with so we have time to make up before we go to bed."

A money order fell out of the letter. Annie picked it up. "It's for ten dollars, Carl! She can't be too mad." They smiled at each other, Annie sat down and relaxed and Carl read the letter aloud.

It started as a routine letter. How was Carl getting along? Did he need anything like woolen socks for winter? And everything was fine at home except Papa's back was giving him a little trouble. That watch she gave him for Christmas: was it all right? Let Mom know before she made the final payments on it.

Then came the gist of the letter.

"I'm surprised," his mother wrote, "that Annie followed you out there. I don't know what kind of mother she has to let her do a thing like that."

Annie was on her feet, choking with indignation. "Take it

easy, sweetheart," he begged. "Please! *Please!*"

"I'm all right. Go ahead. Read more about what's wrong with my mother and me."

"If you're going to act that way, I'll tear it up without reading the rest."

"Read it!"

"Sit down and be quiet, then."

"Of course, you can't be serious about getting married," read Carl. He realized he was getting into the danger zone and hurriedly scanned the next lines before he read them aloud. "Now don't be foolish and let anyone talk you into getting married." He read the next lines to himself. "She's not so dumb. She's smart enough to know you got a good future ahead . . ."

"Read it out loud!" said Annie. "What else does she say?"

Carl improvised the next line. "Now Annie is a very nice girl . . ."

"She didn't say that. You're making it up."

"All right! All *right*, God damn it!" He tore the letter in half and threw it into the wastebasket.

"You should have told her you were married, Carl."

"All *right!* I should have told her. I'll tell her now." He sat down and started to write a note.

"Just write that we were married a week ago, and . . ."

"Okay," he said reasonably. *"You* write it for me." He wadded the sheet and threw it into the wastebasket.

"Now, you just see here, Carl Brown! I'm the one has a right to get mad. Not you."

He wrote the note and gave it to her to read, while he addressed the envelope.

Dear Mom:

Annie and I were married last Saturday and we are very happy. I love her very much and she loves me. When you really get to know Annie, you will love her as much as I do. Love to Papa and Tessie and to you, Mom.   Carl.

He waited until she had read it. "All right?"

"All right," she said.

"Got a stamp on you?" She got one from her handbag. "Annie, do you care if I write a P.S., Love from Annie?"

She thought it over. "No, Carl. She'll feel bad enough when she gets the news. No use rubbing it in." He went out to mail the letter.

Of course, she got the pieces of letter out of the wastebasket and put them together. She read what Carl had evaded reading —how the urgency to marry was all on Annie's side. His mother wanted to know was there a possible pregnancy? She warned him not to be caught in such a trap. Her written words:

> . . . remember, if she let you, she let other men. So send her home right away. I am sending ten dollars for her fare back home so she don't have the excuse of no money to get back home on.

Annie literally saw red! She tore the letter to bits and threw it into the wastebasket. She made confetti out of the money order and threw *that* into the wastebasket. She got her suitcase out of the closet and opened it on the bed. She wrapped her clock in her torn blouse and put that in the suitcase. She added the bitter-sweet, jar and all. Suddenly, she began to sob—loud, hoarse sobs. She ran to the bathroom, locked herself in, turned on the water so no one could hear, and cried herself out.

Carl came back carrying an ice-cream cone for Annie. He looked around the empty room. He saw the opened suitcase on the bed. "Annie?" he called. As if in answer, she came into the room.

"Annie, don't *do* that! You mustn't always disappear the moment I turn my back."

"I was in the bathroom."

"I brought a cone for you."

"Oh, thanks, Carl." She took the cone.

"You got your suitcase out. You weren't thinking of leaving me? Just because of a letter?"

"Where would I go?" she said, licking the ice-cream cone. "But I had to do *something*. You see, I put the letter together and read the rest of it."

"Was it rough, sweetheart?"

"Worse! It was *filthy!*"

"Oh, Annie, don't be too hard on Mom."

"You want me to wire her congratulations or something?" She threw the unfinished cone into the wastebasket.

"Put yourself in her place."

"I'll do just that. Once she was a young girl like me, in love with your father. His mother told him not to marry her because she was pregnant and had slept with a lot of other men, too. All right! How do you think your mother would like that; would have liked it if your father's mother had acted . . ."

"Listen, Annie. Your mother said the same thing and you didn't go crazy about it."

"Maybe she thinks I'm pregnant, but she thinks it's you! Only you! Not a gang." She went to him and pounded her fists on his chest. "But your mother thinks I slept with everybody. Do you understand?" (pound pound) "Do you? But I didn't! I didn't!" she screamed.

"I know, sweetheart. I know."

He took her fists in his hands, held them against his cheek and kissed each little fist.

"Don't make so much of it, Annie. Don't. Someday you might have a son. If he'd spring a sudden marriage on you . . ."

"I'd look at his side of it. I wouldn't be selfish."

"You'd react the same way."

They quarreled, they argued, then got down to plain talking. Carl admitted his mother had done a rotten thing by writing as she had. Contrary Annie said she didn't know about that. After all, Carl owed something to his parents.

"No matter what she does and says now, at least she gave you a wonderful childhood, Carl."

"I don't know about that, Annie. Yes, she was a good mother, gave me everything I wanted . . . No, gave me what *she* wanted *for* me. I wonder more and more as I grow older why she pushed me so hard.

"Summers, when other kids were off to the free camp in the Catskills, she had me go to summer school so I could graduate at twelve instead of fourteen. High school too. I made four years in two and three summer sessions. And it was Mom decided I was cut out for the law."

"But you did like the law, didn't you, Carl?"

"It so happened that I took to it. I wasn't sure, though, until I came here."

"I don't like your mother, Carl, and I never will. But I must say she did an awful lot for you."

"So she told me. Many times. Tessie and Papa told me, too. When I graduated from high school, Tessie happened to say, The next thing you know, Carl will be off and married. And Mom looked at me and said, Not Carl. He's got sense. He's going to be a lawyer and help us get a better home life."

"What did you say?"

"I said, Sure. What else could I say?"

"I wish my mother had been like that," said Annie wistfully. "My mother didn't *make* me go to school. I was thankful that she *let* me. I must be funny or something, but I just loved school." She thought awhile. "Funny, when I think of it, I can't remember having much fun. I never had birthday parties like you; never was allowed to bring girl friends home. She never said, that's nice, when I brought home an all-A report card. Come to think of it, I never was a kid. Not really. I went to work when I was fourteen. I passed for sixteen. But I don't hold anything against Mama. My father was dead and my brothers were so little and Mama and me just had to work."

"Now, Annie, you could have gone to high school when your mother married Dan. You told me."

"Yes. But by that time I didn't want to. I was sixteen. I

didn't want to go to school with kids of thirteen or fourteen. And then there was Dan. There was something about him . . ." She paused. "Oh, never mind. Anyhow, I kept on working because that was my independence.

"I remember how I walked out on my first job. It was in the second basement of a department store on Fulton Street. One day I got this queer idea that I was down in the ground—way down. Like being dead or something. Yes, underground, with people walking above me all day. So after my lunch hour, I didn't go back. But Mama made me go back. She said I had a weak character and mustn't give in to such foolish ideas.

"Still and all, I can't blame her too much. She wanted me to have character, I guess. To be brave or something. And she had such a hard time after my father died."

And it got dark in the room and they didn't turn on the lights. She sat on his lap and she spoke of her childhood. It was as if she were sorting out the materials of growing up and putting the good pieces in one box and the bad ones in another.

He didn't listen very closely, but that was all right. He knew it was good for her to talk out her thoughts whether he listened or not.

He had his own thoughts to cope with. Unlike Annie's, they were of the present and not the past. He thought of his letter arriving and how his mother wouldn't open it until after supper. Then his mother would say she'd had a letter from Carl. His mother and father and sister would sit around the cleared table in the kitchen. And Tessie would say she hoped it was good news and his father would say, it's always good news just to get a letter from Carl. And his mother would open the letter and read: *Annie and I were married* . . .

And just thinking how they would feel made Carl sad, too.

Chapter Six

"I thought it would never get here!" Annie sighed happily.

"Those things take time," the bank teller said. "I entered your interest, Mrs. Brown."

"Imagine," said Annie. "Sixty-eight cents! For nothing! I didn't have to do a lick of work to earn it."

"That's interest for you," said the teller philosophically.

"I want to draw out twenty-five dollars of my own money. But don't touch the interest."

"The idea is," he said, "you want the interest to earn interest."

"Why, yes. Is that all right?"

He shrugged. "It's one way of getting rich," he said.

Annie bought a knee-length, navy-blue, pleated skirt and a sweater to match. The sweater was too loose to suit her. She wanted a tight sweater despite the fashion because she was rather vain of her firm upstanding breasts.

"No, no!" said the horrified saleslady. "It's not chic to wear tight sweaters." She pronounced it "chick." Annie got a loose sweater.

The coat was light brown with a half belt at the back. Annie thought it looked like a boy's coat. Her eyes went longingly to a sleek black coat, with a dyed rabbit collar, on the rack.

"I don't know," said Annie doubtfully. "Do you think this coat makes me look like a boy?"

"Not with those legs."

"Thank you."

"Well!" exploded the saleslady. "You sure hate yourself, don't you?" But she smiled.

"No, I don't. Do you?" Again the saleslady was confused. "I don't have bow legs and I know it. It would be silly to act as though I did, wouldn't it?"

"I don't know," said the saleslady, throwing in the towel.

The shoe clerk was small, slight, and a little on the dainty side. Dapper is the word for him, thought Annie. His black hair was pomaded and he had a wisp of a mustache. His shirt cuffs extended a couple of inches outside his coat sleeves and his cuff links were dramatic, literally so; one being the Mask of Comedy and the other the Mask of Tragedy. But his shoes were unshined and run down at the heels.

That's the way it is, thought Annie. Man that sells shoes can't bother with his own shoes—like a writer can't bother with spelling. Like me.

She looked down at the new saddle shoes on her feet. She had never seen white leather before, and it looked like whipped cream to her. And the saddle of shiny brown leather—I can't stand it, she thought, they are just *too* beautiful.

"I'll take them," she said. "In a box."

"Of course," said the clerk, untying the laces, "they'll look much better when they're dirtied up a wee bit."

"I wouldn't think of letting them get dirty. Not ever!"

"But you *must*, dear," he said, his voice going up on the *must*. "Clean saddle shoes are considered *gauche* on campus."

She had never heard the strange word, but she had an inkling of what it meant. "You mean, like *icky*?"

He didn't know what icky meant but had too much poise to reveal his ignorance. "Why not?" he said debonairly.

Her next stop was the barbershop.

"How do you want it cut?" asked the barber.

"So that it bounces," said Annie.

"You mean when it falls on the floor, it should bounce?"

"No. On my head when it's short."

"You mean a Dutch cut?"

"If that's what you call it," she said dubiously.

She was a prisoner under the voluminous sheet. The barber flexed his shears and waved his comb as if preparing for an attack. She closed her eyes and bit her lip to keep from screaming when the first hank of hair left her head and fell to the floor. It had taken all her life, so far, to grow it and now it was gone.

"You can open your eyes now. It's done," he said, like a dentist after an extraction.

Before opening her eyes, Annie tossed her head to feel if her hair bounced. It did! She sighed happily. The cutting was worth it, no matter how it looked. She opened her eyes. Her head looked strange but not too bad. The barber removed the sheet, shook it out and put it back around her. He put talcum powder on the nape of her neck and dusted it with a soft brush. That was nice. He sprinkled sweet-smelling lotion on her hair and rubbed it in hard. That was even nicer. He combed her hair and little curls formed at the ends and that was the nicest of all.

The barber picked up the shorn hair from the floor and tentatively held it over the tin wastebasket. "You don't want this, do you?" he asked.

"I certainly do!"

"What are you going to do with it?"

"I don't know. I just want it."

He shrugged. "You're the boss." He put it in a paper sack. She paid for the haircut and gave him a nickel tip. He looked at it in the palm of his hand and said, "Sure you can spare it?"

"No, I can't," she said. "But that's the right thing to do."

He smiled, thanked her, and told her to come back soon.

She heard Carl coming up the stairs. She posed, in her new outfit, her back to the dresser mirror. As he opened the door, she tossed her head to make her hair bounce. Carl took one look.

"Oops!" he said. "Wrong house. Excuse me." He went back down the stairs. She ran after him.

"Come back, Carl. Come back!" He came back and looked her over.

"Can you tell me what's become of a girl I knew, Annie Brown?"

"I am she!" she said dramatically.

"Well, Miss Shee, where is your hair?"

"In the bag. See?" She showed him.

"And your bust: Where's that? In another bag?"

"Oh, I still got that."

"Let's see." He pulled up the front of her loose sweater.

"You stop that, now!" She slapped his hands away.

"Just wanted to see if you were all there."

"You never noticed my new shoes."

"I did. First thing. But there's a smudge on the left one."

"I dirtied it on purpose. Clean shoes are not in style."

"It's all over my head." He hung up his coat and pulled down the knot of his tie. He sharpened a pencil.

"You didn't say how I looked in my new clothes," she said sadly.

"You look beautiful in your new clothes. You looked beautiful in your old clothes. But you look most beautiful in no clothes." He dropped the pencil on the table. "Sit on my lap a second, sweetheart."

"Later, Carl. You got to study and I got to go to the store."

"You don't 'got to go' any place and you know it. You just want

91 *

to show off your new outfit."

"Is that a crime or something?" she asked.

Annie was sure the grocer wouldn't recognize her. Without looking up, he said, "Last time you were here, you asked me my name."

"I want a box of soda crackers," she said.

"Well, my name is Henry."

"*And* a box of fig newtons if they're fresh."

"What's your name?" he asked.

"I'll let you know some other time," she said.

She stopped at the drugstore to get Carl a pack of cigarettes and to treat herself to a Coke. Sipping it, she thought of the grocer. She had grown used to his rudeness. In fact, she rather enjoyed the relationship between them. She had asked the landlady and found out that he lived alone. His only son had been killed in the Argonne fighting and his wife had died some years ago. And he was getting old, in his sixties, the landlady had surmised.

Annie had a sudden flash of revelation. *That's* why, she thought, he acts that way. Because he don't want anybody to know he's lonesome and to feel sorry for him!

She went back to the grocery store. It was in darkness, save for the light over the cash register. He was counting his money. She opened the door and stuck her head in.

"Hey!" she called.

"Store's closed," he said, without looking up.

"My name's Annie Brown," she said, then added, "Henry." She scuttled away.

Without looking up from his textbook, Carl patted her hand in thanks when she put the cigarettes on the edge of his study table. She climbed up on the bed with pad, pencil, and *This*

Side of Paradise. But she was too excited to read. She thought of the new people she had come in contact with since her marriage. She decided to list them. She wrote a heading: "New People Who Have Entered My Life." She listed them under subtitles.

New Friends
Mrs. Hansmon—Landlady
Mrs. Ridinski—Cafeteria
Mr. Byrd—Florist & Writer
Henry—Grocery-store man

Enemies
Mr. Felix—Turtle Soup

People I Know to Speak to
Cashier Lunchroom—Female
Waitress Dime Store
Where I Bought Clock—Man
Man in Bank
Saleslady—Dress Store
Shoe Store Man. Also Barber
Drug Store—Cig. Man & Coke Boy

College & Campus People

Here she was stuck, realizing that no one under that heading had so much as spoken to her. She thought of Carl's tennis friend. He's campus, she decided. She wrote down: *Japanese Student.*

She tore off the sheet and held it at arm's length. "Not bad," she said aloud, "seeing I've only been here a short while."

Then, realizing she had spoken aloud while Carl was studying, she braced herself for his battle cry of "Cry-sake, Annie!" But the room remained quiet. She stole a look at him. He was absorbed in his book, but he was smiling. She gave a happy

93   *

sigh, thinking, We're getting along good now, Carl and me. It's what people call adjustment.

The letter came for Carl. His sister, Tessie, had written it—typed it in her office. It was cold and precise.

> Your news came as a great shock to us. Mother almost had to have the doctor and Father was so upset he lost two days' work. Under the circumstances, you cannot expect us to subsidize you any further. Also we want you to pay back all the money we advanced you last year and to date.

"Advance, Carl? I thought they gave it to you." He made no comment. The letter continued:

> I enclose a list of what you owe us. Also if you want to keep the watch Mother gave you for Christmas, you'll have to make the last two payments due on it.
>
> Too bad you have to leave college after you've gone this far.

"But, Carl, you didn't tell them you were going to drop out of school, did you?"

"No, no!" he said impatiently.

He looked at the list. He owed four hundred fifty dollars. The jeweler's slip indicated that there were two more payments, two dollars each, due on the watch. He sat down and worked the palm of his hand back and forth on his forehead.

"I still have fifty dollars in the bank, Carl. We'll send her that right away."

"Don't say anything for a while, Annie. Just don't say anything. Let me think this out."

"All right." She went down the hall to the bathroom so that he could be alone. When she came back, he was pacing the floor and pulling hard on a cigarette. There was a vertical line on his forehead between his eyes. She hadn't noticed that before.

"There's just one way out, Annie."

"Carl, I will not let you leave . . ."

He put his hands on her shoulders. "I am *not* going to drop out of school. And you're not going to contribute your fifty dollars."

"I'll get some kind of a . . ."

"And you will not get a job doing housework. I'm going to give Mom a note, payable over a period of five years at six per cent interest."

"But how can we pay . . ."

"Payments to start one year after graduation."

"But she might get mad. Oh, Carl, suppose she sues us?"

"She won't. You stop worrying now and leave everything to me." He sat down and drafted the note.

The next day, they went into town together. He had the public stenographer at the hotel type the note and notarize their signatures. He had to ask Annie for fifty cents to pay the girl. He sent the note to his mother, registered mail. Annie thought of the ten-dollar money order she had destroyed and wanted to send the money from her bank account. But Carl had included that in the note. Carl pawned his wrist watch for seven dollars and sent off a four-dollar money order to the jeweler, requesting a paid-in-full receipt.

"Damned watch—paid for now," he said. "If I ever catch you buying anything on time . . ."

"It's funny," she said. "Watch on time. Watch—time. Get it?"

"It's funny having a watch all paid for and not owning it. Get it?"

"I'll tell you something even funnier. Married less than a month and already over four hundred dollars in debt. Just get *that*."

"Oh, to hell with it," he said.

"The hell with it," she agreed.

They had lunch in the restaurant where they had had their wedding lunch. They had the fifty-cent lunch this time. Carl took Annie to the College Shop after lunch to buy her a wool scarf. It was made of soft wool in the college colors. It cost a dollar and a half.

The clerk showed Annie how to wear it; wound once around her neck; one end hanging down her back and the other in front. He showed how it could be used as a hood by pulling up the back part over her head. He made quite a production of it, smoothing her hair under the hood and ending up with a "There!" and a pat on her cheek.

"That's just about enough," said Carl. He paid the man and they left the store.

Annie poked her elbow into Carl's ribs and said, "Jealous?"

"Who gave you that idea?"

"You."

"Don't be silly."

She sang a few bars of a song. She sang off-key.

> I'm jealous of the pretty flowers, too.
> I miss the kiss they always get from you . . .

"*Must* you sing on the street?" he asked.

"Yes!"

"Sing out loud and clear, then."

"Oh, Carl!" she hugged his arm. "I'm glad I got you."

"You little nut!" He smiled down at her upturned face.

And many an older person, passing them on the street, sighed and smiled and thought how wonderful it must be to be young and not have a care in the world!

The fourth week of their marriage did not start auspiciously. His interview with the Dean came up, but after he had braced himself for an ordeal, the Dean canceled the appointment—put it off two weeks. Carl worried. Now what? worried Carl. Had his mother written the Dean, in some way berating the man for not preventing the marriage? Was the Dean waiting to make up his mind about expelling him?

He had something else to worry about when he came home

that night. The room was dark. "Annie?" he called tentatively. No answer. He had a clutch of fear. How long had she been gone? Where was she? He switched on the light. She was lying on the bed, fully dressed except for her shoes. She had a folded wet towel on her forehead. She pulled it off and got off the bed.

"What's the matter, Annie? What's the matter, sweetheart?"

"Nothing. I just feel terrible, that's all."

He felt her forehead. It was hot but her hands were icy cold. "You get back into bed," he said, "and cover up good. I'll help you undress." He started to pull off her sweater.

"Don't touch me!" she said sharply.

"Cry-sake, Annie." He stepped back in astonishment.

"Now, I'm not mad at you, Carl, or anything like that," she said. "It's just that I feel like glass—that I'll break in pieces if anybody so much as touches me."

She undressed, got into bed, and pulled the blanket around her. Anxious to do something for her, Carl took off his coat and started to tuck it around her.

"Take that coat away," she said irritably. "That grease smell puts me in mind of Mr. Felix."

Hanging it in the closet, Carl thought that it ought to be cleaned, but he wondered what he'd wear while it was at the cleaner's.

"Did you have supper, Annie?"

"No. I don't want supper. Just a cup of tea."

"I'll get it."

Mrs. Hansmon was in her kitchen. "I don't know how to ask you, Mrs. Hansmon," said Carl, "but Annie—well, she doesn't feel well and she wants a cup of tea and . . ."

"Sit down, Mr. Brown. You're the one who looks sick."

He sat at her kitchen table while she put the kettle on to boil and arranged a cup, saucer, and little brown teapot on the tray.

"It's turning cold," she said. "Wouldn't surprise me if we had snow."

"Snow?" he asked vaguely.

She poured the boiling water into the teapot and put an aspirin on the tray. "Make her swallow it," she said. "It may not do her much good, but it won't do any harm."

Carl got up to take the tray. "I don't know how to thank you," he said. "If I can pay in some way . . ."

"Well, if you're still here in the spring, maybe you'd help me get the screens up?"

"That would suit me fine," he said fervently.

"Here!" She gave him a hot-water bottle which she had filled with water from the kettle.

"What's that for?" he asked.

"Annie will know." As he was leaving, she said, "How old are you, Mr. Brown?"

"Twenty," he said.

She shook her head and smiled ruefully.

Annie appreciated the hot tea, took the aspirin, and was grateful for the hot-water bottle. When she had finished, he put the tray on the dresser and sat on the edge of the bed.

"Don't let me keep you from your studies," she said, as though they were strangers.

"Never mind my studies. I want to stay here with you, Annie."

"Oh, Carl," she said petulantly, "go away and study, will you?"

Worried, and hurt too, he went through his prestudy ritual; checking the matchbook under the wobbly table leg, arranging his textbook and pad, and sharpening his pencils. "Do you think we ought to get a doctor?" he asked anxiously.

"Let me alone, will you?" she said in a high strained voice and turned on her side, her face to the wall.

He tried his best to study, but torts had no meaning for him. He tried to make notes and made doodles instead. He fought down the urge to smoke a cigarette, fearing the smoke would bother her. She was so quiet he wondered whether she was asleep. He listened for her breathing, but couldn't hear it over the clock's ticking. He went to the bed and leaned over to listen. She was asleep and breathing rhythmically.

He undressed in the bathroom so as not to awaken her. Back in the room, he put his hand on the light switch, hoping the click wouldn't awaken her. Carefully, he got into the bed, lying on the extreme edge with a good many inches between them. She turned over and touched him.

"Hold my hand, darling," she said. "Just my hand."

He took it in both his, relieved that now her hand was warm. "Do you get these spells often, sweetheart?" he said.

"Every month," she said wearily. "Every twenty-eight days." He said nothing. "Didn't you *know*, Carl?"

"No, I didn't. I should have known but I didn't. I'm just plain stupid, I guess. No wonder the landlady asked me how old I was."

"I don't know why it comes so hard for me," she said fretfully. "I'm so healthy otherwise. And I get so cranky, then. You'll just have to put up with me, Carl."

"You're fine," he said. "Just fine. And you be just as cranky as you want."

"And I'm sorry, Carl, that for a few nights we can't—"

"Hush!" he interrupted. "That's all right. Everything's all right. Just so you're here nights when I come home."

"Just so you come home nights," she murmured.

He held her hand until she drifted off to sleep. He lay awake a long time, enjoying the relief he felt knowing that she was not pregnant. Then he felt ashamed of his relief. It shouldn't have to be that way, he thought. No. It shouldn't have to be that way.

Chapter Seven

It was a Tuesday in November and there was a "closed" sign on Henry's grocery store. There was a burlap sack outside, which had been rolled down to make half a sack. It was full of walnuts. From across the street, Annie watched a line of squirrels coming around the corner, taking a nut from the sack and then disappearing. It looked like an assembly line. Annie rushed across the street and dispersed them. The little things broke their line and scattered in disorderly retreat, bumping into each other.

Henry came out of the store and asked Annie what in heaven she was doing. A favor, she said. The squirrels were stealing all the nuts and she chased them away.

"But, Annie, I put them there to let the squirrels steal them. Once a year. On my birthday I close the store so people won't bother them."

"Your birthday, Henry?"

"Sixty-one today."

"You certainly don't look it!"

Of course he looked it. He knew it and Annie knew it. But it was a nice thing to say—that he didn't look it.

Now the squirrels were sitting in a crooked line across the

street, their eyes on the nuts. One, braver than the others, hopped over and defiantly took a nut and ran away. The others took heart when he returned unharmed and started up the assembly line again. "Watch!" said Henry. He took a nut, crouched down and held it at arm's length. A squirrel snatched it like a flash. Annie tried it. A little squirrel sat on his haunches, his paws crossed, his nose twitching and his tail quivering. Finally, trembling all over, he snatched the nut, stashed it away in his cheek and was off. Annie was thrilled beyond words. As she continued serving the squirrels, Henry told her he had been giving them this treat for eleven years.

"Ever since I was fifty," he said. "And you know, Annie, they *know* exactly the day to come. They never miss it. There used to be hundreds but now only a handful come."

"What happened to the others, Henry?"

"Well, as the town grew and houses got closer together and the big trees were chopped down to make more house space, most of them went out of town to the woods. Each year they are fewer."

"Know what, Henry? You are a very good person."

"No. It's just that I figure somebody—something will miss me after I'm gone."

He told her how years ago his birthday party for the squirrels had been a big thing. The newspapers wrote it up and took pictures. One was half a page. And there was something in it about his dead son; how brave he had been in the war. He still had the paper.

"I'd love to see it," said Annie.

"Maybe I'll let you see it sometime and maybe I won't," he said.

Annie smiled.

Annie in her conforming outfit felt at ease on the campus. She managed to be on campus when classes let out. She carried her books and mingled with the students and pretended she belonged. She smiled and once threw up her hand and called "Hi!" at no one or anyone. A coed in the crowd, evidently mistaking Annie for someone she knew, waved back. Encouraged, Annie took the next step. She joined a group of students and walked into Casson Hall with them as if she had a class there.

She leaned over the water fountain and took a spurt of water, surprised that it tasted like any other water. With a businesslike frown, she checked the bulletin board. There was a notice stating the deadline of a short-story contest. Someone had a room to let. Someone wanted to sell a camera, slightly used, and someone wanted to buy a typewriter—must be cheap. Someone had lost a galosh, left foot, male. Someone had found a glove and thumbtacked it to the board. Down in the corner was a personal note: *Nancy meet me at 3, Liva's Sweet Shop. Ed.* Under it in various handwritings were: *I'll be there. Doug Fairbanks.* And under that, *Me, too. Walt Whitman.* And a third, *I'll be there, Nancy. Sig Freud.*

Absorbed in the board, Annie had not noticed that the students had dispersed to their various classes. She was alone in the empty hall. On the way out she stopped to listen to a class in session. The door was open, she stood against the wall to listen.

". . . naturalism is just another word for realism."

"Class?" The teacher's voice was a question mark. "You have your hand up, Mr. Boyton?"

"They are two different things."

"Explain."

"Two different things. That's all."

"Miss Decoe? I see your hand."

"Well, realism is naturalism boiled down."

"You mean it's the dregs of realism?"

The class laughed. Annie laughed, too, her hand over her

mouth. She didn't think it was funny, but she wanted so badly to belong. She heard a boy's deep voice.

"Realism is rough and tough. Full of murder and sex."

A boy with a higher voice pitched in. "Naturalism has sex too. Maybe the sex is more natural than real. But . . ."

"We're getting off the subject," said the teacher.

"May I say something?" It was a girl's voice.

"Yes, Miss Downing?"

"Realism is short sentences and few adjectives. Naturalism, the sentences are long and there's more thinking than action. But realism is easier to read."

"Now we're getting somewhere," said the teacher.

He took over for the rest of the hour. He explained the difference between naturalism and realism. He ended the session by assigning books to be read. Annie was familiar with some of the books. She wished she had pad and pencil to write down the foreign names like Zola and Gorki and something that sounded like Duffyetski. However, she memorized the title of the book written by him. She rushed out of the hall and got the book out of the library.

Carl came home at his usual time. She did not run to kiss him. She was lying on her stomach on the bed, absorbed in the book. She turned a page before she looked up.

"You're home early."

"Same time as always." He paused. "Well!"

"Well, what?"

"Here I come home after a hard day's work in the coal mines and . . ."

"Oh, Carl!" She rushed to him, unbuttoned his coat and put her arms about his waist under the coat. "I didn't know it was so late."

"What's the name of my rival?"

"How do you mean, Carl?"

"What would you be reading that made you forget me?"

103 *

"Oh, nothing. Just the best detective story in the world, *Crime and Punishment*."

The next day, this time armed with pad and pencil, Annie took up her station in Casson Hall. But the classroom was empty. She all but wept with disappointment. She had hardly slept the night before, anticipating standing in the hall and listening to the lesson. She told Carl that night. He explained that certain classes did not meet every day, and since the class had been in session on a Thursday, probably it met Thursdays and Tuesdays.

Yes, it was in session the following Tuesday. The teacher gave an assignment for the next session: To turn in a two-hundred-word evaluation of any book they had read in the course. Annie all but ran home, anxious to fulfill the assignment even though it would never be turned in. She gave *Crime and Punishment* a good going over. It took a lot more than the allotted two hundred words.

Carl was having his postponed interview with the Dean. It was a question-and-answer affair.

"You are married." It was a statement, not a question.

"Yes, sir."

"And you've informed your family."

"Yes, sir."

"How did they take it?"

"Not very well."

"I assume, then, you may expect no further financial aid from that source."

"Under the circumstances, no."

"Your wife: has she found work?"

"No, sir. Not yet."

The Dean matched his fingertips and swiveled his chair around to the side. Perspiration broke out under Carl's armpits. He felt it was none of the Dean's damn business how his parents felt or if Annie had a job or not. As long as his tuition was paid and his grades were satisfactory, the Dean had no right . . .

"Has your wife finished high school?" The question took Carl by surprise.

"She never even started high school," he blurted out. "Her formal education ended when she was fourteen."

The Dean's eyebrows shot up. He swiveled back, put both hands on his desk as if to stand up to indicate the interview was over.

"But she is by no means illiterate, sir," said Carl. "She has a good mind."

"What does she do?"

"Do?" Carl didn't quite understand.

"I'll rephrase the question: what is she interested in?"

"Well, reading mostly. She reads a lot. Then she writes a little —or tries to. She sort of—I don't know how to put it—collects people. And she gets a kick—excuse me, sir—a sort of feeling about things; like a clock or the weather . . ." Carl's voice trailed off. He felt he wasn't making a good case for Annie.

"And?" prompted the Dean.

"Well, when a certain class is in session in Casson Hall she stands in the corridor for the hour, listens to the lectures, takes notes, does the assigned reading. I believe it's the class in comparative modern literature."

The Dean picked up a pencil and drummed the rubber tip on his desk as if trying to find a word that eluded him or to come to a decision. Evidently he made up his mind. He dropped the pencil and stood up.

"Bring your wife here."

"Bring Annie *here?*" Carl's voice went up in surprise.

"Bring *Annie* here," said the Dean dryly.

"But sir . . ."

"Tomorrow at four."

The Dean had finished. He started signing letters. Carl said the usual thank you. The Dean continued signing without looking up. Carl left.

That night, when Carl told Annie that the Dean wanted to see her, she got as excited as if she had been invited to a party. She announced that she'd wash her hair so the Dean would think she looked nice; would borrow the landlady's iron and press her skirt, and, and . . .

As arranged, they met next day at ten to four outside the law building. She asked, a little anxiously, if she looked all right. He assured her she looked fine.

"Then I'm ready, if Mr. Dean's ready."

"His name isn't Dean. We refer to him as Dean. His name is Darwent."

"Mr. Darwent, then."

"We don't call him Darwent."

"What do you call him?"

"Sir. We use 'sir' like a name. For instance: 'Sir, if I may ask a question?' If you don't understand something, don't ask. Say 'sir' with a question mark."

"Sir this, sir that! Is he a knight of old or something? Am I supposed to curt-ess-sy to him?"

"Curtsy," he corrected. "And don't be flippant, Annie."

"Who's flip?"

"Another thing: Don't shake hands unless he puts his hand out first."

"Learn me some more," she said ominously.

He fell into the trap. "Well, if he says he's pleased to meet you, don't say 'likewise.' "

"I *never* say that! Cry-sake, Carl, are you ashamed of me or something?"

"No, Annie. Never, sweetheart! It's just . . ."

"Let me be my own dumb self, then, instead of trying to make me over in five minutes."

"I wouldn't want you made over. I just wanted you to make a good impression on the Dean."

"How about him making a good impression on *me?*"

"Oh, Annie, co-operate with me a little. It's so important."

"Carl," she said gently, "you're not afraid of the Dean, are you?"

"Hate to admit it, but I am."

"Don't be. He's only a man. And, Carl, don't you worry about me. I'll be careful what I say."

"That's my girl." He noticed she was carrying a book. "Why the book?"

"In case I get scared, I'll have something to hold on to."

The Dean had not expected Annie to be—well, Annie. He had expected her to be one of two types: an obviously sexy girl who could tease a boy into marriage or an older, more competent woman. Most medics and laws who married while in school seemed to go for the older, more mature type of woman. But this girl! She looked like hundreds of other girls. In fact, she reminded the Dean of his own daughter who was in second-year high.

Annie fixed her eyes on the Dean's eyes. She had read somewhere if you looked an enemy straight in the eye he couldn't get the edge on you. Annie surmised the Dean must have read the same book because he looked her right straight in the eye, too.

Carl introduced her as his wife, Mrs. Brown. Her right hand twitched with the instinct to extend it. But the Dean did not offer his hand. In lieu of shaking hands Annie took a tight grip on her book.

"And how do you do, Mrs. Brown?" he asked.

"And how do *you* do?" she retaliated.

He asked her to sit down. Staring at him she sat down, almost missing the seat. Carl stood behind her, his hand on the top of her chair.

"How do you like our college town, Mrs. Brown?"

"Won't you call me Annie?" she said impulsively.

The Dean almost smiled, but Carl groaned inwardly. There

107 *

she goes, he thought. He pressed her shoulder. Her eyes went a little wild. She brought her book up to her chest and put both arms around it.

"Excuse me," and then, belatedly, "sir." She hit the *sir* a little too hard.

There was a silence. The Dean waited, Annie waited. Carl pressed her shoulder gently to remind her she hadn't answered the Dean. "Oh!" she said, "you want to know—I mean, you asked me how I liked it here?" The Dean nodded. "I love it here. There's so much sky here and the air smells nice."

"Your husband told me you were fond of reading."

"I love to read!" she gulped, and added, "sir."

"What do you read?"

She's going to say books, thought Carl. To try to make him smile.

"I used to read everything I could get my hands on. But now I have a program . . . sir."

"What sort of program?"

"Well, there's a class and I stand in the hall where they can't see me and I write down what books the teacher tells them to read and I get the books out of the library and read them. Oh! Before I forget: Sometimes the teacher tells them to write a composition for homework . . ."

"Composition?" interrupted the Dean. "Do you mean theme?"

"Theme? Thank you, sir. Well, anyway, I go home and write the theme."

"Do you turn it in?"

"Oh, *no,* sir. I just stand in the hall."

The Dean matched his fingertips. He said nothing for a while. Annie clutched her book tighter and Carl patted her shoulder.

"So," said the Dean musingly, "you stand in the corridor and audit a class and fulfill the assignments without benefit of criticism or credits."

"Yes, sir." There was another long silence. "Is that all right, sir?"

He swiveled back to face her. "It's *quite* all right." He stood up. "Thank you for coming."

"You mean," said Annie in incredible relief, "that this meeting is over?"

"Yes, Annie. Your ordeal is over." He extended his hand. She squeezed it fervently.

He shook hands with Carl, too. "Take good care of your asset, Carl," he said.

Out in the hall, she asked anxiously, "Did I do all right?"

"You did just fine, sweetheart. I'm proud of you."

"Were you scared?"

"Just a little in the beginning," he said.

"I was scared all the time. Wouldn't it be funny if the Dean was scared too?"

"Scared? My Dean scared?" he asked incredulously.

"A-*ha!* So it's 'my' Dean now."

"He's all right, Annie. He's all right."

"Carl, what did he mean by 'your asset'?"

"If I told you, you wouldn't be fit to live with."

She looked up the word that night while he was going through his prestudy ritual. ASSET: *A valuable or desirable thing.*

Quick tears came to her eyes. "That," she said aloud, "makes up for the money order to send me home."

Carl, already absorbed in his studies, said, "What you say?"

"Nothing. Excuse me. *Sir!*"

She was at her usual place in the corridor, facing the wall, pad held up against the wall and pencil poised for note taking. The class was in session, but Annie wondered why it was so quiet. A man strolled out of the classroom, hands in his trousers' pockets. He was a little on the shabby side, or perhaps indifferent to what he wore and how he wore it.

"So, Mrs. Brown," he said. "You are the ghost who's been haunting my class."

"*He* said it was all right," said Annie defiantly. "*Quite* all right, was how he said it. The Dean, I mean."

"I am Professor Newcool, known as Prof." He extended his hand.

"My name is Annie Brown."

"I know." They shook hands. "Will you join us?"

"You mean go in there and sit down?"

"It will be more comfortable than standing in the hall, and we have lots of vacant seats."

She sat in the last seat of the empty last row. She just couldn't believe it! Just like I'm a coed, she thought. She fell in love with the chair, which had a broad table-like right arm. She vowed that when she got rich she'd buy a college chair like that and write her first book on it.

It was an hour of ecstasy for Annie. She paid intense attention, nodding in approval when the Prof made a point and frowning when a student gave a facetious answer to a serious question, and she took copious notes. The hour ended all too soon, and when the Prof told her he expected her to sit in on all the classes, she was almost too incoherent with happiness to thank him properly.

"Look at me, Carl," she said when Carl came home.

"I'm looking."

"Do I look different?"

"You look just the same to me."

"Look good!"

"Well, your shoes are a little dirtier, your hair a little longer."

"I thought it would show on me. I am a coed! Well, just the same as one." She told him about being invited to audit the class.

"How'd you work it?"

"The Prof *asked* me. And he knew my name! Carl, how could he know? Who could have told him?"

"You, of course."

"But he knew before I told him. Do you think it could have been—the Dean?"

"Of course. Who else?"

Needless to say, Annie lived for those two hours a week. She listened avidly, made notes, read all the assigned books, and mentally answered all the questions put to the students. Sometimes the Prof looked at her, encouraging her to make a comment. She never presumed to do so, feeling she was not entitled to take an active part since she had paid no tuition.

The class was still tussling with realism and naturalism and seemingly getting nowhere. One afternoon the Prof told them to write a paper of two hundred words or so on realism and naturalism, using *Babbitt* and *Crime and Punishment* as examples of the two styles. Then he went out and got a haircut.

Annie wrote furiously. A lot of it was incoherent because her thoughts raced ahead of her pencil. She was still writing half an hour later when the Prof returned. He began collecting the papers. She folded hers to put in her coat pocket, but he held out his hand for it and added it to the others.

Next session, he read some of the themes aloud. It used to be that the writers read their own work. But he had changed that. Many a bad paper was praised because its author was a dramatic reader. And many a possible literary treasure was lost to the world because its creator read it in a dull monotone. The Prof solved the whole thing by reading all the themes aloud. That way each one got an even break in the reading.

Annie prayed to our Father which art in heaven, not to let him read her theme aloud. Because they will laugh at me because it is no good. They'll make fun . . .

The Prof cleared his throat. "Class! I would like your undivided attention while I read the next paper." He cleared his throat again and read Annie's paper.

Every single person in this world has at least one big fault among many small ones. When a married man has a woman on the side, that is his big fault. Another man's big fault might be that he wants to get rich and don't care whose neck he steps on to do so.

Here is what Mr. Sinclair Lewis did. He did not give Babbitt one big fault, and harp on that. No. He gave him all the little faults there are. He stacked Babbitt. Then he made fun of him. Mr. Lewis never felt sorry for Babbitt because Mr. Lewis had no come-passion.

The Prof paused to smile at Annie's phonetic spelling.

Now take *Crime and Punishment*. In that book the hero had a great fault; the greatest fault in the world. He was a murderer. Now the man who wrote this book does not make you feel sorry for the murderer. But he did write it that in some way you understood why he had to murder this woman who he thought was a louse. And because the writer could make you understand this, it made come-passion.

Now the difference between Realism and Naturalism. I think it is that Realism makes the people in a book seem real and Naturalism makes them seem more human.

When asked, the class as a whole seemed reluctant to comment on Annie's theme. However, one boy did say he thought referring to murder as a fault was the understatement of the year. A girl wanted to know why the writer of the theme hadn't said "mistress," instead of "a woman on the side." There were a few other comments; none very favorable. The Prof took over.

"Strange," he said, "that no one commented on the writer's fresh point of view; the simplicity of her writing; the . . ."

He's talking about me, thought Annie ecstatically. He's talking about me!

". . . making articulate what is inarticulate."

The bell for changing classes ended the Prof's comments on her paper.

That night she kissed Carl with more than her usual tenderness when he came home, and whispered in a new shy way that she loved him very much.

"Now what brought that on?" He was pleased though.

"Nothing. Only I'm so happy I could die."

Chapter Eight

James W. Darwent, Dean of the Law School, and Professor Victor Newcool of the English Department were long-time friends. Both were busy men but they managed to lunch together at the Faculty Club from time to time.

"Yes, thank you, I will." The student waiter refilled the Dean's coffee cup.

Prof Newcool put his hand on his cup and said, "No more for me, thanks."

"You were saying . . ." said the Dean.

"Yes. I'd say she had all the ingredients of a potential writer. Too bad she can't go ahead."

"This beginning class in playwriting next semester: who's teaching it, Vic?" asked the Dean.

"Haise, I believe."

"Could you get him to let her audit it?"

"I believe I could. It would be just the thing. She has quite a flair for dialogue, you know."

"Good!"

The waiter poised the coffee pot over the Dean's cup. "More coffee, sir?"

"No, thank you, Harry. I have a staff meeting this afternoon and a third cup of coffee might keep me awake."

By Thanksgiving Annie's bank account was down to twenty-eight dollars. She had had to use her savings to supplement Carl's five-dollar-a-week income. Oh, yes, it had been so easy to budget their money that wedding day on the campus bench. They had faced the big emergencies that could work havoc with their small income—sudden illness, dental work, pregnancy. But, fortunately, these big dramatic emergencies did not materialize. It was the small nickel and dime things that came up day by day that plagued them.

A pad of paper cost little, but they used a lot of it. Pencils were a bargain at two for a nickel, considering the thousands of words they got out of one pencil. But pencils melted down fast. Razor blades were an item.

And honest, Annie, Carl had to have shaving soap. And no, Annie, the bath soap wouldn't do. And yes, sweetheart, he'd trim *her* hair to save the barber's fee, but no, Annie, she couldn't cut *his* hair. The barber for that. No, he couldn't let it go another week. It was down in his collar already. Did she want the boys to whistle at him?

And she knew it was cheaper than buying new shoes, but imagine! Fifty cents! Just to straighten heels! And yes, he loved her, but the place where she darned his socks was lumpy and he was getting a callus. He *knew* she'd learn, but after all a pair of new socks costs only fifteen cents. She knew it was the last quarter they had, but she just couldn't *live* without a lipstick. And you get that talcum powder, Annie. It makes you smell nice. I didn't like to talk about it, Carl, but sanitary pads . . .

"They never have a sale on that," complained Annie.

"And you can't charge a box of rubbers."

She frowned. "Don't talk dirty, Carl."

"That's one of the privileges of married life. Besides, you know all the dirty words."

"That doesn't mean I like them. It's not that I'm moral or anything, but those words hurt my ears—like chalk scratching on a blackboard."

"Do you know that most of those so-called dirty words come straight from Chaucer?"

"No kidding!"

"Read *Canterbury Tales* sometime."

"I'll get it from the library tomorrow."

"I just don't get it, Annie. For a girl as outspoken as you, you use more silly euphemisms . . ."

"You-for-what? What does that mean?"

"You know damn well what that means: Those cute words you use for going to the bathroom and that oh-you-bad-boy routine when I happen to say a plain Anglo-Saxon word."

"Tell me: do you need dirty words to get excited in bed?"

"No, I don't," he said, mimicking her, "need dirty words. I'll tell you what I do need. I need a quarter—" he looked around pretending he wanted no one else to hear—"for you-know-what."

She laughed at that. As she delved into her always overloaded handbag for nickels, dimes and pennies she said, "I wonder why they call it *free* love. You know: like in Greenwich Village?"

"Annie, can't you find another nickel? I hate to pay with pennies."

"Money is money," she said.

"Gee," he said in exaggerated admiration, "did you think that out all by yourself?"

She spread her arms wide and said dramatically, "Kiss me, my fool!"

He kissed her and went to the door. Hand on knob, he said, "Listen, kid! The way you *won't* say dirty words, as you call them, and the way you keep telling me you won't say them is more exciting than if you *did* say them."

"Why, you . . . !" She picked up the ashtray. He got the door closed after him before it hit. It didn't break this time—it was made of metal.

He opened the door and stuck his head back in. "And, what's more, you *know* it!"

He could run faster than she and was halfway down the street before she was halfway down the stairs.

A few nights later when he got home, she announced dramatically, "I got work, at last."

He had an instant of elation followed immediately by depression. The elation was relief that their financial situation would ease a bit and the depression was shame that he felt this relief. He was old-fashioned in some ways. He had been brought up in a generation where a man was practically considered a bum if his wife had to support him in whole or in part. He felt ashamed—small and insignificant in his own eyes. He did not like to feel this way. He exorcised his shame by being mean to her.

"And where does this work take place?"

"I work all day Saturdays in the dime store, and a couple of nights a week I mind a little girl for a lady who has to go out."

"May I make an appointment to see you sometime?" he asked sarcastically.

"Oh, Carl! I thought you'd be so pleased!"

"How'd you find these jobs? Pardon me: work."

"Well, I asked the dime store manager, and he said he could use me Saturdays with the Christmas rush coming on. And then there was a notice on the bulletin board in Casson Hall saying a lady wanted a responsible girl to look after well-behaved child evenings, and . . ."

"What is the lady's name?"

"Mrs. Karter."

Karter! The name alerted him. "Does she spell it with a 'K' or a 'C'?"

"With a 'K.'"

Karter, he thought, Karter! There was something about that name . . .

"Carl, will you let me sit on your lap? Please?"

They sat in the rocker. She put her arms around him and held him tight. "I had to get work, Carl. I just had to. There's only eight dollars left in the bank."

He buried his face in her neck and said: "I know, sweetheart. I know."

She held him. They said nothing for a while.

After a while he said, "You won't have to drop your class, will you?"

"Oh, no! That's why I looked for work instead of a job."

"I'm glad of that, anyhow. The class means so much to you."

"Oh, Carl!" She straightened up suddenly. "I forgot to tell you. It's the most wonderful thing! You know my prof? Well, he said next term—I mean semester, they repeat the work, and he thinks I should sit in a different class. So he's going to fix it that I sit, I mean audit, the class in playwriting. What do you think of that?"

"I think it's wonderful!"

"Everything's turning out just fine, Carl. Christmas vacation I can work all day every day, the dime store man said."

"And," he said, "I have a job all lined up. Hardware store. From nine to nine. Twenty dollars for the week before Christmas."

"It's going to be a wonderful Christmas. Our first Christmas together, Carl."

"Annie," he said suddenly, "is that Karter woman's first name Beverly?"

"Yes. Why?"

"Oh, I don't know. Somewhere I must have heard something about her. It's not very clear in my mind."

"Why, she's nice, Carl. She has a beautiful home. She has a

little girl, four years old. Joanny. She's such a sweet girl. Not pretty, you know, like her mother. But I like the little thing."

"Karter . . . Bev Karter. Um-m . . ." He shook his head. "Maybe you oughtn't to work for her until I find out . . ."

"What are you trying to tell me, Carl?"

"Something I heard, somewhere, some place . . ."

"You know her!" she said, instantly suspicious. "You're afraid I'll find out something."

"I never laid eyes on the woman."

"That's your story."

"It's the truth, Annie."

"I'm going to work for her. And if I find out anything about you and her . . ."

"Annie, you mustn't be so jealous. It doesn't become you. Suppose I was jealous? You're always talking about that grocer of yours. Suppose I was jealous of him."

"Henry? Jealous of poor old Henry? Why, you're crazy."

"Sweetheart, don't take that job. For my sake."

"I've already taken it," she said.

Chapter Nine

Bev Karter was youngish rather than young. She was drawn a bit too fine. Her cheekbones were prominent and there were two white knobs at the base of her throat. Her breasts were a little on the small, hard side, but she made the most of them by wearing low-cut or very tight dresses. Her backside was flat, as was her stomach. She dressed well and had what Annie thought of as *chick*. She went easy on the accessories—her only ornament was a gold bracelet with a dozen dangling charms which tinkled incessantly as she moved. There was a faint drift of exotic perfume in the wake of her walk.

Her attitude toward Annie was correct. She did not treat the girl as a servant nor as a friend. She liked Annie without being interested in her. Annie liked Bev and was interested in her as well. Annie loved the woman's apartment.

"There's all these windows," she told Carl. "No wallpaper because the walls are painted pale yellow and she has these pictures hanging up. I don't mean pictures like 'Whistler's Grandmother.'"

"Mother," he corrected.

"Anyhow, she don't . . . doesn't have that. She has pictures you have to ask what they are because you can't make them out.

But that makes no difference because the colors get you kind of excited, and Mrs. Karter said you don't have to know what they are. All you got to do is *feel* what they are."

"My!" said Carl in mock admiration.

"She's a widow, I guess."

"College widow," he said.

"And her husband must have left her a lot of insurance."

"The word is alimony."

"How do you know?"

"She's an obvious type. There's one like her in almost every college town. They call them college widows."

"What's a college widow?" asked Annie.

"The college widow, so called," said Carl, lawyer fashion, "is a campus institution. Her home, usually attractive, is, you might say, a haven for lonely but good-looking young men; the more mature student—the medic, the law student, the man working on his Ph.D. She has them over for a social evening. One usually stays behind after the others leave. He spends the night with her —or part of the night if he has an early class the next day."

"Does she charge?"

"No. The pleasure is all hers."

"How do you know all about this?"

"Oh, Annie! It's common knowledge."

Annie thought things over. Mrs. Karter did have one of these social evenings once a week. It was Annie's job to give little Joanny her supper, put her to bed, then help Mrs. Karter get ready. She helped make finger sandwiches, set up the bridge table, place ashtrays in strategic places, and arrange the records Mrs. Karter had chosen in order on a little table. When the boys arrived, Mrs. Karter said, "That will be all, Annie, and thank you." She gave Annie her dollar and Annie left.

"Carl, if you don't want me to work for her, I won't."

"Annie, I love you with all my heart. But you do exasperate me. You *know* I don't want you to work for her and you *say* you'll quit, but you keep right on working."

"We need the money, Carl," she said quietly.

"Yes. The money." He sighed and went to the window and looked out, seeing nothing. She went to him.

"Carl, the dime store man offered me a full-time job. I could take it and quit Mrs. Karter. But then I'd have to give up my class. And oh, Carl, I don't want to do that."

"Don't give up the class, Annie. No matter what else you do."

"But, Carl, don't keep at me all the time about working for Mrs. Karter."

"I can't help it, sweetheart. I'm ashamed that because of me you have to work for a . . ."

She put her hand over his mouth before he could say the word "whore." "Don't say that, Carl. You don't know if she is or not. Anyhow there will be no classes in Christmas vacation, and I'll take the all-day dime store job and quit Mrs. Karter."

"But what about after Christmas?"

"Something else will turn up. You'll see." He sighed and prepared to study. "Carl, before you settle down, could I ask you something?"

"Shoot!"

"Say a woman's not married: she sleeps with a man who is an old friend. If she doesn't charge him, is she still a whore? Or just a loose woman?"

"Now that's a moot question."

"What does that mean?"

"Well, in law . . ."

"Never mind, Carl. You don't have to explain it now. Tomorrow's another day."

"I'd sure be surprised if it turned out to be the same day." He smiled and it was the first time he had smiled that evening. It lightened Annie's heart.

"Don't be so wise, my darling," she said.

She had taken out Milne's *The House at Pooh Corner* because the title was funny. Now she was writing her opinion of

121   *

the book even though no one would read her paper, the book not being required reading in the class.

It's too slick [she wrote]. It's the kind of book grownups read and think how they would love it if they were children again.
But I don't think children will like this book. It looks down on them in a way.
If a child is too little to know how to read and a grownup reads it to him, he won't understand it. If he is old enough to read it himself, he will think it is silly.
Still and all . . . [She crossed that out and started the sentence again.] Yet, the book has a certain charm . . .

Charm, she thought. A dopey word if ever there was one, and this dopey stuff I'm writing. Eyewash. She tore up the sheet. She did not realize it, but she had been thinking of Mrs. Karter as she wrote. And she didn't like her thoughts.

Now: Bev Karter. Annie didn't see anything wrong in her having the boys in for a social evening. It was the man whom Mrs. Karter referred to as an old friend that bothered Annie. He and Mrs. Karter went out every Friday night and didn't come back until midnight. Annie assumed it was a romance and that the friend was young, unmarried, good looking, and had nice ways.

Usually Annie was in the bedroom with Joanny when he came, and they had always left before Annie saw him. One night he was a little late and Annie had a chance to meet him. She was disillusioned. He was literally an old friend; in his late fifties. He was shorter than Mrs. Karter, wore thick-lensed glasses, was just about all bald and had a big paunch.

It was a week after Annie and Carl had had the discussion about Mrs. Karter. It was raining torrents. The rain was mixed with snow and sleet and there was a cold wind. Annie was in the bedroom reading Joanny to sleep when he came. The bedroom door was slightly ajar. Annie heard him say:

"No use going out in this weather. No place like home on a night like this. I brought a bottle of Scotch—the real stuff. I have a contact—gets it for me from Canada." Mrs. Karter closed the door to the child's room and Annie heard no more.

The child fell asleep. Annie wished she had a book or something to read. She became restless. The room was very small, and Annie never could stand being in a small room with the door closed. She stood at the window and watched the steady downpour and noticed the thin coating of ice on the sidewalk. The ice glittered under the street lights. And me without overshoes, she thought. How will I ever get home—all that ice?

She saw the old friend's car parked in front of the adjoining apartment house. It was a long gray car; expensive looking. It had a crystal vase with a red rose in it. Annie wondered whether it was a real rose.

She sat on the low chair next to the child's head and wondered what the child's father had looked like. He must have looked like Joanny, she thought. She hoped she'd have a little girl like that someday. But she supposed Carl would want a boy. She hoped that her children would look like Carl because she thought Carl was better looking than she.

For some time now she had been aware of the constant murmur of conversation in the living room. Now, sitting in the quiet room, she heard words emerge from the murmur.

His voice: ". . . and might as well spend the night here. More comfortable than that hotel." Mrs. Karter said something Annie couldn't hear. His voice again: "Just so I get home by one, so she's not suspicious."

Annie went to the door intending to ask Mrs. Karter if she could go home. Now the voices were distinct. Annie, her hand on the knob, waited for the break in the conversation in order to come out of the bedroom.

"Out of the question, Bev. Not that I don't think a lot of you."

"But who'll be hurt? Your children are grown up now and

123   *

have children of their own. And you admitted you didn't love her any more."

"I don't. But I wouldn't hurt her for anything in the world."

A pause. Annie was about to open the door when Mrs. Karter's voice came up again. "You know I respect you for that? I really do."

"Edna and I don't get along. That's true. But she was a good wife to me in the past and a good mother to the children."

"Conscience bother you, sweetie, that you're cheating on her?"

"Why should it? It's not as if I neglect her. I give her everything she wants; her own car, charge accounts, money . . ."

"That reminds me: my rent's due."

"I took care of that. I put the money on your dressing table."

"I'll need an extra fifty with Christmas coming up."

"I don't have that much on me, Bev."

"Write a check."

"Can't. She might see your name on the canceled check and there'd be hell to pay. But let's see. Yes. I have about thirty in cash. Here. I'll mail you a twenty-dollar bill in the morning."

So she takes money! thought Annie. She takes money for sleeping with that married man. He said: ". . . I'd never divorce her, Bev. Not even for you, and I think a lot of you."

Annie cleared her throat to warn them and came out of the bedroom. She saw them on the sofa. Mrs. Karter had her legs tucked under her and was counting the money in her lap. Old friend had made himself comfortable. He had loosened his belt to ease his paunch. His detachable stiff collar with a gold collar button still on it and his tie were on the coffee table, along with the bottle of Scotch. Old friend's feet were up on the table, too.

"Why, Annie!" Mrs. Karter put the bills on the table and stood up. "I forgot all about you!"

"If you don't need me any more tonight," began Annie.

"Maybe the girl would like a drink," suggested old friend.

"The girl would not like a drink," said Mrs. Karter sharply.

". . . I thought I could go home," said Annie.

"Of course." Mrs. Karter held out her hand to old friend. "I need a dollar for the girl." He indicated the bills on the table. "They're all fives and tens," said Mrs. Karter.

Old friend had to lie on his back, almost, to get a dollar bill out of his pants pocket. Mrs. Karter held out the bill to Annie, and Annie's hand trembled a bit as she took the money, thinking, he pays her and she pays me. It made her feel as if she were a partner to the affair.

She had trouble buttoning her coat. "Here! Let me," said Mrs. Karter. She buttoned the coat and arranged Annie's scarf, making a hood out of the back of it and tucking the ends tightly into the top of the coat. Annie kept her face turned away, aware of the musical tinkle of the bracelet charms and the faint whiff of scent. How can such a clean, pretty young woman like her, thought Annie, who always smells so nice and has such a nice little girl, sleep with a pig like him?

"There!" Mrs. Karter gave the scarf a final pat.

"Thank you and good night, Mrs. Karter."

"Wait! It's pouring out. I'll give you an umbrella."

"I don't need one. But thanks."

"Yes, you do. You can bring it back next time you come."

"I . . . I won't be coming here any more."

"*Annie!*" She grasped Annie's arms. "But you can't *do* that to me," she wailed. "Why, you're the best girl I ever had and Joanny's so attached to you."

"I guess I should have told you before," said Annie lamely.

"But why, Annie? *Why?*" She gave the girl a gentle shake. "Is it money? Don't I pay you enough?"

"It isn't that." Annie's eyes went to the man on the sofa. He took his feet off the table and sat up straight. His eyes met Annie's and she turned away. "It's just that my husband doesn't want me"—she paused—"to work nights."

"Maybe if I talked to him . . ."

Annie shook her head. "Good-by, Mrs. Karter."

Annie had to pass old friend's car. Yes, that was a real rose in the little crystal vase. Imagine, she marveled. A real rose in the dead of winter!

Her shoes, a soggy mess, squeaked and squelched as she went up the stairs. Her woolen scarf was heavy on her head and neck. It had held every drop of rain that fell on it. And to add to her misery, Carl wasn't home. So that's the way it is, she thought. He didn't expect me home until twelve, and he went out.

Just then he came back to the room. They spoke simultaneously. "Where were you, Carl?" and "What are you doing home so early?" He answered first. "I was down the hall shaving." She said, "I should have listened to you, Carl. You were right."

"Look at you standing there," he said, "dripping all over the floor. Cry-sake, Annie, do you want to get pneumonia?"

He removed her scarf and wrung it out in the tin wastebasket. He took off her wet shoes and wrung out her socks, muttering, at least the woman could have lent her an umbrella.

"She tried to, Carl, but I wouldn't take it. You see, I didn't mean to listen, but . . ."

"Tell me later." He rubbed her feet into dry warmth with the bath towel, had her take a hot bath and two aspirins, got her into bed and warmly covered before he asked her what had happened.

"Carl! She takes money!"

"But what happened?"

"Well, I was in Joanny's room. I couldn't help but hear . . ." She told him in detail, ending with, "And you were right about her, Carl."

"It shouldn't have happened," he said. "I shouldn't have let you work there. Cry-sake, Annie, didn't you *know*?"

"Maybe. But I just didn't want to believe it."

"But you're not stupid and, as you say, you know all the words."

"Well, a person can know a thing is true and still not believe it. He has to *see* it to believe it."

*   126

"But I told you," he said stubbornly. "Wasn't that enough?"

"I had to find out for myself."

"You sure could have got yourself in a hell of a lot of trouble. Suppose his wife wanted a divorce; wanted to get something on him so she could put in for a fat financial settlement: why, you'd be a material witness! *The* material witness!"

"But I wouldn't tell the judge what I heard. I'd say I didn't know nothing—I mean anything."

"Then you'd be up for perjury."

She shrugged. "So what!"

"So you'd be put in prison. That's what!"

She scrambled off the bed and clung to him. "Oh, Carl, we'd be disgraced! No one would ever hire a lawyer whose wife was once in jail. Oh, Carl! Why did you let me work for her?"

"Me?" His voice went high in astonishment. "Me *let* you work for her? That's certainly a new one on me!"

"Oh, Carl, what am I going to do? What *am* I going to do?"

"Take it easy, sweetheart. There's only one chance in ten thousand that his wife is on to him and is having him watched."

"Why'd you scare me so, then?"

He threw up his hands. "I give up!"

"Carl, when I get old, you won't have another woman, will you? And run me down to her?"

"Another woman?" he asked incredulously. "God forbid! I have all I can do to handle the one I already have."

Annie couldn't figure out why learning about Mrs. Karter had upset her so. Annie was naïve but not stupidly innocent. Since childhood she had known about prostitutes, whores, and girls who "went wrong." What she didn't know, the other kids had told her.

The prostitutes lived in the nicest, cleanest house in the neighborhood. They had their men at night and charged two dollars. The whore lived in a dirty flat and men came at odd times of day and night. She charged fifty cents. Annie knew of women like that but had never had contact with or been affected by them. She was curious about them but not especially interested.

The girl that went wrong was different. Annie had known some of them as classmates in grade school. The tough girls started going wrong about fourteen or fifteen. They seldom got into trouble. They knew their way around. It was the potentially good girl, the not too pretty girl, the girl whose parents were too strict or too indifferent toward her, who responded too gratefully to the first man who showed an affectionate interest in her. That was the girl who got into trouble—often had an illegitimate child; ended up in a house of correction.

Like poor Ruth, who had lived in the flat above Annie's: she died, giving birth to an illegitimate child. And only fifteen years old! All the night, Annie had lain in bed, awake, and the pillow she put over her face and ears could not shut out the horror of the high, inhuman screams from the rooms above. And the two days that the white crape was on the door (white for children, lavender for adults and black for the old) punched home the fact that the wages of sin were, literally, death.

Ruth had a reason for what she had done. She wanted to *hold* the first human being who she thought loved her. The prostitutes had a reason. Money, yes. And the communal life of the brothel suited them. The whore *liked* being a whore; it was her nature. And the fictional women—*Jennie Gerhardt, Sister Carrie,* and *Maggie, a Girl of the Streets*—had their reasons. Annie firmly believed that everyone had a reason for what he was or wasn't. Moral herself, she did not condone the reasons, but she acknowledged them.

She could find no reason for Bev Karter's relationship with old friend. Bev was not a prostitute, whore, or girl who went wrong. She was well bred. Annie thought of the word "cultured" in connection with Bev Karter. It was obvious that she had come from a comfortable background. Why, thought Annie, why?

Obviously she slept with old friend and took money from him. But money couldn't be the reason. There had to be a better reason. Annie became so tormented and obsessed by this elusive reason that she invented a reason for Mrs. Karter, and old friend too, by writing it out.

She is that way [wrote Annie] because maybe she never had a brother who teased her and shoved her around but grew to think his sister was pretty wonderful. Or maybe her father never told her in so many words that she was the best girl in the world. And maybe the husband she must have had wasn't like Carl. Maybe he never made her sit on his lap so he could rock her and pet her. She never had things like that. So now, she keeps looking for those lost things in her life, always hoping to find them. Tenderness, I guess, is what she never had. That is what she is trying to find.

And maybe that man is truly an old friend. Maybe she knew him long ago when he was young and slim and good looking. When he was full of beans. [She crossed out beans and wrote dreams.] But he married someone else.

Thus Annie got a reason for the way Mrs. Karter was. Maybe it wasn't the real reason, but it served as far as Annie was concerned.

Chapter Ten

She liked working at the dime store at first. It was like being a kid again and playing store for real. She was interested in her customers, patient with them, took pains to wrap their packages nicely, and never failed to say thank you and come again to each customer.

Things changed when the Christmas rush started. The customers seemed to get meaner and meaner as the season of good will got under way. They claimed they had been shortchanged; had been sold broken toys, claiming the girl knew they were broken when the girl sold them.

The manager had to be sent for. He and Annie collaborated in a small production. He knew she was not to blame, but he had to pretend to give her hell because it made the customer feel righteous. Annie played along. At first she apologized so abjectly to the customer that the manager had to warn her not to overdo it.

The cash register drove her crazy. It was high up, and she was only five feet two. She had to stand on tiptoes to work it and the muscles in the back of her legs ached all the time. One day as she was ringing up she turned to reply to a customer's question, and the drawer shot out and clipped her on the chin.

Henry, the grocer, noticed the black-and-blue bruise and asked what had happened. According to their game, it was her cue to say she'd tell him tomorrow. But fearing the grocer might think Carl had beat her up, she told Henry about the cash register. He got a small wooden box from the back room, had her stand on it to see if it would hold her weight. It did. She carried it to the dime store and stood on it to work the cash register.

During the last week before Christmas, the dime store remained open until ten o'clock. In lieu of overtime pay, the girls were given free supper at the lunch counter. Like the bus boys in Carl's cafeteria, Annie saw to it that her plate was well loaded.

Carl, released from the cafeteria for a week, because there wasn't much business there with the students away for Christmas, worked also. He worked full time and overtime in the hardware store where Annie had bought her clock.

Carl and Annie agreed they would not buy Christmas presents for anybody. They needed the money for themselves. But Annie felt she had to send her little brothers a present. Carl said yes. He had been a little boy once himself and he knew how kids looked forward to presents. And they could not overlook the landlady, who was nice enough to let Annie use her iron for Carl's shirts. Carl agreed to that, too, remembering about the tea and the hot-water bottle and the aspirin. And, oh, he felt that he had to give Mrs. Ridinski *something*. She had sort of looked after him before he was married, you know, sewed a loose button on his coat. Things like that. Annie said, of course. He would be a pig if he forgot Mrs. Ridinski. There was something he hated to bring up. But his mother . . . Annie thought that over and came to the conclusion that after all she was his mother, no matter what, and was entitled to a present. Carl urged Annie to buy her mother a gift. Annie said she had thought of it but hadn't liked to bring it up, and she certainly appreciated his not objecting to it.

"But, Carl, I don't want you to get anything for me. I have you and that's enough. Besides, we need the money so bad."

"I won't get you anything if you won't get me anything. Okay?"

"Okay."

Annie had thought of getting a Christmas tree. A little one didn't cost much, but the ornaments ran into money and who could afford to buy them all at once? Ornaments had to be acquired year by year, and often a child grew to maturity before there was a completely filled Christmas tree in his home. She decided to get some sprigs of holly instead.

The florist's window was full of potted poinsettias, red geraniums, and pink begonias. But Annie fell in love with a little hairy-leaved plant in a pink flowerpot. The florist, who was writing in a ledger, looked up at the window. He went back to his book, not having recognized her because he'd never seen her in her new outfit.

When she went into the store, he closed his book before he looked up and asked, "What can I do for you?"

"That hairy plant in the window: what is it called?"

"You!" he said dramatically. "I didn't know until I heard your voice. I thought you were a coed staying over to share our local Christmas. How have you been, Mrs. . . . er . . ."

Pleased at being mistaken for a coed, she said impulsively, "Call me Annie."

"Anthony, here." They shook hands across the counter. "I remember you pleasantly, Annie."

"Me, too, Anthony. I mean the way you spoke about the roots and all."

"What roots?"

"*You* know: *The Rape of the Forest?* I'm glad to see you're writing it." She pointed to the ledger.

"Oh, that! I was merely going over my accounts."

"So you are not writing a book." Her disappointment was obvious.

"I'm not ready for it. I have to think it through first. The writing is nothing. The thinking is all."

"But couldn't you think and write at the same time?"

"And sell flowers also? Frankly, no."

"Frankly, good-by, then." She turned to leave.

"Wait! The name of the plant in the window is saintpaulia, known to the layman as an African violet."

"I don't care what its name is. You're not writing a book."

"You are concerned?"

"Worse than that. Disappointed."

"May I ask why?"

"All my life I wanted to know somebody who was writing a book."

"I see. You don't care to know a florist?"

"I already know a florist. In Brooklyn. He couldn't write a book if he tried. But you . . ."

"I'll write the book!" he announced.

"Oh, will you? Promise?"

"I promise to go into writing January first, 1928."

"Oh, I'm so happy, Anthony."

"I value your faith in me, you see."

They discussed the book a little further before she bought three sprigs of holly for a dime. He wanted her to take the holly as a gift but she refused. He added another sprig as a present.

All of a sudden it was Christmas Eve. The dime store closed at six. Annie got her pay and a new dollar bill in a Christmas folder as a gift. She also received an offer to continue working on Saturdays, from nine in the morning to nine at night, for two dollars and free supper. She accepted.

On the way home she bought a box of chocolate cherries for the landlady and stopped in to wish Henry, the grocer, a merry Christmas. He presented her with a strawberry basket, left over from the summer, filled with walnuts.

133   *

"Oh, Henry! How nice you are!" Then, stricken, "And I didn't give you anything!"

"Ah, they're only nuts," he said.

"Lean over the counter." He did and she gave him a light kiss on his dry cheek.

"Say, Annie! That's the nicest Christmas present I ever had!"

When she got to the room, she heard Carl calling from nowhere, "Where *were* you?"

"Tell me first where you *are*?"

"In the closet."

"What are you doing in there?"

"Brooding."

"Come out and see what Henry gave me for Christmas."

"That's fine. But see what the landlady gave us."

It was a small white cake baked in the shape of a star with a little paper angel on top. Annie read the card that went with it: "Merry Christmas from Margo Hansmon." "It's the most beautiful cake I ever saw. And, Carl, she has a first name!"

"Everyone has a first name. What's so odd about that?"

"Well, you just don't think of landladies having a first name, that's all."

They went down to thank the landlady. She had just finished decorating a small Christmas tree. She asked Carl to carry it out to the hall and put it on the hall table so that they all could enjoy it. Annie thought that was such a nice thing to do and told her so. The landlady thought it was very thoughtful of Annie and Mr. Brown to give her a present and she told them so.

While Annie was hanging the holly upside down on the shade pull, Carl got two boxes and a few Christmas post cards out of the closet. He had asked the landlady to put them aside so Annie would be surprised. He set the boxes and the cards on the dresser. Annie wanted to open the boxes at once, but Carl insisted they go out and have something to eat first—at least a sandwich and coffee. It was only seven o'clock, and if they opened them now, Christmas would be over in ten minutes. He let her open the cards, however.

One was from his family and one from hers. There was a card from Annie's friend, Arlene, and one from an aunt she hadn't seen in years. The last card came in a thick cream-colored envelope. It was a simple card saying: "Season's greetings from James and Janet Darwent."

"Darwent?" Annie said, puzzled.

"The Dean! Well, what do you know!" Carl seemed very pleased.

She ran her finger over the card. "Carl! It's engraved."

"Of course."

"They must be aristocrats from way back. My!"

Back from their hurried supper, Annie threw her coat on the bed, dropped her handbag in the drawer without bothering to shut the drawer and said, "Hurry up! You open yours first."

He decided to tease her a bit. "Hang up your coat first." She did. "Close the dresser drawer." She banged it shut. "Now go wash your hands."

"Why?"

"Because I said so."

"What's the matter? You afraid I'll touch your mother's present and make it dirty?"

"Annie, don't let's fight. Not on Christmas Eve."

She put her arms around him and pressed her face against his chest. "I'm sorry, Carl. And don't mind what I say, darling." Then she spoke one of woman's oldest excuses. "You see, it's getting to be that time in the month when I get on edge for nothing at all."

"I was only teasing you, sweetheart."

"I know. Now open your present."

Mrs. Brown had sent her son two sets of underwear; the kind with long arms and legs and a seat that opened up in the back.

135 *

"I don't know what got into Mom," he said. "She knows I hate long underdrawers—never wear 'em. Never did."

"Well, like people say, Carl, it's the thought, not the gift."

"I suppose so," he said dubiously.

A card attached to the underwear said: "To my son with all my love." There was a small flat box with "Annie" written on the cover. It contained a handkerchief.

"At least Mom remembered you," he said.

"On the package I sent, I addressed it to the whole family and wrote that it was from you and me."

He sighed. "I can't help it, Annie. Mom is the way she is, and there's nothing I can do about it."

Aside from a sharp look, Annie made no comment. She opened the package from her mother. The card read: "For Annie and Carl from all of us." She showed Carl the card. He made no comment, but a muscle twitched in his cheek. The joint gift was a woolen blanket made of alternating large black and red squares.

"But we have a blanket," he said.

"It belongs to the landlady. This one is ours. It will come in handy when we have a house of our own. At least she sent a gift we could share. But not your mother! We can't share the underwear or the handkerchief. It's her way of separating us."

"Very good, Mrs. Freud," he said. "Very good."

There was a dangerous silence. Each waited for the other to say the next mean thing to get a quarrel under way. She spoke first. "Not on Christmas Eve, Carl."

"Not on Christmas Eve," he agreed with relief. He pressed his cheek against hers. "I know, sweetheart. I know how you feel."

She put the boxed handkerchief in the bottom drawer, knowing she'd never use it. He put the folded underwear on the top shelf of the closet, knowing he'd never use it. He asked whether she wanted the blanket put away. She said no, and folded it and put it at the foot of the bed.

"It gives color to the room, don't you think?"

"Annie, if you want my honest opinion . . ." he began.

"Not on Christmas Eve," she said hurriedly. They smiled at each other.

He sat in the rocker. "Well, Merry Christmas, sweetheart." Annie was wedging the Christmas cards in the frame of the mirror. "Come sit on my lap," he said.

"When I finish this, Carl." He got up to get a cigarette. She took advantage of his turned back to get a small package from her handbag.

"Open your hand and shut your eyes and I'll give you something to make you wise," she said. He didn't seem to understand. "Never mind. Here!" She held out the small box wrapped in holly paper and tied with a red ribbon.

"But, Annie, we agreed—promised each other . . ."

"Open it!"

It was Carl's watch, which she had redeemed from the pawnbroker! "I . . . don't know what to say," he faltered.

"Say thanks."

"Many, many thanks, sweetheart. Oh, Annie, you don't know how I missed it! Not because Mom gave it to me, but I was lost without it. I have to time everything so carefully, racing around with the papers, getting to the cafeteria, split seconds to make a class, always worrying whether I'd be late. Well, thanks." He set the time and wound the watch.

She sat on his lap and put it on his wrist. "Annie," he said tentatively, "I don't want to start a fight on Christmas Eve, but I always felt that you hated the watch because Mom gave it to me."

"If I did, I don't now. We made the last two payments, and on the note you put down that you owed her for the other payments. So now I feel that maybe *she* picked it out but *we* bought it."

"Annie, I feel just terrible."

"Don't. Enjoy the watch."

"I mean, I didn't get you a present."

"What?" She was off his lap in a flash. "You mean you didn't get me *anything?*" Her voice went up in indignation.

"But you made me promise not to buy you a present."

"And you believed me?"

"But you *said!*"

"But I didn't mean it! Didn't you know? It's like when you say 'I'm pleased to meet you' when you're not pleased, really. You should have known that."

"I can't say how sorry I am."

"Don't talk to me," she said coldly. She went to the holly and pulled off a leaf that wasn't withered.

"All right, if that's the way you feel," he said in a huff. He went into the closet.

"I didn't mean it, Carl. I didn't mean it. Don't go out. I'm not mad. I was just disappointed for a minute. Carl?"

He came out of the closet with the gift he had hidden there. "Why do you take everything so seriously, Annie? Of course I got you a present."

It was a large loose-leaf notebook. The covers were limp, dark-red leather and her name, *Annie Brown,* was in gold letters on the upper right-hand corner. It took her breath away. Literally! She drew in a breath in a gasp of delight and it wouldn't come back out until he pounded her on the back.

"It's beautiful!" she said. "Like in church. More than beautiful. There must be a word higher than beautiful, and I wish I knew it."

"Look inside."

The first page was blank except for two typed lines in the middle. The first line was *Potpourri.* Under it, *By Annie Brown.*

"What does pot-paw-ree mean, Carl?"

"It's pronounced *po-poo-re.* It means a little of everything nice, I think," he ended dubiously.

He had taken her manuscripts and had them typed up by the hotel stenographer. He had used her title when she had one and made up titles when she didn't. The first manuscript was titled *The Stupid Heart,* the untitled *Babbitt* one he titled *Real Versus Natural.* Her evaluation of the Milne book he called *For Grown-*

ups Only, and the last, the Mrs. Karter one, had her own title: *A Sad Story.*

"But, Carl, I tore up the *House at Pooh Corner* one."

"You tore it very carefully in half and didn't throw it away."

"It's like I had a book printed," she said. "And it makes me happy because you must sort of believe in me."

"You bet I do."

"Would you say it in so many words?"

"You'll be a writer someday."

"Thank you, Carl. But you don't really believe it, do you?"

"*You* believe it. That's more important."

"I know. But a person likes a little encouragement. I know my grammar is bad and my spelling, too. And I can't write a sentence of more than six words without getting lost. So I got to have encouragement."

"Annie, anything you set your mind on doing you will do. With or without encouragement. I know you pretty well by now."

"I'll never be a writer, really. But I love to write all the same. I did get encouragement from this Hemingway. I read *In Our Time* while I ate lunch and supper at the dime store. You know he writes in short sentences? He must have the same trouble I have with sentences. And he writes in conversations because, like me, that's easier. I figure if he can get away with it, so can I."

"That reminds me!" He went into the closet and came out with a package of lined paper to fit the loose-leaf folder. "I forgot this goes with it," he said. "You can write on these sheets and clip them into the book along with your other stories."

"Carl, you think of *everything.* And I've got a new story all figured out; about our first Christmas together. Let's see, what'll I call it? Carl, you're so good on names. You tell me what to call it."

"How about Our First Christmas Together?"

"That's good, Carl. *Very* good! Let me write it down before I forget it! Let me write the first line while it's fresh in my head. Won't take a minute." She wrote:

It started out in great excitement—our first Christmas together. Then it looked as though it would end in grief. Then something wonderful took place—a truly Christmas miracle like in an O. Henry story.

She stood at the dresser, writing furiously, forgetting she meant to write but one line. Carl paced the floor, smoking one cigarette after another. He felt shut out. When he could stand it no longer, he went and took the pencil out of her hand.

"Annie, there is so little time when we can be together and it's Christmas Eve . . ."

She was instantly contrite. "I'm such a dope," she said, putting the book and paper into the drawer. "I don't know why you put up with me." She put her arms around him. "But I'm glad you do."

"It's only a little after eight, and I thought we could celebrate a little. How about the movies? They've got Laurel and Hardy."

"I don't think it's nice to see Laurel and Hardy on the night Jesus was born."

"That's right," he agreed.

"Besides, even if it wasn't Christmas, I don't like the way they keep hitting each other on the head all the time. It makes me sick."

"Well, how about an old-fashioned walk?"

"That would be grand. We can look at all the Christmas trees in people's windows."

It was a lovely night. "Snow on the ground," said Carl. "The stars shining. That's how Christmas should be. Cold and clear."

"I'd like it better if it was a little warm," she said. "And misty. So the stars would be mysterious through the mist. All dreamy. And no snow. It was a warm country where He was born. And in all the pictures of the manger and the shepherds and the Wise Men, I never saw a bit of snow. Did you?"

"Come to think of it, no."

They walked hand in hand, stopping at times to admire a Christmas tree in someone's window. In one they saw children around the tree. A little one held a new doll. "There's my daughter five years from now," said Annie.

"And where's my son?" asked Carl.

"Upstairs, somewhere."

In one place the people had decorated a big live tree just outside the door. "That's what I'll do when we have a home," she said. "Decorate a tree in the front yard with lights and golden balls and tinsel and angels for the whole world to see."

"I believe you'd do just that. You were born an exhibitionist."

"I was not! I was born a Methodist!"

"If that's a joke, pardon me for not laughing."

"Oh, you!" She gave him one of her affectionate shoves.

They came to a church. The door was open. The altar glowed with red poinsettias and white tapers that seemed to breathe out pointed lights. There was a smell of incense. "Let's go in for a minute, Carl."

"But, sweetheart! We're not Catholics."

"Oh, the church don't know that. Come on!" They sat quiet in the back pew for a little while.

They ended the evening with refreshments at the drugstore. She had a banana split, and when the soda boy asked, "The works?" she said, yes, emphatically. Carl had a dish of coffee ice cream.

"I'll be sorry when I get old," she said.

"Who won't be?" he answered.

"I mean, old people don't enjoy things like banana splits."

"I must be old before my time," he said. "I couldn't eat a mixed-up concoction like that."

"You just don't know what you're missing," she said.

Preparing for bed, he emptied his money on the dresser. She got out her earnings and put them with Carl's. Between them, they had almost thirty dollars.

"With this and your five dollars a week paper money and my two dollars a week, why, we'll have enough money to get us through next month and February and March, too, because February's a short month."

"Don't count on it, sweetheart."

"Why, all we need is money for rent and my food."

"You'll need new shoes soon. And I'll need textbooks for the coming semester." The line on his forehead seemed to deepen.

"Don't worry, darling." She tried to smooth out the line.

"You don't count on emergencies."

"There won't be any. If there are, I've still got eight dollars in the bank and you can always loan your watch to the pawnshop for seven or eight dollars."

"But this being poor, the way we are . . ."

"But it's not the tenement kind of poor. That's being poor for *nothing*. But we're poor for *something*. You'll get a law degree out of it, and I'm getting so much out of it right now by being allowed to go to my class."

"But . . ."

"No buts about it. Being poor doesn't bother me too much. I'm used to it, I guess. Besides, I have a feeling that something wonderful will turn up before our money's gone. It's a very strong feeling. So stop worrying now."

As a matter of fact, something quite wonderful *did* turn up.

Chapter Eleven

Like most large institutions, the university had its satellite town. It was too small, actually, to be called a town and too large to be called a village. The university people referred to it as a country town. Lopin was separated from the university by a two-hundred-seat athletic field, which was a baseball field in the spring and a football field in the fall. It was called The Lopin High School Athletic Field. There was a three-room caretaker's cottage and a four-shower clubhouse at the university end of the field. Lopin was at the other end.

The Lopin people were dark-eyed and taciturn. Many had a drop or more of Indian blood. There were few college degrees among them, and they had a contempt for the neighboring university people, who, in turn, ignored the Lopinites, except to patronize them.

Yet, they could not exist without each other. The university needed Lopin and Lopin needed the university. The economy of Lopin depended on the university and the smooth running of the university depended on the people of Lopin. The Lopin men were the university's electricians, plumbers, repair men, grounds keepers, painters, window washers, garbage men, watchmen and janitors. The Lopin women were its seamstresses, laundrywomen, housecleaners, baby minders, and practical nurses. The sons and daughters were clerks, secretaries, typists, and telephone operators in the many offices of the university.

Lopin had been settled long before the university was dreamed of. A little Frenchman had started the settlement. He was one of a party of explorers paddling around the Great Lakes looking for land to claim. The Frenchman got tired of it all, threw in his paddle, swam to the nearest shore, and started walking until he came to a place he liked. A small tribe of apathetic nomad Indians had settled there for the time being. The little white man was enchanted with the land and with a plump Indian girl with swimming dark eyes. He made passionate speeches to the Indians in his native tongue. The Indians hadn't understood a word he said. But one word, Lopin, was spoken over and over in his speeches. He said, *"Un lopin de terre! Un lopin de terre!"* He was asking for a piece of land, but they thought he was saying, "My name is Lopin." So they called him Lopin.

In the fall the squaws struck the tepees and the little tribe strolled away. They were going south, where the living was easier.

The plump Indian girl remained behind, and she and the Frenchman married. He performed the ceremony himself. His Indian bride helped him clear off a bit of land and he built a cabin. His wife called him Lopin, believing that was his name, and in time he got to believing it too.

Seven Lopin sons were born. He baptized them himself and named them Jack, Alan, Paul, Bill, Albert, and Frank. He was out of names when the seventh and last son came along. He called him Lopin. His name was Lopin Lopin.

While the boys were growing up, flaxen-haired, blue-eyed Swedes settled there. At maturity the Lopin boys married the Swedish girls. While Lopin's forty-odd grandchildren were growing up, the railroads were coming through and Irish laborers settled there and their children married the Swedish-French-Indian grandchildren and so on down through the generations and the Indian blood thinned out in time. But there was still a drop or more in nearly everyone who lived in Lopin.

A letter came for Carl. It had a Lopin postmark. It was from one Albert Lopin, principal of the Lopin High School. Mr. Lopin wished to see Carl at Carl's earliest convenience.

"I *told* you something would turn up," gloated Annie. "I bet he's going to give you a job teaching the boys how to play football."

"*Coach* football," he said absently. "I wonder how he got my name?"

"The Dean gave it to him. Who else?"

"Well, I'll go see what he wants."

Albert Lopin was a bright, eager, gregarious little fellow, part French, Swedish and Indian. He told Carl all about his ancestor's settling the place and how, with the aid of his Indian wife, of course, he had founded the Lopin dynasty. Carl fidgeted and worried about missing his next class. Eventually the little fellow came to the point. The athletic coach, who also taught English and algebra and had occupied the caretaker's cottage, had resigned to accept a coaching job in Pittsburgh, where he had to teach but one subject. A new teacher-coach would take over in March. In the interval, someone had to live on the field to keep the fires up in the clubhouse so the pipes wouldn't freeze and to prevent university students and their girls from gaining entrance to the cottage with a skeleton key and using the place for what Mr. Lopin called illicit love.

Well, this started Mr. Lopin on the topic of what were our young people coming to. Now, in his day . . . It was a long monologue on comparative morals. Carl looked at his watch. Knowing he would miss his next class, he thought he might as well relax. He interrupted Mr. Lopin to ask permission to smoke.

Mr. Lopin gave it and accepted a cigarette himself. At last he got to the point.

"Well, sir, I went to Jim Darwent—the Dean's an old friend of mine—and asked him to recommend a steady young man, preferably married and . . . Oh, by the way, I took law for a year."

He was off on that: how he had searched his soul and found that he wasn't meant for the law and the law wasn't meant for him. And . . .

"Excuse me, sir. About the cottage?"

"Oh, yes!" Carl could live in the cottage rent free in return for keeping up the fire in the clubhouse. Electricity and gas for cooking would be supplied free. There was a telephone for his use—no long-distance calls, of course. And he'd have to supply his own fuel for the cottage.

Carl accepted, contingent, of course, upon Annie's approval. Mr. Lopin gave him the key, requested that Carl and Annie look it over immediately, and while Carl was there, would he put some coal on the fire? It would save him, Mr. Lopin, from making the trip. "And keep in mind," he said, over the good-by handshake, "it's only until March."

"It's beautiful!" said Annie breathlessly. "Just beautiful!"

Carl had his doubts. The living room had a table, two chairs, a potbellied stove, and a telephone on the wall. The tiny bedroom had a double bed, and there was hardly room for the pine chest of drawers with a dime store mirror above it. The kitchen also had two chairs and a table, a wood-and-coal stove, a two-burner gas plate, and the minimum of dishes, pots and pans. The lighting in all the rooms was simple: a cord from the center of the ceiling with a naked bulb at the end.

"Where's the bathroom?" she asked. They looked all over but couldn't find it. There was a door in the kitchen. Annie had thought it was a closet. In a way it was. It contained a toilet, a washbowl, and nothing more. "How do we take a bath, Carl?"

"We'll have to go to the clubhouse and use the showers."

"Imagine," she said, "getting dressed to go out to take a bath. That'll be fun!" Carl wondered about *that*. "We'll have to buy sheets and pillow slips and towels, and, say! Mama's blanket will sure come in handy."

"And Mom's underwear. Don't laugh, Annie. We'll each wear a suit as pajamas. That's a mighty cold bedroom."

She paid no attention to that. "You can give up your job at the cafeteria and I'll learn to cook."

"You mean to say that you had nerve enough to marry without knowing how to cook?"

"What's cooking? You boil stuff or fry it or stick it in the oven or else eat it raw. Like lettuce."

"But don't you know that many a homely woman got a man because she knew how to cook well? And don't you know the surest way to a man's heart is through his stomach?"

"But who wants to make a dirty trip like that?"

She was all for moving in the next day but Carl pointed out that their rent was paid up until Saturday and they had to give Mrs. Hansmon some notice.

"All right. That will give me two days to clean up this place. Carl, I have a wonderful idea! I'll buy some paint and a brush and paint the chairs and tables. What color do you think, Carl?"

"Sweetheart!" He put his hands on her shoulders. "Look at me and listen carefully. We will have to give up this house when the new coach comes. We will be here only two months. Do you understand?"

"Sure. But even so, I'd like to make it look nice while we *are* here."

"Don't, Annie! Please! If you make it too nice, it will break your heart to leave it."

"Maybe we won't have to. Maybe the coach won't want to live here. Maybe he'll have six children and it won't be big enough."

"Annie, Annie . . ." He sighed as though he were very weary, and the line between his eyes seemed to deepen.

"All right, darling. I won't paint the chairs then."

She left at six o'clock the next morning, carrying her alarm clock and as many of their possessions as she could. The cottage didn't look so wonderful in cold daylight. It was dusty and shabby, and the windows were so dirty you couldn't see out. And the house was ice-cold. She made a fire in the kitchen stove, using paper, wood and coal from the clubhouse, coal which she expected to return when they got their own supply. She got a good fire going and shut off the other rooms. In a short time the kitchen was nice and warm, but still very dirty. She got broom, mop, and little slivers of soap that smelled like carbolic, from the clubhouse, and gave the kitchen a thorough cleaning.

The cleaned kitchen windows, sans shades or curtains, seemed to bring the whole snow-covered athletic field into the kitchen. There was a long, two-storied factory at the end of the field. Later she'd learn that it was a lamp shade factory. The tops of many small houses could be seen at the north end. She surmised that was the town of Lopin. She decided to walk over and see what the town looked like.

It was a five-minute walk. A street sign read *Main Street*. So there is really such a street, she thought with a thrill. And all the while I thought Mr. Lewis made that name up.

She came upon a little grocery store and paused outside. She thought dramatically, This little store is about to become a part of my life. I will buy our food here. The people who run it will either get to be my friends or they'll just put up with me. But at least they'll do *something*.

It was a combined grocery and butcher store. A man with a wide mouth and narrow eyes and coarse black hair was behind the counter working on a portion of a cow on the meat block. He must be an Indian, surmised Annie. At least she thought he was descended from one. She anticipated the new heading on her list,

* 148

Indians I Know, and his name under it when she found out what it was.

There was also a woman with pretty blond hair and a heavy sullen face. She was swollen with a child soon to come and held another, who looked big enough to walk, astride her hip. This one had two handfuls of his mother's hair which he used as reins, and from time to time he dug his heels into her and hollered "Gidd-yop" as though his mother was a horse.

"Yes?" said the woman. The word was like a challenge. Annie asked for a pack of cigarettes. The woman put a pack on the counter. "Ten cents. Two for nineteen." Annie took two, delighted at saving a penny.

"You have a nice place here," said Annie.

The man and woman looked at each other as though Annie had said something startling. "You bastard!" said the woman suddenly.

Annie almost jumped out of her skin and her face got hot. But the epithet was meant for the baby, who had bitten his mother's ear. Annie had another heading for her list: *Strange Mothers.* Under it, she'd write: *Mother Who Calls Baby Bastard.*

"And just think," she told Carl that night, "we'll save half a cent on each pack. Only those people are going to be hard to know. But I'll work on it."

"You just hold still, Annie, and let them make the overtures. If they want to be friends they'll do it their own way. They think you're from the university, and they don't care much for university people. So just go easy about making friends in Lopin."

The next morning, burdened down with things to take to the cottage, she stopped at Henry's store and bought a half pound of coffee, a box of prunes, and a loaf of bread.

"What's the best way to make coffee, Henry? And tell me now, not tomorrow."

"You don't *know* how to make coffee?"

"Now listen, Henry: I didn't say *how,* I said *best.*"

"For two cups you put in three cups of water. When it boils up, you put in three tablespoons of coffee. Let it be until there is chocolate foam on top, then take it off the stove and throw in a little cold water."

"But I like coffee hot."

"The cold water settles it. The prunes, now, follow the directions on the box, and the bread you cut with a knife."

"Now stop it, Henry. I'm not *that* dumb."

"I'll miss you, Annie."

"Oh, I'll have to come on campus twice a week, and I'll drop in to see you. It's only a few blocks out of the way."

"It won't be the same like running in for jelly when I'm closing up."

"No, it won't," she said. "But that's life."

He agreed, and on that philosophical note they shook hands fervently as though they were parting forever.

"One more thing, Henry: why do you have to use three of everything to make only two cups?"

"I'll tell you next time I see you," he said.

Among the items she had brought to the cottage was a box of her summer dresses, which her mother had mailed to her. Two of the dresses, a red-checked gingham and a blue, were too worn to wear. Annie made kitchen curtains out of the skirts, the blue check for one window and the red for another. She was an indifferent seamstress. The skirt hems served as curtain hems. For the top, she folded down an inch of material and basted it. It took her ten minutes to make the curtains. Fortunately, there were curtain rods attached to the windows. She hung the curtains, and they looked fine except they needed pressing. That reminded her she had to get an iron for Carl's shirts.

She had a dozen dried prunes for lunch and a slice of bread warmed in the oven and two cups of coffee. She sat at the table for a long time trying to figure out where the third cup of water and spoon of coffee went to. How did three cups of water turn into two? She got it straight after a while. The wet grounds had absorbed a lot, and some of the water had gone off into steam. So many things to find out, she thought; so much to learn, I'll be dead and buried before I learn half of it.

She went into Lopin to get some eggs for her supper. The baby was riding his mother's other hip this time, and the man was grinding meat for hamburger. Annie asked for four eggs, and the woman put the eggs and a paper bag on the counter. Annie put a dime on the counter.

Putting the eggs in the bag, Annie asked: "Is there a dry goods store in town?" The man stopped grinding, and he and the woman exchanged looks before the woman said, "Two blocks." The man extended his arm and said, "That way."

Annie thanked them. On the way out she tweaked the baby's bare foot. Swift as lightning, the woman transferred the child to her other hip, away from Annie. "Excuse me," said Annie, "but he's so cute." At least they talked to me in a way, she thought as she left.

Aggie Lopin, spinster, owner of the dry goods store, was to become another item on Annie's list. Miss Aggie had an old woman's face and a perennially young-looking body. It was as if standing where the brook and river met, she went no further. The little hard knobs on her chest had never turned into breasts; her hips had never swelled to indent her waistline, and her legs were the thin straight legs of a child. There was an aura of expectancy about her, as if she'd burst into bloom any moment.

Unlike the grocery people, Miss Aggie was very loquacious. The principal of the high school was her nephew, and he had a degree from the university. This made Miss Aggie Town and Gown, as it were. Annie asked her about the grocery store people.

"Those Lopins! You see, my dear, he's part Indian and she's a white woman, and she's too proud to marry him. So they just live together and have children. What a woman won't do to save her pride!"

Annie told Miss Aggie they were going to move into the little cottage the next day. "Thank God!" Miss Aggie said fervently. "The things that go on in there when it's vacated! You see, my dear, I take a walk around there after I close the store. I look in the bedroom window just to check if everything's all right. And the things I've seen!" She raised her hands and rolled her eyes. "The sinful goings on, my dear. I wouldn't dare tell you." But she told her anyhow and advised Annie to get a new mattress. She had a nice one in the back room that she'd sell cheap.

But Annie didn't want a new mattress. She wanted two sheets, two pillow slips, two bath towels, and two dish towels. She almost had to beg Miss Aggie to sell her these items. The woman would rather talk than sell. Annie asked her where she could get a secondhand iron. Miss Aggie told her to try the secondhand store around the corner. Annie got away but not before Miss Aggie had told her all about the secondhand store man.

It wasn't a store, really. It was a junk shop. Annie found a rusty iron in the corner, and the man wanted fifteen cents for it. She paid for it. He took the iron and started rubbing the rust off with a piece of sandpaper.

"That's nice of you to do that for me," she said. Immediately he handed her the iron and the sandpaper. Me and my big mouth, she thought. Now I'll have to do it myself.

She saw a rocker. It was in good condition except that three legs matched and the fourth was a stick of new wood. It was a dollar and a half. She paid a quarter deposit, explaining that her husband would pay the balance when he came to pick it up. She wrote out a receipt for the quarter and asked him to sign it. He made a cross on the paper.

Following directions on the box, she put the prunes in a pot, put a cup of water over them and placed the covered pot on the back of the stove to cook slowly all afternoon. She went to make up the bed with the new sheets and slips. First she checked the one window in the bedroom. Yes, the sill was low enough that even a small woman like Miss Aggie could look in. I've got to do something about that, she decided, so that when the moon is bright Miss Aggie can't look in and watch us in the act of sin. She hung the two bath towels on the curtain rods.

She looked at the mattress which, according to Miss Aggie, had been so much sinned upon. The mattress looked innocent enough to Annie, but she decided to turn it over to get rid of the idea of other couples having used it.

It was a terrific job. She pulled and pushed and used her head as a ramrod and broke two fingernails before she got it turned. She threw herself on the bed in exhaustion. She was flushed and her heart was beating rapidly. She soon relaxed, though, and was about drifting off to sleep when the phone rang, flooding the cottage with its raucous demand for attention. She got up to answer it. "Who is it?" she asked.

"Me. I'm calling between classes. How are you doing?"

"Carl! They're not married!"

"Who's not married?"

"The grocery people."

"Annie, that's none of our business."

"But they already have a baby and another one on the way and the children will grow up to be bastards."

"Stop worrying. They're married."

"But Miss Aggie said . . ."

"Who? Oh, never mind who said it. They are married."

"No, they're not because she's proud."

"Listen, Annie, if they live together for a certain number of years and have children, they are married by common law."

"Honest, Carl?"

"Honest. So stop worrying."

"But—"

"Listen, Annie, I called to tell you I'll be home a little late tonight."

"Our last night in our room?"

"Well, after the cafeteria I have to go out there to bank the clubhouse fire."

"I'll do it, Carl. I'll be here until dark anyhow." She wanted to talk more, but he had to run to make his class.

She made the bed, using the Christmas blanket as a bedspread. It gave the chilly room a warm look. She pressed the curtains and rehung them. She prepared her supper. She put two eggs into boiling water, took one out after three minutes and the other out after five. The three-minute one was a little runny; the five-minute one, a little on the hard side. Four minutes would be just right, she concluded. I'll cook them for four minutes forever now. Who said cooking was hard?

She had the boiled eggs, stewed prunes, the three-for-two coffee, and a slice of bread for supper. She was proud of her supper. It will make a fine breakfast too, she decided. She put coal in the clubhouse furnace and went home.

Since she had to work in the dime store the next day and would go directly to their new home from there, she said her good-bys to Mrs. Hansmon. It was a tearful farewell. She embraced her and wept when the landlady said she'd miss having Annie to talk to. Annie promised faithfully to visit her, and the landlady said they could have their room back any time on one day's notice.

And for the last time Annie had to run around to the grocery store before it closed. "A jar of raspberry jam, Henry, for old time's sake." He wouldn't let her pay for it, for old time's sake. They parted again, as if forever, with a warm handshake.

She took off her locket and asked Carl to put it on again as he had done on their wedding night, and she asked to be rocked for the last time in their room. He suggested she take a bath first. Her hands were grimy with coal dust. She'd put the coals on the fire one by one, she explained. And why hadn't she picked up each one with a piece of paper? Because she hadn't thought of it, she said. A person couldn't be born knowing *everything*, could they?

She was so long in the bathroom that Carl started to worry. She had looked so tired, supposing she had fallen asleep in the tub full of water? Supposing . . . He rushed down the hall to the bathroom. He pounded on the locked door and begged her to open it. She opened it suddenly and he all but fell into the room. The water was out of the tub, but there was a black ring around it. She was getting it off with toilet tissue because she didn't want to ruin the landlady's towel. He helped her. They used up most of the roll.

He rocked her and patted her and she told him in detail of the happenings of the day. He listened. The rise and fall of her low-pitched voice almost lulled him to sleep.

"And, Carl, today I learned to cook!" she said triumphantly.

"Thas good," he said drowsily.

It took Carl some time to get used to one kitchen window curtained in blue checked gingham and the other in red. But Annie was proud of the curtains and bet that she was the only one in the world who had curtains like that and Carl said he was sure of it. They lived in the kitchen to save fuel, closing off the other unheated rooms. The bedroom was always ice-cold, and they tried wearing Carl's Christmas underwear in bed but that didn't work out. The woolen material made Annie itch, and her constant scratching kept him awake and he had to abandon his because the buttons on the back flap dug into his back.

They showered together in adjoining stalls in the clubhouse, and Annie was delighted with the shower because there was no bathtub ring to clean up. After a thorough rubdown, they dressed and raced each other back to the cottage in the snow, so they wouldn't catch cold.

Annie learned to cook simple, uncomplicated meals. Usually she put everything in the oven early in the afternoon and let the food cook until suppertime. She was adamant about one thing, however. She refused to fry anything. She wouldn't even have lard in the house because the smell of grease reminded her of Mr. Felix and his turtle soup.

Things were easier for Carl. He had given up his cafeteria job because they could get along all right with his five dollars a week paper money and Annie's two dollars from the dime store. He was able to do most of his studying in the hours the cafeteria job had taken. Most days he was home at four o'clock—at the latest five. He thumbtacked a notice on the bulletin board that he was available for tutoring at fifty cents an hour. With mid-year exams coming up, there were quite a few frat men who could use a little tutoring, and Carl made a couple of extra dollars.

Everything was just fine except that Annie's monthly period was one week overdue.

Chapter Twelve

In the excitement of moving and fixing up the cottage and meeting new people, Annie had had little time to be concerned. A day or two late? It had happened before, hadn't it? Ah! But she hadn't been married then! This was different. When she was two weeks overdue, she began to worry. Her first impulse was to tell Carl, but his mid-year exams were coming up and the news might throw him off his studies. And maybe it was all a mistake and things would adjust themselves the next month and she would have upset Carl for nothing at all.

Two weeks late didn't necessarily mean she was pregnant. It could be a mistake; it *had* to be a mistake. Things were going so well. They had their own little home, they had their meals together, more time together; they could get along fine on their joint earnings of seven dollars a week, and she was about to audit the class in playwriting. Everything was working out so wonderfully, if only . . .

Please, God, she prayed, don't let it happen. Not right now. Give us a year of grace. Just one year. And I'll never ask You for another thing as long as I live. And I promise to give up my writing forever if only You . . .

Mr. Haise treated Annie like a registered student working for a degree. It was a small, rather informal class. Teacher and students sat together in the front of the room and talked drama. They talked about plays and playwriting and theme and characterization, crisis and climax, titles and curtain lines, and about dialogue—especially dialogue. They were like friends spending a social hour together, and Annie enjoyed it.

She took to the medium heart, soul, and mind. Dialogue came easy to her. In the play form her short, often unfinished sentences were an asset rather than a drawback. She had an instinct for characterization and a sure feeling about building up to a crisis and making it flow easily into a climax.

A whole new world of reading opened to her; she read all the plays she could get hold of. Her favorites were *The Lower Depths* and *Riders to the Sea*. She all but memorized the latter play. She couldn't keep the book out forever, so she copied the play word for word and clipped it into her loose-leaf book. Yes, she had promised her God that she wouldn't write if . . . But He won't mind, she thought, if I copy someone else's play.

Near the middle of February she knew she was pregnant. Her first instinct was to keep it secret from Carl, give him less months of worry. Her condition would not be obvious until summer, and he would, by then, have completed his third year. But she had to see a doctor—not for her sake but for the sake of the unborn baby. She'd just *have* to tell him. Maybe it wouldn't be too bad. She could continue working at the dime store once a week until summer vacation; Carl would have finished his next to last year. He could get a steady job in the summer.

But what about his last year? The baby would come in the autumn. Carl couldn't possibly get through his last critical year with the burden of a wife and child to support. Well, they'd have the summer together and when the last year started she'd go home to have her baby.

But how could she go home? There was Dan. She winced inwardly at the hearty off-color remarks he'd be sure to make about her pregnancy. Even if she could put up with him, would her mother take her in? She could hear her mother saying, "You made your bed, now lay in it." Or: "I told you and told you. But no! You wouldn't listen. Go back to your husband. It's his place to take care of you and support you and the baby. Not mine."

Annie heard herself begging: "If you let me stay, Mama, I won't get in the way. I won't fight with Dan. I'll mind the boys so you and Dan can go out nights. I'll do all the housework and the cooking. I know how, now. And, Mama, I love you. And you got to love me."

The other alternative was that Carl drop out of school for a year. But if he did, how could he go back? All the money he could earn that year would be used up for living expenses, doctor bills, hospital bills, and all the things a baby needed. There'd be no money left over to finance the last year in school.

And even if he could get back after a year away—even if he *could!* Would he be able to take up where he had left off? Carl was not a variable person. He had made—was still making—a hard push to be a lawyer. Away from school he'd make a hard push to be a breadwinner. The great push of his life would be diverted from law to the adequate support of his wife and child.

No! He'd have to finish school and she'd have to go back home. That was the only way.

She'd have to tell him right away. How was the best way to tell him? What could she say to lighten the news? It was Annie's theory that there were compensations to everything. The way she thought of it was: Every cloud has a silver lining. And this had been brought home to her very vividly in *The Lower Depths* and *Riders to the Sea*. In *Lower Depths*, when the people got as low down as they could possibly get, there was the compensation that they couldn't get any lower. In *Riders to the Sea*:

> They're all gone now, and there isn't
> anything more the sea can do to me.

159   *

Yes, Maurya wouldn't have to cry and pray any more when the storms came over the seas. She had no more sons for the sea to take. That was her compensation.

But what compensation was there for Carl? For her? There was the big wonderful compensation for both—that a human being would be created out of their love, a living soul to love and protect; a new life to guide.

And, dreamed Annie, I'll read to her every day until she can read for herself because I want her to grow up to be a reading girl. And colors. I'll get a water color set and put the brush in her little hand and guide it and let her make a mark on the paper and I'll tell her, "This is blue, darling, like the sky. And this is red, like a rose is red."

But what about small, individual compensations? As for her, she didn't have to worry any more as to whether she was or wasn't pregnant. Now she *knew!* And that was a sort of relief. And she could write again! Her promise to God no longer held.

Mr. Haise was always urging her to write a play. I'll write a one-act play and call it *The Marriage.* That judge with his big stomach will make a fine character and the businesslike clerk. And I'll use Miss Aggie for Miss Vi—the way Miss Aggie talks a lot and all. And I'll direct that the stage be in two parts. One part will have only a counter to show it is the judge's office. The play will start there. Then I'll direct that the lights go down there and come up on the other side where there is a kitchen table and chairs and two little boys are eating oatmeal, and there's the girl and her mother and the stepfather, and by the way they talk you will find out why the girl left home at eighteen. That will give the girl compassion and . . .

Annie had two compensations now. But it was sure hard to find a compensation for Carl. She thought of the contraceptives. She knew Carl hated to use them. Now he wouldn't have to. That could be a small compensation. And the money they'd save, not having to buy . . .

Suddenly she laughed aloud. It was a hysterical laugh. Imagine, she thought, thinking about a thing like that; about saving a few pennies at a time like this!

She made up her mind to tell Carl that night. His exams were over and tomorrow was Saturday and he'd have no classes. First she would prepare a nice supper and then she'd tell him.

She bought two pork chops and two apples for a pie at the grocery store. She bought a fresh tomato. It was a luxury at ten cents, but how pleased Carl would be! As usual, the woman, the child on her hip, said nothing.

On an impulse, Annie said, "Would you let me hold him for a minute? I haven't held a baby since I was a little girl. I'd like to know again how it feels."

To her surprise, the woman said, "You can hold him and keep him." But she gave the baby an "umph" kiss before she turned him over. "His name is Lester. But we call him Less."

The child tried his best to get into the saddle, but Annie didn't have enough hip. She was still a slender twenty-two around the waist. The baby twined his legs about it and grabbed her tight around the neck like a monkey in a tree. He stared into her ear and then tried to get his nose into it. Failing, he gave her ear a thorough licking with his tongue. Annie laughed, the woman smiled, and the man behind the meat counter looked up for a second.

"Tell me, Mrs. Lopin," said Annie. "How does a girl, a woman, who's never had a baby before, know for sure she's going to have a baby?"

The woman came directly to the point. "Do you throw up mornings?"

"No."

"Ah, you'll have a hard birth, then." As if she had said too much and was angry at herself, the woman jerked the baby out of Annie's arms. But she did walk to the door with Annie. "Listen, missus . . ." She paused.

"Won't you call me Annie? Please?"

"Well, listen, Annie. You want to know anything, ask me."

"Oh, thank you. I've been dying to talk to someone about it. I haven't even told my husband. You're the first one I've told."

The woman thought that over before she said, "My name is Goldie—after my hair, you know." She patted her pretty blond hair.

Annie hugged her packages all the way home. We're friends! she thought. Now I have a friend. That is three silver linings I got out of that dark cloud.

Carl came home in great high spirits. "Guess what, sweetheart! Guess what!"

"What, Carl?"

"I made straight A's on all my exams!" He lifted her off her feet and swung her around. He put her down and held her at arm's length. "And guess what else."

"Tell me."

"I made the Dean's List!"

"Is that something important?"

"It's a great honor. The Dean called me in to his office and shook my hand and called me Carl. You know, last year, before you were here, I had all the time in the world to study and didn't have to worry too much about money, and I never could make the Dean's List? The Dean said you were an influence—a good influence, he said."

It's going to be awful hard to tell him, thought Annie. Awful hard!

She squeezed the baked potatoes until they gave way and opened enough to accept a lump of butter. She sprinkled paprika over them like, she told Carl, they do in swanky restaurants. The pork chops were baked just right and the chilled tomato slices! Carl became quite lyrical about them. And the cinnamon-spiced apple pie! How did Annie ever guess that was the way he liked apple pie? And was there some more of that good coffee? There was. And could he have another piece of that pie? Or was she saving it for tomorrow? She wasn't.

Replete with food, he leaned back in his chair and sighed happily. "If life could always be like this; like this day—this hour. I wouldn't ask for more. I'd rather have this than be governor."

I can't tell him tonight, she thought in anguish. No! Not tonight. She shook her head sadly.

He put his hand on hers. "What, sweetheart? What's troubling you? Tell me."

"Nothing. I was just thinking . . . Carl, while I'm working tomorrow, why don't you go ice skating?"

"I wouldn't feel right enjoying myself while you're working."

"You owe yourself something getting those high marks and getting on that list. Take advantage."

"Tell you what. I'll skate for an hour or so and meet you at the dime store when you're through and we'll eat supper out so you won't have to cook after being on your feet all day."

"We'll eat at the cafeteria. I'd like to see Mrs. Ridinski again."

"Good! Oh, I meant to tell you, she lives in Lopin. Maybe you could go and see her sometime on her day off."

"I'd like to. Where does she live?"

"We'll ask her when we see her." Helping her with the dishes, he said, "You know I'll miss all this when we have to go back to Mrs. Hansmon's a couple of weeks from now?"

That's when I'll tell him, she decided. We'll both be upset anyhow on account of moving to start with. Might as well add on the news of the baby then.

She waited out the two weeks until they'd be told that they'd have to vacate the cottage. In the meantime she wrote her one-act play about the wedding. It was the first play turned in that semester, and when Mr. Haise read it aloud in class, it sounded pretty good to Annie. She had a new kind of thrill when the class

163 *

laughed at something funny that Miss Chip, alias Miss Aggie, said. Mr. Haise told the class that the standard set by this first submitted play was high, and he hoped the playwright could sustain it.

Annie ran all the way home to meet this challenge by writing another play. The setting was a slum street in Brooklyn; the characters, a couple of derelicts, names unknown, who slept in various tenement cellars—a different one each night so they wouldn't be caught—and begged pennies on the street, pretending they were blind.

This play was not well received. It was severely criticized and, what was worse, laughed at. The title, *Callous Flesh,* got a big laugh when a student said it sounded like a play about a bunion. The curtain line got a bigger laugh. One of the derelicts had been found dead in a cellar and had been brought up and laid out on the sidewalk. A man in the crowd surrounding the corpse said, "Well, we all got to go someday." *Curtain.*

Annie was bitterly humiliated, and ashamed too. Mr. Haise had a hard time getting the class in order. "I am going to be very severe," he said, "because I know the writer is capable of better work." Capable of better work! Annie's humiliation lightened a bit. "The play is derivative," he said. "It is an inept imitation of *The Lower Depths.*" Annie wished the floor would open up so that she could fall through and disappear. "It is a combination of sordidness and sentimentality," he continued. "The two do not mix well. However," and here Annie's heart lifted a little, "the dialogue is authentic."

Annie held on to that little crumb of praise: The dialogue is authentic. Self-criticism replaced shame. She realized she'd been too self-confident—had assumed she knew all there was to know about playwriting. But I've still got lots to learn, she concluded. And I *will* learn. By the end of the semester . . .

But would she be able to finish the semester? When her pregnancy became obvious she'd have to drop out. A pregnant woman just wouldn't fit in a class of raucous young men and curious girls. How much time did she have to learn how to write a one-act play?

"Goldie, when will I show?" she asked the grocery woman.

"Five months." Annie counted. That would make it the month of May. I won't be able to finish, she thought. "But," added Goldie, "you're so skinny it won't show till six months."

June! She might make it at that. "Honest, Goldie?"

"You heard me say it."

Annie patted the baby's backside. "Your mother made me very happy," she told him.

Annie went to class, the library, stopped in to see Mrs. Hansmon once in a while and did not neglect Henry. Once or twice she dropped in at the florist shop for five minutes to check on the progress of *The Rape of the Forest*.

To Carl she seemed quieter. She didn't talk to him so much—didn't ask him so many questions. It was as if he were losing her somehow. His old fear. I shouldn't encourage her so much in this playwriting business, he thought. That's one way of losing a wife. Then he was ashamed of the thought.

February ended with a premature warm spell. The snow melted, there was more sun. One afternoon three high school boys in baseball uniforms came and asked her if she knew where the coach was.

That night she told Carl that the new coach must have arrived. Carl said it was sure going to be a hell of a job carrying all those books back to Mrs. Hansmon's. Annie wondered whether the junk man would buy back the rocker.

"I wonder why we haven't heard from that principal," she said.

"I'll see him tomorrow. I've got to know because I have to see about getting back my cafeteria job."

"Will you be sorry to leave here, Carl?"

"You know I will. But I was prepared for it. Being prepared for something takes some of the curse off it."

There was some truth in that, she thought. Maybe she ought to try to prepare him for the baby. "Carl, suppose someday—just suppose, mind you—I told you I was going to have a baby, what would be the first thing you'd say? The very first thing?"

"I'd say, damn those cut-rate drugstores." He grinned.

I wonder, she thought.

It turned cold again in late afternoon. She was starting to prepare supper when the phone rang. From the kitchen she heard Carl say, "How are you, Mr. Lopin? I was planning on seeing you tomorrow about the new coach."

Annie went into the chilly living room to stand next to Carl. She heard the muffled rise and fall of the principal's voice but couldn't make out what he was saying.

After a long time of listening, Carl said, "Why, that's fine, Mr. Lopin. Just fine!" More listening before Carl said, "I'd be glad to, Mr. Lopin, and we sure appreciate it." Some more of Mr. Lopin's muffled voice, then Carl's "Thanks a lot. Good-by, Mr. Lopin." He hung up the receiver and turned to Annie, all smiles.

"What do you know, sweetheart! We don't have to move after all. The new coach has a wife and three kids and the cottage is too small for him. So Mr. Lopin said we could stay as long as we want! Of course I'll have to do a little work around the place—keep the field in order, clean up the clubhouse, and take tickets when there's a game, and . . ."

Now! thought Annie. Now! This is the time to tell him. Get it over with.

"Carl, I'm going to have a baby."

He misunderstood. "Sure, I know you want a baby. But let's not start one right away. We have time. Wait until I'm in practice."

She started to tremble. It was going to be harder than she had thought.

"Look at you shivering! Why do you wear thin summer dresses in this cold house? What's the matter with your woolen skirt and sweater?"

"I have to save them for my class."

He took her into the kitchen where it was warm and rubbed her cold hands, trying to stop what he thought was her shivering.

"Carl, listen to me. Please listen. I am pregnant." She raised her voice. "Pregnant! Do you understand?"

He dropped her hands and moved back a step. "What did you say?" he asked, bewildered.

"*I am going to have a baby!*"

He said what many another husband had said: "*Are you sure?*"

"I am two months on the way."

"I see," he said quietly. "Well . . . I'll be right back, sweetheart. I have to check the furnace."

The locker-room furnace did not need checking, but Carl wanted to be alone a few minutes to think things out. He sat on one of the narrow benches and did some very hard thinking.

How could it have happened? I took care. It's going to be tough. Very tough. I don't think she knows how tough. Or does she? The poor little thing—keeping it all to herself! Well, I've got to take hold now. I mustn't let her worry.

He hurried back to the cottage.

"Why didn't you tell me, sweetheart? I had a right to know. You shouldn't protect me so much. I'm a man, not a kid any longer. I'm your husband, not your son."

"I was afraid you'd worry."

"I worry anyhow. Let me have something important to worry about. You feel all right?" he asked suddenly.

"I feel fine."

"And you want the baby?"

"So much! I can hardly wait!"

"That's good, sweetheart. Now I'll figure out what—"

"I have it all worked out, Carl," she interrupted. "We'll be

167   *

together until September. Then I'll go home and have my baby and you can get through your last year in school without worrying and live in the dorm again. We'll be apart only a year and I'll write to you every day and . . ."

Suddenly she broke down and wept. She put her arms around him. "But I don't want to go back," she sobbed. "I want to stay with you . . . I want to stay with you." She couldn't control her sobs. He pretended anger as an antidote.

"Cry-sake, Annie, what do you mean by making foolish plans without asking me? You'll do this—you'll do that! What are you trying to do? Take my manhood away from me? At least give me a chance to handle things." Her sobbing subsided. "Come sit on my lap, sweetheart."

He rocked her and patted her until she calmed down and relaxed with a shuddering sigh. "Listen, sweetheart, you are *not* going back to your mother. You are my wife and you belong to me. And don't you tell me to go live in a dorm. I want to live with you. Ah, Annie, I couldn't get along without you—without talking to you—without sleeping with you . . . without . . ."

"But how can we . . ."

"Be quiet. I'll take care of everything from now on."

She was quiet awhile before she said, "But, Carl, you didn't say anything about my baby."

"I can't quite take it in yet. I've only known for ten minutes about it. You've known for two months. You kept it all to yourself. Yes, you shut me out. And you're still doing that. You act as though it's all yours: *My* baby, you keep saying. *I'm* going to have a baby. Never *our* baby or *we're* going to have a baby. Remember it will be mine as much as yours."

"I don't mean I own it by myself, Carl, it's just my way of talking." Her voice seemed tired.

"You feel all right, Annie?" he asked anxiously.

"I feel wonderful."

"So I'm going to be a father! How about that! It's just begin-

* 168

ning to get through to me. The more I think of it the better I like it. The idea of having a son of my own . . ."

"*Our* own. If it's a girl, I hope she looks like you because you're prettier than I am."

"You know, Annie, I feel like celebrating."

"Too bad we're fresh out of champagne. But I tell you what: Go get a bottle of near-beer while I fix supper. And get one for me, too. The Germans say beer is good for a baby."

"Nothing to that. Just propaganda to sell surplus beer."

"Get me a Coke, then."

Preparing to leave, he said, "You'll be all right while I'm gone?"

"Why, sure."

"From now on I want you to take special care of yourself. Don't overdo. Let the housework go."

"Carl? Will you tell me not to move heavy furniture?"

"Especially heavy furniture. Don't move any heavy furniture."

"Thank you, Carl." Her eyes filled with tears. "I wanted somebody to say that to me so *bad*."

Chapter Thirteen

"Yes, I grant you that," said the Dean. "We do have some married students. But they are mature men whose wives have already completed their own education and have well-paying work which enables them to support a husband. Or they are financed by their parents. The question as to whether they are eligible for financial aid does not come up."

"But, sir," said Carl, "there is a definite trend toward early student marriages. Man and wife go to college together, or marry while still in school."

"Yes. And, unfortunately, most of them have to drop out of school because of financial difficulties."

"But, sir, nowhere in *The General Catalogue* does it specify that a married student may *not* apply for a loan." Carl had the catalogue with him. He read from it: *"Financial aid for tuition and necessary textbooks is available to almost every student who can show superior academic achievement and definite financial need."* Carl closed the book. "I believe I qualify, sir."

"You overlooked the word 'almost,' Carl. *Available to almost every student* . . . That one word 'almost' means we may discriminate if we see fit."

"If you'll pardon me, sir, 'almost' is an ambiguous word."

"True. I'll call it to the attention of the editors."

"I believe that I qualify academically."

"No question about it."

"I also qualify under *definite financial need.*" Carl swallowed hard. "My wife is going to have a child."

The Dean's eyebrows went up in astonishment. "Annie's going to have a baby?" he asked increduously.

"In September, sir."

"But she's a mere child herself."

"She'll be nineteen this fall."

"Has she seen a doctor?"

"Not yet, sir."

"That should be attended to immediately. I suggest Dr. Marson. He's the best gynecologist in the state. He's on the School of Medicine faculty but retains a small private practice." The Dean picked up his pencil and asked Carl what time he was free the next day. Carl's last class was at three. "Good! I'll arrange an appointment for three-thirty." He wrote the time on a pad, then carefully arranged the pencil on top of the pad. He was silent for a long time. Carl broke the silence.

"I shall not be able to register for my last year, sir, without a tuition and textbook loan."

"Tell me, do you intend to practice in this state?"

"Yes, sir."

"You were married in the state. I take it your child will be born in the state."

"Of course. And I'll cast my first vote in this state. I'll be twenty-one the latter part of next month."

"Good! I believe you qualify as a state resident. This is a state university. I like to believe we take care of our own. Tuition fees are lower for state residents and I am certain a loan can be arranged. Three per cent interest and ten years to pay."

Carl's sudden relief made him almost incoherent in thanking

the Dean. He thanked him for putting him on his list, for the cottage, the doctor, the loan—for Annie's class. The Dean frowned and raised his hand in a "stop" signal.

"I'm told," he said, "that Annie is a great asset to the class in playwriting. I hope she will be able to finish the semester."

"She plans to," said Carl.

"I am pleased to know that. Too bad she cannot forge ahead. She seems to have so many potentialities for . . ." He left the sentence unfinished. "Good luck, Carl," he said abruptly. He picked up the telephone. Carl was dismissed.

Carl chain-smoked in the waiting room while Dr. Marson gave Annie the preliminary examination; lungs, heart, blood pressure, reflexes, and so on. When he had finished, the nurse took Annie into a cool cubicle, had her undress and helped her onto the table. She draped a sheet over Annie's nakedness, told her to relax and left, saying the doctor would see her in a few minutes.

Annie had never had a complete physical examination. In fact, she had never been to a doctor except for something trivial—a cinder in her eye, a wart to be removed, a vaccination and other minor things. She had never been examined while naked. She was embarrassed and ill at ease.

The doctor came in, followed by the nurse. "Now, Mrs. Brown," he said cheerfully, "let's see you slide down to the bottom of the table with your knees raised. That's it! All the way now. That's good. Now put your feet in the stirrups." Annie didn't know *where* the stirrups were or *what* they were, for that matter. The nurse guided her feet into the stirrups. Suddenly the doctor threw back the sheet and spread her legs wide apart.

"No!" Annie cried out. "No! Don't!" She put her legs together and slid back up the table, clutching the sheet about her.

"Now, Mrs. Brown, now . . ." said the doctor soothingly.

"Maybe she'll be more relaxed with her husband here," said the nurse. "I'll get him."

* 172

"Don't get him. Please!" said Annie. She did not want Carl to see her in that ugly position. "I will do what the doctor says." She assumed the position.

"That's a good girl," said the doctor.

The nurse handed him an instrument. Annie flinched at the first impact of the cold instrument on her inner flesh.

"I know it's a position of great indignity," said the doctor, "but it's necessary."

Indignity. It was a new word to Annie. It sounds exactly like what it means, thought Annie.

Soon it was over and the doctor left. The nurse helped her off the table. "There, that wasn't too bad, now, was it?" said the nurse.

"No," lied Annie.

"Doctor wants to see you and your husband in his office when you've finished dressing."

Carl was waiting for her in the corridor. Mutely she took his hand and held it tight as they went into the office.

"Your wife is in her third month of pregnancy," said the doctor cheerfully. "She's in a good physical condition—nothing to worry about there." Annie was alerted at the word "there." "Of course, she has a very narrow pelvis." Annie felt a quiver of fear. "But I don't think that will give us too much trouble."

He gave instructions: Check with the dentist . . . lots of milk . . . for calcium that the baby takes away from a mother. Do everything she was accustomed to doing, but at the first sign of exhaustion lie down and rest. Diet? As usual. But avoid fattening foods.

"We want a small baby," he said.

Again Annie felt that quiver of fear.

Carl asked his fee.

"My fee, Mr. Brown? Fifty dollars." The doctor saw Annie and Carl exchange looks. "But don't worry about it. Pay as we go along. Or take a year. I can wait."

"How much for the hospital?" asked Carl.

"Private hospital, ten dollars a day." Annie made a gasping sound. "However, I prefer my patients to go to the University Hospital."

"That ten dollars a day, too?" asked Annie.

"No charge, except for anesthetics, special diets . . ." Carl and Annie beamed at each other. "Provided," he continued, "*provided* you permit two of my graduate students—interns—to observe the birth process from beginning to end. Perhaps to assist . . ."

"I don't want any student to experiment on my wife," said Carl quickly.

"No, no! I'll deliver the baby. The boys may help out in routine things . . . checking during preliminary labor, pulse . . . so on."

"Annie?" said Carl, indicating that the decision was hers to make.

Ten dollars a day, she figured. Ten days a hundred dollars. Where would we get the money? she thought.

"I guess I wouldn't mind, Carl," she said.

"Now that's sensible," said the doctor.

"You're sure, Annie?" asked Carl.

"I'm sure. I trust Dr. Marson because the Dean recommended him."

The doctor put his hand over Annie's. "Ah, thank you, Mrs. Brown."

"I'd feel more at home, though, doctor, if you'd call me Annie."

"Annie it is then," he said. "I'll take good care of you, Annie."

Chapter Fourteen

Spring in the Middle West, wrote Annie, does not come all of a sudden as if it had been waiting all the time around the corner. No. It takes a long time to get ready. First, it has to clean up after Winter.

"You got any snow left, old man," Spring says to Winter, "you get rid of it now because it won't keep until next year. And make it snappy! I want to move in."

Then it snows like it never snowed before. Old-timers sit around the stove and say it's Winter's last howl. Winter is pretty tired by then—getting rid of all that snow—and he limps up north to join other Winters waiting there.

Then Spring hollers: "Hey, Sun! Let's go!"

Sun leans down and breathes hard on Snow and makes it change into water. First, Water fills people's basement, then the street gutters. Then it fills up the river.

"Take it easy, Spring, will you?" says River. "I'm getting high on water. I can take just so much and no more."

The Old-timers say, "Worst flood in years! It's in all the papers."

Spring says, "Okay, Sun. That's it! Get lost for a few days."

Spring calls in the Four Winds. They all blow in at once. "Hey, fellers, clean up that mess down there, will you? And make it quick. I'm running late this year."

And Winds blow every which way. They get rid of the water all right, but they get excited and knock off chimneys and pull up trees and lift up houses and set them down on River. Old-timers say, "I'll take a blizzard any day. They can keep their tornadoes."

Spring says, "Hold it, Winds. Don't overdo it. You can beat it now. But you, South Wind, stick around. I need you."

"Anything I can do for you, Spring, just ask," says South Wind.

"Okay! Blow me in, boy. Blow me in gently and blow around me when I'm in."

And then it is Spring.

"Spring at last," said Annie, tugging at a stuck window frame.

"Here! Let me do that," said Carl. "You know what the doctor said."

"I know. Don't strain, he said. Open all the windows, Carl, that little breeze smells so sweet. I bet it comes from the south."

Now after school hours the field overflowed with high school boys in uniform with *Lopin H.S.* stenciled on the back of each jersey. Now the clubhouse where Annie and Carl took their showers smelled of sweat shirts and jock straps and the shower drains had forbidden cigarette butts pushed down into the holes.

On the field the coach was everywhere at once; crouching next to the shortstop, behind the pitcher, and running along with the batter to make base after a hit, and in addition, umpiring all the time.

The coach had the privilege of using the cottage phone. He was very polite about it. He always said, "I hate to trouble you,

* 176

Mrs. Brown," and she always said, "That's all right, Mr. Stevens."
Usually, he called his wife to ask if she wanted him to pick up
something from the store on his way home. Annie thought it was
nice of him to be so thoughtful.

When Carl got home in the afternoon, he first asked Annie
was she all right. Then he asked could he do anything for her.
If there was nothing for him to do, he went out on the field and
spent an hour with the coach. Sometimes Mr. Stevens stopped
running around and stood awhile with Carl. Often Annie
watched from the window as they talked together. Each seemed
interested in what the other had to say. She wondered what they
talked about aside from baseball. She felt there was a side to Carl
that she knew nothing about: a man's side.

He had a world of his own, apart from her. She knew he had
played baseball in high school; had won a trophy in a hundred-
yard dash; had broken a Y.M.C.A. swimming record. She had
watched him play tennis; had stood at the edge of a frozen pond
with other onlookers watching him do the perfect figure skating
that had once won him a medal.

She wondered about the people he knew outside of his life
with her. Had he had close friends in the dormitory? Did he still
see them from time to time? And his classmates: Was he part
of a group that gathered for a few minutes on the steps after a
class to talk about corporate law or torts? Did he ever adjust his
stride to that of one of his professors as they walked across the
campus, and did Carl converse with him in a different kind of
way than the way he conversed with her, Annie?

It got Annie to wondering why she had no friends of her own
age except Arlene. But that was a routine office friendship, inevitable, because their desks were side by side. Yes, thought
Annie, all my friends are older than me. Why is that? Because I
had to say I was older, had to act older to get jobs? The girls in
the playwriting class: now, they are very nice to me, but not
what you would call friendly. I guess I don't fit in with them—

especially now, with a baby on the way. I am the same age the girls are, but I'm so much older somehow.

It made her a little sad. She felt that somewhere along the way she had lost something out of her life.

She had moods like this as her pregnancy advanced. They didn't bother her too much; she considered the moods as part of pregnancy. Actually, she had never felt better.

They had written their respective mothers about the baby. Annie's mother wrote it was no news to her—she had been sure Annie was pregnant before Annie had left home. And Annie mustn't feel ashamed. At least she's married, and the child will have a father. And twenty years from now, who will know or care, she wrote, that the baby had come ahead of time?

Carl's mother made no mention of the coming baby. She assumed Carl would come home and spend the summer with his family as usual. She would pay his fare both ways. And surely Annie's mother wanted her daughter home and would pay *her* fare?

Annie's first reaction was that there was something wistful about his mother writing as though things hadn't changed with Carl's marriage; that her boy would come home as usual for the summer. But soon enough that first reaction was replaced by anger. So! His mother still felt she owned him, didn't she! Could tell him what to do! Could tell Annie what to do! Annie's mother what to do! And wouldn't that be dandy! Like old times—she at her mother's home and he at his mother's home. Maybe they could get together, she and Carl, some Saturday evening?

Carl didn't argue with her. In a way, he saw her side—saw his mother's side. In law, one had to see both sides; not necessarily to approve of the other side but to understand it. So he let Annie carry on about the letter until she got it out of her system.

Annie got a letter from Arlene. The girl had finally received the long-waited-for "ring." Only it was a diamond ring and they'd be married in the fall.

"It's a load off my mind," Annie told Carl. "Now I don't need to feel sorry for her any more."

Annie wrote a play about it, changing all the names of course. *Time:* The present. *Place:* Brooklyn. *Scene:* An average Brooklyn living room. She titled it: *Waiting for the Ring.* She appraised the play as better than *Callous Flesh* but not as good as *The Marriage.* The class and Mr. Haise felt the same way about it.

Goldie Lopin was now so swollen with child that Less could no longer ride his mother's hip. Now, wearing only a diaper, he trotted around the store in circles, his always-saturated diaper hanging low and almost touching the floor. When he tired of being a centaur, he lay flat on the floor, arms and legs outstretched, and took his rest. Customers had to step over him to get to the counter.

"When do you expect to go to the hospital, Goldie?" asked Annie.

"Who goes to the hospital? My man will bring the baby. Like he brought Less."

"Oh, no!" Annie was shocked. "Not your husband!"

"*Somebody* has to tie the cord. Otherwise I wouldn't need *anybody*."

"What'll you do about Less?" Goldie shrugged. "I could keep him for a few days."

"Would you, Annie? Just for a day or two until I got on my feet?"

"It would be fun and give me a chance to find out how Carl takes to children. So you just send him over when the time comes."

"I'll do that and thanks, Annie."

"What does he eat?"

"Anything that won't eat him."

Annie laughed. "But seriously, Goldie."

Seriously, he had a can of vegetable soup three times a day.

"Let him eat from the can," said Goldie. "Don't thin it with water. He likes to eat with his hands, and if it's thinned out he won't be able to hold it."

A few days later when Annie came home from her class, Less, surrounded by canned goods, was sitting in a little express wagon outside the door. His father was peering in the window to see if anyone was at home. When he saw Annie coming, he started to walk away. "Hey!" she called. "Where's the blanket and his diapers?" He pointed to the blanket on which Less was sitting and a paper bag of diapers wedged in with the canned goods. "How is Goldie doing?" she asked. The man gave her a narrow-eyed look, grunted, and walked away.

Less refused Annie's help in getting out of the wagon. He got himself out by overturning the wagon and crawling out from under. He grinned smugly as Annie chased the rolling cans. He refused to mount the three steps to the door, holding out his arms for Annie to carry him.

"Nothing doing," she said. "I'm not allowed to lift heavy furniture, and you're as heavy as a baby grand piano. Now, you take Annie's hand and walk up like a good boy." His response was to spread-eagle himself on the ground. Annie coaxed and pleaded. Finally, she lost patience. "You get up now and walk or—" she made her voice very sugary—"Annie will knock ooh 'ittle head off."

The idea charmed him. He gave Annie an angel's smile, got up, took her hand and went into the cottage. For a moment he stared around the room in open-mouthed awe, then thoroughly wet his diaper. This time, when she *wanted* him to lie on the floor in order to change his diaper, he wouldn't. When again she threatened to knock his head off, he stretched out happily on the floor and the change was made. He trotted and galloped around the house until he was exhausted, then crawled under the kitchen table and went to sleep.

"Why under the table?" asked Carl when he came home.

* 180

"It's his Indian blood," said Annie. "He thinks it's a wigwam."

Carl got on his hands and knees and crawled under the table. The child awakened instantly and assumed the same posture. Carl backed out, Less following. Like a flash, he was on Carl's back. He grabbed Carl's ears for reins, dug in his heels and hollered, "Gid-yup!" Carl shook an imaginary mane and whinnied like a horse. The child laughed in delight, which so flattered Carl that he played "horse" with him until Annie announced that supper was on the table.

Less refused to eat at the table. He refused to eat his stewlike soup from a bowl. Annie had to push it back into the can. He sat on the floor with the can between his legs. Annie gave him a spoon. He threw it across the room. He was a methodical eater —one handful went into his mouth, the next one on the floor, and so on, until the can was empty.

"If he was mine," said Carl, "I'd beat the bejesus out of him."

"No, you wouldn't," said Annie. "You'd think he was generous—wanting to feed the poor hungry floor."

At bedtime the problem came up as to where he was to sleep. "I suppose he could sleep with us," said Carl dubiously.

"Sure! If you like to float while you're sleeping."

"He's got to sleep somewhere." Suddenly Carl said, "Hey! Where'd he go?"

They couldn't find him anywhere. He wasn't under the kitchen table; he couldn't have got out because the doors were locked. They found him at last, spread out under their bed. They covered him with his little blanket and went to bed with the problem solved.

The next day Annie got Less into his wagon and pulled him around to the grocery store. She was anxious to find out how Goldie was getting along. The store was locked! Annie got all upset, afraid that things hadn't gone right with her friend. She hurried to the dry goods store to find out if Miss Aggie could give her any information.

"What makes you think anything could happen to her?" said Miss Aggie scornfully. "Her kind has babies like a cat has kittens. Just drop 'em anywhere."

"But if she was all right, he'd be in the store, wouldn't he?"

"Not Lopin Lopin." (That was his full name.) "Think he's going to do all the work alone? He'll keep it shut until she's on her feet and able to wait on customers."

The next morning the three of them, Carl, Less and Annie were crowded in the little cubicle that held the toilet and the small washbasin with a cracked mirror over it. Carl was shaving. Less was standing on the toilet seat; he was shaving, too. Carl had lathered Less's face and given him a tin spoon to use as a razor. Annie was wringing her hands.

"I forgot it was Saturday and I have to go to work," she wailed. "Who's going to look after him?"

"Take the day off," said Carl.

"But, Carl, we need that two dollars."

"I suppose I could take care of him for the day," said Carl. But his heart wasn't in the offer.

"I wouldn't let you," she said. "A day with him and you'd be off children for life."

Well, who knows—what way is there of finding out—the thoughts in a child's mind? Less grinned at himself in the mirror as though it was a great compliment to sort of not be wanted. Then he turned, put his arms around Annie's neck, buried his face, lather and all, in her neck, and in a small broken voice said, "Gid-yup!"

"What's two dollars?" said Annie, her voice a little broken, too. "I'll call up the manager and tell him I'm not coming in today."

While she was looking up the dime store's number in the book, Less's father walked in. He didn't knock or anything—he just opened the door and came in. He put a bag of apples on the kitchen table as payment, or perhaps as an award, for Annie's care of the child. He picked up his son and started for the door.

"Wait a minute," called Annie. "Did Goldie have a boy or a girl?" Lopin Lopin ignored the question. "You ask him, Carl," she said. "He's too proud to talk to a woman."

"How's the wife?" asked Carl in a hearty, man-to-man voice.

"She ketch a girl off me," said the Lopin of few words.

Monday, business was as usual at the Lopin Grocery Store. Lopin was sawing bones behind the counter, and a slimmer Goldie was allowing people to buy groceries.

Three days! And she's up and around, thought Annie. Childbirth can't be so bad, then. Even if a person does have a narrow pelvis.

Less, of the dragging diaper, greeted Annie as an old friend. He threw himself on his stomach and twined both hands around her leg and hung on. He wouldn't let go when his mother took Annie into the back room to see the new baby. He slid along on his stomach, holding her leg as she walked.

"He might get a splinter in his belly button," Annie said.

"If he does, I sure feel sorry for the poor splinter," said Goldie.

The Lopins lived in one room. It had a double bed, a sink, a cookstove, a round table and chairs and a big icebox for meat, milk, butter, and other perishables sold in the store. Four inverted wooden boxes in a row, with a thin pad, served as stoic Less's bed. Three walls were lined with canned goods, packaged goods, sacks of potatoes, onions and apples, and other produce.

The new baby, asleep in a washbasket on the table, was a beautiful thing—like, thought Annie, a rosebud ready to open any minute. It had straight black, wet-looking hair, heavy eyelids, and its legs were in the position of a frog about to leap. Annie asked how much the baby weighed. Goldie didn't know, but obligingly took the baby out to the store and weighed her on the meat scales.

"Eight and a half," she announced. "Say, eight and a quarter because Lopin keeps the scales a little ahead."

Annie was permitted to carry the baby back to its basket. Instinctively she held it correctly; her arm a reclining chair and her spread hand a seat for its little backside.

"She fits!" said Annie. "Fits against me like I had a place made for her."

"God shapes women for babies."

"Why, Goldie! You're religious."

Goldie shrugged. "No harm in that."

"What are you going to call the baby?"

"Lily Pearl."

"Lily Pearl! Oh, how beautiful! It sounds like clear, cool water running over smooth white stones."

"My man—he picked out the name," said Goldie.

It was hard for Annie to believe that the dark, brooding Indian could think up such a light, airy name. "The world is full of surprises," said Annie. Another shrug was the only comment from Goldie.

On her way home Annie waved at Miss Aggie, who was standing in the store window putting a housedress on a headless dummy. Miss Aggie did not wave back. *Now* what? muttered Annie to herself.

The phone was ringing as Annie entered the cottage. A woman's voice, obviously disguised, said, "Mrs. Brown?"

"Speaking!"

"You better watch yourself, Mrs. Brown. You're new here, and you won't get along with us Lopin people if you keep on being friends with that woman who lives in sin with a man and births babies in sin."

"Who are you?" said Annie.

"I am, shall we say, a friend?"

"That's a moot question," said Annie, using one of Carl's sayings. "And the woman *is* married, my friend."

"Married?" The caller was so indignant she forgot to disguise her voice. "Married? Just because they stood under a tree with a couple of Indians and one of them said some hocus-pocus over them, they are *married*? Huh!"

"*Good* and married! Married in the Indian religion and in law religion. Common law. My husband told me, and he knows because he's going to be a lawyer." Annie paused to sock home the curtain line. "Thanks for calling . . . *Miss Aggie*." She grinned wickedly as she hung up the receiver. I guess I fixed her wagon for her, she thought smugly.

Chapter Fifteen

Too soon it was June. Annie was aware of the change of atmosphere on campus and in the college town as commencement drew near. She spent hours thinking out the ingredients that made the change. She was aware of a mixed mood of bright intense excitement and sad sentimental nostalgia. The upcoming graduates set the mood.

It might well be, thought Annie, that the four years here made the in-between place of the past and the future. In that time they changed from boys and girls to men and women. They came from home when they were very young, seventeen and eighteen, and a few smart ones were only sixteen. Maybe they didn't know it, but the day they left home to go to college they ended the home part of their lives.

And now they are going out into the world and begin the lives that they will live until they die. The thought of it awed Annie. And they can't go back again, she thought. Sure, they can go home again. But only the outside part of them will be home; not their minds; not their thoughts.

Now I know, she thought, why they call it commencement. Because they have to commence this new life.

Lying awake on still June nights, Annie heard snatches of close harmony singing as boys walked across the campus. They sang sad songs about "Dear Old Alma Mater" to the melody of the saddest and oldest of all college songs: "Far Above Cayuga's Waters." To Annie it was all deliciously sad.

One especially quiet night when the wind was right she heard the words of the song very clearly, and she sat up in bed and sang "Dear Old Alma Mater" along with the boys. She wanted to belong to it all. Carl woke up and asked if she was practicing lullabies. No, she told him, she just wanted to get the feeling of commencement. Then she told him how she had figured out why they called it commencement.

"Because they commence a whole new life," she concluded.

"But, Annie, everybody knows that. It's not new."

"But, Carl, I first felt it by myself and I figured it out by myself, so it is new to me."

In a way, the last session of the playwriting class was Annie's commencement. The college part of my life is over, she thought. Too soon—too soon. And too soon I will start my life as a mother. The thought was sad, but exciting too.

The last session reminded her of a story she had read as a child—its title eluded her—about the last class taught in French. On the next day the children had to learn German. She had cried when she read it; it had been sad and seemed so real; the way the last playwriting class session was sad and real.

It was an informal hour. Mr. Haise sat on the edge of his desk, swinging one leg, the other touching the floor. The students grouped in the first two rows of seats. Mr. Haise led them in reminiscing. Plays written in the semester were recalled, and some were praised anew and others were good-naturedly condemned. Once more, Annie's *Callous Flesh* got a going over, and Annie laughed along with the rest. For the first time she spoke out in class.

187 *

"I apologize," she said. "And I'm willing to forget it, if you all are."

And Mr. Haise said once more what he had said many times before: that one could learn as much from a bad play as from a good play. Annie did not believe that, but felt it wasn't her place to challenge the statement.

Then it was time for the wonderful announcement!

An alumnus, who had put in four years of college taking every writing course available, had turned out to be a well-known and prosperous engineer. But he still had that old feeling for his first love: writing. He had donated a sum of money to defray the cost of publishing a volume of seven one-act plays written in the class. There were no strings attached except that the book be dedicated to him.

In two years Mr. Haise had garnered four plays that were worthy. He stood up now, took a sheet of folded paper from his inside coat pocket. He unfolded the paper, looked at each student in turn, cleared his throat and said:

"I am pleased to announce that two plays written this semester are worthy of publication. That makes six plays we have. One more, and we have the book."

Two plays! There was no doubt as to who had written them. A pretty girl named Sylvia Connel and a frat boy named Thomas Buchanon exchanged triumphant looks.

"We have a third play. Now, with a good rewrite, it could give us our seventh play, and we could get the book out in the fall."

Annie was alerted. Could it possibly be *her* play? Please God, she prayed, let it be my play. I'll work on it night and day! I'll do anything . . .

"The first play," said Mr. Haise, and the class was still, "is—" he paused for suspense "—is, *A Night in the Trenches* by Thomas Buchanon!"

All turned to face Tom and politely applauded. The boy next to Tom shook his hand.

"The second play was written by a young lady of great promise." The beautiful Sylvia sat up straight, smiled and modestly dropped her eyes as the class turned to her, ready to applaud. "The second play . . ." Mr. Haise paused and looked directly at Annie. "The second play: *The Marriage* by Annie Brown!"

An involuntary murmur came up from the class. Annie turned ice-cold! Simultaneously with the announcement something totally unexpected happened. The child within her moved. For the first time she felt its life! For an instant Mr. Haise's announcement meant nothing. Then reaction set in and she trembled all over.

Sylvia started to rise as if in protest, but sat down again and applauded Annie the loudest of all. Annie tried to smile; to say thank you all, but she just couldn't make it.

An undersized, bushy-haired boy, wearing thick-lensed glasses and unpopular with class and teacher because he split too many hairs when plays were discussed in class, was on his feet.

"Her play is out," he said. "She is not registered in the university."

Annie's little world collapsed. She looked appealingly at Mr. Haise. "The specifications," he said dryly, "are two, Mr. Cronth. One: That it be a good play. Two: That it be written in class. Mrs. Brown qualifies. Any other questions, class?"

"If I may say so," said Tom, who was enamored of the beautiful Sylvia, "I think Miss Connel's play should be published."

"It's not quite right," said Mr. Haise. "It has all the elements of a good play but somehow it does not come to life." He turned to Annie. "Mrs. Brown, you made no comment when it was read in class."

"But you didn't ask me, Mr. Haise."

"I ask you now. Can you suggest what it lacks to make it a good play?"

"It's the dialogue," said Annie. "It's wrong. There are these sorority girls and it's Saturday night and it's raining out and they're sitting there talking about their boy friends. These girls all come from the same class—background, I mean. That makes them think and talk in the same way. And that's how Miss Connel wrote it. But it seems to me that even if they talked in the same way they would, each one, talk different in the same way. I know what I mean, but I'm not saying it right."

"You are doing very well, Mrs. Brown," said Mr. Haise. "What you are saying is that the play lacks characterization. The dialogue is at fault because through dialogue we get our characterization." He enumerated the elements of dialogue. "Each line of dialogue must: one, characterize the person speaking; two, advance the plot; three, be interesting in itself. Perfect dialogue has all three elements. Good dialogue has two. Miss Connel's dialogue has but one: advancement of plot. Now, Miss Connel, if you would be willing to rewrite your play, it would make the seventh, and we could get the book out in the fall."

"I don't see why I should, Mr. Haise. My father read it and said it was all right. As you know, he's a Broadway producer."

Mr. Haise turned his arms, the palms of his hands facing the class, and shrugged in an I-give-up gesture. The campanile struck the hour and the last class session of the year ended.

"That's it!" said Mr. Haise. "And I hope you all have a nice summer."

"The same to you," chorused the class.

Annie remained after the others left to thank Mr. Haise for choosing her play. Gallantly he said, not at all, and wished there were more plays like Annie's around. He hoped she'd be able to audit his other class in full-length playwriting in the fall and he said he was disappointed when Annie told him she couldn't take classes in the fall because she'd have a baby then.

She said good-by and shook his hand and had to try very hard to keep from crying.

Tom and Sylvia were waiting for her outside and invited her to have a Coke with them. Tom, anxious to have his play published, begged Sylvia to rewrite hers so as not to hold up publication for another year.

"Let's gang up on her, Annie," he said, "and *make* her rewrite so you and I can brag about being published playwrights."

"Look!" said Sylvia. "My play's all right as it is. I'm not going to fuss over it any more."

"Not even to get it *published?*" asked Annie. "This may sound funny to you, Sylvia, but I think to have something published is the most wonderful thing in the world."

"You said it for me too, Annie," said Tom.

"You're very sweet," said Sylvia. "Both of you." She put a hand on Annie's arm and her other hand on Tom's. "And I wish you both all the luck in the world, you budding playwrights. But honest! I don't intend to make a career out of writing. I took the course only because I intend to be an actress and I thought I ought to know a little something about how a play is put together. Now let's have another Coke and talk about something else."

They reminisced about the class and recalled the funny things that had happened in it and Tom gave an imitation of the student named Cronth who had always objected to everything; found no merit in anything at all. "God's little angry man," said Tom.

And they laughed and talked and Annie listened and smiled and felt she was part of them and of the university, and wistfully wished it had happened sooner when it would have meant so much to her.

"I can't believe it, Carl! I just can't believe it! I can't take it in! To think a person like me . . . *Me,* Carl! Never went to high school even; never had a job where I could use my mind. And my mother and father never had an education—and the way we were poor and lived in a tenement—and Mama always telling me I didn't know anything and didn't have sense. And your mother. The way she thinks I'm nobody—not good enough for you. Me! Me! *I am going to have a play I wrote printed in a book!*"

Carl wanted to warn her not to get her hopes too high—that sometimes those things did not pan out. The University Press might not think the book worthy of publication even if subsidized; the needed seventh play might not materialize for a year or two. Or with the growing popularity of the playwriting course and larger enrollments, superior plays might turn up and Annie's might be withdrawn to make room for a better play.

He let her talk. No use spoiling her great happiness.

"Oh, and Mr. Haise invited me to come to the three-act class next year. He said I would be a—"

She stopped short. She drew in a long, trembling breath and her face froze in an intense waiting look.

"Annie! What's the matter?"

She took his hand and placed it on her stomach. "Feel, Carl! Feel!"

The child within her moved under his hand. He gave a great start and pulled his hand away as though he had touched fire. "Good God, Annie!"

"It's the baby! It's alive and it moves!"

"Does it hurt you?" he asked anxiously.

She laughed. "Of course not! It just feels funny, that's all. Funny . . . the idea that I'm living two lives."

"Well, it sure scared hell out of me, all right." He groped in his pocket for his cigarettes. The pack was empty. He wadded it up and threw it into the wastebasket.

"Oh, Carl," she said, contrite, "in all the excitement of the play and the baby moving, I forgot to get you cigarettes!"

"Oh, that's all right, sweetheart."

"No, it's not! You go and get a pack. Get two. That saves a penny."

"I don't need to smoke."

"Yes, you do and you know it. Besides, I need a loaf of bread and I'm too tired to go to the store."

"Are you sure you're all right, Annie?"

"Oh, Carl!" she said in a long-suffering voice.

When he got back she was hunched over the table writing furiously. He was relieved. I guess she's all right, he thought, or she wouldn't be writing. He took it for granted that she was writing down her reaction to the possibility of having a play published. She's lucky, he thought, having an outlet like that. Nothing will ever throw her—no matter what happens to her—if she can get it down on paper.

He kissed the top of her head and looked over her shoulder. He expected the title to be *My First Publication* or something similar.

The title was *My First Baby*. Space, space, then the first sentence: *Today, I felt life . . .*

She could have written *Our First Baby*, he thought as he put the bread away in the cupboard.

Chapter Sixteen

In the week between the end of the regular school year and the beginning of summer school, the university lay fallow. The library and school cafeteria were closed; the chairs in classrooms seemed to ache with emptiness and even the campanile rested. Literally, time stood still.

The campus dog, who had been wined and dined all year by the frat boys, had been left behind to shift for himself. He roamed the campus and patrolled the empty classrooms, wondering, probably, when the life that he had become accustomed to would start up again.

He was a pure-bred Airedale with skid-row whiskers, and, as Annie phrased it, no one knew from whence he came. Some years back, lost or abandoned, he had shown up on the campus, liked it, had taken up with the frat boys, and wiped from his canine mind whatever "whence" he had known. He had come footsore, his pelt tangled with burs and wearing a rope collar, the end dangling, showing evidence it had been chewed off. The boys got him in shape. They fed him, cleaned him up, put iodine on his sore footpads and gave him a name.

After an all-night party, they poured the dregs from a bottle of needle-beer on his flat dome and intoned in chorus, "We hereby christen thee Michelangelo."

Inevitably the name was shortened to Jello.

Jello became a campus character. He took up with everybody; he belonged to nobody. He was courteous to all but intimate with none. He stayed a week or two with each fraternity in turn, but he had no home.

He went everywhere, including classes, with the boys, lying on the floor in the no man's land between teacher and class. In some classes the session did not officially begin until the thump came, indicating Jello had settled down to sleep through the class. He went to lectures given by visiting men of prominence and slept at the foot of the rostrum. He went to night concerts and slept at the back of the auditorium because up front the sudden clash of the cymbals kept waking him up.

Annie knew all about Jello because he had visited the play-writing class once or twice with Tom Buchanon, who was a frat man.

Now in the quiet of between sessions, Jello roamed the deserted campus with an uncomprehending look in his small amber eyes, wondering where the boys were; where his next meal was coming from. Annie came upon him one morning, sitting under a tree with his head down on his forepaws. He was whimpering a little. When he saw her he got up and looked ashamed. He had not wanted anybody to see him that way.

Annie walked over to a bench and sat down to rest. He sat down, too, with that classroom thump. She spoke to him. She told him all about the library and the books in it and all about the baby she was going to have. She spoke in a low monotone so he would think it was a class lecture and go to sleep. Jello slept. When it was time for Annie to go home, he woke up and went home with her. She wrote it all down under the title of *Campus Dog*.

No one knows from whence he came. He turned up one day on the campus and never went away. All year the frat boys wine and dine him as the saying goes. Suddenly it is summer and the boys go away and leave Jello to shift for himself.

Although they abandon him each summer, Jello never gets used to it. Each June he grieves anew at man's inhumanity to dog. . . .

The first morning he walked home with me he wouldn't come in the house. So I put a pan of water in the yard and gave him a slice of bread and butter, because that was all there was.

You are too sentimental, said my husband. The dog got along in the summers before you came here and will get along after you leave. I showed my husband some white hairs on Jello's snoot to prove that the dog was getting too old to shift for himself in summer.

Then my husband said we could keep Jello for a while but I must not get too much attached to him because when the boys got him back in the fall, I would suffer.

I do not intend to suffer because I do not intend to give up Jello. When the boys come to get Jello, I will charge them with woeful neglect of a dumb animal. If that doesn't work, I will bring up corruption—the way the boys make him drink beer out of a saucer and the way they laugh when Jello drinks too much and falls down.

If that doesn't work, I will mention the words *Humane Society* in a mysterious way. I will fight to keep Jello.

He is my dog.

Summer school got under way. Annie told Carl there wasn't much "college" about summer school. Carl asked did she mean atmosphere and she said he knew what she meant.

The first opening days of the session, Annie mingled with the young men and women—teachers, mostly—who had come from all over the United States, making use of their vacation to garner credits added to what they had, which would lead to a higher degree which would increase their salaries a couple of hundred dollars a year.

Although most of them had at one time been college undergraduates, they no longer fitted into college life—proof that while you could go back again you couldn't go back in the same way. The young women did not become coeds again; the young men did not hang out in near-beer places or walk about on campus coatless, tieless, shirt unbuttoned, and sleeves rolled up. They were sedate. They did not call out to each other across the campus; did not club up in groups. It was always two and two; two women walking together; two men walking together.

Carl registered in summer school. He had not intended to do so. He had planned to get an eight-hour-a-day job over in Herdstone, in an auto factory. He had made arrangements for transportation with Mrs. Ridinski's son, who had a steady job in Herdstone. Carl would share gasoline costs with him. But the Dean of the Law School changed all that.

"It's her first baby," said the Dean. "You can't leave her alone eight to ten hours a day in that isolated cottage."

Carl wanted to say that Annie wouldn't be alone; she would have the dog. But he knew the Dean would consider that irrelevant.

"I suggest you take two of next year's courses now. In the summer session."

"But . . ." Carl began in objection.

The Dean held up his hand in a "stop" gesture. "Aside from being at home with your wife, there are other advantages. Your schedule will be lighter next fall. You'll have more time to be"—he paused and smiled—"with your family. More time for outside jobs.

"And," continued the Dean, carefully matching his fingertips, "if circumstances force you to drop out of school—"

"I do not anticipate . . ." interrupted Carl.

"Neither do I, Carl. But in life, as in law, we cannot overlook any contingency." He waited.

"I agree, sir," said Carl, a little dubiously.

"If you have to drop out of school for financial or other reasons, you can make up the year's work in the next summer session and take the bar examinations along with your class in September, 1929, thereby not losing a year."

Carl saw the logic of the plan and wondered why he hadn't thought of it himself.

Annie was so pleased when Carl told her he wasn't going to be away. "I guess Dr. Marson must have told him the baby was coming earlier. In September."

"Annie!" He grabbed her arms. "Has something gone wrong? *Is* something wrong? Does he think you aren't strong enough to make it full term?"

"Oh, no!" she smiled. "It's just because I felt life ahead of time and he said . . . how did he say it? Yes! Miscalculated the time when I first became pregnant."

"Why didn't you tell me, Annie?"

"Didn't want to worry you."

"Annie, Annie! You must not keep such things to yourself. Had I only known I wouldn't have told the Dean I planned to work away from you. He must think I'm a heel."

"Ah, no, Carl. He thinks you're grand the way I think you're grand."

"He thinks *you're* grand."

"Let me sit on your lap, Carl."

"I don't know about that," he said, teasing her. "I don't like girls who keep things from a husband to sit on my lap."

The tuition loan had been arranged and Carl registered for summer school, taking trade regulation and labor law. These classes were scheduled for Friday in the fall semester. By taking them now, Carl would have Fridays free in the fall and might be able to pick up a steady weekend job.

With the opening of summer school, Annie decided to go into retirement. Her pregnancy was quite obvious now and she waddled awkwardly when she walked. She gave up her Saturday job at the dime store. Her ankles were liable to swell when she was on her feet too long. With her last pay she bought several yards of flannel to make diapers for the baby, taking advantage of the 10 per cent discount the dime store gave the workers. She also bought a skein of pink floss. Miss Aggie was going to teach her how to hemstitch. She visited each of her friends to tell them good-by for a while.

"So I won't be seeing you, Mrs. Hansmon, until after the baby is born."

"Why not, Annie? I know it's a long walk from Lopin but walking's good for you."

"It's not that. I don't like people staring at me—the way I look and all. I feel ashamed."

"Don't be foolish. It's no crime to have a baby. You ought to be proud."

"I know. But when I was a little girl and a pregnant woman passed on the street, the boys said dirty things in dirty words about, you know, how she got that way? I used to feel so ashamed. Oh, I know nobody would think or say those things about me. Still and all, I have this strong hangover from when I was a child."

Mrs. Hansmon shook her head. "I can't make you out, Annie."

"But I'll phone you once in a while so you don't forget me."

"How could I ever forget you? But you do that—give me a call every now and then."

Henry, the grocer, was very careful not to look at her, not out of delicacy, but it made him wince inwardly. She was so small and fragile to carry such a seemingly heavy load.

"But I'll be here with the baby when the squirrels come for the nuts in the fall."

"You won't forget?"

"I won't. And I'll bring Jello with me."

"Don't bring that son-of-a-gun. He'll scare the squirrels away."

"All right." She looked around the store as though for the last time. "Well, take good care of yourself, Henry."

"You too, Annie."

"Thanks." Again the survey of the store.

"Will you take a jar of raspberry jam from me for old time's sake, Annie?"

"For old time's sake I will."

Once more they shook hands and said their good-bys as though they would never meet again.

She saved the florist for the last. "I won't be seeing you again, Anthony, until fall."

"You're leaving us?"

"Oh, no! I'm going to have a baby."

"I see!"

"You'd be blind if you didn't," she said, smiling. His face flushed deep red.

"How are you coming along with your book?"

"Owing to circumstances . . ."

"You mean you haven't written a word."

"I'm afraid not."

"But you promised! You said you would start January first. And here it is nearly July . . ."

"I simply cannot do it, Annie."

"Why? Tell me *why*."

"If I don't write it, I can think that I'll be a writer someday. If I do write it, I may find out I'll never be a writer. Then what would I have to dre—" He bit off the word.

"You mean to dream on?" He lowered his head. "Say it, then."

"Something to dream on," he said.

Annie pondered on it. It was a new conception to her. Was it better to think you *might* than to test it; to take the big chance to find out you *couldn't?* She concluded it might be better for some people not to put the dream to the test.

While she was thinking that out the florist went into the back room and returned with a handful of seeds. "Nasturtiums," he said. "Require no care. Grow and blossom in the poorest of soil." He opened her handbag, which she had placed on the counter and emptied the seeds into it.

"I think I see," she said slowly. Then out of the blue she said, "You know, Anthony, there's just a little bit of woman in you."

He laughed. "I had hoped no one would ever know," he said jokingly.

"Well, I know. And that's all right. It lets me like you without being in love with you."

"Oh, I *say!*" he blurted out, astonished and embarrassed.

"Good-by, Anthony." She smiled and left.

One more trip. "Have you heard anything," she asked the clerk in the bookstore, "about a book of one-act plays to be published this fall?"

"No, I haven't," said the clerk. "But Mr. Whorl might know." He called for Mr. Whorl.

Mr. Whorl knew that such a book was going to come out sometime but didn't know when. She could call the University Press. Annie said she didn't like to do that. Obligingly enough, Mr. Whorl called the Press. And, no, the book would not be published this year; perhaps next year.

So, thought Annie bitterly as she walked home. That Sylvia just wouldn't rewrite! How can she be so mean and still so beautiful?

They settled down for the long hot summer. Carl went to classes and worked at whatever odd jobs he could get. He had tried to get a part-time job in some stores, but with the close of the regular school session, many of the stores closed for the summer and business wasn't brisk enough in those remaining open to hire a part-time worker.

Carl had had a hundred circulars mimeographed, stating that he was available for lawn mowing, window washing, minor household repairs, and cellar whitewashing at twenty-five cents an hour. He had distributed the circulars along his old paper route. He got work and earned four or five dollars a week, which at least paid for their food.

Jello, the dog, slept the summer away. At first, he had attended Carl's classes but had given that up. It wasn't the same without the frat boys. He did go to the grocery store with Annie and carried home his own bone—high-stepping, with the bone held high.

Annie went nowhere except the grocery store and once in a while to Miss Aggie's. Miss Aggie let her use the sewing machine in the back room and helped her make a couple of maternity smocks. By unspoken agreement, neither mentioned the anonymous phone call, and they got along all right.

Once in a while Annie took Less off Goldie's hands for an afternoon. He had calmed down a lot since the arrival of sister Lily Pearl. He wore pants now, instead of diapers, and could talk a little—at least enough to say "pee-pee" a split second before he wet his pants.

Carl worried about Annie not getting out more. He felt she could use summer school recreation. Now, the summer school students didn't seem able to make their own recreation so the university manufactured fun for them.

There was a "Folk Sing" on Thursday nights, where they sat on the dewy-dewy grass and sang songs like "On Top of Old Smoky," the young ladies wondering all the while what *would* remove grass stains from the seat of a summer dress.

Saturday nights there was "Down Country Dancing" on the asphalt in front of the Administration Building. The dancers bounced and shuffled around in circles to the sinister monotony of a fiddle taking a beating from an angry bow.

Carl, then, feeling that Annie needed recreation, took her to one of the Folk Sings. She hadn't wanted to go, saying she "showed" too much. Carl talked her into going, assuring her that she didn't show at all when she wore a smock, and he was sure she'd like the folk stuff. It was right up her alley, he said.

Annie *didn't* like it. She didn't like to sit on the grass; she didn't like to sing with a lot of other people because, then, nobody could hear her. And she thought the songs were too dreary.

"But, Annie," Carl explained, "they are the songs of the people. They've come down to us through the generations by word of mouth. They are part of the cultural inheritance of America."

"Oh, baloney!" she said.

He took her to a folk dance and she tore that apart, too. She said it wasn't dancing. It was physical ed. without credits.

"My idea of dancing," she said, "is somebody's arm around you, holding you a little tight—but you like it, and cheek to cheek, while soft music plays something like 'Shine on, Harvest Moon.' You get memories out of that. But what do you get out of stamping around and grabbing sweaty hands and that fiddle banging out 'Jimmy Crack Corn' and hurting your ears like scratchy chalk on a blackboard? You get tired. That's what you get."

"What makes you so cranky, sweetheart?"

"Am I cranky, Carl? I don't mean to be. It's just that the summer school students are so nice and it *is* their vacation. So why can't they have fun instead of recreation?

"Oh, cut it out, Annie. You don't *have* to go to these things. You don't have to go to the lecture tonight, either."

But she wanted to go to that. A much-publicized poet was to recite some of his poems. Annie had never seen a poet in the flesh. To her disappointment, he didn't look as she thought a poet should look. His gray pants were baggy at the knees, his coat was rumpled, and his tie was awry. The color of his hair matched the color of the suit.

"He looks like a day laborer out of a job," she whispered.

"Oh, Annie," he said in a very tired voice, "we don't have to listen to him. Let's go."

203   *

"No! I want to hear him." She put her arm through his. "I'm sorry, Carl."

"I don't like poetry. I'm here for your sake, not mine," he said.

"I know. I won't run him down. I promise."

She thoroughly enjoyed the first half of the recital. The poet's work was good and he had a beautiful reading voice.

The second half of the program was given over to the long narrative poem that had made him famous. It was titled: *How Dark Is My Africa*. The poet started out quietly enough but began working himself up into a frenzy. He cakewalked around the stage, flung his hands in the air; grabbed his hair and made it hang over his eyes. He displayed his teeth in an ugly grimace.

Chong-a-long! Chong-a-long! *Boom!* he chanted. Chong-a-long! Chong-a-long! *Boom!* Each time he hit the *Boom,* Annie's unborn child leaped within her.

"We got to get out of here!" Annie hissed in Carl's ear.

"Cry-sake!" said Carl out loud. Fortunately it coincided with a piercing scream from the poet and no one heard. With the scream, the baby did a double leap. Annie got Carl's hand on her stomach just in time to have him feel the second leap. He jumped up.

"Wait!" she said. The poet threw himself on the floor, and screaming, pounded his hands on the boards. "Now's our chance!" said Annie. They left the auditorium.

Annie was through with summer school. She seemed very contented to stay close to home. She sewed diapers, read a lot. She tried her hand at writing poetry. She washed the dog and brushed his stiff hair. She had Less as a guest once a week. She watched her nasturtiums grow. She wrote to her mother once a week. She tried new ways of cooking and baking, and best of all, Carl was with her a lot. The days were hot and still and the nights were cool. She had never known such quietly happy serenity.

Then one of those contingencies came up.

Chapter Seventeen

It was a simple, logical contingency. They ran out of food because they ran out of money because Carl ran out of work.

He had thoroughly cleaned out cellars and/or basements that had needed cleaning for years and now wouldn't need cleaning for years. He had made all the minor repairs that had come his way; nipped the trouble in the bud before they became major repairs. Soon there was only lawn mowing, and soon that gave out. There was a long drought and lawns dried up. Then came a long, hot, rainy spell, and foot-high weeds grew lavishly. Homeowners said, To hell with it! Cheaper to start a new lawn next spring.

Another item: Most of Carl's work had come from faculty people—many of whom left on belated vacations when the first summer session ended.

Carl tried the little town of Lopin. No work there. Shopowners and their wives tended their own stores; homeowners mowed their own lawns, made their own minor and major repairs, and saw nothing out of the way in a dusty cluttered cellar. And twenty-five per cent of the Lopinites were out of work themselves and would be until the university opened full time in the fall.

Carl and Annie had to—as she put it—get their two aces out of the hole. Regretfully, she closed out her eight-dollar-plus-interest pennies account. Carl pawned his wrist watch but got only five dollars. It was half a year older than at the last pawning.

"Thirteen dollars," said Carl, "won't last forever. Be very careful what you buy, sweetheart."

"Oh, stop worrying, Carl. By the time the money's gone, something else will turn up. It always does, you know."

They had already paid Dr. Marson eight dollars on his fifty-dollar fee—a dollar or two at a time. On her next visit to the doctor, Annie gave him two dollars out of their precious thirteen.

"Why, Annie? Why?" said Carl desperately. "When we need the money so bad! And he *said* he'd wait. Please tell me *why*."

"Because," said Annie, "I wanted to make it a round sum."

"Oh, Annie," he said wearily, "will you ever grow up?"

Not so long ago, thought Annie, he had said, Stay the way you are. Don't ever change. And now he don't like me the way I am. They say, she thought bitterly, that trouble brings people together. It don't. It splits them wide apart. Is he getting tired of me? Will he leave me in time? What will I do then? Tears came to her eyes and the child within her moved. My baby! she thought. She spoke out of her thoughts, her words full of tears.

"Anyhow, I'll have my baby if you leave me."

"Ah, sweetheart!" He took her into his arms and let her cry a little.

"I'll grow up," she said. "You'll see. From now on, I'll try not to be so dopey." She paused. He had told her to grow up and here she was talking like a kid! "What I mean to say is that I will make an effort to be more sensible in the future."

Carl was amused and somewhat touched by the pompous little statement. "Make no efforts," he said lightly. "You just stay the way you are."

"Oh, Carl!" She was happy again. "For a minute I thought you didn't like me."

"I don't like you at all," he said. "I just happen to love you."

It was only a week later that they had another flare-up about money. The sum was also two dollars, and Carl was the villain this time. It had to do with the drafting of the will of a prosperous farmer named Friend Hawkner. "Friend" was his real first name. It had been given him by his mother, a renegade Quaker who had married a Lopinite.

Friend Hawkner was getting into the years and was anxious to make a will—that is, his wife was anxious to have him make a will, which is the same thing. But Hawkner did not want to pay the usual attorney's fee. High School Principal Lopin, who was Friend's brother-in-law, said he knew just the fellow, good as any lawyer, who'd be glad to draft the will for a dollar or two. The fellow was Carl Brown.

Carl, feeling obligated to the principal, drew up the will. On a Saturday afternoon, the principal picked up Annie and Carl in his Ford and drove them out to the farm. There was another passenger: the banker who had taken care of Annie's small account. He was a cousin of Principal Lopin. He was also a notary public and the means of saving the farmer from paying a notary fee.

Carl read the will aloud. It satisfied Friend Hawkner and, what was more important, Mrs. Hawkner. Annie and a neighbor woman were witnesses. Annie signed her name carefully, feeling very important. The banking cousin notarized the document and it was done.

They shook hands all around. The neighbor woman went home. Mrs. Hawkner, now legally assured of a prosperous widowhood should her husband predecease her, excused herself and went out to the barn to milk the cows.

"What do I owe you, counselor?" said the farmer jovially. He pronounced *counselor* as though the word were full payment in itself.

"Nothing," said Carl. "I did it as a favor to Mr. Lopin here."

The farmer's relief made him expansive. "None of that now! I'm a man who pays his just debts." The banker smiled. "Would a dollar be all right, counselor?" asked the farmer.

"God's sake, Friend," said the banker. "Make it two. You saved on me, you know."

"Two?" said the farmer. His voice trembled.

Carl hesitated a second before he said, "Thank you, Mr. Hawkner, but I can't accept a fee."

Annie gasped audibly. "Carl, I want to see you for a minute," she said. "Outside."

The banker and the principal exchanged knowing looks as a red-faced Carl followed his wife out to the porch. The farmer looked worried.

Annie grabbed Carl's arm and fiercely whispered, "You take that two dollars! You hear me?"

"I hear you. And I won't take it."

"You *will* take it. You earned it. I read somewhere that a laborer is worthy of his hire. And the man said he pays his just debts, didn't he? Now you go in there and get that two dollars."

"I can't, sweetheart. Aside from depriving a legitimate lawyer of a fee, I am not a member of the bar and I can't accept a fee."

"But the bar will never know."

"It isn't that, Annie. It's a question of ethics."

"To hell with ethics! We need money for food. *I* can live on boiled onions and bread and weak tea, but my baby can't." She paused. "Now, will you take the money?"

"No!"

"All right, then. I'll go in and get that two dollars." She started to go into the house.

Carl grabbed her arms and gave her a little shake. "You'll do no such thing! This is my business and you keep out of it. I let you run me in most things. But I won't let you run me this time. Law is—will be—my life's profession, and you are never to interfere in my law work as long as we are together. Do you understand?"

"No!" she said sullenly.

"Now you sit here in this porch chair and be quiet."

"I won't!"

"Please, sweetheart." He placed her in the chair.

"Why don't *you* grow up?" she mumbled as he went into the house.

Through the open window she heard Carl talking. "No, I can't take money."

"You and your damn ethics," she mumbled to herself.

"But," continued Carl, "I'll take it out in vegetables—potatoes, apples . . ."

"Sure! Sure!" said the farmer happily.

Annie smiled and relaxed.

She stood with Carl and watched the farmer put the fee into the car: a bushel of Irish Cobbler potatoes; a bushel of apples, and a dozen ears of Country Gentleman corn. Annie gave Carl's arm an ecstatic hug each time an item was stashed in the car.

"I don't think Ramona would mind," said the principal, "if you threw in a jar of her pickles."

"And," suggested the banker as the farmer started for the cellar, "how about a bottle of your homemade Royal Duke cherry wine, Friend?"

"Whoa up, there!" protested the farmer.

The banker carefully examined his fingernails as he said, "I usually get fifty cents when I bring my stamp out to the country."

The farmer got a quart jar of pickles and a quart bottle of wine out of the cellar.

Annie held up the bottle of dark rosy wine. "It's beautiful!" she said. "Too beautiful to drink."

209   *

"You drink it all yourself, my dear," said the banker. "It'll put roses in your cheeks, and in the baby's too."

Annie was touched. "If we ever get a lot of money," she said, "I'll put it all in your bank and nobody else's." They all laughed.

As Carl helped her into the back seat of the Ford, she whispered in his ear: "That stuff is worth much more than two dollars."

It was hard to brag in a whisper, but Carl managed it. "I knew what I was doing," he said.

Carl and Annie were just about down to rock bottom prior to his drafting the will. He had managed once in a while to earn a quarter or thirty cents washing windows. A quarter didn't go very far—that is, not far for the year 1928. It bought a couple of eggs, a loaf of bread, an onion, and a nickel sack of Bull Durham tobacco.

At the start of what, with grim humor, they called the Famine of '28, Carl had given up smoking cigarettes. After a few days of deprivation, he was jumpy and cranky and found it hard to concentrate in class. Annie got him a clay pipe for a nickel—the kind children used for blowing bubbles—and a sack of Bull Durham. He didn't like the pipe. He wasn't used to it. His jaws hurt from gripping the pipestem. Eventually he clamped his teeth so tight on the stem that the end broke off. This gave Annie an idea. She recalled how the old Irishmen in Brooklyn smoked clay pipes with just an inch or two of stem. She cut Carl's pipestem down to two inches, filled it with tobacco and told him to try it.

"The idea is," she said, "to suck on it. Not bite it." She watched anxiously as he took a few puffs. "How is it, Carl?"

"Well, it's better than a kick in the pants," he said grudgingly.

"You mean you have a choice?" She smiled.

"Don't get so wise, Annie." She turned away with a sigh. "I was just joking, sweetheart. It's fine!"

And so it was, except that the bowl of the pipe was so close to his face that most of the smoke went up his nostrils.

Jello, the dog, fared well in the Famine. He had his full quota of free meat scraps and a succulent bone from Goldie every day or so. As Annie said, he was waxing fat. Often she looked enviously at Jello's bones and meat scraps. Annie was used to a rather heavy meat diet and missed meat terribly. Even back in her childhood, before her mother married Dan, there had always been meat. If there was only fifteen cents in the house, her mother bought a dime's worth of chopped meat and a loaf of bread and it made a satisfying supper.

One day at the grocer's, Goldie gave Annie a package of scraps and said if she'd wait a few minutes, there'd be a bone for Jello as her man was cutting up a quarter of beef.

Annie watched as Lopin Lopin cut away the meat from a large bone and sawed out the bone. He held it up. To Annie it looked like a miniature ivory tower and her mouth watered at the bits of good red meat clinging to it. Goldie must have noticed. She didn't put the bone with the scraps. She wrapped it separately.

"I'll take Less for the afternoon, Goldie, if you'll let me."

"Now, Annie, don't feel you have to put yourself out just because . . ."

Annie broke in before Goldie could say the rest. "Oh, Less is no trouble. He's good company, and you ought to see how he and Jello play together. They take turns being the horse."

With a nickel's worth of dried beans, the bone made a wonderful soup, and the bit of meat on it was a small luxury. Annie cooled off the bone and went out to give it to Jello. He sat down, the bone on one paw and the other paw over it. He sniffed it, then looked up at Annie with eyes full of hurt reproach as if mutely asking, Why did you have to monkey with my bone?

With the advent of farmer Friend's largess, Jello went back on raw bones and Carl and Annie ate well again.

The corn didn't last very long, but it seemed as if the potatoes and apples would last forever. They had potatoes: boiled, mashed, baked, or what Annie called "scalped" potatoes. There was potato salad, too—as long as the pickles lasted, which wasn't long as they seemed to have an insatiable hunger for pickles. The salad, made of cubes of cold boiled potatoes and chopped pickles marinated in the spiced pickle vinegar, went off the menu when the pickles gave out. Very soon, the diet of potatoes, apples, bread, and weak tea (cheaper than coffee) got awfully monotonous; especially since everything was boiled or baked. As tactfully as possible, for Annie was very much on edge these days, Carl suggested that she fry something once in a while.

"Instead of keeping that hot oven going in this hot weather, Annie, we could have something fried once in a while, couldn't we?"

"Like what, Carl?"

"French fried potatoes or hashed brown. Mom used to make the best potato pancakes," he said wistfully.

"Naturally," she said.

"I had fried apples once. They were quite good."

"Mom make those, too?"

"Oh, Annie! Can't I make a suggestion without being dragged over the coals?"

"You know I can't stand the smell of frying grease."

"Oh, don't be so neurotic!"

"Now I'm neurotic as well as childish. Soon I'll need to make a list of all the new things I am since we got married."

"Don't be so sensitive."

"Item three on the list. So sensitive."

"Annie, I'm going to be frank with you."

"When people say they're going to be frank, that's a sign they're going to say something mean."

"Let's stop all this, sweetheart. Okay?"

"Okay," she agreed.

"You know, it's a long time since you sat on my lap?"

"I'm getting too big to fit in the rocker."

"Let's try it."

It was a tight fit. She had to assume an awkward position, half sitting, half lying back, to accommodate her swollen abdomen.

"My mother used to fry everything in bacon fat. Funny! That doesn't bother me at all. She used to dip a slice of bread in beaten egg and fry it in this bacon fat and it was wonderful!"

"Couldn't we?"

She shook her head. "Bacon's too dear. Forty cents a pound. Mama couldn't afford bacon either. But she bought the bacon end. All the ladies waited for the bacon to get near the end. But the butcher saved it for Mama because he liked her. She was very pretty then, Carl. He didn't want to charge her for it, but Mama wouldn't take it for nothing. Because he was married, you know, and she was a widow.

"Funny," she said, "it seems like years ago, but it was only last fall when we sat on the campus bench and I said a baby wouldn't cost much; that I could nurse it." She sighed. "What a dope I was!" She got off his lap. "I guess the potatoes are baked by now." They sat down at the table.

"I don't feel much like eating," she said. "It's so hot here with the oven and all."

"You've got to eat, sweetheart."

"I can't!" She pushed her plate away. "I'm getting so I can't look a potato in the eye any more." She smiled wanly.

"Do we have any ice, sweetheart?"

"A little."

"I tell you what. Let's eat outside on the back steps where it's cooler and I'll make some iced tea. You'd like that, wouldn't you?"

"Oh, I'd love it! I'm glad you thought of it."

They had their supper on the back steps. A dozen or so girls came out of the lamp shade factory at the end of the Athletic Field. Some got into beat-up family cars waiting at the curb, the others walked away in groups of twos and threes. One girl walked alone. The last one out of the building was a man, evidently the boss or owner. He stood looking at the building for a while before he got into his almost new Ford and went home.

"Good God!" said Carl. "Right under my nose!" He beat his fist against his temple. "*I'm* the dope of this family. A fourteen-karat dope!"

"What's the matter, Carl?"

"That factory! Why didn't I think of it? Where there is a factory, there's bound to be a job."

"Only girls work there. No men."

"Bound to be men—janitor, night watchman . . ."

"Only girls. Sometimes in the afternoon I walk over there with Less and Jello and the girls come to the windows and talk to us. They tease Less and whistle at Jello. Then the boss comes and shoos them back to work. Then he waves at us. But he's the only man in the place."

"I'll go see him in the morning about a job. No harm in trying."

"Watch out for the girls," she said. "Some of them are awfully pretty. The other day the prettiest one of all threw a caramel out of the window for Less. But Jello caught it and ate it—paper and all." Jello, hearing his name, came from behind the clubhouse and sat at their feet. "Didn't you, Jello?" The dog thumped his tail in verification.

"You know, it's going to be a lovely night, Carl. It's getting cooler by the minute. Here, no matter how hot the days are, the nights are always cool. Back home in Brooklyn it stays hot all night because the sidewalks and buildings hold on to the heat. And people sleep on the roof and on the fire escape and babies cry in their cribs because it's so hot.

"Oh, Carl, I'm so glad I am here in this nice place where the nights are so cool and quiet."

He put his arms about her and held her close. "Oh, Annie, I love you so," he whispered.

* 214

Chapter Eighteen

The small factory manufactured parchment lamp shades appliquéd with flower cutouts. These shades were in vogue at the time and threatened to replace the long-popular silk and ribbon shades.

The owner bore the noble surname of Pulaski. He was American-born of Polish immigrant parents who had settled in River Waddy, a satellite town of the great automobile city of Herdstone. Although in his early thirties, Pulaski looked drained out —played out too soon was Carl's first impression of him.

"Yep, Pulaski's the name," he said. "And I'm a Polack from way back. Couldn't deny it if I wanted to. Got the Polish trademark." He touched his gray, pockmarked face.

"You the manager?" asked Carl.

"Manager, bookkeeper, shipping clerk, salesman, chief cook, and bottle washer. To make a long story short, I own the dump."

"Brown. Caretaker of the Athletic Field," said Carl. They shook hands across Pulaski's untidy desk.

"Hey! Then that kid with the big dog must be your wife."

"That's right."

"What do you know! She don't look more than sixteen and

already's got one kid on the hoof and another on the way. Oh, boy! You must have got her young. That's the way I like 'em, too. Most guys go for the chickens. But me? I'll take a pullet any day."

"My wife," said Carl very precisely, "happens to be going on nineteen, and the little boy does not belong to us."

Pulaski was aware of Carl's cold distaste. "Okay!" he said. "O-kay! Keep your shirt on. And now," he said jauntily, "What can I do you for?"

"Could you use a part-time janitor?"

"Nope!"

"Night watchman?"

"Nope."

"But you need a night watchman—all this highly inflammable stock."

"Which I got highly insured. Wouldn't make me no mind if the joint burned down tonight. I'd stay cool, calm, and collect my insurance."

"You might have trouble collecting it if it burned down at night and no watchman on the job. The company would charge willful neglect."

"You're telling *me*? I wasn't born yesterday. I got me a night watchman."

"But who takes over on his night off?"

"He don't take no night off. Where would he hang out? A home . . . friends, he ain't got. Pop's just an old souse with no relations. Sleeps down in the stockroom. Works for bed and bottle. Can't get 'em cheaper than that," he said smugly.

"I see," said Carl, not knowing what else to say.

Pulaski walked to the door with him. " 'Preciate you dropping in, Brown. If Pop comes down with the dee-tees some night and can't make the rounds, I'll give you a ring."

Carl didn't tell Annie of his interview with Pulaski. He knew she'd start hoping too high; she'd make plans what to do with the money and then if no job materialized . . . But something's got to break, he thought desperately. They weren't exactly starving—there were still apples and potatoes left, but Annie couldn't stand the diet. She existed mostly on broth made from Jello's daily bone and on cold tea.

"Oh, what I'd give," she said, "for fresh-caught fish cooked in sweet butter! Broiled sirloin steak, not too well done, mind you, and fresh asparagus. And oh! Half an ice-cold ripe mush-melon!"

"*Musk*-melon." His correction was automatic. "But they don't call them that any more, sweetheart. Now they're cantaloupes."

"*Mush*-melon! Can't-elopes! What difference does the name make when you haven't got it to eat?"

"I know. But, sweetheart, if we can hold out just two weeks longer . . ."

"What's going to happen then?"

"Summer school exams will be over and I can sell my textbooks. Then we'll have steak and mushmelon."

"You mean, can't-elope." She sighed and smiled simultaneously. "If it was just myself, Carl, I'd put up with the potatoes and apples. Food is food. But I got to think of the baby. She's growing on what I eat. I should drink milk and eat stuff like liver and fresh vegetables, the doctor said."

"I know." He sighed too. "I hate to do it, but there's no other way out. I'll write to Mom and ask for a loan."

"Good luck!" she said bitterly.

"Now, Annie, Mom is sure to come through. I *know* it."

"Oh, sure!" she said with no conviction.

He had long since pawned his tennis racket, ice skates, and watch. There was nothing more to pawn and they had nothing to sell, so he wrote to his mother and asked for a loan of twenty-five dollars. Annie wrote to her mother and asked for ten, begging her mother not to tell Dan of her need.

His mother answered immediately. "Sure hate to read it to you,

Annie," said Carl. "You'll find something in it to fight about. Now, I don't mind if you take me over the coals, but it can't be good for the baby—the way you get so fighting mad."

"I know, Carl. And I'll try to hold myself in. Open it and read it."

There was no enclosed money order.

. . . sorry as I can be [she wrote], that you're in such a fix and a baby on the way and all. It's hard on you both. But times are hard with us, too. Papa ain't working steady and besides he is getting old so quick. If it wasn't for your sister helping out I don't know what we'd do. But I can't ask too much of her. Tessie is in her forties now and has to save for her old age. She has no husband to fall back on.

"There's something in what your mother writes, Carl," Annie said. "I feel so sorry for them. Especially poor Tessie."

Carl gave a great sigh of relief. But the letter's ending spoiled everything.

Son, I could say I told you so but I'm not going to rub it in. But I will say you married too quick. You should have thought of all this before you married. Now you're stuck.

Papa and Tessie send their love . . .

Annie folded her arms on the ledge of her protruding stomach and let out an explosive *"Well!"*

"Take it easy, Annie," he said apprehensively. "Think of the baby."

She fought for self-control, got it, but couldn't resist muttering, "If people figured out all the things that could happen, who'd get married?"

"We would. And we did and I'm not sorry. You?"

"Ah, no, Carl. Never! It's just that I'm worried a little."

So like everybody else you got money troubles [wrote Annie's mother].

I know how that is.

Your father was out of work when you came in the world.

We had to owe the midwife so she had money troubles then.

That's the way it goes. Yes.

You come to the wrong party to ask for money because I got none.

Dan is a good husband and no faults only he likes to handle all the money by his self.

He gives me so much every day for the table and he always wants meat for supper and sometimes the money don't reach that far even.

Now I tell you to do this.

Write to Dan and ask him.

Write with a feck shown and he will send you money.

He always had a feck shown for you like you was his own daughter and he will send money I know.

The letter ended with a prayer that the coming baby be a boy. Annie's mother wrote she wouldn't want Annie to have a daughter who would grow up and run away and hurt Annie the way Annie had hurt her mother.

Annie considered her mother's instructions to write an affectionate letter to Dan and ask for a loan. She didn't want to do it. But for the sake of the baby . . . She got pen and paper and wrote:

Dear Dan,
    How are you anyhow? Often I think of you—how nice to me you were and all. I guess I was a bad girl. I did not appreciate you the way I should have, Dan. Why, you were more of a father to me than . . .

She paused. *Father to me!* She thought of how he had come into her bedroom . . . *father to me.* Suddenly her mouth filled with bitter-tasting bile. She tore the sheet of paper in two and went into the little cubicle and spit out the bile into the toilet bowl and rinsed out her mouth. "I can't do it," she moaned. "I can't write that letter. I'd rather die!"

She placed herself flat on her back on the bed, and put her

arm over her eyes. Yes, I'd rather die, she thought. The unborn child turned in her womb. It seemed like an omen. She was frightened. "I didn't mean it, God! I didn't. Please forgive the thought."

Outside, Jello stood on his hind legs, paws on the window sill, and looked in on her lying on the bed. She got up and went to the window.

"Want your bone, Jello?" He thumped his tail once. That meant yes. "Okay. Want to go to the store with me to get it?" Sedately he walked around once in a circle to indicate he was ready for a stroll. "All right. Soon as I get my shoes on, then." He yawned, collapsed on his stomach, put his head down on his paws, and went to sleep. He knew that "shoes" meant lipstick and powder, hair combing and what not.

Carefully Annie prepared for the trip to the grocer's. It was a way of getting up courage. She was going to do what, to her, was an unprecedented thing: She was going to get steak, a cantaloupe, a couple of ripe tomatoes, lemons, and a pack of real cigarettes for Carl. And she was going to say, "Charge it!" She went to the window and told Jello about it. Not that he'd understand, but she wanted to get it out in words.

"I've got to take a chance, Jello, at losing her as a friend. Shakespeare said it. Don't borrow, don't loan, for loan oft loses a friend. Knowing I owe Goldie, I will start ducking her because I'm ashamed and she'll think I don't like her any more and . . ."

The phone rang. A man's voice asked for "Brown."

"He's in class," Annie said.

"What class? First class or no class?"

"*Law* class."

"What do you know? When do you expect the lawyer?"

"Four o'clock."

"Tell him to give Pulaski a ring soon as he gets home. Goodby." He hung up.

It's a job. I *know* it's a job, she thought. Thank God I didn't ask Goldie for credit! "Come on, Jello. Let's go get your bone. This time I won't cook it. You can have it raw." He looked up at her with his head cocked as if trying to say, you mean it? She laughed. "Ah, Jello, you're *such* a funny dog."

Carl phoned Pulaski as soon as he got home. Annie heard Carl say, "Sorry to hear that." A pause. "Sure! Be glad to. Be right over. Good-by."

"Oh, Carl, is it about a job?"

"Tell you when I get back, sweetheart."

He was back in half an hour. He told her about his former interview with the factory owner and about the night watchman.

"Poor fellow's in the hospital. In bad shape. Didn't have money for bootleg so he drank nearly a bottle of rubbing alcohol flavored with grapefruit juice."

"Good God!" Annie shuddered.

"Pulaski asked me to take over tonight. Said he'd give me a dollar. If anything happens to the old man, I can have the job full time, five dollars a week."

"Oh, Carl!" She smiled ecstatically. "With that five and the five for delivering papers when school opens—ten dollars a week! We can live fine!"

"And with my light schedule . . . Fridays no classes . . ."

Suddenly ashamed, they looked away from each other.

"It's ugly . . . ugly," she said. "Don't ever let anybody tell you poverty makes people noble. Here we are hoping that a man will die . . ."

"No, Annie, no! Don't say that."

"It's true," she muttered.

They had an early supper. They ate in silence, having nothing to say to each other. At a quarter to seven, armed with his textbooks, planning to study during the night, Carl prepared to leave.

"Annie, I don't like to leave you alone all night . . ."

"I have the dog," she said.

"Phone me if . . ."

"I'll be all right," she said sharply.

He phoned her from the factory at eight and asked how she was doing. She phoned him at ten and wanted to know if there was any news about the night watchman. After Carl had made his eleven-o'clock inspection, he slipped home for two cups of tea and two slices of bread spread with applesauce. She had a cup of tea to keep him company. They had little to say to each other.

He was through at seven in the morning. They had a breakfast of tea and unbuttered toast and applesauce. She waited for him to tell her about the watchman, he waited for her to ask.

He broke the deadlock. "I better get some sleep," he said. "Got to work tonight. And two classes today . . ."

"Then the watchman . . . ?"

"He'll pull through," Carl said too casually. "They got his stomach pumped out just in time."

"When's he coming back to work?"

"He's not coming back."

"Why?"

"Well, he's old, you know. Got a widowed daughter out in . . ." Carl paused to think of a name. "Yes. In Kenosha. That's right! Kenosha."

"That must be an Indian name."

"That's right!" he said too eagerly. "I believe that's in Wisconsin. Anyway, he's going to live with his daughter." Carl gave a sigh of relief, thinking he had got away with it.

"*The Death of a Derelict!*" she said. "I bet they wouldn't laugh at that the way they laughed at *Callous Flesh*, in class."

"All right, Annie. All *right!* It wasn't my fault. I didn't kill him. I need the job. I can't bring him back by not taking it."

"I know, darling. I know. It just seems . . ." She paused a

second. "Oh, never mind. Get some sleep now, Carl. I'll get you up in time for your class."

He put a dollar on the table. "Advance on my first week's pay. Let's have a *good* supper tonight, sweetheart."

She had an impulse to say, "To celebrate?" Instead she said, "What would you like? Steak?"

"It's only a dollar. Better get hamburger. And one of those 'mushmelons.'" He pinched her chin.

"And I'll get us a fresh tomato," she added. "And I'll put the card in the window for a ten-cent piece of ice. It's so long since we had ice. And lemons for lemonade . . ." She paused. "But, Carl, you need a haircut so bad!"

"That'll wait." He yawned as he unbuttoned his shirt.

She followed him into the bedroom. "A quart of milk. The doctor said I should drink milk. And eggs! I love eggs and they're so cheap now."

He looked around vaguely. "What did you do with my . . ."

She got his pajamas from under the pillow and held the jacket as he got into it. She turned him around and buttoned it up. "Know what, Carl?"

"Sure," he said sleepily. He pulled back the sheet and got into bed.

"Listen to the way people talk and you'll find out what they haven't got."

"Umm!" he murmured deliciously as his head made contact with the pillow.

"Like people who don't have enough to eat always talk about food. And people who don't have money always talk about how much things cost." She covered him with the sheet. "And people who never had any children write the *best* children's stories. And people who . . ."

He turned over on his side and was instantly asleep.

She asked to go to the factory with him that night. She accompanied him on the seven-o'clock checkup. He punched the clock

223   *

on each floor. The clocks automatically recorded the time of inspection.

"Proof," he explained, "there was no negligence in case of fire. That's for the benefit of the insurance investigators."

He took her to Pulaski's office, where he had his books, pad and pencil set up on the desk. He would spend the first part of the night in study. He told her to wait there while he went down into the stockroom to punch the clock there. Annie insisted on going with him, however.

"It's no place for you, Annie. You won't like it."

"Who says I should *like* it. I just want to see it."

"Annie . . ."

"It's where the watchman lived, isn't it?"

"Yes."

"I want to see it."

"Why?"

"I don't know."

He sighed and led her down to the basement. The cellar was without windows. A bulb hanging from the middle of the ceiling gave light. Large heavy rolls of parchment paper were stacked against the walls. There were bales of wire and a pile of decal sheets to decorate the lamp shades. In a corner there were five wooden soapboxes in a row, turned upside down with a thin mattress pad covering the boxes. There was a dirty pillow and a dirty torn blanket.

"So here is where he lived."

"Yes."

"Where he slept."

"Yes, Annie. He had no home, no folks."

"Where did he come from, Carl?"

"No one seems to know."

"Who is going to bury him then?"

"Pulaski didn't say."

"Will they give him to the medical school to experiment on like they do dead prisoners that nobody claims?"

"Why this morbid interest, Annie?"

"It just seems so terrible that a person lived and died and nobody cared."

"Maybe that's the way he wanted it, Annie. Who knows?"

Something moved in a corner. Annie thought it might be a rat. She shuddered and clung to Carl. "Let's get out of here, Carl. It's spooky."

"I'll walk you back to the cottage, Annie."

"No. It's still light and Jello's somewhere around the field."

He walked out the back door with her. Jello bounded into view. "Atta boy," said Carl, patting the dog's head. "Old Johnny on the spot."

Annie started off, Jello walking at her side. She paused, turned and said, "What was his name?"

"Didn't have any—far as I know. Pulaski called him 'Old Pop.'"

She opened her book to her play *Callous Flesh*. She crossed out that title and inserted, *The Death of a Derelict*. She read the play she had written, then tore it from the book, shoved it into the stove, and got her pad and pencil. She started a new play.

THE DEATH OF A DERELICT

BY

ANNIE BROWN

Time: The present.

Place: A box factory in a small midwestern town.

CHARACTERS

Morongski: Owner of factory. He is a dapper little man with a scarred face. His talk is very breezy and he is free with the slang of the times.

David: A self-help pre-med student. He is tall, blond, the athletic type. Very serious. His speech is precise.

Alice: His wife, who has recently had a baby. She is small, thin, with a worried look. She has a broad southern accent because she comes from Kentucky.

Pop: Night watchman at the factory. He is old and bent, with sparse gray hair. His face is lined and most of his teeth are gone. He wears a dirty shirt and old black pants with a button off in the front. Wears somebody's ragged and discarded tennis shoes. Talks in whining voice.

Setting: Stockroom in cellar. No windows. Light from bulb in center of ceiling. Stacks of flat cardboard all over. Makeshift bed. Filthy dirty.

At curtain: Stage in darkness. Voices heard off stage.

That was as far as Annie went. She knew the material would not adapt itself to the play form. She had formed the habit of starting all her writing in the play form. She felt she got better characterization if she started out in dialogue; kept the best of it in the story, discarded the rest or put it into exposition and description. She began to rewrite it as a short story.

He was a trembling old man. No one knew where he came from. He had no friends or relations. If he had a name—had ever had a name—he kept it to himself. The girls in the factory and the boss called him Pop.

Annie spent the night in writing the story. She wrote under great compulsion. She couldn't stand it that a human being had lived and died and there was no record that he ever had *been.* She felt that in writing about him she was establishing the fact that he *had* lived and walked the earth and had once been a man.

She had breakfast ready when Carl came home in the morning. They had cold cantaloupe and eggs scrambled in butter and buttered toast and good hot coffee. It had been so long since they had had coffee for breakfast. Carl said it was the best breakfast he'd ever had.

She went to bed with Carl. He had no class until three in the afternoon, and they slept most of the day away.

Chapter Nineteen

Carl's nights changed into days and the days into nights. He went to work at seven in the evening, sneaked home after the eleven P.M. checkup for a cup of coffee and a sandwich, went back to the factory until seven in the morning, came home, had breakfast with Annie and went to bed to sleep until it was time for a class. Usually Annie slept through the morning with him. Naturally, she wasn't tired at night and sometimes stayed up until two or three o'clock.

One night at two, she stood at the window, looking across the Athletic Field at the dark bulk of the factory. She wondered why the lights didn't go on and off from room to room. She phoned the factory. The phone rang a long time before Carl answered. As she had surmised, he had fallen asleep and missed the checkup.

From that time on she remained awake as long as she could. When she got really tired and went to bed she set the alarm for each hour and got up to make sure Carl was making the rounds.

"This has got to stop, Annie," he said. "You need your sleep."

"How can I sleep, worrying the factory might burn down while you're asleep over there? Isn't there a clock in the office?"

"Sure. But what good is it if I happen to fall asleep? I need an alarm . . ." His eyes went to the clock on the mantelpiece.

"Oh, no, you don't!" she said.

"Wouldn't my beautiful Linda lend stupid-heart Lance her alarm clock from seven to seven inclusive?"

She laughed. "Imagine, Carl! It seems years and years since I wrote that play. I was only a dopey kid then."

"You still are."

"Dopey?"

"A kid."

He carried the clock to the factory and brought it back each morning. During the night he set the alarm to ring each hour to awaken him if he happened to fall asleep. But even without a clock Annie awoke every hour to be sure he was making his rounds.

The university just about closed down in the two-week hiatus between the end of summer school and the beginning of the regular session. Again, the campanile was silenced, and the library, after ordering all books turned in, locked its doors and left Annie without reading material.

Annie fussed about it. "Does that campanile have a motto that says: 'I count only the student hours'? And the library: They could open it for at least an hour a day. This college is just like a ghost town after all the gold is dug up. Why?"

"Well, repairs have to be made. People who work in the library and offices have to have a vacation. Which reminds me the U. Bookshop closes tonight and if I want to sell my summer texts I've got to do it now."

"We could use the money. You need a haircut."

"Want to come with me?"

"And have everybody stare at me?"

"There won't be many people on the campus."

"You go, Carl. I'll stay home."

"Aw, come on, Annie. We haven't been anywhere together in a long time."

"I don't want to, Carl."

"You've been complaining about having nothing to read. We might pick up a book for you."

"They loan out books?"

"No. But sometimes you can pick up a good book cheap. Secondhand, of course."

"You mean a book I can keep?"

"That you can own."

"I'll be just a minute, Carl. I got to put lipstick on."

While Carl waited for the clerk to examine his texts in order to place a value on them, Annie went over to the secondhand book area. A clerk came and asked could he be of help.

"No, thank you," she said. "Do you care if I just look?"

"No, ma'am. Browse all you want." He left.

Browse! Annie savored the word. To her, it had meant cows looking for grass. Imagine! It also applied to books! She had never heard the word sounded before. Now *she* was anxious to say it and make it her own.

Carl came over. "Found anything yet?"

"I haven't even started to look. Carl, why don't you go get a haircut while I *browse* in the books?"

He grinned. "Okay. Take your time," he said. He went down the street to the barbershop.

Where to start? Oh, where to start? she thought in delicious indecision. I can't browse all the books, so I better start with the big fat ones.

She pulled out the biggest, fattest one of them all. Immediately she fell in love with the strong, terse title: *War and Peace.* She noted the author's name. *Count Leo Tolstoi.* It must be a Russian story, she decided, like *The Lower Depths.* She recalled Professor

229 *

Newcool saying: . . . *Russian writers—second to none.* War and Peace: *The greatest novel ever written!*

"Oh, I *must* have you!" she whispered to the book.

Then she noticed the hard back cover was missing—had been torn off and the last page was torn and wrinkled.

"Now what slob did that?" she said aloud. She took the book over to the clerk. "Look what somebody did!" she said indignantly.

"A shame," he agreed. "That's why it's priced so low."

"How much?"

"You can have it for a quarter."

"A what?" she said incredulously.

"Twenty-five cents and it's yours."

"Mine?" The unborn child moved within her. "She's going to be a reading girl," said Annie.

The clerk's eyebrows shot up. "Pardon me?" he said.

"Nothing. Will you save it for me till I come back? I got to get the money."

"You bet!" He put the book on top of the cash register.

Halfway to the door, she turned and came back. "Would you loan me your fountain pen?"

He pulled it from his shirt pocket, unscrewed the top, and handed it to her, point toward him. How nice and polite he is, she thought. She took the book down from the cash register and wrote on the flyleaf: *My book.* And under it: *Annie Brown.* She returned the pen and book with a thank you. "I'll be right back."

"No hurry," said the clerk.

Carl seemed like a stranger sitting in the barber's chair. He was swathed in a sheet with only his head and feet showing. He had one leg crossed over the other under the sheet and a couple of bare inches of flesh showed above his sock. His head was lowered and tilted to one side. He looked sheepish—the way most men look in a barber chair.

"A quarter!" she announced breathlessly. "I bought a book."

The sheet billowed as Carl groped in his pocket. It was as though a Houdini was struggling under it to get out of handcuffs. The barber poised his hands, comb in one, shears in the other, in the air, waving them as though he didn't want to lose his hair-cutting rhythm. Carl came up with a quarter, the sheet calmed down and the barber laid his comb on the nape of Carl's head and resumed his art.

Walking home, Carl said, "What'd you get for a quarter?"

"I got *War and Peace* for a quarter. That's what I got! But look!" They stopped walking while she pulled the book out of the blue-striped paper bag. "Just look what some slob did to my book!"

"*Vandal,* sweetheart. That's a better word."

"All right, then. Look what a vandal did!"

"I think I can fix it, Annie."

"Honest, Carl?" She clutched his arm. "*Honest?*"

"There's a lot of scrap parchment around the factory. Maybe I can glue four or five sheets together—one on top of the other and make a back."

As they resumed walking, she hugged his arm and said, "Oh, Carl!"

"What?"

"I own a book at last. Don't have to take it back to the library. I'm so happy! Just think! The first book I ever owned!"

At eight that night she phoned him at the factory. "My book fixed, Carl?" she asked anxiously.

"Not yet. But I found four pieces of parchment just the right size."

She phoned at nine. He reported that the parchment sheets had been glued together, but as yet not attached to the book. Have to dry first, he explained.

At eleven she stood in the open kitchen door waiting for Carl.

231   *

When she saw a moving shadow looming up larger as it came toward the house, she ran out to meet him. She was bitterly disappointed that he hadn't brought her book home.

"But there was more to fixing it than I bargained on," he said. "I had to take the strip of leather off the spine. Then I had to make a sort of hinge to attach the parchment to the spine, glue back the strip of leather. I'll bring it home in the morning if it's good and dry."

He did bring the book home in the morning. Annie cuddled it in her arms as she would a lost child who had found his way home again.

"Who else but you, darling, would think of making such a strong beautiful cover—even better than the one the vandal tore off, I bet. Oh, I'm so glad I married *you*, Carl, instead of someone else."

He grinned with pleasure and said, "You mean you had a choice?"

"You know what I mean and if I wasn't so fat I'd sit on your lap."

"It rhymes!" he said. "Let's see now:

> She got so fat,
> This Annie Brown!
> No sit on lap,
> Poor Annie Brown!"

Like a flash, she topped his rhyme:

> Stick to the law,
> I say to thee.
> For a poet
> Thou ne'er will be.

"*Touché!*"

"What's that?" she asked.

"That's French for: You had the last word."

"Aw, shut up!" she said affectionately. "You *and* your French."

After breakfast Carl prepared for bed while Annie washed the dishes. He got into bed and waited for her to come, too. He waited for what seemed a long time.

"Aren't you coming to bed, Annie?" he called. There was no answer. He called again. Silence.

"Now what?" he grumbled. Where could she have gone this time of the morning? I thought she was all through with that disappearing act. With a couple of sighs and a grunt he got out of bed and went to the kitchen. To his relief she was there. She was sitting at the kitchen table hunched over the book.

"Annie," he said gently, "come to bed with me." She didn't seem to hear him. "Annie!" he said sharply.

She gave a great start and looked up at him. Her eyes were blank. "What?" she said vaguely.

"I want you to come to bed with me."

"Just a minute," she said. "Let me finish this page."

"Now, Annie, don't make me beg you."

"But I don't *want* to go to bed." She looked up at him pleadingly. "Please, Carl?"

"If that's the way you feel about it . . ." He waited.

Annie wet her middle finger with her tongue, turned a page and huddled over the book. He waited for what seemed a long time. She turned another page.

Carl went back to bed and viciously punched the unoccupied pillow next to his. "God-damned book!" he muttered. "I should have thrown it in the God-damned factory furnace!"

Annie found that *War and Peace* was by no means easy reading. It was bewilderingly rich in all the elements of writing—had so much life, so much color. It was stuffed with action. It spilled over with incident and the plot was stupendous in its scope. And the characters! Enough to populate a place as big as Canarsie, she figured. All those names to keep in mind! She thought it

233   *

wouldn't be so bad if the names stayed put. They didn't. They changed into other names from time to time.

She decided there was but one thing to do: Take the book apart and rewrite it in her own way. She had a theory that if she rewrote enough of it, the time would come when she could read straight from the book and sort of translate it in the reading without writing it down. She started with page one.

Anna Paviovna was also known as Annette Scherer. She belonged to the Russian court. She had a good job. She was maid-of-honor to the Empress. She was in her forties but she didn't look it —the way she dressed and all.

She was very shrewd but charming. She knew all about politics. This made her an interesting talker as far as the court nobles were concerned. Women didn't know quite how to take her. When they were at one of her parties and got into little bunches to talk to each other or to a man, Anna always broke it up. She thought that was the way to be a good hostess—let the conversations be general and not private.

Well, Anna had a party one night in July in the year 1805. She had sent out invitations that she had the grippe and wanted company. Now, carefully dressed and made up, she waited for her guests. Prince Vassily was the first to arrive. . . .

Annie was obsessed by the book. When Carl left at night, she was working on it. When he came home in the morning, she was working on it. She talked of nothing but the book. Carl felt that her tense absorption couldn't possibly be good for her and told her so. She claimed it was *very* good for her because she enjoyed it so much. He begged her then not to overdo it.

"A person can't overdo what he likes to do," she said flatly.

In the week before the fall semester started, Principal Lopin showed up one afternoon with a bucket of white paint and a brush and asked Carl to give the bleachers a quick paint job.

"There might be a little something extra in it for you," he hinted.

"I could use a little extra something, all right," said Carl.

"We'll see," said the principal mysteriously.

Next day Coach Stevens came onto the field. He had been away all summer. They shook hands and asked each other what kind of summer he'd had. The coach asked when the baby was expected.

"In a week or two," said Carl. "We hoped it would come before classes started. It would be something if it came while I was on campus and Annie alone in the house."

"Don't worry. Babies always come in the middle of the night. At least my three did."

"That's another problem. I work nights—watchman in that factory over there. Suppose it comes in the middle of the night and she hasn't time to phone me at the factory?"

"If she could only be that lucky! Babies take a hell of a long time to be born. Especially the first one. She'd have plenty of time to phone. Don't worry, son," he said paternally. "When her time comes, phone me. Never mind what hour of the day or night. I've got a car. We'll get her to the hospital in plenty of time." He looked at his watch, whistled and announced it was six-thirty and he was already half an hour late for supper. "See you," he said, and rushed off.

Methodically, Carl pressed the cover down on the paint can and ran the brush back and forth on a rail to get out the surplus paint. That would make cleaning the brush easier. Suddenly he remembered the time. Six-thirty, the coach had said. What was the matter with Annie? She always came out at six to call him for supper. Did she forget? No. She was always so aware of the time. Clock stopped? Never! Not the way she wound it two or three times a day. Something must be wrong, then.

Paintbrush in hand, he raced across the field to the house and threw himself in through the door, fully expecting to see Annie on the floor writhing in birth pains.

She was sitting at the kitchen table hunched over book and pad and seemed to be reading and writing simultaneously. His relief made him weak. The brush dropped from his hand. The sound got Annie to her feet.

"Carl! You scared me!"

From fear to relief was a big comedown. He had worried for nothing. It made him irritable. "Do you know what time it is?" he said.

She looked up at the clock. "Good heavens! I forgot all about supper!"

"Well, what about supper?"

"Just a minute, Carl. Let me finish this sentence." She wrote standing up.

"Annie, I've got to put my foot down." Firmly, he closed the book and stacked her papers. "I don't want you working on this day and night. An hour or two a day is enough."

"Now, you let me be, Carl. Some people do crossword puzzles. I do books."

"That's fine. But you don't have to go at it as if it was your last day on earth. You have your whole life ahead of you to, as you say, do books."

She got two pork chops from the icebox, dusted them with salt and pepper and put them in the pan before she answered. "Ah, no, Carl. You're the one has your life ahead of you. The life you'll have as a lawyer. It will be a new life—different from the one now. But my life is fixed. It will be home, children . . . a book to read once in a while . . . Do you want coffee or ice tea?"

"Iced tea will be fine."

"Good!" She put the kettle on the little gas plate. He put her book on the stacked papers. "What are you going to do with my things?"

"Why, I'm just clearing the table for supper, sweetheart."

"All right. It'll be ready in five minutes."

"Could you hold it back a little, Annie? It's ten to seven and I better get over there to punch the clocks."

"Okay."

"I'll be back in fifteen minutes."

He came back and they sat down to supper. Annie resumed talking as though he hadn't been away. "Yes, you'll get to know hundreds of different kinds of people through your work. I'll always know the same kind. Like the people where I'll buy groceries, like Henry and Goldie, and people like the florist . . ."

"*Especially* the florist," he said teasingly.

She paused to think of the florist. Yes, she liked him—she often had wondered why. Now it came to her why.

He has a dream, she thought. And what's a dream? A kind of promise that will never be fulfilled. Anthony, the florist, had it. She had it. Carl didn't have it.

But, yes, in a way he had it. He had ambition. I suppose you could call that a dream, she thought. A practical dream. He can and will make that come true.

"Yes," she said, "you'll have a new and different life. Like you'll join a country club and play golf . . ." He laughed. "Oh, yes, you will, Carl. You'll be part of something—belong to something. But me? I'll never belong to things like a country club. I'll never be easy among the kind of people who do. I'll never fit in."

"Why, Annie, you'd be the most popular girl in the club."

"No, Carl. For one thing, I never went to college. That puts me to one side right away. I'll just never fit in with the people you will get to know as a lawyer." She put her hand on his arm. "Ah, Carl, let me be, then. Let me read and let me write down things."

"I'm afraid you'll read and write me right out of your life." He said it lightly. "You'll get to be a famous author . . ."

She shook her head. "No, Carl. Nothing will ever come of **my** writing. I'll never write a great book like, say, *War and Peace*. And I know I never will. But I like to dream that I might. It keeps me excited."

They ate in silence.

She's slipping away from me, he thought. It used to worry me —the way she had of disappearing on a street; slipping quietly out of a room. But this is worse. In her thoughts she goes away from me . . . leaves me . . .

"Talk to me, Annie."

"What about, Carl?"

"Anything. Don't shut me out."

"Let me see. Oh, yes! I know something to talk about. Soon I'll be nineteen. Can you believe it?"

"You're growing up."

"Oh, I've always been grown up. I never had that time when a person changes from a child to a grownup. And I guess I'm still waiting for it. I guess that's why I say dopey things now and then. Now you say something."

"Soon we'll be married a whole year. Think of that!"

"Funny," she said, "but I feel that we've always been married. I don't mean it in the wrong way, Carl. It's just that I can hardly remember how it was *not* to be married to you. Like the baby. It seems there never was a time when I *wasn't* carrying her. It will feel funny when she's on the outside."

"I love you, Annie," he said.

"I love you, Carl."

He looked up at the clock, finished his tea and stood up with a sigh. "Well, back to the salt mines. See you at eleven, sweetheart."

"I'll be waiting for you."

He paused at the door and said, "Annie?"

"What is it, Carl?"

"Oh, nothing, I guess."

"Tell me."

* 238

"You'll laugh."

"Stop teasing and tell me. I want to know."

"If you must know, I have no intention of ever joining a country club. And I *don't* like golf."

She waited. She knew he was offering her a promise in exchange for a promise from her. But what promise? What did he want from her? She led him on, saying:

"Oh, I don't think I'd mind. Just so you wouldn't overdo it."

"Exactly!" he said. "I don't mind if you lose yourself in a book or a story you're writing. But don't overdo it."

She smiled, remembering how once her little brother Tommy had tried to exchange promises with her:

"Play marbles with me, Annie?"

"I'm reading."

"I'll give you the B.B. gun I might maybe get for Christmas if you play with me."

"Play with Freddy. Why me?"

"Because you don't ever play with me no more. You always read by yourself."

That was it. Carl was lonesome the way Tommy had been lonesome. On an impulse, she said, "Carl, is it all right if I go to the factory with you tonight?"

His face lit up. That's it, she thought. He's lonesome.

"Why? Are you afraid alone here nights?"

"Not with Jello."

"Lonesome, then?"

"Just lonesome for you, Carl. Married people should always be together nights."

"It won't be much fun for you sitting in that dismal office all night."

"Yes, it will. We'll be together and we can just sit and talk. Soon there won't be much time for that, you know."

"You have no idea how long the nights are, Annie. How time drags over there."

"I'll get my coat."

As he helped her on with her coat, she said, "Carl, if it bothers you, I won't read so much any more. And I'll give up trying to write. Nothing will come of it anyhow. And, after all, you come first. You and the baby."

She means well, he thought. But she'd never give it up. She couldn't! Why, if she were capable of giving that up, she'd be capable of giving me up. She seems so simple, he thought. And she's so outspoken in her ways, and, yes, she's even childish sometimes. But there's a rod of steel in her somewhere.

She waited, praying, Please, God, make him say no! Please!

Carl said nothing. He's thinking it over, she thought. She said, "It's near the hour to check. We better go." She looked around the room. "Carl, if I let the dishes stand until morning, do you think I'll get mice?"

"No, you won't get mice, you dope." He smiled.

"I'm all ready to go, then."

"Annie?" He paused a second. "Take your book along. And your papers."

She clasped her hands in ecstasy and looked up at him. "You mean it, Carl? Honest?"

"Why, sure! I might want to catch a little sleep toward morning. Between checkups. And I wouldn't feel like such a pig if I knew you had something to do while I slept."

Chapter Twenty

"Do you think you'll lose your job, then?" she asked anxiously.

"That depends on whether Pulaski checks my rounds. If he doesn't, okay. If he does, I might or might not lose the job. It depends."

"But didn't the clock go off at two?"

"I didn't hear it. I was sound asleep. After all, Annie, I had only five hours' sleep in twenty-four hours. Went on that all-night job after putting in six hours painting those damned bleachers."

"Oh, Carl! You *can't* lose that job with the baby due any day, now."

"I know! I *know!*" The line between his eyes deepened. He pushed his coffee cup aside, got up and started to pace. From old habit, he searched his pockets for his cigarette pack. Naturally, he didn't find it. It had been weeks since he'd had a pack in his pocket.

"God *damn* it!" he said.

She got his stubbed clay pipe from the mantelpiece, filled it with tobacco, and handed it to him. He looked at it, looked at Annie, and threw the pipe across the room. It hit the stove and shattered.

She knew better than to say anything. But she thought, How will he manage when school starts? He'll have to go direct to delivering papers when he gets out of the factory. Then classes. When *will* he get any sleep?

As if answering her thought, he said, "I'll have to switch around. Do the painting in the morning and sleep in the afternoon. Might as well get used to it. That's how it will be when classes start next week. Get out of factory, deliver papers. Then go to classes. Sleep afternoon, go to factory. Leave factory in morning, deliver papers, and so on and so on."

"I won't see much of you, then."

"That's the way it's got to be," he said grimly.

"Maybe we can get together weekends." She said it as a joke but he didn't take it that way.

"You don't need to be so damn sarcastic about it," he said.

"I'm not, Carl. It's just that I'll miss you."

"I doubt it. You'll have the baby and . . ." He paused.

"And what, Carl?"

"Nothing."

"You were going to say, 'And you have your books and your writing,' weren't you?"

"Oh, Annie, why do you take everything I say—even things I don't say—so seriously?"

"Because you're a serious person."

"I'm a tired person." He put his head down on his arms and closed his eyes.

"What are we fighting about, Carl?"

He gave her no answer.

I'm tired, too, she thought. I've been carrying the baby *so* long. And you're so heavy, baby—so big. I can't see my feet when I look down. You hide them from me. And I can't get stockings on because you won't let me bend over. You've got to come soon, baby. Soon.

She put her hand on Carl's bowed head. He didn't move. He was sound asleep. "Sleep, Carl, my darling," she whispered. The baby turned inside her. "I know," she whispered. "Maybe it's hard on you, too. But it's only for a day or two more. Then you'll be here."

She closed the bedroom door behind her as she went in to make up the bed. She stepped out of her shoes so there'd be no sound to awaken Carl from his brief sleep. It took her quite a time to smooth out the sheets and pull up the blanket. She went from one side of the bed to the other, back and forth, until the bed was made. She felt like lying down to rest but decided not to because it would be too hard to raise herself up again. So she sat on the edge of the bed to catch her breath.

When she had rested she stood up and groped for her shoes with her feet. She got a foot into one of the shoes, but in doing so accidentally pushed the other shoe under the bed. Unable to bend over, she got down on her knees, and, torso upright, tried to fish out the shoe but couldn't quite reach it. With a sigh she got flat on her back and inched her way under the bed. Like swimming on my back, she thought. Only there's no water. She got the shoe and pushed it out. She noticed a crumpled cigarette pack wedged behind one of the bed legs. She "swam" to it, pulled the wadded pack apart and found one forgotten cigarette!

"Carl!" she called out. "I found a cigarette for you. Come and get it! And get me, too!"

She waited. No answer. Inch by inch she backed out from under the bed, got her feet into her shoes, and went to the kitchen. Carl was gone. Through the window she saw him on the top row of the bleachers. Putting the cigarette in her apron pocket, she went out to the field.

"Hello, up there!" she called.

"Hey!" he called back. "Does your mother know you're out?" He put the paintbrush on top of the can and came down to her.

That's one nice thing about him, she thought. He never stays mad long.

"You never told me when you left," she said.

"I thought you were sleeping."

"And I thought *you* were, Carl."

"What do you think of my paint job?"

"It looks grand! You nearly done?"

"Just about. Say! Quite a view from up there—Lopin, the campus, town. . . . You ought to see it, Annie."

"Wish I could. But I couldn't get up there—the way I'm so heavy in front."

"I could get behind you and sort of boost you up." She shook her head. "Let's give it a try anyhow."

They started up the other end where the paint was dry. He got behind her and held her elbows and pushed. He leaned forward, she leaned backward shifting most of her weight on him. With each upward step, she leaned back more. He told her to take it a little easy—he was having trouble keeping his balance.

"First thing you know I'll be flat on my back and you on top of me—you and the kid."

This got her to giggling so hard that they had to sit down for a few minutes. Finally they got to the top. She looked around and clasped her hands together the way she always did when something pleased her.

"Oh, it's beautiful, Carl!"

Lopin looked like a toy village with its buildings set symmetrically apart—flower or vegetable gardens back of each home and trees like sentinels along the edges of the dirt sidewalks.

She looked the other way and there was the campus with its high flat-roofed buildings; the winding slate paths and low bunched trees. The library stood out with its stately Greek pillars. And the campanile! Up! Up! Up! As though it wanted to mingle with a cloud.

"Beautiful! Oh, beautiful! Just think, Carl. It was here all the time and I didn't know it. You know, if someone charged a dollar to see all this, I would be glad to pay a dollar—if I had a dollar."

"But it's all free, my girl." He stretched out his legs and from old habit delved into his pocket for a cigarette.

"Oh, Carl! What is the matter with me? I forgot all about it."
She took the cigarette from her apron pocket and gave it to him.

"No!" he said. "A real live cigarette!" It was a little bent, to be sure, and he carefully straightened it. "Where did you get it?"

"It was under the bed all the time. Lucky I'm a sloppy house-wife or I would have swept it out long ago." He took a matchbook from his pocket. "Here! Let me light it for you, Carl. That will make it seem more like an occasion. There!"

He took a long pull and blew out the smoke almost voluptu-ously. "It's been a long, long time!"

"You've been a good boy holding out so long even if you were cranky at times. And the minute the principal pays you for painting this . . . this . . . balcony, you go buy a pack of cigarettes right away."

"As long as I did without cigarettes so far . . ."

"Oh, be a little weak instead of so strong all the time. Go ahead, treat yourself to a fault once in a while."

"But money . . ."

"How much do you think he'll give you for this job?"

"Not much. A dollar, maybe."

"That all?" Her disappointment was obvious but she shrugged philosophically and said, "Oh, well, it's better than a kick in the pants."

"You mean I have a choice?"

It was an old gag between them but they laughed as though it was brand new.

The campanile, mute all summer, now tolled out the hour.

"Happy New Year, Carl!" She held up an imaginary glass. "A toast! Click with me, Carl." A little sheepishly, he held up an imaginary glass and aimed it at hers. She made a clicking sound with her tongue. "To your last college year!" She pretended to drain champagne. A little ill at ease, he lowered his arm. "Why'n't you drink with me?"

"Because . . ." He was about to say, Because it's silly, but he

245   *

thought that might hurt her feelings. He said, "Because I'm a teetotaler."

"You're that, all right," she said fervently. "Whatever *that* means."

Before he sat down to lunch Carl phoned the principal to announce that the painting job was finished. As soon as the receiver clicked back into place, Annie, all excited, asked:

"What did he say?"

"Good!"

"That's all?"

"That's all. *Good!*"

"Nothing about money?"

"*Nothing* about money."

"Well, we might as well eat then," she said, disappointed.

As soon as the dishes had been done and Carl was asleep, Annie arranged her book, pad and pencil on the kitchen table, anticipating an exciting afternoon with *War and Peace*. But the principal came by. He wanted to see Carl. Annie told him Carl was sleeping and that she didn't like to wake him up unless it was important. The principal allowed it was important but it would keep and would she give this to Carl when he woke up? He gave her a folded slip of paper and left. The second the door closed after him, she unfolded the paper.

It was a check for five dollars!

She ran into the bedroom. "Wake up, Carl! Wake up!" He groaned and turned over on the other side. "Wake up!" She shook him roughly.

"Wha's a matter?" he asked groggily.

"Something wonderful! So wonderful! Wake up, Carl! Oh, I can hardly stand it!"

He was awake in a flash. He all but fell out of bed. "It's all right, Annie. All right!" He staggered around the room. "What did you do with my pants?"

"Never mind your pants. I'm so excited . . ."

"Take it easy, Annie. Everything will be all right. I'll call Coach Stevens right away. We'll get you to the hospital in ten minutes."

"What hospital? Oh!" She laughed. "Oh, the baby's not coming yet."

"What?" He sat on the bed, one leg in his pants. "You mean . . . ?"

"Oh, it's just a little surprise."

"Cry-sake, Annie! What do you mean waking me up out of a sound sleep and scaring hell out of me for nothing?"

"Nothing? Nothing, he says. Just take a look at *this*." She gave him the check.

He gave a whistle of surprise. "Five dollars! What do you know!"

"It's like . . . *you* know. When apples fall off a tree and people can have them for nothing?"

"Windfall?"

"Windfall! This check is a windfall." She liked the word and said it again. "Windfall."

"Sure is," he agreed.

"Let's waste the windfall!"

"But why?"

"Because I never wasted money in all my life, Carl, and I'd like to know how it feels."

"What would you like to waste it on?"

"A whole carton of cigarettes for you. Those Avalon ones. Save a nickel buying them that way and we'll have more money to waste."

"How else do you want to waste it?"

"A haircut for me. My hair don't bounce no more. I mean *any* more."

247 *

"What else?"

"Let's see: eighty-five for cigarettes, fifty for haircut. One-thirty-five. No. One-forty with nickel tip. Leaves three dollars and sixty cents. Now what else? Oh! The carriage!"

"What carriage?"

"Oh, I told you, Carl." He shook his head. "About how it could be a crib for the first month or so?"

"You never told me."

"Well, anyhow, the junk man wanted three dollars for it. Imagine! So, I just—you know—happened to mention this in conversation with Miss Aggie. And it just happened that she's related to this here junk man. So she spoke to him and now he will let me have it for two-fifty."

"My!" said Carl in mock admiration. "How wonderful! If it only had wheels!"

"Now you stop it, Carl. It's in perfect condition. Only all the paint's peeled off."

"Well, you buy it, I'll paint it."

"But paint's dear, isn't it?"

"It's quite inexpensive. There's a half can of bleacher paint left over."

"Honest?" She was delighted.

"Not quite. It belongs to the high school."

Her face fell. "We can't use it then. For a minute I thought it was another windfall."

"We'll have to do it quick—before the principal comes and takes it and the brush away," he said.

"No! I made up my mind. We can't take it because that would be stealing."

"What about the high school coal you swiped last winter, Annie?"

"That was different. The house was icy and we were out of coal. And I only did it once. And I did not take it from a person. That *would* be stealing. It was the high school's coal and the high school is not a person."

"The high school owns the paint, too, Annie."

"That's right! So if we used just a little bit, it wouldn't be stealing, would it?"

"No comment."

"Then we'll use it."

"That's what I said to start with, Annie. I don't know why we had to thrash it out."

They went to town the following morning to cash the check. The streets were crowded with freshmen who were buying tin wastebaskets, desk blotters, ashtrays, pennants, and other items that would make a dormitory room a home. It was Thursday and classes didn't begin until Monday, but the freshmen had to come a week ahead of time to register and get oriented. They were children just out of high school and on their own for the first time. In nine months they'd be adults. It was like the birth cycle: conceived by the university as children, and at termination of pregnancy reborn as young men and women.

They wore little skullcaps with the university letters in blue and white—the college colors.

"Did you ever see so many pee-wee hats, Carl?"

"They're beanies."

"They call them pee-wees in Brooklyn."

"But I'm not in Brooklyn."

"But you're still a Brooklynite."

"I wouldn't want that to get around, Annie."

"You don't mean that, Carl."

"Ah, we might as well call them beanies, Annie."

"Why?"

"When in Rome do as the Romans do."

"Do they call them beanies in Rome?" she asked artlessly.

"This is the silliest conversation . . ."

"It's not a conversation, Carl. It's what they call banter. We are bantering."

"Good night! Where'd you get that word?"

249   *

"Wouldn't you like to know!"

"And wouldn't you like to tell me!"

"It's when people . . ."

"Never mind. Here's the barbershop. Go in and get your hair bounced and banter with the barber. He's good at it. Seriously, Annie, we ought to get home as soon as possible and get that carriage painted before the principal comes for the paint and brush."

"All right. And you go get your carton of Avalons."

"I'll just get a pack."

"A carton. Hear?"

"I'll get Wings. They're longer."

"But skinnier. Same amount of tobacco. But you get what you want, Carl."

"Gee, thanks!" he said, pretending servile gratitude.

"Any time!" she said grandly.

They had to pass the florist shop on the way home. Again there was bittersweet in the window as there had been the year before.

"Bittersweet! Let's go in and get a bunch."

"We haven't time, Annie."

They had time but he didn't want her in there jabbering with the man. He had never met the florist but had a distaste for him because Annie seemed to admire him so much.

Annie thought it was a question of money. "But it's only a dime, Carl, and what's a dime?"

"The price of a large loaf of bread, for instance."

"But a person can't live on bread alone. He should buy hyacinths to feed his soul. I read that somewhere. They don't have hyacinths in the window but I like bittersweet better."

"Some other time, Annie. Let's go."

Just then the florist saw them through the window and waved at Annie, who naturally waved back.

"We've got to go in now because he saw us and it will look funny if we don't go in," she said.

"Okay. But don't get started on a talking jag."

The florist shook her hand and said, "Why, Annie! What a delightful surprise! I thought I'd never see you again."

"How have you been, Anthony?"

So, thought Carl, it's Annie and Anthony now.

"Oh, so-so," said the florist. "And you?"

"Just fine! I'd like you to meet my husband." She turned to Carl. "Carl, this is Anthony Byrd. You heard me speak of him?"

And how! thought Carl.

"A pleasure, I'm sure." The florist gave Carl a limp hand to shake.

What the hell does she see in that weak sister? thought Carl.

"Anthony, those seeds you gave me last spring?"

"Nasturtium, I believe?"

"Yes. Well, they came up. And one plant had a round leaf that was as big as my hand." Wishing to get Carl into the conversation, she said, "Wasn't it, Carl?"

"Wasn't what?" said Carl.

"Oh, never mind."

So, thought Annie. He can't stand the sight of the man. I'd better watch my step.

"Bittersweet time again," said the florist.

"Yes. Carl and I saw them in the window. Didn't we, Carl?"

Instead of answering, Carl walked to the other end of the shop and stared at some garden tools hanging on the wall. Annie noticed that the florist flushed.

"You must have been up in the north country, then," she said.

"Indeed, yes."

"And how did you find it?"

Carl almost said: He looked around and there it was. But he controlled himself.

"I found that the jack pines are taking over, but the wounds heal slowly . . . slowly."

God, thought Carl, what a lot of eyewash! Aloud he said, "I don't want to interrupt, but we've got to get on home." He spoke directly to the florist. "We happen to have a lot of things to do, you know," he said coldly.

"I see," said the florist. The flush deepened in his cheeks.

Carl, how could you? wailed Annie inwardly. Can't you see that he's sensitive—like a woman is sensitive?

"Let's go, Annie." Carl went to the door.

"I'm sorry, but we do have to go, Anthony."

"Wait!" He wanted to hold her attention a little longer. He thought of their common interest—writing. "I started writing my book, Annie."

"Honest, Anthony? Honest?"

"A moment, please." He got a big ledger from under the counter, opened it and read:

This was the forest primeval. But no more do the murmuring pines and the hemlock . . .

Carl couldn't take any more. "Annie! *Do* you or *don't* you want that baby carriage painted?"

Annie saw all the color drain out of the florist's face. "Oh, Carl!" she said pleadingly.

The florist took over. With great dignity, he said, "I won't keep you any longer. Thank you for dropping by. Both of you."

He put the opened ledger down on the counter and Annie saw that the page was blank. She knew then he had ad-libbed the beginning of a book. Her eyes filled with tears. He noticed and turned his head away.

"You have a fine beginning, Anthony," she said. "You keep it up, now."

"I will."

"Promise?"

"On my honor!"

"And you'll keep that title: *The Rape of the Forest?*"

"*Indeed,* I shall."

Cry-sake! thought Carl. He left.

"Good-by, Anthony."

"Good-by, Annie."

In the middle of the block Carl stopped and waited for Annie. By now he had cooled off and he was ashamed of himself for being so churlish. He walked back to her. I'll let her give me hell, he thought, and I'll take it and won't argue back. It'll do her good to take me apart and put me together again.

"Annie . . ." He was about to say how ashamed he was but she didn't give him a chance.

"You ought to be ashamed of yourself," she said.

"All right! I am. Now, can we drop it?"

"No."

"Do you want me to get down on my knees?"

"You walk on ahead. I want to be by myself."

He cradled her arm in his and put his hand over hers. Furiously she pulled her arm away. He took her arm again and pressed it close to his side, so she couldn't withdraw it.

"Let me go!"

"Let me hold on to you, sweetheart. It will make walking easier for you." She stopped struggling but made her arm rigid.

He waited for her to lash out at him and get it all out of her system before they got home. But she said nothing. After two blocks of silence, he forced the issue.

"Listen, Annie. It's not that I'm jealous . . ."

"Thanks for the compliment," she said bitterly.

"All right, then. I am."

"Why?"

"Well, he's a man." He paused. "Isn't he?"

(She didn't like the way he said, "Isn't he?")

"Of *course* he is. But that doesn't mean I want to sleep with

253   *

him. And imagine him *wanting* to—the ugly way I look!"

"But you seemed to know each other so well."

"I *like* him."

"Why?"

"Because I understand him. And I understand him because he's like me. About wanting to write, I mean. And other things. Men . . . manly men like you don't like him because he's a little bit womanish and women don't like him for the same reason. He has no wife, no children. I judge that he's very lonesome."

"Therefore, you are obligated to be all in all to him."

"Oh, stop it, Carl." Her arm in his relaxed a little, but instead of drawing it out she hugged his arm and entwined her fingers with his. "Maybe *like* is the wrong word for the way I feel about him. It's compassion I feel. That's what." She smiled, recalling the way she had spelled it *come passion* the time she wrote the paper on *Babbitt*. "Yes, I have *compassion* for him."

"I just don't get it," he mumbled.

They walked another block before he broke the silence.

"So you like him because you can look down in pity on him. Just like a woman."

"No, no! Compassion is not pity or feeling sorry for a person or overlooking bad things he does. Compassion means knowing how it *is* with people—like you can understand a person without liking him. I know what I mean but I don't have the right words to say it in."

"You could have said it all in one word: tolerance."

She frowned. "But I don't like that word 'tolerance.' It's a looking-down-on-a-person sort of word." She paused and looked at him suspiciously. "All in one word! Why are you making fun of me?"

"I'm not. I thought I was helping you. You asked me to correct your mistakes, you know."

"But I wasn't *making* mistakes."

"Oh, Annie, let's cut it out. I could say I was sorry for everything but you wouldn't take that. You'd say something like: 'Sorry: A word that's as handy as an eraser on a pencil.'"

"Well, isn't it?"

"I give up! I admit I acted like a dope—and made too much out of the damned episode or whatever you want to call it. And you didn't get your bittersweet. All right! I'll drop in tomorrow, get your bittersweet, and talk to him the way I'd talk to any other man. How's that?"

"No, Carl. It's better to hate him than to patronize him."

"But your bittersweet . . . ?"

"I don't want it. I don't like it any more."

Another long silence. Finally he said, "Am I walking too fast for you?"

"No."

"Ah, cheer up, Annie. That baby will be along soon and he wouldn't want to meet a sad mother."

"The baby, yes. I guess God don't like me. For everything I get, He takes something away."

They stopped before a drugstore that had a soda fountain. He put his arm around her waist and mopped up the tears on her face.

"Take your arm away, Carl. People are looking at us."

"What do we care? Remember when you kissed me on Forty-second Street right in the middle of a great big crowd?"

"That was a hundred years ago!"

He had an idea. "Look! How'd you like to go in here and waste some money on an old-time banana split?"

"Oh, I'd love to. Haven't had one of those since last Christmas."

She ordered a banana split and to her astonishment, he ordered the same. "Why, Carl, I'm surprised! I thought you hated banana splits."

"I do."

"Then why . . ."

"Penance. Mortify the flesh . . . eat crow. Something like that."

"You don't *have* to, Carl. Change the order before the boy makes it up."

He ordered a Coke instead. He watched her eating the banana split. She seemed very slow about it and made no ecstatic comment.

"Good?" he asked.

She put her spoon down. "Funny," she said, "I don't seem to like it any more. Can it be that I'm growing old? Old people don't like . . ."

"Nonsense! You're all worked up about your little lecture on compassion." He picked up the spoon and put it back into her hand.

Compassion, she thought. Easy to say it means you know how it is with a person even if you don't like him. Does it work? In books, yes! Maybe. But in real life? Carl's mother: I don't like her but I know how it is with her. Like me, she carried a baby. Had the same dreams. . . . Yes, for her I have compassion. And for my mother too. And for Bev Karter. But what about my stepfather? I know how it is with him. He's a pig. That's how it is with him. And I have no compassion for a pig. So the way I figured out compassion has a hole in it.

Will it be that as I get older all the things that I'm figuring out now and thinking are so right . . . all . . . all will have holes in them? Is that what getting old means? That you realize what a dope you were when you were young?

"I don't want to get old," she said aloud.

"Who does?" Carl said cheerfully. "And what brought that on?"

She pushed the plate away. "Carl?" she said pleadingly.

"Okay!" he said. "You don't have to eat it if you don't want to." He looked around and caught the soda clerk's eye. "Can we have our check?" he said.

Chapter Twenty-one

The paint was dry on the baby carriage but there were quite a lot of bare spots that hadn't taken the paint. Paint meant for wood didn't stick very well on metal—rusty metal at that. Except for the wheels, which were in fair condition, the carriage was fit for nothing but the junk pile. Annie had described the carriage as a windfall; a windfall at the price of only two dollars and fifty cents. He wondered how she could fool herself that way. She must know better. He took the carriage into the kitchen.

"I can't say much for my paint job," he said, "or for this carriage either."

"It'll do," she said brusquely.

"Back home the kids would pay a quarter for a buggy like this."

"We called them go-carts."

"Go-carts, then. For a quarter. For the wheels. Used to use them for soapbox scooters."

"I *said* it will *do!*" Her voice went high and shrill.

Dreading another quarrel, he tried to soothe her. "It will do just fine. Sure it will. It's just that I wish we had a lot of money and could buy one of those big ones—you know the kind the rich people in the Flatbush section had? What did they call them? They looked like a gondola on wheels?"

"What's a gondola, Carl?"

He relaxed and thought he was pretty smart in diverting the expected quarrel.

"Why, it's a boat that they use on the canals in Italy."

"I know. It has an awning with fringe on. And the boatman wears a straw hat with a ribbon on it and he stands up and rows it with one oar and sings 'O Sole Mio.' "

"That's it!"

"I know the kind of carriage you mean. Perambulator."

"You're right!"

"In England, they call them 'prams' for short."

"Well, this old wagon isn't exactly a pram but, as you say, it will do." Absent-mindedly he kicked one of the wheels. That's all Annie needed to set her off.

"Okay! *Okay!*" she shouted. "So it's *junk!* So I *know* it's junk! So *shut up!*"

"Now, Annie . . . now, sweetheart . . ." he said soothingly. He put his hand on her cheek and she slapped it away.

"Sometimes I make myself believe something is wonderful even if it ain't, because I *want* it to be wonderful. I knew as well as you that the carriage was junk. But I had to believe it was wonderful because it was the only carriage I could get. And you had to go and spoil everything!"

"I didn't mean to, Annie. Honest, I didn't."

"I saw myself on a nice spring day, wheeling the baby in the carriage down the street and people passing by smiling at her in the carriage and maybe somebody would stop and say, 'Oh, what a cute baby!' and I'd say, 'Oh, all babies are cute,' just to keep myself from bragging about her. Did I ask for the moon? No. All I wanted was a run-down carriage for my baby. Was that too God-damned much to ask for?"

She grabbed the carriage's handle bars and with all her

258

strength gave a mighty shove. It careened across the kitchen. As it hit the wall and fell over on its side, she wailed, "I feel like killing the whole world!"

Jello, tail between his legs, crawled under the table and whimpered. Furiously she turned on him.

"And you too! *You* shut up! Nobody's hollering at you."

Carl righted the carriage and picked up a slab of hardened paint which had fallen off it. He turned the slab over and over, looking at it searchingly as though the answer to everything was in that slab.

"Don't just stand there!" she screamed. "Do something!"

"What do you want me to do?"

"Burn it up! Bust it up! Throw it on the trash pile!"

"Now you just take it easy, Annie, or I'll swat you one." He looked her over and added, "Big as you are."

"You wouldn't dare!" she said, absolutely shocked.

"No, I don't believe I would. But the idea makes me feel good."

"Enjoy yourself then!"

She went into the bedroom, slammed the door and locked it.

He wanted to smash the carriage to bits but thought it would be more sensible to bring it back to the junk man and try to get some of the money refunded.

"Annie," he said to the closed door, "are you all right?" He waited. No answer. He rattled the doorknob. "Answer me!" he said sharply.

"I'm all right," she said sullenly. "And don't apologize."

"You bet your life I won't! God damn it! A man has to assert himself once in a while."

"I know, Carl," she said. "That's all right."

He let out a sigh of relief because she sounded like her old self. "Listen, Annie, I'm going out for a while."

"Where?"

"Never mind where. Now! Will you be all right while I'm gone?"

259   *

"I'll be all right. I'll be fine. But don't take too long, Carl."

She stood at the window and watched him stride across the field with the carriage. He did not push it before him as was common procedure. He pulled it behind him. Just like a kid pulling a wagon, thought Annie. She smiled, unlocked the door, and went to the kitchen. Jello, still quivering under the table, gave a doubtful thump of his tail.

"Poor Jello! You can come out now, Jello. The fight's over."

Coach Stevens was raking his lawn. He saw Carl coming down the street, pulling the dilapidated baby carriage. He stopped raking, folded his hands on the top of the rake handle, put his chin down on his folded hands, and waited. When Carl came within hailing distance, he called out:

"What's the big idea? Lose an election bet?"

"Annie bought this from the secondhand store and I'm taking it back."

"How much did he take her for?"

"Two-fifty."

"He sure saw her coming. Why, for two-fifty down, you can get a new one."

"I don't believe in buying on time."

"Time? Oh, you mean installment."

"Back home they say 'on time.' A dollar down and a dollar when they get you. I don't believe in buying anything you can't pay for outright."

"You don't, eh?" The coach placed his rake against a tree before he continued. "I do. How do you think I got my car? Where would I get fifteen hundred dollars for a car? I'm buying it twenty dollars a month. After the down payment, of course."

"It will be old before you get it paid."

"I know that. I look at it this way: I'm *renting* it for twenty dollars a month. Getting my money's worth, too."

"I couldn't see it that way," Carl said. "My mother was always buying things on time. My father's pay was spoken for before he earned it."

"What did she buy?"

"Things like a new cook stove when the old one went on the blink. And . . ." He thought a second. "Well, stuff for me. The best ice skates to be had, tennis racket, track shoes. Even a new outfit, suit, shoes, and overcoat when I left for the university." He thought of the wrist watch and smiled sheepishly. "Mostly things for me, I guess."

"Which you'd have had to do without if it wasn't for the good old installment plan."

"I still don't see it, Steve. Get tied up in time payments and you don't own the money you earn."

"Don't get tied up and you don't own things like—say—a baby carriage."

"You might have something there," said Carl. "But I don't know . . ."

The junk man admired the paint job on the carriage. "Good!" he pronounced. "Like new."

"Glad you think so. You can have it back. You had some nerve charging my wife two-fifty for this hunk of junk. I want my money back now."

Carl girded himself for a long argument. To his surprise, the junk dealer shrugged and gave him a two-dollar bill.

"What about the fifty cents?"

"Charge two days' rent carriage."

"Oh! Well, okay."

The raked leaves had been stacked into a mound and the coach had set fire to it. Now, hands folded on top of the rake, he stared at the flames. Carl joined him. They said nothing to each other. They watched with prehistoric awe and civilized satisfaction the miracle of combustion.

"No wonder kids like to play with matches," said the coach.

"Yeah!" agreed Carl.

They watched until the flames lost their fire and were transformed into billows of curving smoke.

"How'd you make out, Carl?"

"He refunded two dollars."

"Not bad."

"Better than I expected."

"If I were you, Carl, I'd use that two dollars as a down payment on a new carriage."

He didn't have to talk Carl into it. Carl figured that since he was already in debt to his mother, the university, and Annie's doctor, he might as well go the whole hog.

"How do you go about it, Steve?"

"Go to Glick's Furniture Mart. It's on the block behind the dime store. Tell him Steve sent you. He knows me well. But for God's sake, don't let him know you're a student. Students are considered bad credit risks in town. If he wants a reference, give him my name."

Carl went through the formalities of becoming a debtor.

"Name?"

"Carl Brown."

"*E* on end?"

"No *e*."

"Address?"

"Lopin High School Athletic Field."

"Good!" Mr. Glick looked up from the form on which he was writing down Carl's answers. "When you walked in here, I thought you were one of those damned college boys. Now: married?"

"What would I want a baby carriage for if I wasn't?"

"Just a technicality, Mr. Brown. Employment?"

"I'm holding down two jobs at present: caretaker of the field and night watchman at the Pulaski Lamp Shade Factory."

"How about that!" said Mr. Glick admiringly. "Income?"

"What?"

"Pay. Salary. In plain words, how much do you earn?"

"Mr. Glick: All I'm here for is to buy a ten-dollar carriage: two dollars down, a dollar a week. I have the two dollars. If I thought I couldn't scrape together a dollar a week, I wouldn't be here."

"It's just a form . . ." began Mr. Glick when the telephone rang. "Excuse me." He said hello into the mouthpiece and waited.

"Speaking! Who? Oh! How's tricks, Steve?" Pause. "Yeah! He's here." Mr. Glick turned to stare at Carl. "Yeah! Just came in." Pause. "I see . . . I see." Pause. "You bet!" Pause. "Think nothing of it. Glad to do it. Good-by."

Mr. Glick hung up the receiver and went back to the counter and tore up the form. "If Coach Stevens vouches for you, that's plenty good enough for me. Now: which was the carriage you wanted?"

"That ten-dollar one over there."

"Twelve. Two dollars carrying charges."

"Okay. I'll take it."

Mr. Glick pulled it out from the line of carriages. "Want to take it with you?"

Carl had no desire to pull the empty carriage across the campus. "Could you send it out?"

"Sure thing! You'll have it first thing in the morning. And say hello to Coach Stevens for me."

"I'll do that," said Carl.

Annie was a little too ecstatic about the new carriage. She used superlatives—such as "sweet" and "darling"; words she abhorred. She was too glib; her voice was too squeally. She was trying too hard to be enthusiastic.

So she really wanted that junk carriage, he thought. Wanted to take nothing and make something out of it. She doesn't like the new carriage—had no hand in creating it.

". . . no hand in creating it," he said aloud out of his thoughts. "That's it!"

"What's *it?*"

"Oh, nothing, Annie."

"Why did you say it, then?"

"Because I picked up your habit of speaking my thoughts out loud."

No doubt about it. Annie was very hard to live with and she was getting worse every day. Nothing seemed to please her. She complained about being house-bound but refused to go out anywhere except to the store. She begged him to tell her what he'd like for supper. When he said pork chops, she said too much pork wasn't good for a person's system. She challenged just about every remark he made—had him walking on eggs, as it were.

It had started with her pregnancy and the more obvious her pregnancy became the more things displeased her.

She had been against the summer session—couldn't find anything to commend it. She felt that the students came for credits only and not for learning, and Annie would have given her eyeteeth just to *learn* and to hell with credits.

And then that fighting interest in the florist as a potential writer: Why? Did she want to create a writer? As sort of insurance in the event that she herself might fail?

Maybe. She seemed to have given up her own great project of rewriting *War and Peace*. Just because he, Carl, had told her not to overdo it? Because he hadn't encouraged her enough and she was punishing him?

Carl admitted to himself that he wasn't easy to live with either. He worried a lot and worrying made him irritable. And he felt he had a lot to worry about. For instance, he had banked on the baby coming before school started, so he'd be on hand. But now it might start to come when he was in class and she was all alone in the house with nobody . . . He trembled just thinking of it.

And he worried whether he'd be able to hold down three jobs, the field, the factory, and newspaper delivery, and in addition get through his studies and be a helpful husband and father. Away all night and most of the day. The few hours at home had to be given up to study or to sleeping.

When would he and Annie ever have a chance to sleep together again? A few stolen minutes on a Sunday afternoon, providing the baby was asleep? Ten minutes between the eleven- and twelve-o'clock factory checkup?

Things were tough enough now. They had not slept together for two months now, because of Annie's condition. That kept him on edge—made him cranky. Maybe it kept Annie on edge, too. Like him, she had become accustomed to a rhythmical sex life. Now they were no longer lovers; they were two people living in the same house and getting on each other's nerves.

He came out of his reverie. Annie was fussing with the new carriage, making the awning go up and down.

"Twelve dollars it cost," she said petulantly, "and the damn shed won't go up and down."

"It's stiff because it's new. A few drops of oil will fix it up."

He got the oilcan from the clubhouse and knelt down and oiled the joints of the carriage. The awning went up and down like a charm.

"There you are. Try it, sweetheart." She tried it. "Works fine now, doesn't it?"

"I guess so," she admitted grudgingly.

Still kneeling, he looked up at her and said, "Do you miss sleeping with me, sweetheart?"

"Oh, yes, Carl, I do!" She smoothed back his hair in a caressing way. "It's just terrible the way I *do* miss you . . . this sleeping alone after being *so* used to you!"

"Well, it won't be long now." He put his arm around her legs and she leaned against him.

265   *

"I hope not, Carl, but I don't know . . ."

"How soon after the baby is born can we start sleeping together again?"

"Maybe a month? Six weeks?"

"You're sure?"

"Just guessing. I suppose I could ask Goldie, but I don't like—*you* know—to ask when they start up again."

He pressed his cheek against her legs and smiled up at her. "I bet you they're at it an hour after the baby is born."

"Don't talk like that!" she said sharply and jerked away from him. "You know how I hate smutty talk."

The nice moment between them was over. His smile faded. He got up and went out to put the oilcan back on the shelf in the clubhouse.

The next day was Friday. It was the last day Carl could register. Classes started Monday. It was also the day Annie was to have her last appointment with the doctor. They left a little early because Annie wanted to stop by and say hello to Henry, the grocer, and to their former landlady.

"How are you, Annie?" Henry's voice trembled a little.

"I'll tell you tomorrow," she said tearfully.

It was a tearful visit and ended in a tearful parting.

"And you will come to see me when I'm in the hospital?"

"Even if I have to close up the store." He blew his nose very hard. "And you will come to see my squirrels steal nuts?"

Annie choked up, trying to answer, and Carl took over. "She'll come, Henry. I'll mind the baby—even if I have to cut two classes."

Henry thanked them both and they left. Annie borrowed Carl's handkerchief (she never seemed to have one of her own) to wipe her eyes.

"Why, Annie! I thought you and Henry were playing a little game. I didn't think you were taking it seriously."

"I guess you think I'm sentimental and you don't like that. You always say there's no logic in sentimentality."

"But did I say it was a crime?"

"The way Henry looked at me and how his voice was shaky made me cry. Because I got this feeling that we would never see each other again. That's why I cried when he said about coming to see the squirrels. I felt he knew that would never be and that's why I couldn't say I would be there."

"Be sentimental all you want, sweetheart, but try not to be morbid. Nothing's going to happen to you. The Dean told me your doctor was the best in the state."

"I wasn't thinking of me. I was thinking of Henry. He doesn't look so well."

"He's getting older. That's all."

The landlady was glad to see them and insisted they have a quick cup of tea with her.

"And what are you going to name the baby?" she asked Annie.

"Rosie Maria."

"Rosie Maria?"

"Yes. I think it sounds like a string of pretty beads, and Rosie Maria Brown will make a nice monogram for her handkerchiefs. R.M.B. It will look like the initials of a princess."

"You're a funny girl, Annie. What are you going to call him if it's a boy?"

"It won't be a boy. Because I'm a girl."

"Girls *do* have boys, you know." Mrs. Hansmon winked at Carl.

"Only big strong women have boys. Small women have girls."

"Well, I never!"

"No use arguing with her, Mrs. Hansmon," said Carl. "If Annie wants a girl, she'll see to it that she gets a girl." Although the watch wasn't there, he looked at his wrist. "We'd better go. Don't want to be late for our last appointment with Annie's doctor."

"Henry said he'd come to see me at the hospital. Will you come too, Mrs. Hansmon?"

"You just bet I will, Annie."

Carl went to register and Annie sat on a campus bench to wait for him. As she had done a year ago, she noticed with wistful envy the casual air of "belonging" of the old and new students. How she had wanted to be part of it!

That's all over now, she thought. Anyway, I'll have something those coeds don't have. A baby. But then they can have babies, too, after college. They can have both: wonderful college years and a baby too. I can just have one of those things.

It was true Carl had said that after graduation he'd practice over in Herdstone and they could hire someone to stay with the baby while she commuted to the university and took classes as a special student not eligible for a degree. But even if that did work out, and Annie doubted it, it wouldn't be the same.

In a couple of years, she thought, with the baby and all, I might not want to come back. I won't care so much then. It's now. *Now!* I'll never feel again like I felt this year. So excited about learning things—so excited about writing—one inspiration after another. It could never be the same again.

She saw a coed coming toward her. The girl looked familiar. Sylvia! She was back then! And she had rewritten her play and now the book could be published and Annie would have the baby and a published play too. She was suddenly very happy. She stood up to greet the girl who was coming toward her.

But it wasn't Sylvia—just someone who looked like Sylvia from a distance.

Carl came upon a classmate of his, a frat man from the South. His name was Culpepper. Once in a while, Jello had come to class with Culpepper.

"How's your schedule?" he asked Carl.

*   268

"Light. Worked off two classes in summer school."

"Different with me. I flunked two subjects last year. Have to take 'em this year along with the other subjects. I'll never make it and I don't give a damn. Who wants to be a lawyer? Not me."

"How come you took the law course then?"

"My old man wants me to be a lawyer. That's what *he* wanted to be. But I want to be what he *is*—a breeder of race horses. Breeds the best horses in Kentucky."

"Tough on you, all right," said Carl.

Culpepper shrugged and changed the subject. "How's the dog?" he asked.

"What dog?" asked Carl as if he didn't know.

"Our frat dog. Jello."

"Oh, he's around."

"Nice of you folks to take him in during the summer. We'll be around soon to take him off your hands."

"My wife is very much attached to him."

"She can have him back Christmas vacation. See you around."

Carl had another worry on his mind. But then, she'd have the baby and might not care too much about losing the dog.

Carl reported to Miss Kingsten, the Dean's secretary. She was a small, thin, immaculate, middle-aged spinster. She was also a very efficient secretary. Carl filled out the blank she gave him.

"How is the baby, Mr. Brown?"

"Hasn't come yet."

"No? That complicates things, doesn't it? The Dean and I discussed it. He hoped the baby would arrive before classes started. You might be difficult to contact if you're in class when it happens."

"No difficulty. The baby will come at night when my wife can get in touch with me in seconds."

"But supposing it comes in the day?"

"All babies are born at night, aren't they, Miss Kingsten?"

"I wouldn't know," she said. Her face flushed pink.

Why, thought Carl, surprised, she must have been very pretty when she was a girl.

He smiled at her the way he'd smile at any pretty girl. Her pink cheeks deepened to red. She fumbled through some cards on her desk.

"I'd like to make a suggestion. Give Mrs. Brown the phone number here"—she paused to write it on a card—"and have her call me. I have your schedule and will personally go on campus to get you out of class. That is—" the color in her cheeks ebbed and flowed—"if the baby decides to make a daytime debut."

He took the card and smiled at her as if she were a *very* pretty, young girl. "You are very nice," he said.

Impulsively, she looked up and smiled into his eyes. He smiled into *her* eyes. Flustered, she lowered her eyes. She felt she had gone quite too far with a student. And even if he was very handsome, that was no excuse.

"I don't know how to thank you," he said.

"You're doing very well," she said, making her voice cool.

She took his schedule card and went to the filing cabinet. Expertly she riffled through the cards until she came to "B." She put the card, *Brown, Carl,* at the head of the half dozen *Browns* in the file.

Carl knew a dismissal when he saw one. He left.

"All set, sweetheart! I am now a senior." He took her hands to help her get up from the bench. "Ready for your ordeal?"

"What ordeal?"

"Oh, you know. The doctor?"

"Well, why didn't you say doctor, then?"

"Aw, Annie, have a heart. *Please!*"

Dr. Marson examined her and found the fetus had dropped down considerably.

"You can go home now, Annie, and pack your suitcase. That baby's due any day now—in fact any hour. Soon it will be all over." She started to tremble. "Cold?" he asked.

"Not cold. Scared!" she said.

"Oh, come now, Annie. I know you're a brave girl."

"I'm only brave in my mind. Not outside."

"Now you put your mind to being brave outside, too."

"A person like me could wear herself out trying to be brave and get nowhere. It's easier to *be* scared than to *fight* being scared."

"You'll be all right. You have my promise that there is nothing to get scared about."

"If you say so," she said dubiously.

She packed her little red suitcase as soon as they arrived home. She put in a baby blanket, a dozen diapers, and two baby shirts. She added her bridal nightgown and robe. On top of them she placed her comb, brush, tooth powder, toothbrush, talcum powder, face powder, and lipstick.

"I can't get my woolen skirt and sweater in. Will you bring them to me at the hospital, Carl? So I have something to go home in?"

"Sure. But why pack up now?"

"Any day, any hour, the doctor said."

"He didn't say any *minute*."

She fixed a very nice supper for Carl but would eat nothing herself. She said it would interfere with the delivery of the baby. When it came time for him to go to work, she insisted on going with him; insisted on taking her suitcase along, so she could go right to the hospital from the factory. She insisted that Jello go to the factory with them—in case of rats, she explained.

"I might see a rat and the baby might be marked," she said.

271 *

"Cry-sake, Annie!" he exploded. "You don't believe that non-sense, do you?"

"Of course I don't! I'm a civilized person. But it costs nothing to be on the safe side."

After the eleven-o'clock checkup, they went back to the house for coffee and a sandwich. The suitcase went with them. Just before twelve they went back to the factory with the suitcase. When the night was over, both were on the ragged edge. He was afraid to say, It's going to be a nice day for the high school's first football game, fearing it would start a big fight.

They had breakfast—at least he did. She announced she'd have nothing but a cup of weak tea. He talked her into having a slice of toast, saying maybe the baby needed nourishment.

Immediately after breakfast he went to bed. He had to be up at noon on account of the football game. Annie went to bed, too, utterly exhausted after a night of waiting for the baby to be born. He awakened a little before noon. She was still asleep.

He heated what was left of the previous night's lamb stew, scorching it somewhat. He brought a plateful into the bedroom for Annie. She sat up in bed and ate it, saying she felt like a rich person—having stew in bed.

"I guess I burned it a little," he said apprehensively.

"No one would ever notice it. Stew always tastes better warmed over."

It took her less than five minutes to empty her plate. He was so pleased. Happy, too. She was so much like her old self this morning.

"Sure glad you ate it all," he said.

"I was hungry."

He disposed of the plate and fork and sat on the edge of the bed. He took her hand. "How do you feel today, sweetheart?"

"I feel funny. Do you know this baby of mine hasn't moved for hours?"

Sweat broke out under his armpits. The baby's dead then, he thought. Dead inside of her! Good God!

He ran to the phone, lifted the receiver, replaced it. He couldn't call the doctor from home. Annie would know the baby was dead and go into hysterics. He'd phone from the grocery store.

"Is it all right with you, Annie, if I run down to the store for a pack of cigarettes?"

"Go ahead." She noticed his hands were shaky. "You need a cigarette. But don't take too long. If they have oranges, get two."

The doctor was neither at home nor in his office. His wife didn't know where he was but expected him home in an hour. If Carl would leave his phone number . . . Carl said he'd call back in an hour.

Goldie noticed that he had trouble putting the receiver back on the hook. Lopin had a half-smoked cigarette dangling from his lips. She took it from him and put it in Carl's mouth.

"First, take a good drag on this," she said. He did. "Now! Is it Annie?"

"The baby stopped moving! I'm afraid . . ."

"Don't be like that."

"But it must be dead!"

"Dead, my foot! It's ready to pop out, that's all."

"Honest, Goldie? *Honest?*"

"Ain't that right, Lopin?" Her man affirmed her statement with a deep grunt. "See? You got nothing to worry about."

"Gee!" He wiped the sweat off his face with his coat sleeve. "Give me a pack of Avalons, then, and two oranges."

She had to open the pack for him and light his cigarette—he was that nervous. He inhaled deeply, suddenly dropped the cigarette and made for the door.

"Hey! You forgot your oranges!"

"Never mind! I got to get home. She might be having the baby right now." She put the oranges in his pocket.

"Not for a couple of hours or so. The bag of waters has to bust first."

"The bag of what?"

"You'll find out!"

"What must I do?"

"Just wait. That's all. And keep her mind off the baby."

"How can I . . . With what?" Just then Less made an appearance. If anyone, anything, could take Annie's mind off herself, it was Less.

"Could I take Less home with me?"

"Only if you promise not to bring him back." Maybe the child understood what she said and maybe he didn't. But just the same he stamped down hard on her instep. "Ouch! you little bastard!" But she swooped him up and gave him a smacking kiss before she turned him over to Carl.

"Tell Annie he's housebroken now."

Annie was glad to see Less. Jello was anything but glad. He scrambled under the bed. He didn't feel like being a horse that day.

"He's housebroken," said Carl.

"Really? At last?"

To affirm it, Less said, "Pee-pee."

Annie took him to the toilet. He functioned. She came out beaming. "He's housebroken!"

"Ow-bo," said Less.

"What did he say?" Carl asked.

"He said he was housebroken and I say it's high time. He's almost two years old."

"Do!" said Less proudly.

"Well, be that as it is in May . . ." Carl waited for her to smile. She smiled. "I have to get out on the field and collect tickets."

"And you better get out fast. They're beginning to come."

"First game of the season, you know. We'll have a crowd."

"Hope we win. For the coach's sake," she said.

"Yes. Well, if you need me, just holler out the back window. I'll hear you." Jello came out from under the bed, rushed to the back door and gave short barks of happy excitement. "No, Jello, you can't go with me this time." To Annie, "Keep him in the house. The frat boys might come to get him."

"Just let them try!" she said grimly. "Just let them!"

It was a long afternoon. Annie watched the game awhile but soon lost interest. She'd never seen a football game before and had no idea how it was scored and who was winning. Less played "horse" with the dog. Only Less was the horse, and on hands and knees under Jello's belly, he tried to get the dog to mount him.

Soon after the third quarter started, there was a knock on the front door. Annie shooed Less into the bedroom and pushed a reluctant Jello in after him.

"Listen, Less: You stay in here with Jello and *don't open the door!* No matter what! Understand?"

"Pee-pee!" said Less.

"Don't give me that now." She closed the bedroom door and went to the front door.

There were two casually well-dressed frat boys on the steps. "I'm Stacy Culpepper," said the more handsome boy of the two.

Annie savored the name. It must be real, she thought. A person couldn't make up a name like that.

"I have some classes with your husband . . ." He looked at the other boy for verification.

"That's right," said the other boy.

"And," said Stacy, "we've come to get our dog, please, ma'am."

"That's right," said the other boy.

Annie had no chance to mention Humane Society in a mysterious voice. The bedroom door opened and Less trotted out. Jello shot out like a missile from a cannon. He shot past Annie, all but knocking her down, and whined and coughed and barked; ran around in circles and rolled over on his back; leaped in the air. He was that happy to see his old friends again.

"How are you, feller?" said Stacy, rubbing Jello's head.

"Yeah!" seconded the other boy.

"Thanks, ma'am, for taking him in," said Stacy.

The boys left and Jello left with them. He ran in joyous circles around them as they walked. Once he stood on his hind legs and hopped along waving his paws.

"Come back, Jello! Come back!" she cried out.

The dog paused in his wild gyrations to look back at Annie and give her one thump of his tail before he trotted around the corner after his friends.

"You Benedict Arnold!" she shouted and slammed the door. She turned on Less. "And you! You! It's all your fault. Didn't I tell you to stay in there? Why'd you have to come out and let the dog out, too?"

"Pee-pee!" said Less.

"That's just an excuse and you know it."

"Ow-bo," he said proudly.

"Oh, come on then." She took him to the toilet. He really had to go. "You!" she said. "You couldn't be ow-bo last week or next week. No! You had to be housebroken just today!"

Carl had anticipated that she'd cry her eyes out if she lost Jello. But instead of weeping she was fighting mad. She slammed the dishes down when setting the table for supper and banged the pots down on the stove.

"But, Annie! After all, you didn't own Jello."

"I had squatter's rights to him like in real estate law."

"But, Annie! The boys took him in, fed him, petted him. After all, he was a stray . . . had nobody to care for him until he showed up on the campus. Now you wouldn't want him to be disloyal, would you?"

"Yes, I would! Disloyal to everybody in the whole world! But loyal to me!" She poured coffee into the two cups on the table, slammed the pot back on the stove and said, "Eat!"

"Oh! Orange Jello for dessert. With real oranges!"

"Don't say that name in this house!" she shouted.

He tried to divert her. "Well, we won the game today."

"Who cares?"

"The coach cares. His job depends on wins."

"All right! I'm glad then," she said sullenly.

He reached across the table and put his hand on hers. "Let me eat!" she shouted.

"Listen, Annie. Jello just wanted to spend an evening with his friends for old time's sake. He'll come back. You'll see."

"Just let him try to come back! Just let him try! I'll kick him out so *fast* . . ."

Right then there was a scratch on the door accompanied by a tentative bark. Carl and Annie stared at each other. "See?" he said. He got up and opened the door. Jello, tail wagging so hard that it nearly threw him off balance, rushed in, plopped down at Annie's feet and licked her saddle shoe.

"My Jello!" She started to weep. "He came back to me! Oh, you beautiful dog! Here!" She put her plate of supper on the floor for him.

"Don't let him eat out of the plates we use, Annie."

"Just this one time, Carl. To celebrate. I'll wash it good."

She watched the dog wolf down the food. She wiped her eyes with her paper napkin and smiled across at Carl. "I'm awfully glad we won today, darling. *Honest!*"

Jello finished his supper, crawled under the table and went to sleep with his head on Annie's shoe. Annie finished her dessert. It was all she had for supper. Carl insisted she eat his dessert, saying he didn't want it.

"Are you sure, Carl?"

He swore he didn't want it and handed it over to her. "I'm so glad Goldie had fresh oranges." She lifted a full spoonful to her mouth, but it never got there. Her hand started shaking so hard that she was forced to drop the spoon.

"Carl!" she said in a stricken voice.

"Did you swallow a pit?"

"Carl!" her voice went high.

"Tell me, sweetheart."

"I'm all wet and it won't stop coming."

He jumped up, overturning his coffee cup, and ran to the phone. He gave the number and waited for what seemed ages before the coach said, "Hello?"

"Steve?" Before he could say another word, the coach said, "Be right over!" and hung up.

"Steve will be right over with the car," he told her.

"What am I going to wear?" she said. "I'm all wet and I haven't got another dress."

"Just put your coat on over it. No one will see in the car."

He got her winter coat from the closet, helped her on with it.

"Do you hurt, sweetheart?" She shook her head. He was trying to button her coat over her swollen stomach when the coach came. He had left the motor running. Each took one of her arms and walked her to the door.

"I can walk by myself," she said petulantly.

"Don't deny me the privilege of holding your arm, Annie," said the coach gallantly.

She smiled up at him and said, "Hold it tight, then."

"Shame on you, Annie," said Carl. "Flirting with a strange man on your way to the hospital!" They all smiled.

At the door she paused and said, "What about Jello?"

"The hell with Jello!" said Carl. "No, I mean, don't worry about him. He won't go away any more." (The dog was still sleeping under the table.)

About to get in the car, she stopped. "My suitcase! We forgot it!"

Carl ran back to the house. The suitcase seemed unnecessarily heavy. He opened it. *War and Peace,* a thick pad of paper and two pencils lay on top of her toilet articles. He grinned in relief. She expects to come through safely, then, he thought.

They sat in the back seat. He had his arms around her and she leaned against him. She shuddered from time to time.

"You're not afraid, Annie, are you?"

"A little. I've never been in a hospital before."

"It will be over before you know it and tomorrow you'll wake up with a beautiful baby girl."

"You don't care, then, if it's a girl?"

"Not at all. Especially if it's a wonderful girl like my Annie. Can't have too many of that kind around the house."

She took his hand and held it to her cheek. "Oh, Carl, you're so wonderful the way you let me always have what I want. The next baby will be a boy for you. And *that's* a promise."

Chapter Twenty-two

She was big, gusty, and busty and had what were called back in Queen Victoria's time rosy cheeks. Her name was Christina Olson, but she was affectionately known as Nurse Treener. She got Annie out of her wet clothes, sponged her down and dried her. She held up a clean, white, unironed garment which looked like an apron that tied in the back.

"I brought my own nightgown," said Annie.

"Save it for company," said Nurse Treener. "Now jump into this number."

Annie thrust her arms through the armholes and the nurse tied the string. "But my back's all naked," protested Annie.

"The better to spank you, my dear."

"It gives me the creeps. It reminds me of something"—Annie paused to shiver—"that I don't want to talk about."

"It makes things handy for the doctor." She got Annie into bed and covered her with a sheet. "Now I'll leave you."

"Oh, no!" Annie had formed a liking for the nurse the moment she saw her.

"I'm supposed to go off duty at six but Dr. Marson asked me to stay over and get you settled. He thinks you're something special."

"Oh, he's *so* nice."

"Oh, yes. Now the next time you see me, I'll be coming through that door with your baby."

"Honest?"

"So help me!"

Carl came in and Annie introduced him to the nurse. "My husband, Nurse Treener."

"So this is the villain who did it." The nurse smiled at Carl. "No longer than ten minutes, Mr. Brown." To Annie, she said, "I'll send in the night nurse and your doctor is on the way over. Good luck!" She left.

Carl didn't have much of a visit with his wife. He left when a new nurse came in.

She was a spritely little thing. "My name is Tilly Shawn." She touched a little card with her name on it, pinned to her breast. "I'm your night nurse. Any time you need me, press the button and I'll be here in a gypsy."

"Gypsy?" said Annie.

"Jiffy. A little hospital joke. Now I'll take your temp."

She inserted the thermometer and put two fingers on Annie's wrist. Her lips moved in time to the pulse and Annie's lips moved in time to the nurse's lips. She tucked Annie's hand under the sheet, removed the thermometer, frowned at it, shook it down and placed it in a small tumbler on the table.

"Oky-doke!" she said cheerfully and jotted down her findings on the chart attached to the foot of the bed. "Remember now. Press the button if you need me."

"Oh, I will!" said Annie gratefully.

Nurse Shawn left and Annie never saw her again.

A nurse came in carrying a douche bag with a long rubber hose. She was followed by a nurse carrying an agate pan covered with a clean towel.

"Time for our enema," said the first nurse brightly.

281   *

"I don't need one," said Annie, "because I didn't eat any supper because Jello came back." She saw the nurses exchange looks and felt she had to explain. "Jello's my dog, you know."

"Yes, dear," said the douche nurse. "Now turn over on your side."

"I will not!" said Annie emphatically.

The other nurse set her pan down, turned Annie on her side, and held her down during the whole process.

"This is . . . this is . . ." Even in her humiliation Annie searched for the right word. "Indignity! A great indignity!"

"That's right," said one nurse soothingly. The other said: "Doctor's orders."

Carl came in at seven-thirty and announced he was going to stay with her until the baby came.

"What about the factory?"

"The hell with the factory."

"Go back, Carl. No sense both of us going through this. It's enough that I have to."

"I want to be with you, sweetheart."

"I'd rather be by myself. If I let you go through this with me, I'd be sort of punishing you. I wouldn't want you to see. . . . You might never want to sleep with me again."

"Oh, nonsense!"

"Let me have it my way. *Please!* I love you, Carl, but I don't want you to see me in childbirth. So, *please!*"

He left.

A nurse entered with a flurry of skirts. She plumped up Annie's pillow, straightened the sheet, smoothed back a hank of hair hanging over Annie's eye, and said, "Your doctor's here." She was Miss Spirus, who would assist at the baby's delivery.

Dr. Marson came in with two young men in white jackets with stethoscopes in their top pockets. One was tall and good-looking and had a simple name: Robert Moore. It became him. The other intern was a little fellow, slight of body and gaunt of face. His expression was one of worried eagerness and he had the magnificent name of Lazarus Levine.

Annie acknowledged the introductions with a nod for intern Moore and a smile for Lazarus Levine because she liked his name.

Dr. Marson pulled up her eyelids, shone a light in her eyes, listened to her heart through his stethoscope, felt her pulse and took her blood pressure. The doctor then put a rubber guard on his right forefinger and nodded to the nurse. The nurse helped Annie turn over on her side. The rubber finger was inserted. It was over in seconds.

"That's the worst indignity of all," said Annie.

The doctor laughed, put his big hand over her small one and said, "Everything's fine, Annie. The baby's in the correct position . . . it should be a normal birth."

"Oh, I'm so glad, Dr. Marson."

"Nurse Spirus will take good care of you."

It came suddenly—a sharp, warning pain. She clamped her teeth together and waited. The pain vanished as suddenly as it had come.

It left her with a nice drowsy feeling. The beginning of a dream and the beginning of sleep came simultaneously. She was walking through a park . . . or was it the campus? Carl was with her. There was a wind . . . She shivered and opened her eyes. Her sheet was down and her bared legs were cold.

Suddenly she wanted her husband. She wanted to tell him that she had sent him away because she loved him so and that his suffering would double her suffering. She wanted to tell him how afraid she was—that she was the biggest coward . . .

Ah, well, she thought, I'll write it all out someday and let him read it. Then he'll know.

She heard a man's voice outside the door. ". . . see my wife."
And a nurse's voice: "Not now. She's resting."

The voice sounded like Carl's. She called out his name and
waited. She heard footsteps recede down the corridor.

Intern Levine came in, followed by Miss Spirus. "How are you
coming, Mrs. Brown?" he said.

"Oh, I'm fine, Dr. Levine."

He went to the foot of the bed to check the chart. The nurse
pulled the sheet down and told Annie to turn on her side. Annie
said, "Oh, no! Not again!"

"It won't be necessary, nurse," said the intern.

"Then what are you here for?" asked the nurse bluntly.

"I'd like to have a talk with the patient."

"Go ahead." The nurse went to the window, leaned against
the ledge, and folded her arms.

"I'll let you know when I've finished," he said, and added,
"Thank you." It was a dismissal.

He pulled a chair closer to the bed, sat down, and started a
question-and-answer conversation as if they were two people
meeting for the first time at a cocktail party.

"I hear you're from Brooklyn, Mrs. Brown."

"*Flatbush* Brooklyn."

"I have never been there."

"A lot of people have never *been* there. But a lot of people *are*
there."

"It sounds like an interesting place."

"Oh, it is. That's where Ebbets Field is, you know."

"So I've heard."

After some more getting-acquainted talk, he said, like a polite
guest at a cocktail party, "Can I get you something, Mrs. Brown?"

"Like what?" That was the end of the cocktail mood.

"Like a glass of cool water?"

"Not like a sandwich? I'm awfully hungry."

"I'm afraid not. It's best to go to the delivery room on an empty stomach."

"It's better to go on a stretcher."

It was a testing remark. If he laughed, or even smiled, she knew they'd be friends.

He smiled. "I agree with you, Mrs. Brown. Nothing like a stretcher."

"Call me Annie."

"Only on condition that you call me Lazarus."

"I will. But only when we're alone—not when the nurse is here."

"It's a deal."

"I guess I'm keeping you from your supper," she said.

"Oh, I ate."

"But I *didn't*."

"And you're hungry. Well, maybe this will tide you over." He took a stick of gum from his pocket and removed the wrapper.

"Oh, thanks!" She paused and a little awkwardly added, "Lazarus." She took a chew. "Umm! Spearmint! My favorite." Chewing contentedly, she said, "Did you know there's a big building in Chicago named after this gum?"

"I know. I came from there. And I'm going to practice there when I finish interning—in the tenement district where I was brought up."

"You won't make much money."

"No. But I'll have a big practice. Poor people have lots of children, you know."

"How well I know! In my neighborhood . . ."

Sweat broke out on her forehead. She bared her clenched teeth and made an animal-like sound. He took her hand and held it tight.

"Don't fight it, Annie. Yell if you want to."

It was over in seconds. He jotted the time down on the chart, went back to her, and wiped her face with a clean handkerchief from his pocket.

"Well, we're on our way, Annie."

The next time Carl went back to the hospital, the desk nurse said, "Mrs. Brown is in the delivery room." She smiled.

Carl turned pale. "In the delivery room?"

"Now, Mr. Brown, there is nothing to worry about. She's in good hands. Would you like to wait in your wife's room? It will only be an hour or two."

"I'll do that," he said gratefully.

"Room four-o-five."

"I know," he said.

The narrow bed was made up, the covers turned down as if waiting for Annie. Her special scent was in the room, emanating from her opened suitcase. It was as though she had left for a few minutes and would soon return. He saw the writing on her pad, picked it up and read it.

I do not like this hospital gown. It doesn't even come down to my knees and it leaves me naked in the back. It reminds me too much of when I was a kid.

There was this undertaker store. There was this shroud in the window. It was a tuxedo, pants and coat in one piece, just the front part of a collar and a real black bow tie and a fake handkerchief in a fake pocket.

But it had no back—just string to tie it around the neck and waist and feet. The dead man would have to lie in the casket with his bare back on the puffed-up silk.

Us kids stood around and made fun of it and one boy said that he felt sorry for the stiff that had to wear that—that he would sure freeze his backside off on the way to heaven. And we all laughed.

That was a terrible thing to do. To laugh. Why did we laugh? I didn't know it then but I know it now. We laughed because we were afraid of death and didn't want each other to know it.

That's why I don't like this gown. It reminds me.

* 286

Carl smiled as he read and was comforted. Annie is still Annie, he thought.

He rested awhile, then went back to the factory.

It was nearing the fifth hour of her labor. Annie had been screaming for an hour. Nurse Spirus had called in another nurse to help her—Annie tried from time to time to throw herself off the table. The nurse was named Maida. She kept urging Annie not to scream so much—it was wasting her strength.

Between screams Annie moaned, "Why must I suffer like this? What did I do that was bad? I love my husband—I wanted this baby . . . Why, why, why?"

"It's God's will, my dear," said Maida.

"You mean He looks down and sees the little sparrow fall and don't see me?"

Suddenly Annie was surrounded by people. The doctor and the two interns were there in white gowns, masks, and rubber gloves. The nurses also wore white gowns, masks, and rubber gloves. Annie thought she heard the doctor say . . . got to take it. She heard the rustle of a starched apron. She knew someone was standing behind her. Annie saw the nurse wheeling a tray of instruments toward her.

"No! No!" she screamed. "Don't!" She raised herself up and tried to get off the table. Intern Moore held her down.

"Listen, Annie," said Dr. Marson. "Listen to me. You are very tired. We have to help you."

"Don't cut me open," she whimpered. "You'll crush her head."

"Now . . . now," he said soothingly, "we're going to put you to sleep for a little while. When you wake up you'll have your baby."

"Let me try once more! I beg . . . I beg . . ."

The doctor sighed. "All right. Grab her hands, Laz."

287   *

The little intern had to lean far over the table to grasp her hands. He held them tight. She bore down.

Nothing happened!

The doctor held out his gloved hand. The nurse placed a scalpel in it. Someone behind Annie placed a light, stiff, concave thing over her face. A strange voice said: "Count up to ten please. Very slowly."

Annie knocked off the thing with her arm and screamed in a high, thin voice. "One more time! It's coming . . . coming . . ."

She took a deep shuddering breath and from some unknown source the strength of a giant came to her and she bore down once more.

She felt that all her bones had torn apart. She heard someone say, "Good God!" She heard Intern Levine say in a voice of high triumph, "No tears!" She thought she heard the doctor say, "Here. Take the baby, nurse." Then everything went black.

Dr. Marson was slapping her face. "Wake up, Annie! Wake up!" She opened her eyes. "Bear down once more, Annie."

"Twins?" she said wearily.

He laughed. "No. Afterbirth. This will be easy." He pressed his hand down hard on her stomach. "Now!"

It was over in an instant. "There! That's enough out of you, Miss Annie."

She smiled at the feeble joke. "Where's my baby?" she asked.

"He's getting cleaned up."

"*He?*"

"You have a whopping eight-pound son."

"You mean a *boy?*" she said incredulously.

"A handsome boy."

"How can that be? I was so sure it would be a girl."

"If you don't want him, I'll take him," said the doctor.

"Oh, no, you won't! It's not every woman can get a boy the first time," she bragged. "Have I got stitches?"

"You tell her—" he paused and smiled—"Dr. Levine."

Dr. Levine cleared his throat, stood up straight, and proudly proclaimed: "No sutures."

Annie was back in her narrow bed. The nurse had finished sponging her off and dried her. She got Annie's hairbrush and smoothed out the damp snarls in Annie's hair.

"Ah, you are so nice, Miss Spirus."

"Oh, everybody tells me that," said the nurse, smiling. "Except the interns."

"Can I see my baby now?"

"He's only a little over a minute old and shouldn't be moved just yet. Also, the doctor wants you to get some sleep first. He wants you to take this." She helped Annie hold a glass with a bent glass tube. "Drink it all up like a good girl. It will make you sleep, and when you wake up they'll bring the baby to you." Obediently Annie sipped the sedative. "Good night, Mrs. Brown."

A delicious drowsiness came upon Annie. She reached for her pad and pencil and wrote a few words, but fell asleep before she could put the pad back on the table.

"Congratulations, Mr. Brown! How does it feel to be a father?" said the desk nurse.

"Fine. But could I see my wife?"

"She's under sedation."

"I won't wake her up. I just want to look at her."

"Well . . ." began the nurse dubiously. Then: "All right. But just for a moment."

"Thank you."

He looked down on her. She was sleeping peacefully. Her face was drained of color and her cheeks seemed sunken. Her closed eyelids seemed more transparent than usual. A lock of damp hair hung over her face. He put out his hand to smooth it back but desisted. He picked up the pencil which had fallen to the floor and put the writing pad back on the bed table. He read the few words she'd written before the sedative took over.

They say He looks down and sees the little sparrow fall. But did He look down and see me? I'm more important than a sparrow.

His eyes smarted with tears as he wrote under her words:

Yes, you are! And I love you, Annie.

He knelt at her bed, buried his face in his arms, and wept.

Chapter Twenty-three

He was long and skinny and had straight, black hair like an Indian. His complexion was a dull turkey-red and his skin seemed to need a pressing job. And Annie thought he was beautiful!

"Isn't he *beautiful*, Nurse Treener?" she asked. "*Isn't* he beautiful! He's so beautiful I could cry." And Annie cried because he was so beautiful.

"He's beautifully soaking wet," said the nurse. She undid the baby's diaper.

Annie saw his infinitesimal penis. "Isn't that cute?" she said. "And no bigger than a thimble."

"I've heard it called a lot of things in my time," said the nurse, "but never a thimble." She changed his diaper and wrapped him in his blanket. "Let's go, Buster."

"Can't I have him a little longer? *Please?*"

"Later. Doctor wants to see you now."

Dr. Marson came in with the two interns. "You came through just fine, Annie," he said.

"I'll say!" said Intern Levine.

"I'm proud of you," said the doctor.

"We all are," said Intern Moore. And his voice didn't sound so cold.

"Did you tell Carl, doctor?" she asked.

"I did."

"What did he say?"

"He said, 'So what!' and hung up."

"He did not!"

"Doctor's only teasing you, Annie," said the nurse.

"What *did* he say, doctor?"

"Annie, that boy was so overcome that he was too incoherent to say much. He's waiting outside now."

"Oh, nurse! Get my lipstick and my comb, please?"

"I guess we can take a hint, can't we, boys?" said the doctor. They left.

"It's true, Annie. I was so excited I couldn't say anything when he told me I had a son."

"*We* had a son."

"Right! Now let's find a good name for him."

"I've already named him."

"Without asking me?"

"Was I supposed to ask you?"

"Listen, Annie. After all, I *am* his father."

"I *know*. And I named him after his father. His name is . . ." she paused. "Carlton!"

"Carlton?" His grin of pleasure was almost too big for his face. "Honest, sweetheart?" She nodded. "Carlton! I always liked that name. I sort of held it against my father that he changed it to Carl. Now I have it back again in my . . . I mean *our* son."

Suddenly he felt ashamed of his pleasure. He knew how she had counted on having a girl. "I'm sorry, Annie—so sorry that you didn't get the girl you wanted."

"That's all right. I'll get a girl the next time."

*   292

"There won't be a next time. I'll see to that."

"Don't talk silly."

"They told me how you suffered. I won't let you go through that again."

"Sure I suffered. But did I die? Next time will be easier. I'll know what I'm up against and I won't be so scared."

A few days later Carl brought her a clipping from the Lopin *Clarion*, a weekly newspaper. It had a column headed: *What Goes On Here*. It listed the births, marriages, and deaths of the week.

BORN: To Carl and Annie Brown, a son, Carlton. Mr. Brown is caretaker of the High School Athletic Field.

Her reaction surprised Carl. She raved about seeing her name in print for the first time. She thought it looked wonderful. Gallantly, he said she'd see her name in print many a time as the years passed. "Thank you," she said modestly, as if it were a foregone thing—her name in print.

She asked him to send a clipping to his mother and to her mother. The item was proof that she hadn't been pregnant prior to her marriage to Carl. Carl wanted to know who cared. Annie did. When Carlton grew up, she didn't want any grandmothers telling him that his father had been forced to marry his mother.

Her friends came to see her: Mrs. Ridinski, Miss Aggie and Mrs. Hansmon. They brought gifts. Young Carlton ended up with two pairs of pink bootees and a celluloid rattle.

Goldie came and brought Less as her gift. Annie was glad to see him. "And here's Less," she said.

"Ear Ess," he said.

"He talks a lot now," said Goldie proudly.

"Talk to me, Less," said Annie.

He gave her his whole vocabulary: "Horsy! Howb'oke," and a whole sentence. "Ess no more pee-pee pants!"

"Ah," said Annie, "you're a sweetheart!"

"Me is eat hard," he agreed.

"See how the little bastard picks up new words?" said his proud mother.

Annie received a lavish card with the words of Brahms's *Lullaby* in gold letters entwined with rosebuds. Beverly Karter's name, in bold black letters, sprawled diagonally across the card. Annie smiled and gave a thought to Old Friend.

The Dean of the Law School sent his secretary over to give Annie his compliments.

But the two friends she liked best did not come to see her. Henry had left for Minnesota the day Annie entered the hospital. He went to keep an appointment with a great midwestern clinic. He needed a complicated operation.

And there was no reason, of course, why the florist should come to see her.

It was a memorable week. The baby's birth, their first wedding anniversary, and Annie's nineteenth birthday all came in that week. Carl bought her a secondhand book of poetry for her birthday. She was delighted.

"My library is growing. I own two books now." She opened the book. "Robert Burns! Oh, wonderful! That song we sang at graduations . . . *thy murmuring stream* . . . something . . . What a lovely word! Murmuring!"

"I don't go much for poetry," Carl said, "but if I did, this would be my favorite." He opened the book and read:

> She is a winsome wee thing,
> She is a handsome wee thing,
> She is a lo'esome wee thing,
> This sweet wee wife o' mine.

He closed the book and said, "And her name is Annie Brown."

"Hold me, Carl! Hold me!" He put his arms around her and

*   294

held her tight. "I'm so glad I married you," she whispered, "and nobody else."

"You mean you had a choice?" he whispered back.

"Oh, you! Always making fun of me." She gave him an affectionate shove.

She hated to leave the comfortable hospital, but she was so anxious to get home and have the baby all to herself.

"I'll miss you, Annie," said Nurse Treener. "You and the baby."

"But I'll be back to see you with the baby."

"That's what they all say. But they never come back to visit."

"But I'm different. I'll come back."

Jello just about jumped out of his pelt—he was that glad to see Annie again. But when he saw the baby in her arms he put his tail between his legs and crawled under the bed.

"Jello is jealous," she called out. "Shame!"

"He'll get over that," Carl said. "Before you know it, it will be one of those a-boy-and-his-dog affairs."

"Folks write, Carl?"

"Both of them."

"What did they say?"

"I haven't read the letters."

"Well, I'll get the baby settled and we'll have a cup of coffee while we read them."

Her mother had written a long letter. She described each step of the birth of Annie—even how the midwife had stolen the caul from Annie's head and sold it to a sailor for a dollar so he wouldn't be drowned if he fell off the ship into the ocean. She ended her letter with a sort of plea. Now that Annie had suffered in childbirth, she must know how her mother had suffered too. *I hope this will make you treat me better,* ended the letter.

"Poor Mama," sighed Annie.

Poor Carl was afraid to open his letter. "Promise me you won't start a fight."

"I won't. It might spoil the baby's milk," she said.

The letter addressed to *Dear Son* was brief. Mrs. Brown was surprised to learn she was a grandmother and who did he look like and would Carl be home for Christmas?

"There! That wasn't so bad, was it, Annie?"

"It wasn't so good. She didn't even mention my name."

"Now, Annie . . ."

"I'm not mad. It's just that I'm a person who doesn't like to be ignored all the time."

"I know. Come sit on my lap, sweetheart. It's been so long . . ."

She sat on his lap and he rocked her and patted her. "It seems like old times," she murmured dreamily.

But old times didn't last more than a moment or two. The baby started to cry. She stiffened. He tightened his arms around her.

"Don't go, Annie. He'll stop crying in a minute or so."

But Annie released herself, got off his lap, and went to attend to her baby.

Chapter Twenty-four

"Annie?"

"What, Carl?"

"I don't know how to tell you . . ."

"Is it about Henry?"

"The doctors did all they could. But the cancer was too far gone."

Her eyes searched his face. "I see," she said quietly. Then her face contorted and the tears came. "He was my friend—my good friend. And God took him from me."

"He suffered terribly, Annie. Death came as a relief."

"How do you know it came as a relief?"

"I *don't* know," he said miserably. "It's just something one says because there is nothing else to say."

"Yes, well . . ." She looked around vaguely, then said, "Don't be late for your class, Carl."

She had to endure a lesser sorrow. The doctor put the baby on a formula because the child needed more nourishment than Annie could supply. She wept on Carl's shoulder.

"I'm only half a woman," she sobbed. "Can't even nurse my own baby!"

The baby thrived on the formula. After he lost the hair he'd been born with, he turned out to be quite a handsome baby. He had a beautifully formed head. And sometimes his mouth widened into something almost like Carl's grin.

"He looks so much like you, Carl, it isn't funny."

"Aw, you can't tell yet, sweetheart." But Carl sounded awfully pleased.

When it got through to Jello that the baby was there to stay, he made the best of it. He did not fall in love with the baby, but at least he tolerated him.

"What more can you expect?" said Annie. "After all, Jello was here first, wasn't he?"

There is nothing lovelier than Indian summer in the Middle West. On a day that was especially lovely Annie bundled the baby into his carriage and went to Henry's store. She bought a nickel's worth of peanuts along the way. Not that she expected the squirrels to come, but just in case they did.

The store was being remodeled. A fast-growing grocery store syndicate had bought the building. When they are finished with it, she thought, there won't be anything left of what once was Henry. I wish everybody could know what kind of man Henry was.

She went home, fed the baby, and put him to bed. She wrote a letter about Henry and mailed it to the "Letters to the Editor" department of the Herdstone *Press*—a newspaper that had a state-wide circulation.

The *Press* did not use it as a letter. They put a title on it: *My Friend, Henry,* and ran it as a human-interest story. They sent Annie a tear sheet and a check for two dollars.

"I can't believe it!" she gasped. "My *story*, my *name* in print! It can't be true! And they *paid* me!"

"That makes you a professional writer," said Carl.

*   298

"I didn't write it for money. I wrote it because I wanted people to know that once there was a man like Henry. I feel like sending the check back."

"He'd be so proud if he had a way of knowing, Annie. I think Henry would want you to keep the check and get something for the baby with it. As a gift from him."

Annie agreed and bought a beautifully illustrated book of Robert Louis Stevenson's poems. Each night, instead of singing a lullaby to the baby, she read a poem to him. She didn't know about the baby, but *she* enjoyed the poems.

Carl was having a hard time of it. Twelve hours at the factory, two hours delivering papers, and attending classes and studying gave him about four or five hours of sleep. And he worried about money. Ten dollars a week wasn't enough. The baby was getting too big to sleep in the carriage. He needed a crib. He was outgrowing his shirts and nightgowns. There had to be a fire in both living room and kitchen to keep the baby warm. This doubled the fuel bill. And Carl needed new shoes and Annie needed . . .

Work and worry. Work and worry. No relief. He seldom had the solace of a cigarette or the consolation of sleeping with his wife. The baby was a month old now, but Annie gave no indication as to when they would sleep together again. And, to tell the truth, Carl was too tired to care.

The inevitable happened. He slept through a couple of time-punching hours. The boss found out. "Do it again," said Pulaski, "and I'll have to get me another boy."

Carl started to doze off in class. He couldn't concentrate on Real Estate 2. "Am I boring you, Mr. Brown?" asked the instructor. The class laughed; Carl was humiliated and began cutting the class.

He failed an important quiz and his grades went down.

Of course, these things got to the Dean and he called Carl in for an explanation. Carl was reluctant to tell the Dean his troubles. But the Dean, by adroit questioning, got it all out of Carl.

"Your wife: Does she know all this?"

"No, sir. She's so happy with the baby I didn't want to tell her."

The Dean got up and put his hand on Carl's shoulder. "A young man of your intellect should not be required to work as night watchman in a factory. We will have to do something about it."

Carl's face contorted. Good heavens, thought the Dean, I hope he's not going to break down and cry!

But Carl got control of himself. "Sir, I don't know how to thank you."

But the Dean was signing papers and didn't even look up when Carl left.

And the Dean did do something about it. Carl got a job in the rare-book room of the library. He worked there afternoons and Friday; that day, he had no classes. He earned ten dollars a week. He kept his newspaper route and they had an income of fifteen dollars a week. Since few people used the rare-book room, Carl had ample time to study.

They paid off the carriage and bought a crib. The baby got new woolen shirts. Carl got a new pair of shoes and eventually was able to get his watch out of pawn. He was able to have a pack of cigarettes now and then, too. His grades went up. He had his evenings and his nights at home and really got to know his son.

Best of all, he and Annie were sleeping together again.

"Last New Year's Eve, Carl, did you ever think we'd have a baby this New Year?"

"I sure didn't. Gosh!"

"Just think! Another few minutes and it will be nineteen-twenty-nine!"

"Hard to believe it."

"You know, Carl, a lot of things are going to happen in nine-teen-twenty-nine? I'm going to be twenty years old in that year. The baby will be walking and talking and you'll be in practice. And Jello's whiskers will change from gray to white." She patted the dog's head. "Won't they, poor Jello?" Jello yawned.

"And a girl named Annie Brown will have a play published in nineteen-twenty-nine," said Carl.

"I've given up all hope that there ever will be such a book. But, still and all, how wonderful it would have been if . . ."

Just then the campanile began to chime. Carl threw open the window and Annie ran to close the bedroom door so the baby would not be exposed to the draft. The night was cold and still. There were stars . . . a crescent moon; unsullied white snow which glittered in the moonlight like a carpet of diamonds.

"Like they say in books," said Annie, "it's breath-taking."

Aloud, they counted the strokes: nine—ten—eleven . . . "Happy New Year, sweetheart!" he shouted. "Happy New Year, darling!" she shouted back.

The campanile started to go into "Auld Lang Syne." They stood, arms about each other's waist, and sang along with it, Annie as always blithely off-key.

The song ended. They closed the window. "Did you get the marshmallows?" she asked.

"Get what?"

"*You* know. I was going to make cocoa to celebrate the New Year? Champagne would be better, though."

"Let the cocoa go for a while and sit on my lap for 'Auld Lang Syne.' "

"We'll take a cup of cocoa yet for 'Auld Lang Syne,' " said Annie.

"Now you come and sit on my lap, Annie."

"Try to make me!"

He chased her around the kitchen table. She ran, laughing,

into the living room, he ran after her. Jello took part in the chase, scurrying after them and barking as loud as he could. Of course the baby woke up and began to cry.

"Now look what you've done," she said, and went into the bedroom and took up the baby.

"What's the matter, baby-mine?" she crooned. "What's the matter?" He cried louder. "Your fault," she said to Carl. "Now he won't sleep all night."

"Give him to me, Annie. I'll rock him back to sleep."

"You're not supposed to rock a baby. It spoils him."

"Oh, to hell with that eyewash! Hand over my son!"

He took his son and rocked him and patted him, and after drooling a little on Carl's shirt the baby went back to sleep.

Annie stood off and watched her husband rocking his son.

"Jealous?" asked Carl.

"Just sad. Because somebody else has taken my place."

She was really pleased, though. I'm glad, she thought, that Carl likes to take care of him. Because, then, if I died or something I wouldn't have to worry about what might become of my baby.

Chapter Twenty-five

All of a sudden it was June and time for Carl to graduate!

Annie had a new dress, a white one, because she wanted to feel that she was part of graduation day. She couldn't go to the stadium to applaud when Carl was given his diploma, on account of the baby. But she could see him marching on his way to the stadium and wave to him. She'd be on the left side of the walk, she told him, and he mustn't forget to wave back. He promised.

Both sides of the walk leading to the arch that led to the stadium were crowded. But people were nice enough to make room for Annie, the baby in his carriage, and Jello.

The Engineers swaggered along, gowns unbuttoned, mortar-boards askew, and waving and shouting at people they knew or didn't know. Following the rioting Engineers came the Laws, gowns fastened, mortarboards on straight and marching in straight lines. They were very solemn compared to the Engineers.

It so happened that the one lone coed in the graduation class was marching next to Carl and they were talking to each other. The girl was poised and handsome and Annie had that old pang of not belonging—even if she did wear a white dress.

She lifted the baby from the carriage and held him up. But Carl was searching for her and the baby on the *right* side of the walk. He was about to pass through the arch without seeing them when Jello recognized him and began barking furiously. Carl turned his head and grinned happily at his family. The baby grinned back, displaying his two brand-new lower teeth. Annie waved. And Jello wagged his tail so frantically he had to pant. The handsome coed turned, smiled, and waved at Annie and the people standing near Annie smiled at each other and everything was suddenly all right with Annie.

Annie sat on the front step of the cottage waiting for Carl to come home with his diploma. Young Carlton sat on the lawn trying to feed grass to Jello. He extended a blade of grass, Jello took it in his mouth, then set it down on the lawn. Young Carlton picked it up and again gave it to Jello, who again took it and again set it down. This went on and on and the baby chuckled each time it happened.

It was to be their last night at the cottage. They were leaving in the morning for Seneca up in the north country. It was a small country town, named for a wonderful type of cherry which was grown and harvested there. It had but one lawyer, A. H. Seaborne. He and his wife—now that their children were grown up and gone from the home—wanted to take a year's vacation and see the world. But Mr. Seaborne didn't want his practice to die out or, what was worse, have a new lawyer set up a practice there. He wrote to his old friend and classmate, the Dean, and asked him to send a bright young man, preferably married, to take over the practice for a year. There were furnished living quarters attached to the office, and all Mr. Seaborne asked was that the young man pay a nominal rent of twenty-five dollars a month. All that he earned in fees would belong to the young man.

The Dean recommended Carl Brown. The lawyer accepted Carl on the Dean's say-so.

The Dean explained to Carl that it was a general practice—

wills, contracts, a divorce now and then, defending alleged moonshiners, and so forth. Mr. Seaborne took in five thousand a year in fees, and the Dean was sure Carl could take in between three and four thousand. Yes, the Dean understood that Carl wanted to practice corporate law, but a year of general practice would do no harm. When the year in Seneca was up, he had something else in mind for Carl. There would be an opening in a well-known Herdstone firm that specialized in corporate law. The Dean was sure he could place Carl there.

It would be on salary for the first few years. After that percentage and eventually a junior partnership. They could live in Lopin. The Dean understood that was what Annie wanted. Half an hour of commuting twice a day. And he'd see about getting Annie into the university as a special student. Five hours a week.

Annie, sitting on the steps, was thinking about that. Of course, she thought, I'd have to get somebody good to mind the baby.

Carl came through the gate, carrying his diploma, a rented box camera, a book, and a carton of ice cream. Jello rushed at him. Young Carlton got up on his hands and knees to get to his father, but after falling twice, gave up. Carl put his diploma and the camera on the steps and went inside to put the ice cream in the icebox and the book under his pillow.

They took pictures. One of Carl in cap and gown holding his diploma; another of Carl holding the baby and the baby holding the diploma. Then he took one of Annie holding the baby; another of Jello and the baby sitting on the grass and *not* looking at each other.

Carl put the camera on the step and said he'd be right out and they'd take another picture. He went into the cottage and came out carrying a little book in both hands.

"Annie, you've graduated too. Here is your diploma." He held out the book.

Her eyes widened and she backed away from him. "No!" she said. "No! It can't be . . . it just can't! It *can't* be . . ."

"It is. It came out a few weeks ago. I saved it for graduation."

"You wouldn't fool me, would you, Carl?"

"Ah, no, sweetheart."

"Is . . . is my play in it?"

"I forgot to look," he said, teasing her.

"*Carl* . . ." she wailed.

"Of course it's in." He turned a few pages. "Here it is: Third play. *The Marriage* by Annie Brown."

"Honest?"

He placed the book in her hands and put his mortarboard on her head. "You have graduated *magna cum laude!*" He had her stand on the steps and hold the book high on her breast. He focused the camera, then lowered it. "Annie, stop crying. You're making the film all wet."

"I can't help it," she sobbed. "I'm so ha-happy!"

They had a nice supper. They divided the ice cream into three parts so Jello could have an equal share.

"What time is he coming in the morning?"

"Anthony? He'll be here at seven sharp. He said it's a four-hour drive."

"I could get along without *him* just fine."

"Now, Carl, that's no way to talk. I didn't ask him. I just went in to say good-by and told him we were going to Seneca and he said he was going up to the north country for stock and he had to pass through Seneca anyhow. I thought that was awfully nice of him."

"What about our stuff? Will it all fit in that bitsy baby truck he has?"

"What have we got all? A crib, a carriage, a rocker, two suitcases, books, sheets, towels, and a blanket. Lots of room. And we can all sit in the front seat."

"*You* can sit in the front seat. Young Carlton and Jello and I are going to sit with the furniture."

"Don't be like that, Carl."

"You and he can talk about writing for four whole hours."

"He's going to let me read his book about the rape of the forest."

"You mean he's finished it?"

"Well . . . he's got five pages done, he said."

"Pretty good! Pre-tee good for a year's work."

"Now you stop it, Carl. He's doing us a great favor."

"Okay."

"Carl, don't go to sleep yet. I want to talk."

"All right, sweetheart." He put his arm over her. "Cry-sake, Annie, what've you got in bed with you?"

"My book. I took it out from under my pillow."

"It won't run away."

"I want to hold it so that if I dream I have a play in a book I want to have it in my hand when I wake up so I know it's no dream."

"What do you want to talk about?" He yawned.

"Is there a library in Seneca?"

"I don't know. But there must be one at the county seat and I'll be going there a lot. What else have you got on your mind?"

"We'll have to get a high chair for the baby, first thing, and . . ." She paused. "Listen!" She sat up in bed.

From somewhere a quartet was singing:

> The girl of my dreams
> Is the sweetest girl . . .

When the singing stopped, she said, "Oh, Carl, hasn't this been a wonderful year?"

"Well, it was an exciting year. I'll say that much for it."

"It was wonderful! Wonderful! We'll never have another such wonderful year."

"We'll have lots of wonderful years, lots of them."

"But not as wonderful . . ."

307　*

"Annie, I love you. But it's after eleven and we must be up before six. Let's get some sleep, sweetheart. It's been a big day and I'm awfully tired."

"I won't keep you awake a minute longer, darling. Kiss me good night."

"Good night." He turned over on his side.

"Carl?"

"Now what?" he groaned.

"What does Maggie-come-louder mean?"

"What does *what* mean?"

"Oh, you heard me, Carl."

"You mean *magna cum laude?*"

"That's what I just said. What does it mean?"

"I'll tell you tomorrow."

Betty Smith was born and raised in Brooklyn. Barely out of her teens, married, and already a mother, she entered the University of Michigan, where she won the Avery Hopwood Award for drama and fiction. Later she studied at the Yale Drama School under George Pierce Baker, then was sent to the University of North Carolina by the Federal Theater Project. She wrote and had published seventy-two one-act plays during the latter period, and decided to make Chapel Hill her permanent home.

It was there that she wrote her first book, *A Tree Grows in Brooklyn,* her two subsequent novels, *Tomorrow Will Be Better* and *Maggie-Now,* and also her latest, *Joy in the Morning.* Miss Smith says of *Joy in the Morning:* "I started the novel on January 1st, 1960. My locale was a composite of the three college towns in which I had lived for a total of twenty-five years, also a bit here and there from college towns I had visited. As I wrote, I realized to my delight that the book was more than a novel of college life. It was the anatomy of a marriage; the story of victory over odds."

Format by Katharine Sitterly
Set in Linotype Fairfield
Composed, printed and bound by American Book–Stratford Press, Inc.
HARPER & ROW, PUBLISHERS, INCORPORATED